A. P. Russell

Library notes

A. P. Russell

Library notes

ISBN/EAN: 9783743328495

Manufactured in Europe, USA, Canada, Australia, Japa

Cover: Foto ©Andreas Hilbeck / pixelio.de

Manufactured and distributed by brebook publishing software
(www.brebook.com)

A. P. Russell

Library notes

LIBRARY NOTES.

BY

A. P. RUSSELL.

NEW YORK:
PUBLISHED BY HURD AND HOUGHTON.
Cambridge: The Riverside Press.
1875.

RIVERSIDE, CAMBRIDGE:
PRINTED BY H. O. HOUGHTON AND COMPANY.

CONTENTS.

I.

INSUFFICIENCY.

In every object there is an inexhaustible meaning; the eye sees in it what the eye brings means of seeing. — A remark of Sterling on La Rochefoucauld's maxims. — How a man, especially, should be looked at. — A habit of Fuseli. — Illustrations from Richardson, Dr. Johnson, Emerson, Burns, Landor, and Dryden. — What you think of a man depends upon how you look at him. — Diversity. — Illustrations from nature and literature. — Sentences from Cervantes, Emerson, and Montaigne. — Interspaces betwixt atom and atom, differing atoms. — Public opinion the atmosphere of society. — Lowell's definition of common sense. — The history of human opinions the history of human errors. — Observations of John Foster, Swift, Montaigne, Pope, Emerson, Voltaire, and Motley. — Anecdote of Voltaire. — Nollekens and the widow. — Christopher North to the Ettrick Shepherd. — Illustrations from Gilbert White, Darwin, Youatt, Voltaire, and Digby. — Lowell's remark upon Montaigne and Shakespeare. — Self-knowledge. — Self-love. — Vanity. — Thoughts of Erasmus, Norris, Plutarch, Pascal, Sir Thomas Browne, Jeremy Taylor, and Thackeray. — An anecdote Cicero told of himself. — Southey's anecdote of the Jesuit Manuel de Vergara and the seventh commandment. — Opinion of old Indian women as to the cause of the earthquake at Talcahuano. — Tenterden-steeple the cause of Goodwin Sands, related by Bishop Latimer. — Darwin's story of the fox on the island of San Pedro. — Voltaire's remark upon insects in the garden, illustrating our limited knowledge of the globe we inhabit. — Similar remark of Horace Walpole, comparing man to a butterfly. — Exclamation of Dr. Livingstone's African servant, upon his first experience of the sea. — Ignorance, and some of its effects. — Credulity, and one of its uses. — Exclamation of Thackeray. — Remarks of Horace Walpole. — Fancy of Crabb Robinson, when a child, for the book of Revelation, and his reasons therefor. — Robert Robinson and the trinity. — Rebuke of a clergyman to a young man, who said he would believe nothing which he could not understand. — John Foster's analysis of an atheist. — Coleridge's account of one just flogging. — Difficulty of doing good. — A pattern within ourselves. — Conscience. — Our vices and our virtues.

II.

EXTREMES.

In man there will be a layer of fierce hyena, or of timid deer, running
through the nature in the most uncertain and tortuous manner. —
Cruelty and tenderness of the Tlascalans of Mexico. — The good
and the evil lie close together, and alternate. — Metals and rags. —
A terrible Voltaic pile. — The claw nicely cushioned. — Illustrations.
— Lady Mary Wortley Montagu's remark of the Duchess of Marlborough. — Madame de Maintenon's remark to Madame de Montespan. — Conduct of the women at Goa. — Conduct of Pietro Della
Valle. — Conduct of the Chinese. — Conduct of the ladies of the court
of Paris after the massacre of St. Bartholomew. — John Howe's
method of conducting public fasts. — How the rector of Fittleworth
lost his living. — Puritanism in the early history of New England.
— Some customs of the Irish when Ireland was called the Isle of
Saints. — Prayers for revenge in North Wales. — An account of the
death of a cock-fighting squire, by Mrs. Gaskell. — Man a strange
mixture of generosity and meanness, of kindness and severity, even
of dishonesty and nobleness. — A passage from Helps. — Neither
the vices nor the virtues of man are his nature. — A passage from
Taine. — The three sects at Rome. — A passage from Middleton's
Cicero. — The same lecturer there publishes the rules of temperance,
and at the same time discourses of love and wantonness. — A remark of Montaigne. — A saying of the courtesan Lais. — Pericles and
Aspasia. — A passage from Bayle. — Good and bad men are each
less so than they seem. — Some devil and some God in man. — An
observation of Coleridge. — Separating good qualities from evil in
the same person. — A remark of Boswell. — A good preacher and a
bad liver. — Nicholls, a Yorkshire clergyman. — A Quaker's invective. — Luther's and Calvin's violence. — Anger the sinews of the
soul. — A remark by Luther.   Opinions of Burke, Sir Gilbert El-

III.

DISGUISES.

Man, poor fellow, would be a curious object for microscopic study. — An account by Addison, of a gentleman who determined to live and dress according to the rules of common sense. — Custom doth make dotards of us all. — A passage from Carlyle. — Very few spontaneous actions. — A passage from Emerson. — Every man is conscious that he lives two lives. — A passage from Lowell. — We keep on deceiving ourselves in regard to our faults, until we at last come to

IV.

STANDARDS.

V.

REWARDS.

VI.

LIMITS.

VII.

INCONGRUITY.

The most delightful picture of home and homefelt happiness drawn by Goldsmith, a homeless man. — Byron thought it contradictory that the ancients, in their mythology, should have represented Wisdom by a woman, and Love by a boy. — The French theory of three sexes : men, women, and clergymen. — A recumbent statue in an old church in England, which every one believed was a woman, till Flaxman, the sculptor, examined it, and satisfied himself that it was a priest. — A lady's opinion of the poet Thomson. — Savage's correction of it. — Sydney Smith pronounced a naturalist, and Lord Lansdowne a visionary. — Jeffreys painted with a sweet countenance. — An observation by Evelyn. — Lavater's and Horace Walpole's opinions of Lord Anson. — Portrait of Addison. — Happy accidents. — Petrarch's Sonnets. — Chesterfield's Letters. — Boswell's Johnson. — Rabelais. — Cervantes. — Fielding. — Robinson Crusoe. — The Vicar of Wakefield. — Paradise Lost. — Tristram Shandy. — Books that never were published. — Great things rarely appreciated at first view. — Niagara. — Mountains. — The sea. — London. — Sir Joshua Reynolds and the works of Raphael. — Observations by Goethe and Gainsborough. — Persons engaged in the same departments of literature or art dislike one another, and can-

VIII.

MUTATIONS.

IX.

PARADOXES.

Ignorance bold and knowledge reserved. — Good books unprofitable to printers. — A thing so obvious as the vanity of the world little known. — Marriage, that least concerns other people, most meddled with by other people. — The most delicate friendships most sensible to the slightest invasion, and jealousy ever attendant upon the warmest regard. — Labor scarce in China. — Spaniards few and

X.

CONTRASTS.

XI.

TYPES.

XII.

CONDUCT.

XIII.

RELIGION.

Ah! sighed Shelley to Leigh Hunt, as the organ was playing in the
cathedral at Pisa, what a divine religion might be found out if
charity were really made the principle of it instead of faith. — Story
to the same effect of Samuel Rutherford and Archbishop Usher,
related by Dean Stanley. — Legend of the beloved disciple,
recorded by St. Jerome. — Love would put a new face on this
weary old world. — An observation of Emerson. — The Holy
Ghost came down, not in the shape of a vulture, but in the form of
a dove. — A suggestion of old Thomas Fuller. — A passage from
the Persian. — The author of Ecce Homo urges that we ought to

LIBRARY NOTES.

INSUFFICIENCY.

It was well said by some one that "in every object there is an inexhaustible meaning; the eye sees in it what the eye brings means of seeing." Here is a copy of La Rochefoucauld: William Gowans, Nassau Street. The duke gives us a true picture, not of human nature, but of its selfishness. "He works," said Sterling, "like a painter who paints the profile, and chooses the side of the face in which the eye is blind and deformed, instead of the other, which is unblemished. Yet the picture may be a most accurate copy." So do we all. Those of us that see at all, see but a small part of anything at a time. Only a nice line upon the column is distinctly visible; all the rest is hidden, or obscured in the glaring light or eclipsing shadow. A man, especially, must be looked at all around, within, by a fair light, and with a good eye, to be seen truly or judged justly. We put a narrow and fine sight upon him naturally, and can hardly avoid estimating him meanly. We have too much the habit of Fuseli, who preferred beginning his sketch of the human figure at the lowest point,

2

and working from the foot upward. "The wisest amongst us," said Richardson, "is a fool in some things, as the lowest amongst men has some just notions, and therein is as wise as Socrates; so that every man resembles a statue made to stand against a wall or in a niche; on one side it is a Plato, an Apollo, a Demosthenes; on the other, it is a rough, unformed piece of stone." "Both," said Dr. Johnson of the remarks of Lord Orrery and Delany on Swift, "were right, — only Delany had seen most of the good side, Lord Orrery most of the bad." There is a curious life of Tiberius, with two title-pages, both taken from historical authorities; two characters — one detestable, the other admirable — of one and the same person; made up, both, of recorded facts. "A man," said Emerson, "is like a bit of Labrador spar, which has no lustre as you turn it in your hand, until you come to a particular angle; then it shows deep and beautiful colors." What you think of him depends so much on how you look at him. As a creature of small ways and little achievements, he seems fit only for "stopping a bung-hole;" as an embodiment of every manly trait and of every Christian virtue, he appears indeed "a noble animal, splendid in ashes, and pompous in the grave." The petty tyrant of a family, he satirizes Cæsar; the canting bigot of the church, he brings reproach upon religion. Now a gentleman, he makes you think of Sidney; now a beast, of Swift's revolting Yahoo. When truly humble and consciously ignorant, he hath the aspect of a child of God; when conceited, dogmatic, aggressive, all the forgotten orthodox teachings of the

fate of the hopeless come back to you with the force
of apostolic thunder. As the splendid immortal he
is destined to be, you hasten to apotheosize him ; as
the monster he sometimes appears, you wonder that
he exists. Even Burns, who was a master in human
nature, and a lover of woman, characterizes *her* as
"great for good, or great for evil ; when not an
angel, she 's a devil." It seems to be nearly impossible to be moderate. If we are calm or deliberate
enough to be just, we are almost sure to be indifferent. Our ignorance, our education, our interests, our
prejudices, blind our eyes, darken our minds, or drive
us to violence. There is nothing half and half about
us. The little that we see, we see so differently and·
so partially. Ignorance finds its complement in feeling. " The eyes of critics," said Landor, " whether
in commending or carping, are both on one side, like
a turbot's." Dryden affirmed of some of the judges
of his day, that, right or wrong, they always decided
for the poor against the rich ; and he quoted a saying
of Charles II., that the crown was uniformly worsted
in every case which was heard before Sir Matthew
Hale.

Perhaps the thing which astonishes us most, when
we fairly open our eyes upon the world, is the
diversity in all things. Out in the forest, under
the spreading tree, looking up at the luxuriant foli-
age, you may not think of the difference between
the leaves ; but pull down a limb, and spend an
hour comparing them ; you find, much as they resemble, that no two are precisely alike. Examine the
plumage of the owl you cruelly brought down with

your rifle ; every feather of his beautiful dress differs
from every other; and, what is more remarkable,
every fibre of every feather is another feather, still
more delicate, differing from every other, all of which
together yield to the pressure of your hand like floss
of silk.   No wonder he fell upon the mischievous
mole or mouse as noiselessly as the shadow of a cloud.
Go down to the sea-shore; the tide is out; there is
an apparent waste of white sand, a dull extent of
uniformity; but stretch yourself on the beach, which
the innumerable differing waves have beaten to incomparable smoothness, and examine leisurely, with
a good glass, a few hundred of the infinite grains
which you thought to be the same, and you discover
that they differ, that each is differently shaped, each
holds the light differently, and, what is more wonderful than all, each appears to be a shell, or part of a
shell, which was once the abode of a creature, and a
different creature from every other inhabiting or that
ever inhabited any other shell of the ocean.   Look
into the crowded street; the men are all men ; they
all walk upright; they might wear each other's clothes
without serious inconvenience ; but could they exchange souls ?   " Clothe me as you will," said Sancho, " I shall still be Sancho Panza."   The soul is
not twin-born, but the only begotten."   " And there
never was in the world," said Montaigne, " two *opinions* alike, no more than two hairs or two grains.
The most universal quality is diversity."

" The nerve-tissue," said an acute physiologist,
" is never precisely the same in two men ; the blood
of no two men is precisely alike ; the milk of no two

women is identical in composition—they all vary (within certain limits), and sometimes the variation is considerable. It is in this that depends what we call the difference of 'temperament,' which makes one twin so unlike his brother, and makes the great variety of the human race." "Give Professor Owen part of an old bone or a tooth, and he will on the instant draw you the whole animal, and tell you its habits and propensities. What professor has ever yet been able to classify the wondrous variety of human character? How very limited as yet the nomenclature! We know there are in our moral dictionary the religious, the irreligious, the virtuous, the vicious, the prudent, the profligate, the liberal, the avaricious, and so on to a few names, but the comprehended varieties under these terms — their mixtures, which, like colors, have no names — their strange complexities and intertwining of virtues and vices, graces and deformities, diversified and mingled, and making individualities — yet of all the myriads of mankind that ever were, not one the same, and scarcely alike; how little way has science gone to their discovery, and to mark their delineation! A few sounds, designated by a few letters, speak all thought, all literature that ever was or will be. The variety is infinite, and ever creating a new infinite; and there is some such mystery in the endless variety of human character."

Molecular philosophy shows interspaces betwixt atom and atom, differing atoms, which can hardly be said to touch; so bodies are formed, and so society and public opinion are compounded. "The single individual is to collective humanity," says Alger, " as the little column of mercury in the barometer is to the whole atmosphere. They balance each other, although infinitely incommensurate. A quick-silver sea, two and a half feet deep, covering the globe, would weigh five thousand million tons. That is the heft of the air, — that transparent robe of blue gauze which outsags the Andes and the Alps. Its pressure is unfelt, yet if that pressure were annulled all the water on the earth would immediately fly into vapor. Public opinion is the atmosphere of society, without which the forces of the individual would collapse and all the institutions of society fly into atoms." Common sense has been defined to be the " average intellect and conscience of the civilized world, — that portion of intelligence, morality, and Christianity which has been practically embodied in life and active power. It destroys pretense and quackery, and tests genius and heroism. It changes with the progress of society; persecutes in one age what it adopts in the next; its martyrs of the six-teenth century are its precedents and exponents of the nineteenth ; and a good part of the common sense of an elder day is the common nonsense of our own."

" The history of human opinions," says Voltaire, " is scarcely anything more than the history of hu-man errors."

John Foster, in one of his thoughtful essays, has this suggestive passage: " If a reflective, aged man were to find at the bottom of an old chest — where it had lain forgotten fifty years — a record which he

had written of himself when he was young, simply
and vividly describing his whole heart and pursuits,
and reciting verbatim many passages of the language
which he sincerely uttered, would he not read it with
more wonder than almost every other writing could
at his age inspire ? He would half lose the assurance
of his identity, under the impression of this immense
dissimilarity. It would seem as if it must be the tale
of the juvenile days of some ancestor, with whom he
had no connection but that of name." Says Swift,
" If a man would register all his opinions upon love,
politics, religion, learning, etc., beginning from his
youth, and so go on to old age, what a bundle of
inconsistencies and contradictions would appear at
last." Says Montaigne, " Never did two men make
the same judgment of the same thing ; and 't is impossible to find two opinions, exactly alike, not only
in several men, but in the *same men*, at different
times." Says Pope, " What is every year of a wise
man's life but a censure or critic on the past? Those
whose date is the shortest live long enough to laugh
at one half of it; the boy despises the infant; the
man, the boy ; the philosopher, both ; and the Christian, all." Diet, health, the weather, affairs, — a
thousand things, — determine our views. " I knew
a witty physician," says Emerson, " who found the
creed in the biliary duct, and used to affirm that if
there was disease in the liver, the man became a Calvinist, and if that organ was sound, he became a Uni-
tarian." Voltaire declared that the fate of a nation
had often depended on the good or bad digestion of a
prime minister; and Motley holds that the gout of

Charles V. changed the destinies of the world. Our views change so often that the writer who would be consistent would never write at all. The sentence that would express his thought at one time would fail at another. Alteration would confuse. An attempt to find words to express his thoughts upon any one thing at all times would be given up in despair. Voltaire once praised another writer very heartily to a third person. " It is very strange," was the reply, " that you speak so well of him, for he says *you* are a charlatan." " Oh," replied Voltaire, " I think it very likely that *both* of us are mistaken." Smith gives an account of a lady in weeds for her husband who "came drooping like a willow to Nollekens, the sculptor, desiring a monument, and declaring that she did not care what money was expended on the memory of one she loved so. 'Do what you please, but, oh, do it quickly!' were her parting orders. Nollekens went to work, made the design, finished the model, and began to look for a block of marble to carve it from, when in dropped the lady; she had been absent some three months. 'Poor soul,' said the sculptor, when she was announced, ' I thought she would come soon, but I am ready.' The lady came light of foot, and lighter of look. 'Ah, how do you do, Mr. Nollekens? Well, you have not commenced the model?' 'Ay, but I have, though,' returned the sculptor, 'and there it stands, finished!' 'There it is, indeed,' sighed the lady, throwing herself into a chair; they looked at one another for a minute's space or so — she spoke first: 'These, my good friend, are, I know, early

days for this little change,' — she looked at her dress,
from which the early profusion of crape had disap-
peared, — ' but since 1 saw you, I have met with an
old Roman acquaintance of yours who has made me
an offer, and I don't know how he would like to see
in our church a monument of such expense to my late
husband. Indeed, on second thought, it would be
considered quite enough if I got our mason to put up
a mural tablet, and that, you know, he can cut very
prettily.' ' My charge, madam, for the model,' said
the sculptor, ' is one hundred guineas.' 'Enormous !
enormous !' said the lady, but drew out her purse
and paid it." The mutability of human nature !
Change, change is the rule. " I wish the world,
James," said Christopher North to the Ettrick Shepherd, " would stand still for some dozen years — till
I am at rest. It seems as if the very earth itself were
undergoing a vital change. Nothing is unalterable,
except the heaven above my head, and even it,
James, is hardly, methinks, at times, the same as
in former days or nights. There is not much difference in the clouds, James, but the blue sky, I
must confess, is not quite so very blue as it was sixty
years since ; and the sun, although still a glorious
luminary, has lost a leetle — of his lustre." Gilbert
White, in his Natural History of Selborne, says he
" saw a cock-bullfinch in a cage, which had been
caught in the fields after it was come to its full colors. In about a year it began to look dingy ; and
blackening each succeeding year, it became coal-black
at the end of four. Its chief food was hemp seed.
Such influence has food on the color of animals !"

Darwin, in his Voyage, says that Captain Sullivan
told him that "the wild cattle in East Falkland Isl-
and, originally the same stock, differ much in color;
and it is a remarkable circumstance, that in different
parts of that one small island, different colors pre-
dominate. He remarked that the difference in the
prevailing colors was so obvious, that in looking at
the herds from a point near Point Pleasant, they appeared from a long distance like black spots, whilst
south of Choiseul Sound they appeared like white
spots on the hill-sides. Round Mount Usborne, at a
height of one thousand to fifteen hundred feet above
the sea, about half of some of the herds are mouse or
lead colored." "From the westward till you get to
the river Adur," wrote White, "all the flocks have
horns and smooth white faces, and white legs, and
a hornless sheep is rarely to be seen; but as soon as
you pass that river eastward, and mount Beeding
Hill, all the flocks at once become hornless, or, as
they call them, poll-sheep; and have, moreover,
black faces, with a white tuft of wool on their fore-
heads, and speckled and spotted legs, so that you
would think that the flocks of Laban were pastur-
ing on one side of the stream, and the variegated
breed of his son-in-law, Jacob, were cantoned along
on the other." Youatt speaks of the two flocks of
Leicester sheep kept by Mr. Buckley and Mr. Bur-
gess, which "have been purely bred from the original stock of Mr. Bakewell for upwards of fifty years.
There is not a suspicion existing in the mind of any
one at all acquainted with the subject, that the owner
of either of them has deviated in any one instance

from the pure blood of Mr. Bakewell's flock, and yet the difference between the sheep possessed by these two gentlemen is so great that they have the appearance of being quite different varieties." " We may, in truth," says Voltaire, " be naturally and aptly resembled to a river, all whose waters pass away in perpetual change and flow. It is the same river as to its bed, its banks, its source, its mouth, everything, in short, that is not itself; but changing every moment its water, which constitutes its very being, it has no identity; there is no sameness belonging to the river." Said Sir Kenelm Digby, long before Voltaire, " There is not one drop of the same water in the Thames that ran down by Whitehall yesternight; yet no man will deny but that it is the same river that was in Queen Elizabeth's time, as long as it is supplied from the same common stock, the sea."

Lowell, in one of his critical essays, says that "'all men are interested in Montaigne in proportion as all men find more of themselves in him ; and all men see but one image in the glass which the greatest of poets holds up to nature, — an image which at once startles and charms with its familiarity." Montaigne himself says, " Nature, that we may not be dejected with the sight of our deformities, has wisely thrust the action of seeing outward." " Know thyself," that Apollo caused to be written on the front of his temple at Delhi, appeared to him contradictory. We are vain of our knowledge, vain of our virtue, vain of everything that pertains to ourselves in the slightest. Reading Rochefoucauld's maxims at twenty, one is a little surprised that the first and longest should be upon self-love ; at forty, one is not astonished at the rank and importance it has in the philosopher's system. " Oh, the incomparable contrivance of nature," exclaims Erasmus, " who has ordered all things in so even a method that wherever she has been less bountiful in her gifts, there she makes it up with a larger dose of self-love, which supplies the former defects, and makes all even." " Could all mankind," says John Norris, " lay claim to that estimate which they pass upon themselves, there would be little or no difference betwixt laps'd and perfect humanity, and God might again review his image with paternal complacency, and still pronounce it good." " Blinded as they are as to their true character by self-love, every man," says Plutarch, " is his own first and chiefest flatterer, prepared therefore to welcome the flatterer from the outside, who only comes confirming the verdict of the flatterer within." " Vanity has taken so firm hold in the heart of man," says Pascal, " that a porter, an hodman, a turnspit, can talk greatly of himself, and is for having his admirers. Philosophers who write of the contempt of glory, do yet desire the glory of writing well ; and those who read their compositions would not lose the glory of having read them. We are so presumptuous as that we desire to be known to all the world; and even to those who are not to come into the world till we have left it. And, at the same time, we are so little and vain as that the esteem of five or six persons about us is enough to content and amuse us." " We censure others," says Sir Thomas Browne, " but as they

disagree from that humor which we fancy laudable
in ourselves, and commend others but for that wherein
they seem to quadrate and consent with us. So that
in conclusion, all is but that we all condemn, self-
love." We think ourselves of great importance in
the eyes of others, when we are only so in our own.
Calmly considering it, what can be more astonishing
than vanity in a middle-aged person? Know as
much as it is possible for a human being to know in
this world, he cannot know enough to justify him in
being vain of his knowledge. Good as it is possible
for a human being to be, he cannot be good enough
to excuse a conceit of his goodness. Yet how common it is for full-grown ignorance to have conceit of
wisdom, and for ordinary virtue to assume the airs of
saintship. How we shall one day wonder, looking
back at the world we have left, at the nearly invisible
mites, like ourselves, tossing their heads in pride, and
gathering their skirts in self-righteousness, that we
were ever as vain and shameless as they, and that the
little things of life ever so engrossed us! Alas, to
learn and unlearn is our fate; to gather as we climb
the hill of life, to scatter as we descend it; empty-
handed alike at the end and at the beginning.

> "Youth's heritage is hope, but man's
> Is retrospect of shattered plans,
> And doubtful glances cast before."

" All the world, all that we are, and all that we have,
our bodies and our souls, our actions and our sufferings, our conditions at home, our accidents abroad,
our many sins, and our seldom virtues," says Jeremy

Taylor, "are as so many arguments to make our souls dwell low in the valleys of humility." We are not what we think ourselves, nor are other people what we think them, else this were a different world. We know not ourselves, nor others, nor anything, so well as to avoid misapprehending everything. Our condition is ignorance and humility, and better it were if we kept modestly in our beaten paths. Whatever we do or are, we are of chief importance to ourselves. " The world," says Thackeray, " can pry out everything about us which it has a mind to know. But there is this consolation, which men will never accept in their own cases, that the world does n't care. Consider the amount of scandal it has been forced to hear in its time, and how weary it must be of that kind of intelligence. You are taken to prison and fancy yourself indelibly disgraced? You are bankrupt under odd circumstances? You drive a queer bargain with your friend and are found out, and imagine the world will punish you? Psha! Your shame is only vanity. Go and talk to the world as if nothing had happened, and nothing *has* happened. Tumble down; brush the mud off your clothes; appear with a smiling countenance, and nobody cares. Do you suppose society is going to take out its pocket-handkerchief and be inconsolable when you die? Why should it care very much, then, whether your worship graces yourself or disgraces yourself? Whatever happens, it talks, meets, jokes, yawns, has its dinner, pretty much as before." Depend upon it, the world will not hunt you, nor concern itself much about you. If you want its favors you must keep yourself in its eye. Cicero left Sicily extremely pleased with the success of his administration, and flattered himself that all Rome was celebrating his praises, and that the people would readily grant him everything that he desired; in which imagination he landed at Puteoli, a considerable port adjoining to Baiæ, the chief seat of pleasure in Italy, where there was a perpetual resort of all the rich and the great, as well for the delights of its situation as for the use of its baths and hot waters. But here, as he himself pleasantly tells the story, he was not a little mortified by the first friend whom he met, who asked him how long he had left Rome, and what news there, when he answered that he came from the provinces. "From Africk, I suppose," says another; and upon his replying, with some indignation, "No; I come from Sicily," a third, who stood by, and had a mind to be thought wiser, said presently, "How? did you not know that Cicero was quæstor of Syracuse?" Upon which, perceiving it in vain to be angry, he fell into the humor of the place, and made himself one of the company who came to the waters. This mortification gave some little check to his ambition, or taught him rather how to apply it more successfully; and did him more good, he says, than if he had received all the compliments that he expected; for it made him reflect that the people of Rome had dull ears, but quick eyes; and that it was his business to keep himself always in their sight; nor to be so solicitous how to make them hear of him, as to make them see him: so that, from this moment, he resolved to stick close to the forum, and to live perpetually in the view of the city ; nor to suffer either his porter or his sleep to hinder any man's access to him.

As capital in trade must be constantly turning to accumulate, so intelligence must be constantly in use to be useful. Its value and utility and accuracy can only be known by constantly testing it. A false light leads straight into the bog, and misinformation is worse than no information at all. Curiosity has need to be on tip-toe, — but cautious, nevertheless. Southey tells a story in his Doctor which the Jesuit Manuel de Vergara used to tell of himself. When he was a little boy he asked a Dominican friar what was the meaning of the seventh commandment, for he said he could not tell what committing adultery was. The friar, not knowing how to answer, cast a perplexed look around the room, and thinking he had found a safe reply, pointed to a kettle on the fire, and said the commandment meant that he must never put his hand in the pot while it was boiling. The very next day, a loud scream alarmed the family, and behold there was little Manuel running about the room, holding up his scalded finger, and exclaiming, "Oh dear ! oh dear ! I've committed adultery ! I've committed adultery ! I've committed adultery ! "

Men are most apt to believe what they least understand. What they are most ready to talk upon, if they knew just a little more about, they would be dumb. We are told that shortly after the shock of the famous earthquake at Talcahuano, a great wave was seen from the distance of three or four miles, approaching in the middle of the bay with a smooth outline ; but along the shore it tore up cottages and trees, as it swept onward with irresistible force. At the head of the bay it broke in a fearful line of white breakers, which rushed up to a height of twenty-three vertical feet above the highest spring-tides. The lower orders in Talcahuano thought that the earth-quake was caused by some old Indian women, witches, who, two years before, being offended, stopped the volcano of Antuco !

Bishop Latimer says that " Master More was once sent in commission into Kent, to help to try out, if it might be, what was the cause of Goodwin Sands, and the shelf that stopped up Sandwich haven. Among others, came in. before him an old man with a white head, and one that was thought to be little less than one hundred years old. Quoth Master More, How say you in this matter ? What think you to be the cause of these shelves and flats that stop up Sandwich haven ? Forsooth, quoth he, I am an old man. I think that Tenterden-steeple is the cause of Goodwin Sands ; for I am an old man, sir, quoth he, and I may remember the building of Tenterden-steeple, and I may remember when there was no steeple at all there. And before that Tenterden-steeple was in building, there was no manner of speaking of any flats or sands that stopped the haven, and therefore I think that Tenterden-steeple is the cause of the destroying and decay of Sandwich haven ! " (The centenarian's re-ply crystallized at once into a proverb and synonym for popular ignorance ; but what if the old man had in his mind the half of the story omitted by Latimer — that the obnoxious steeple had been built by a bishop with fifty thousand pounds appropriated to build a breakwater!)

The fox that, Darwin tells us about in his Voyage was *dumb* in the presence of wonders. "In the evening," says the naturalist, "we reached the island of San Pedro. In doubling the point, two of the officers landed, to take a round of angles with the theodolite. A fox of a kind said to be peculiar on the island, and very rare in it, was sitting on the rocks. He was so intently absorbed in watching the work of the officers, that I was able, by quietly walking up behind, to knock him on the head with my geological hammer!"

"We on this globe," said Voltaire, speaking of the slender acquaintance of Europe with the Chinese empire, "we on this globe are like insects in a garden — those who live on an oak seldom meet those who pass their short lives on an ash." "We are poor, silly animals," says Horace Walpole; "we live for an instant upon a particle of a boundless universe, and are much like a butterfly that should argue about the nature of the seasons, and what creates their vicissitudes, and does not exist itself to see an annual revolution of them." When Dr. Livingstone returned from Africa, after a stay of sixteen years as a missionary, he was induced to bring with him an intelligent and affectionate native, Sekwebu, who had been of great service to him. When they parted from their friends at Kilemane, the sea on the bar was frightful, even to the seamen. This was the first time Sekwebu had seen the sea. As the terrible breakers broke over them, he asked, wonderingly, "Is this the way you go? Is this the way you go?" exclaiming, "What a strange country is this—all water together!"

At sea, a person's eye being six feet above the surface of the water, his horizon is only two miles and four fifths distant; yet his tongue will as freely wag of the world as if it were all spinning under his eye. We freely discuss the ignorance of those we believe to be less intelligent than ourselves, never thinking that we are unconsciously the cause of like amusement to those who are more intelligent than we are. Fewer laugh with us than at us. The grades are so many that contrast is more natural than comparison. Unfortunately, too, it is only in the descent that we can see, and that but a little way. We know it is up, up, that we would go, but the rounds of the ladder are but vaguely visible. But a small part, indeed, we perceive of the prodigious sweep from the lowest ignorance to possible intelligence. Happily, credulity fills the empty spaces, erects itself for original wisdom, and satisfies us with ourselves and ours. Thackeray, in one of his best novels, thus satirically screams out one of its uses: " Oh, Mr. Pendennis! if Nature had not made that provision for each sex in the credulity of the other, which sees good qualities where none exist, good looks in donkeys' ears, wit in their numskulls, and music in their bray, there would not have been near so much marrying and giving in marriage as now obtains, and as is necessary for the due propagation and continuance of the noble race to which we belong!" "I desire to die," said Horace Walpole, "when I have nobody left to laugh with

me. I have never yet seen, or heard, anything serious that was not ridiculous. . . . . Oh! we are ridiculous animals ; and if angels have any fun in them,
how we must divert them."

" I had taken, when a child," says Crabb Robinson,
" a great fancy to the Book of Revelation ; and I
have heard that I asked our minister to preach from
that book, because it was my favorite. 'And why is
it your favorite, Henry?' 'Because it is so pretty
and easy to understand !' "

Writing to Toulmin, Robert Robinson, a witty and
distinguished clergyman in the last century, biogra-
phied by George Dyer, gives the following : " Says a
grave brother, ' Friend, I never heard you preach on
the Trinity.' ' Oh, I intend to do so as soon as ever
I understand it !' "

This recalls the rebuke of a clergyman to a young
man, who said he would believe nothing which he
could not understand. " Then, young man, your
creed will be the shortest of any man's I know."

John Foster's analysis of an atheist you remember,
—" one of the most daring beings in the creation, a
contemner of God, who explodes his laws by denying
his existence. If you were so unacquainted with
mankind that this character might be announced to
you as a rare or singular phenomenon, your conject-
ures, till you saw and heard the man, at the nature
and the extent of the discipline through which he
must have advanced, would be led toward something
extraordinary. And you might think that the term
of that discipline must have been very long ; since a
quick train of impressions, a short series of mental

gradations, within the little space of a few months and years, would not seem enough to have matured such an awful heroism. Surely the creature that thus lifts his voice, and defies all invisible power within the possibilities of infinity, challenging whatever unknown being may hear him, was not as yesterday a little child, that would tremble and cry at the approach of a diminutive reptile. But indeed it is heroism no longer, if he *knows* there is no God. The wonder then turns on the great process by which a man could grow to the immense intelligence that can know that there is no God. What ages and what lights are requisite for *this* attainment! This intelligence involves the very attributes of the Divinity, while a God is denied. For unless this man is omnipresent, unless he is at this moment in every place in the universe, he cannot know but there may be in some place manifestations of a Deity by which even *he* would be overpowered. If he does not know absolutely every agent in the universe, the one that he does not know may be God. If he is not in absolute possession of all the propositions that constitute universal truth, the one which he wants may be, that there is a God. If he does not know everything that has been done in the immeasurable ages that are past, some things may have been done by a God. Thus, unless he knows all things, that is, precludes another Deity by being one himself, he cannot know that the Being whose existence he rejects does not exist. And yet a man of *ordinary* age and intelligence may present himself to you with the avowal of being thus distinguished from the crowd!"

"I had one just flogging," says Coleridge. " When I was about thirteen I went to a shoemaker and begged him to take me as his apprentice. He, being an honest man, immediately brought me to Boyer, who got into a great rage, knocked me down, and even pushed Crispin rudely out of the room. Boyer asked me why I had made myself such a fool? to which I answered that I had a great desire to be a shoemaker, and that I hated the thought of being a clergyman. 'Why so?' said he. 'Because, to tell you the truth, sir,' said I, 'I am an infidel!' For this, without more ado, Boyer flogged me, — wisely, as I think, — soundly, as I know. Any whining or sermonizing would have gratified my vanity, and confirmed me in my absurdity; as it was, I was laughed at, and got heartily ashamed of my folly."

"It is one thing to see that a line is crooked, and another thing to be able to draw a straight one," says Conversation Sharpe. "It is not quite so easy to do good as those may imagine who never try." Says Montaigne, "Could my soul once take footing, I would not essay, but resolve; but it is always leaving and making trial." " 'T is an exact and exquisite life that contains itself in due order in private. Every one may take a part in the farce, and assume the part of an honest man upon the stage; but within, and in his own bosom, where all things are lawful to us, all things concealed, — to be regular, that is the point. The next degree is to be so in one's house, in one's ordinary actions, for which one is accountable to none, and where there is no study or artifice." " We chiefly, who live private lives, not exposed to any other view than our own, ought to have settled a pattern within ourselves, by which to try our actions." " Conscience," cries Sterne, " is not a law ; no, God and reason made the law, and have placed conscience within you to determine."

How often our virtues and benefactions are but the effects of our vices and our crimes ; and as often do our vices disguise themselves under the name of virtues. " We ought not," says Montaigne, " to honor with the name of duty that peevishness and inward discontent which spring from private interest and passion ; nor call treacherous and malicious conduct courage. People give the name of zeal to their propensity to mischief and violence, though it is not the cause, but their interest, that inflames them. Miserable kind of remedy, to owe a man's health to his disease. The virtue of the soul does not consist in flying high, but walking orderly ; its grandeur does not exercise itself in grandeur, but in mediocrity." The greatest man is great in matters of self-conduct ; the wisest is wise in little matters of life ; the one is never little, the other never foolish.

" The superior man," says Confucius, " does not wait till he sees things, to be cautious, nor till he hears things, to be apprehensive. There is nothing more visible than what is secret, and nothing more manifest than what is minute. Therefore, the superior man will watch over himself when he is alone. He examines his heart that there may be nothing wrong there, and that he may have no cause for dissatisfaction with himself. That wherein he excels is simply his work which other men cannot see. Are you free from shame in your apartment, when you are exposed only to the light of heaven ? "

"Most men," says Alger, "live blindly to repeat a routine of drudgery and indulgence, without any deliberately chosen and maintained aims. Many live to outstrip their rivals, pursue their enemies, gratify their lusts, and make a display. Few live distinctly to develop the value of their being, know the truth, love their fellows, enjoy the beauty of the world, and aspire to God."

"Life is a series of surprises," says Emerson, "and would not be worth taking or keeping if it were not. God delights to isolate us every day, and hide from us the past and the future. We would look about us, but with grand politeness He draws down before us an impenetrable screen of purest sky. 'You will not remember,' He seems to say, 'and you will not expect.'"

Goldsmith, in one of his delightful Chinese Letters, gives this illustration of the vanity and uncertainty of human judgment : "A painter of eminence was once resolved to finish a piece which should please the whole world. When, therefore, he had drawn a picture, in which his utmost skill was exhausted, it was exposed in the public market-place, with directions at the bottom for every spectator to mark with a brush, which lay by, every limb and feature which seemed erroneous. The spectators came, and in general applauded ; but each, willing to show his talent at criticism, marked whatever he thought proper. At evening, when the painter came, he was mortified to find the whole picture one universal blot; not a single stroke that was not stigmatized with marks of disapprobation. Not satisfied with this trial, the next day he was resolved to try them in a different manner, and, exposing his picture as before, desired that every spectator would mark those beauties he approved or admired. The people complied; and the artist, returning, found his picture replete with the marks of beauty; every stroke that had been yesterday condemned now received the character of approbation."

Irving, in his Knickerbocker's New York, thus refers to the habit of criticising and complaining in the time of William the Testy: " Cobblers abandoned their stalls to give lessons on political economy; blacksmiths suffered their fires to go out while they stirred up the fires of faction; and even tailors, though said to be the ninth parts of humanity, neglected their own measures to criticise the measures of government. Strange! that the science of government, which seems to be so generally understood, should invariably be denied to the only ones called upon to exercise it. Not one of the politicians in question but, take his word for it, could have administered affairs ten times better than William the Testy."

Socrates used to say that although no man undertakes a trade he has not learned, even the meanest, yet every one thinks himself sufficiently qualified for the hardest of all trades, that of government.

" Whoever would aim directly at a cure of a public evil," says Montaigne, " and would consider of it before he began, would be very willing to withdraw

his hands from meddling in it. Pacuvius Calavius,
according to Livy, corrected the vice of this proceeding by a notable example. His fellow-citizens were
in mutiny against their magistrates ; he, being a man
of great authority in the city of Capua, found means
one day to shut up the senators in the palace, and
calling the people together in the market-place, he
told them that the day was now come wherein, at
full liberty, they might revenge themselves on the
tyrants by whom they had been so long oppressed,
and whom he had now, all alone and unarmed, at his
mercy ; and advised that they should call them out
one by one by lot, and should particularly determine
of every one, causing whatever should be decreed to
be immediately executed ; with this caution, that
they should at the same time depute some honest
man in the place of him that was condemned, to the
end that there might be no vacancy in the senate.
They had no sooner heard the name of one senator,
but a great cry of universal dislike was raised up
against him. 'I see,' says Pacuvius, 'we must get
rid of him ; he is a wicked fellow ; let us look out a
good one in his room.' Immediately there was a profound silence, every one being at a stand who to
choose. But one, more impudent than the rest, having named his man, there arose yet a greater consent
of voices against him, a hundred imperfections being
laid to his charge, and as many just reasons being
presently given why he should not stand. These
contradictory humors growing hot, it fared worse
with the second senator and the third, there being as
much disagreement in the election of the new, as

consent in the putting out of the old. In the end, growing weary of this bustle to no purpose, they began, some one way and some another, to steal out of the assembly; every one carrying back this resolution in his mind, that the oldest and best known evil was ever more supportable than one that was new and untried."

" Among all animals man is the only one who tries to pass for more than he is, and so involves himself in the condemnation of seeming less." " The negro king desired to be portrayed as white. But do not laugh at the poor African," pleads Heine, " for every man is but another negro king, and would like to appear in a color different from that with which Fate has bedaubed him."

It is even harder, when he is most barbarous and besotted in his ignorance, to disturb his complacency and self-conceit. " It was most ludicrous," says Darwin, " to watch through a glass the Indians, as often as the shot struck the water, take up stones, and, as a bold defiance, throw them towards the ship, though about a mile and a half distant! A boat was then sent with orders to fire a few musket-shots wide of them. The Fuegians hid themselves behind the trees, and for every discharge of the muskets they fired their arrows ; all, however, fell short of the boat, and the officer as he pointed at them laughed. This made the Fuegians frantic with passion, and they shook their mantles in vain rage. At last, seeing the balls cut and strike the trees, they ran away, and we were left in peace and quietness."

You remember the famous contest of Dr. Johnson,

in Billingsgate.   He was passing through the market, as the story goes, with Goldsmith, when he was
rudely jostled and profanely addressed by a monstrous fish-woman.   " See how I will bring her down,
Goldy, without degrading myself," whispered Johnson.   Looking straight at the creature, he said to her,
deliberately and emphatically, " You are a triangle ! "
which made her swear louder than ever.   He then
called her " a rectangle ! a parallelogram ! "   That
made her eloquent; but the great moralist with his
big voice again broke through her volubility, scream-
ing fiercely, " You are a miserable, wicked *hypothe-
nuse !* "   That dumfounded the brute.   She had
never heard swearing like that.

Curran, we are told, used to relate a ludicrous encounter between himself and a fish-woman on the
quay at Cork.   This lady, whose tongue would have
put Billingsgate to the blush, was urged one day to
assail him, which she did with very little reluctance.
" I thought myself a match for her," said he, " and
valorously took up the gauntlet.   But such a virago
never skinned an eel.   My whole vocabulary made
not the least impression.   On the contrary, she was
manifestly becoming more vigorous every moment,
and I had nothing for it but to beat a retreat.   This,
however, was to be done with dignity; so, drawing
myself up disdainfully, I said, ' Madam, I scorn all
further discourse with such an *individual !* '   She did
not understand the word, and thought it, no doubt,
the very hyperbole of opprobrium.   ' Individual, you
wagabone ! ' she screamed, ' what do you mean by
that ?   I 'm no more an individual than your mother

was!' Never was victory more complete. The whole
sisterhood did homage to me, and I left the quay of
Cork covered with glory."

A wise man, who lived a long life of virtue, study,
travel, society, and reflection; who read the best
books and conversed with the greatest and best men ;
the companion of philosophers and scientists ; familiar with all important discoveries and experiments ;
after he was three-score and ten, wrote, "It is remarkable that the more there is known, the more it
is perceived there is to be known. And the infinity
of knowledge to be acquired runs parallel with the
infinite faculty of knowing, and its development.
Sometimes I feel reconciled to my extreme ignorance, by thinking, If I know nothing, the most
learned know next to nothing." "Had I earlier
known," said Goethe, "how many excellent things
have been in existence, for hundreds and thousands
of years, I should have written no line ; I should
have had enough else to do." Cardinal Farnese one
day found Michel Angelo, when an old man, walking alone in the Coliseum, and expressed his surprise
at finding him solitary amidst the ruins; to which he
replied, "I go yet to school, that I may continue to
learn." Mrs. Jameson once asked Mrs. Siddons
which of her great characters she preferred to play?
She replied, after a moment's consideration, "Lady
Macbeth is the character I have most *studied*." She
afterward said that she had played the character
during thirty years, and scarcely acted it once without carefully reading over the part, and generally the
whole play, in the morning; and that she never read

over the play without finding something new in it; "something," she said, "which had not struck me so much as it *ought* to have struck me." Dugald Stewart said of Bacon's Essays that in reading them for the twentieth time he observed something which had escaped his attention in the nineteenth. "I don't know," said Newton, "what I may seem to the world; but as to myself, I seem to have been only like a boy playing on the sea-shore, and diverting myself in now and then finding a smoother pebble or a prettier shell than ordinary, whilst the great ocean of Time lay all undiscovered before me." Said Bossuet, "The term of my existence will be eighty years at most, but let us allow it an hundred. What ages have rolled before I had my being! How many will flow after I am gone! And what a small space do I occupy in this grand succession of years! I am as a blank; this diminutive interval is not sufficient to distinguish me from that nothing to which I must inevitably return. I seem only to have made my appearance for the purpose of increasing the number; and I am even useless — for the play would have been just as well performed, had I remained behind the scenes." Wrote Voltaire, "I am ignorant how I was formed, and how I was born. I was perfectly ignorant, for a quarter of my life, of the reasons of all that I saw, heard, and felt, and was a mere parrot, talking by rote in imitation of other parrots. When I looked about me and within me, I conceived that something existed from all eternity. Since there are beings actually existing, I concluded that there is some being necessary and necessarily eternal. Thus the first

step which I took to extricate myself from my ignorance overpassed the limits of all ages — the
boundaries of time. But when I was desirous of
proceeding in this infinite career, I could neither
perceive a single path, nor clearly distinguish a single object ; and from the flight which I took to con-
template eternity, I have fallen back into the abyss
of my orginal ignorance." " Heads of capacity, and
such as are not full with a handful, or easy measure
of knowledge, think they know nothing till they
know all; which being impossible, they fall," says
Sir Thomas Browne, " upon the opinion of Socrates,
and only know they know not anything." Hiero,
tyrant of Sicily, asked old Simonides to tell him
what God is. The poet answered him that it was
not a question that could be immediately answered,
and that he wanted a whole day to think upon it.
When that term was over, Hiero asked the answer;
but Simonides desired two days more to consider of
it. This was not the last delay he asked ; he was
often called on to give an answer, and every time he
desired double the time he had last demanded. The
tyrant, wondering at it, desired to know the reason of
it. I do so, answered Simonides, because the more I
examine the matter, the more obscure it appears to
me. " I am a fragment, and this is a fragment of
me," says Emerson. . . . . " I am very content with
knowing, if only I could know. . . . . To know a
little, would be worth the expense of this world."
" You read of but one wise man," says Congreve,
" and all that he knew was — that he knew nothing."
" The curiosity of knowing things has been given to

man for a scourge." " If God," said Lessing, " held
all truth shut in his right hand, and in his left nothing but the restless instinct for truth, though with
the condition of forever and ever erring, and should
say to me, Choose! I would bow reverently to his
left hand, and say, Father, give! Pure truth is for
Thee alone!"

II.

EXTREMES.

" IN man there will be a layer of fierce hyena, or of
timid deer, running through the nature in the most
uncertain and tortuous manner. Nero is sensitive to
poetry and music, but not to human suffering : Marcus Aurelius is tolerant and good to all men but
Christians." The Tlascalans of Mexico loved, and
even worshiped, flowers ; but they were cruel to
excess, and sacrificed human victims with savage delight. The good and the evil lie close together; the
virtues and the vices alternate; so is human power
accumulated ; alternately the metals and the rags ;
a terrible Voltaic pile. In the well-bred animal the
claw is nicely cushioned ; the old Adam is present-
able. Overhear a beautiful young woman swear,
and meet her an hour afterward, all smiles and loveliness, in the drawing-room. Speak with unreserved
kindness of one lady to another, — both of them very
lovely creatures, so far as you know, — and receive in
reply, " Don't ! She, of all persons I know, is the
only one I hate to hear praised." Lady Mary Wortley Montagu said of the Duchess of Marlborough,
" We continue to see one another like two persons
who are resolved to hate with civility." Madame de
Maintenon and Madame de Montespan met in pub-

4

lic, talked with vivacity, and, to those who judged
only by appearances, seemed excellent friends. Once
when they had to make a journey in the same carriage, Madame de Montespan said, " Let us talk as if
there were no difference between us, but on condition
that we resume our disputes when we return." Pietro
Della Valle says that when the *Ecce Homo* was exposed during the sermon in the Jesuit church at Goa,
the women used to beat their servants, if they did
not cry enough to please them. The distinguished
Italian traveler referred to had such an absorbing
fondness for his wife that, when she died, on the
shore of the Persian Gulf, he embalmed her body,
and spent one whole year conveying it back through
India to Rome, where he celebrated her obsequies by
pronouncing a funeral oration, during the delivery of
which his emotions became so violent as to choke his
utterance. Not long after, in a fit of anger, he killed
his coachman, in the area before St. Peter's, while the
pope was pronouncing a benediction. In China, not
long since, the goddess of small-pox was worshiped
and prayed to preserve the dying emperor, but, having failed to do so, was flogged and burnt. It is
recorded that after the massacre of St. Bartholomew
the ladies of the court of Paris went out to examine
the long row of the bodies of the Huguenot cavaliers
who had been slain during the tumult, and curiously
turning them over, when half-stripped of their garments, said to each other, " This must have been a
charming lover; that was not worth looking at; "
and when a fanatic assassin was brought out in the
square of the Louvre to undergo during four hours

the most frightful tortures which human ingenuity or malignity could devise, or the human frame endure, all the ladies of the court assembled to witness the spectacle, and paid high prices for seats nearest the scene of agony. John Howe's method of conducting public fasts was as follows: "He began at nine o'clock with a prayer of a quarter of an hour, read and expounded Scripture for about three quarters of an hour, prayed an hour, preached another hour, then prayed half an hour; the people then sang for about a quarter of an hour, during which he retired and took a little refreshment; he then went into the pulpit again, prayed an hour more, preached another hour, and then, with a prayer of half an hour, concluded the services." The clergy, too, were sometimes victims. An instance: "The rector of Fittleworth, in Sussex, was dispossessed of his living for Sabbath-breaking; the fact proved against him being, that as he was stepping over a stile one Sunday, the button of his breeches came off, and he got a tailor in the neighborhood presently to sew it on again." In the early history of New England the law compelled the people to attend church, the services commencing at nine o'clock and continuing six to eight hours. Near the church edifice stood the stocks and the whipping-post, and a large wooden cage, in which to confine offenders against the laws. The congregation had places assigned them upon the rude benches, at the annual town-meeting, according to their age and social position. A person was fined who occupied a seat assigned to another. The boys were ordered to sit upon the gallery-stairs, and three constables were employed to keep them in order. Prominent before the assembly, some wretched male or female offender sat with a scarlet letter on the breast, to denote some crime against the stern code. Fleeing the mother-country for peace and freedom, the descendants of the Puritans persecuted the Quakers, and burnt the incorrigible eccentrics of society for witches. We are told that at the time Ireland was called the Isle of Saints, " when a child was immersed at baptism, it was customary not to dip the right arm, to the intent that he might strike a more deadly and ungracious blow therewith ; and under an opinion, no doubt, that the rest of the body would not be responsible at the resurrection for anything which had been committed by the unbaptized hand. Thus, too, at the baptism, the father took the wolves for his gossips, and thought by this profanation he was forming an alliance, both for himself and the boy, with the fiercest beasts of the woods. The son of a chief was baptized in milk ; water was not thought good enough, and whisky had not then been invented. They used to rob in the beginning of the year as a point of devotion, for the purpose of laying up a good stock of plunder against Easter ; and he whose spoils enabled him to furnish the best entertainment at that time was looked upon as the best Christian ; so they robbed in emulation of each other ; and reconciling their habits to their conscience, they persuaded themselves that if robbery, murder, and rape had been sins, Providence would never put such temptations in their way ; nay, that the sin would be, if they were so ungrateful as not to take advantage of a good opportunity when it was offered them." In North Wales, it is stated, when a person supposes himself highly injured, it is not uncommon for him to go to some church dedicated to a celebrated saint, as Llan Elian in Anglesea, and Clynog in Carnarvonshire, and there to offer his enemy. He kneels down on his bare knees in the church, and offering a piece of money to the saint, calls down curses and misfortunes upon the offender and his family for generations to come, in the most firm belief that the imprecations will be fulfilled. Sometimes they repair to a sacred well instead of a church. Mrs. Gaskell, in her biography of Charlotte Brontë, tells of a squire of distinguished family and large property, who died at his house, not many miles from Haworth, only a few years ago. " His great amusement and occupation had been cock-fighting. When he was confined to his chamber with what he knew would be his last illness, he had his cocks brought up there, and watched the bloody battle from his bed. As his mortal disease increased and it became impossible for him to turn so as to follow the combat, he had looking-glasses arranged in such a manner around and above him, as he lay, that he could still see the cocks fighting. And in this manner he died." Says Helps, " Qualities are often inserted in a character in the most curious and inharmonious way ; and the end is that you have a man who is the strangest mixture of generosity and meanness, of kindness and severity, even of dishonesty and nobleness. Then the passions enter. Sometimes these just fit in, unfortunately, with good points of character, — so that

one man may be ruined by a passion which another
and a worse man would have escaped unhurt from.
Then there are the circumstances to which a character
is exposed, and which vary so much that it hardly
seems that people are living in the same world, so
different are to them the outward things they have to
contend with. Altogether, the human being becomes
such a complicated creature, that though at last you
may know something about some one specimen, —
what it will say and what it will do on a given occasion, — you never know enough about the creature to
condemn it." "Neither the vices nor the virtues of
man," says Taine, "are his nature; to praise or to
blame him is not to know him; approbation or disapprobation does not define him; the names of good or
bad tell us nothing of what he is. Put the robber
Cartouche in an Italian court of the fifteenth century; he would be a great statesman. Transport
this nobleman, stingy and narrow-minded, into a
shop; he will be an exemplary tradesman. This
public man, of inflexible probity, is in his drawing-
room an intolerable coxcomb. This father of a family, so humane, is an idiotic politician. Change a
virtue in its circumstances, and it becomes a vice;
change a vice in its circumstances, and it becomes a
virtue. Regard the same quality from two sides; on
one it is a fault, on the other a merit. The essential
of a man is found concealed far below these moral
badges. A *character* is a force, like gravity, weight,
or steam, capable, as it may happen, of pernicious or
profitable effects, and which must be defined otherwise than by the amount of weight it can lift or the

havoc it can cause. It is therefore to ignore man, to reduce him to an aggregate of virtues and vices; it is to lose sight in him of all but the exterior and social side; it is to neglect the inner and natural element." " The three sects that at one time chiefly engrossed the philosophical part of Rome were the Stoic, the Epicurean, and the Academic; and the chief ornaments of each were Cato, Atticus, and Cicero, who lived together in strict friendship, and a mutual esteem of each other's virtue." " Yet," says Montaigne, " in all the courts of ancient philosophy this is to be found, that the same lecturer there publishes the rules of temperance, and at the same time discourses of love and wantonness." " I know not," said the courtesan Lais, " what they talk of books, wisdom, and philosophy; but these men knock as often at my door as any others." Says Bayle, in his Critical Dictionary, " It was reported that Pericles turned out his wife, and lodged with Aspasia, a Magarian bawd, and plunged himself into lewdness, and spent a great part of his estate upon her. She was a woman of so great parts that Socrates went to see her, and carried his friends with him; and, to speak more clearly, she taught him rhetoric and politics. That which is most strange is, that those who frequented her carried their wives to her house, that they might hear her discourses and lectures, though she kept several courtesans at home. Pericles went to see Aspasia twice a day, and kissed her when he went in and when he came out; which was before he married her. She was accused of two crimes by the comedian Hermippus. He made himself a party against her in due form, and accused her before the judges of impiety, and of drawing women into her house to satisfy the lust of Pericles. During the trial of Aspasia, Pericles used so many entreaties with the judges, and shed so many tears, that he obtained her absolution. The Athenians said that Phidias, the most excellent sculptor in the world, and surveyor-general of all the works which Pericles ordered to be made for the ornament of the city, drew in the ladies under pretense of showing them the works of the greatest masters ; but in truth, to debauch and deliver them to Pericles."

" Good and bad men are each less so than they seem."

> " When man's first incense rose above the plain,
>   Of earth's two altars, one was built by Cain."

" As there is," said Coleridge, " much beast and some devil in man, so is there some angel and some God in man. The beast and the devil may be conquered, but in this life never destroyed." " I have ever delighted," said Boswell, " in that intellectual chemistry which can *separate* good qualities from evil in the same person." Hart, a Calvinistic Baptist minister, in Crabb Robinson's time, was so good a preacher and so bad a liver that it was said to him once, " Mr. Hart, when I hear you in the pulpit, I wish you were never out of it ; when I see you out of it, I wish you were never in it." One Mr. Nicholls, a Yorkshire clergyman in the days immediately succeeding the Reformation, who was " much addicted to drinking and company-keeping," used to say to his companions, " You must not heed me but when I am got three feet above the earth," that was, into the pulpit. Cotton Mather has preserved a choice specimen of invective against Dr. Owen, by one of the primitive Quakers, whose name was Fisher. It was, says Southey, a species of rhetoric in which they indulged freely, and exceeded all other sectarians. Fisher addressed him thus: " Thou fiery fighter and green-headed trumpeter; thou hedgehog and grinning dog; thou bastard, that tumbled out of the mouth of the Babylonish bawd; thou mole; thou tinker; thou lizard; thou bell of no metal, but the tone of a kettle; thou wheelbarrow; thou whirlpool; thou whirligig; oh, thou firebrand; thou adder and scorpion; thou louse; thou cow-dung; thou moon-calf; thou ragged tatterdemalion; thou Judas: thou livest in philosophy and logic, which are of the devil." The good Luther was a violent saint sometimes. Hear him express himself on the Catholic divines: " The papists are all asses, and will always remain asses. Put them in whatever sauce you choose, boiled, roasted, baked, fried, skinned, beat, hashed, they are always the same asses." Hear him salute the pope: " The pope was born out of the devil's posteriors. He is full of devils, lies, blasphemies, and idolatries; he is anti-Christ; the robber of churches; the ravisher of virgins; the greatest of pimps; the governor of Sodom, etc. If the Turks lay hold of us, then we shall be in the hands of the devil; but if we remain with the pope, we shall be in hell. What a pleasing sight would it be to see the pope and the cardinals hanging on one gallows, in exact order, like the seals which dangle from the bulls

of the pope! What an excellent council would they
hold under the gallows!" And hear him upon Henry
VIII.: "It is hard to say if folly can be more foolish,
or stupidity more stupid, than is the head of Henry.
He has not attacked me with the heart of a king, but
with the impudence of a knave. This rotten worm
of the earth, having blasphemed the majesty of my
King, I have a just right to bespatter his English
majesty with his own dirt and ordure. This Henry
has lied." The good Calvin was alike violent. He
hated Catholic and Lutheran. "His adversaries are
never others than knaves, lunatics, drunkards, and assassins. Sometimes they are characterized by the familiar appellatives of bulls, asses, cats, and hogs."
Beza, the disciple of Calvin, imitated his master.
Upon a Lutheran minister, Tilleman, he bestowed
these titles of honor: "Polyphemus; an ape; a great
ass who is distinguished from other asses by wearing
a hat; an ass on two feet; a monster composed of
part of an ape and wild ass; a villain who merits
hanging on the first tree we find." As to the Catholics, there is no end to the anathemas and curses of
the Fathers.

One of the old bishops called anger "the sinews
of the soul." It helped to fortify the rugged reformer in his conflicts, and illuminated the perilous
way he trod. "We oft by lightning read in darkest
nights." It is said the finest wine is pressed from
vintages which grow on fields once inundated with
lava. "I never work better," said Luther, "than
when I am inspired by anger; when I am angry I
can write, pray, and preach well; for then my whole

temperament is quickened, my understanding sharpened, and all mundane vexations and temptations depart." Burke said, "a vigorous mind is as necessarily accompanied with violent passions as a great fire with great heat." "No revolution (in public sentiment), civic or religious," said Sir Gilbert Elliot, "can be accomplished without that degree of ardor and passion which, in a later age, will be matter of ridicule to men who do not feel the occasion, and enter into the spirit of the times." "Our passions," said John Norris, "were given us to perfect and accomplish our natures, though by accidental misapplications to unworthy objects, they may turn to our degradation and dishonor. We may, indeed, be debased as well as ennobled by them; but then the fault is not in the large sails, but in the ill conduct of the pilot, if our vessel miss the haven." When one commended Charillus, the king of Sparta, for a gentle, a good, and a meek prince, his colleague said, "How can he be good who is not an enemy even to vicious persons?" Erasmus said of Luther that there were two natures in him: sometimes he wrote like an apostle, sometimes like a raving ribald. "When he was angry, invectives rushed from him like bowlder rocks down a mountain torrent in flood." But of *vanity* he had no trace. "Do not call yourselves Lutherans," he said; "call yourselves Christians. Who and what is Luther? Has Luther been crucified for the world?"

"The Latin tongue," says Montaigne, "is, as it were, natural to me; I understand it better than French, but I have not used to speak it, nor hardly

to write it, these forty years; and yet, upon an
extreme and sudden emotion, which I have fallen
into twice or thrice in my life, and once on seeing
my father, in perfect health, fall upon me in a swoon,
I have always uttered my first outcries and ejacula-
tions in Latin; nature starting up and forcibly
expressing itself, in spite of so long a discontinua-
tion." "Nature," says Bacon, "will be buried a
great time, and yet revive upon the occasion or temptation; like as it was with Æsop's damsel, turned
from a cat to a woman, who sat very demurely at the
board's end till a mouse ran before her." "A frog,"
said Publius Syrus, "would leap from a throne of
gold into a puddle." Layard relates an incident of
the party of Arabs which for some time had been
employed to assist him in excavating amongst the
ruins of Nineveh. One evening, after their day's
work, he observed them following a flock of sheep
belonging to the people of the village, shouting their
war-cry, flourishing their swords, and indulging in
the most extravagant gesticulations. He asked one
of the most active of the party to explain to him the
cause of such violent proceedings. "O Bey!" they
exclaimed almost together, "God be praised, we have
eaten butter and wheaten bread under your shadow,
and are content; but an Arab is an Arab. It is not·
for a man to carry about dirt in baskets, and to use a
spade all his life; he should be with his sword and
his mare in the desert. We are sad as we think of
the days when we plundered the Anayza, and we
must have excitement or our hearts must break.
Let us then believe that these are the sheep we have

taken from the enemy, and that we are driving them
to our tents." And off they ran, raising their wild
cry, and flourishing their swords, to the no small
alarm of the shepherd, who saw his sheep scamper-
ing in all directions. Hazlitt related an Indian
legend of a Brahman, " who was so devoted to abstract meditation, that in the pursuit of philosophy
he quite forgot his moral duties, and neglected ablu-
tion. For this he was degraded from the rank of
humanity, and transformed into a monkey. But even
when a monkey he retained his original propensities,
for he kept apart from other monkeys, and had no
other delight than that of eating cocoanuts, and
studying metaphysics." " Perhaps few narratives in
history or mythology," says Carlyle, " are more significant than that Moslem one of Moses and the
Dwellers by the Dead Sea. A tribe of men dwelt
on the shores of that same asphaltic lake ; and
having forgotten, as we are all too prone to do, the
inner facts of Nature, and taken up with the falsi-
ties and other semblances of it, were fallen into sad
conditions, — verging, indeed, towards a certain far
deeper lake. Whereupon it pleased kind Heaven to
send them the prophet Moses, with an instructive
word of warning out of which might have sprung
' remedial measures ' not a few. But no : the men of
the Dead Sea discovered, as the valet-species always
does in heroes or prophets, no comeliness in Moses ;
listened with real tedium to Moses, with light grinning, or splenetic sniffs and sneers, affecting even to
yawn ; and signified, in short, that they found him a
humbug, and even a bore. Such was the candid

theory these men of the asphalt lake formed to
themselves of Moses, that probably he was a humbug, that certainly he was a bore. Moses withdrew ;
but Nature and her rigorous veracities did not withdraw. The men of the Dead Sea, when we next
went to visit them, were all changed into apes, sitting on the trees there, grinning now in the most
*un*affected manner ; gibbering and chattering very
genuine nonsense ; finding the whole universe now
a most indisputable humbug ! The universe has *become* a humbug to those apes who thought it one.
There they sit and chatter, to this hour : only, I
believe, every Sabbath, there returns to them a bewildered half-consciousness, half-reminiscence ; and
they sit with their wizened, smoke-dried visages,
and such an air of supreme tragicality as apes may,
looking out through those blinking, smoke-bleared
eyes of theirs, into the wonderfulest universal smoky
twilight and undecipherable disordered dusk of
things ; wholly an uncertainty, unintelligibility,
they and it, and for commentary thereon, here and
there an unmusical chatter or mew, — truest, trag-
icalest humbug conceivable by the mind of man or
ape ! They made no use of their souls ; and so
have lost them. Their worship on the Sabbath now
is to roost there, with unmusical screeches, and half-
remember that they had souls." The shark is said
to have been the god the Sandwich Islanders, in their
savage state, chiefly worshiped, or sought to propi-
tiate. In their present semi-civilized, semi-Christian-
ized condition, it is said, they pray, and sing, and
moralize, in fair weather ; but when they get into

trouble they call upon the shark-god of their fathers for help or deliverance. Sir Walter Scott used to tell a story of a placid minister, near Dundee, who, in preaching on Jonah, said, "Ken ye, brethren, what fish it was that swallowed him? Aiblins ye may think it was a shark; nae, nae, my brethren, it was nae shark; or aiblins ye may think it was a sammon; nae, nae, my brethren, it was nae sammon; or aiblins ye may think it was a dolphin; nae, nae, my brethren, it was nae dolphin." Here an old woman, thinking to help her master out of a dead lift, cried out, "Aiblins, sir, it was a dunter" (the vulgar name of a species of whale common to the Scotch coast). "Aiblins, madam, ye 're an auld witch for taking the word of God out of my mouth," was the reply of the disappointed rhetorician. As Dr. Johnson was riding in a carriage through London on a rainy day, he overtook a poor woman carrying a baby, without any protection from the weather. Making the driver stop the coach, he invited the poor woman to get in with her child, which she did. After she had seated herself, the doctor said to her, "My good woman, I think it most likely that the motion of the coach will wake your child in a little while, and I wish you to understand that if you talk any baby-talk to it, you will have to get out of the coach." As the doctor had anticipated, the child soon awoke, and the forgetful mother exclaimed to it: "Oh! the little dear, is he going to open his eyesy-pysy?" "Stop the coach, driver!" shouted Johnson; and the woman had to get out and finish her journey on foot. Frederick William, of Prussia, father of the great Frederick, had a way of addressing, familiarly, the people he met in the streets of Berlin, utterly indifferent, we are told, to his own dignity and to the feelings of others ; if he could devise something that was not quite agreeable, it was sure to be said. The fear of such encounters sometimes made nervous people indiscreetly evade the royal presence. One Jew having fairly taken to his heels, he was pursued by the king in hot haste. " Why did you run away from me ? " said the king, when he came up with him in breathless dudgeon. " From fear," answered the Jew, in the most ingenuous manner ; but the rejoinder of the king was a hearty thwack with his cane, who roared out that he wished himself to be loved and not to be feared. Dr. Livingstone, when he first went into Africa, as a missionary, attached himself to the tribe of Bakwains. Their chief, Sechele, embraced Christianity, and became an assiduous reader of the Bible, the eloquence of Isaiah being peculiarly acceptable to him, and he was wont to say, " He was a fine man, that Isaiah : he knew how to speak." But his people were not so ready for conversion, although he calmly proposed to have them flogged into faith : " Do you imagine," he said, " these people will ever believe by your merely talking to them ? I can make them do nothing except by thrashing them ; and if you like I shall call my head men, and with our litupa (whips of rhinoceros hide) we will soon make them believe altogether." We have it upon authority that when a fugitive from one of the early Protestant missions in New California was captured, he was " brought back again to the mission, where he was bastinadoed, and an iron rod of a foot or a foot and a half long, and an inch in diameter, was fastened to one of his feet, which had the double use of preventing him from repeating the attempt, and of frightening others from imitating him." Southey says that " one of the missionaries whom Virgilius, the bishop of Salzburg, sent among the Slavonic people, made the converted serfs sit with him at table, where wine was served to them in gilt beakers, while he ordered their unbaptized lords to sit on the ground, out of doors, where the food and wine was thrown before them, and they were left to serve themselves." " Seeing a large building," relates Robinson, " I asked a man who looked like a journeyman weaver what it was. He told me a grammar-school. ' But, sir,' he added, ' I think it would become you better on the Lord's day morning to be reading your Bible at home, than asking about public buildings.' I very quickly answered: ' My friend, you have given me a piece of very good advice; let me give you one, and we may both profit by our meeting. Beware of spiritual pride.' The man scowled with a Scotch surliness, and, apparently, did not take my counsel with as much good humor as I did his." " In one of the debates on the Catholic question," said Lord Byron, " when we were either equal or within one (I forget which), I had been sent for in great haste to a ball, which I quitted, I confess, somewhat reluctantly, to emancipate five millions of people." Some ladies bantering Selwyn on his want of feeling, in attending to see Lord Lovat's head cut off, " Why," he

said, "I made amends by going to the undertaker's
to see it sewn on again." "I have," says Heine,
"the most peaceable disposition. My desires are a
modest cottage with thatched roof — but a good bed,
good fare, fresh milk and butter, flowers by my window, and a few fine trees before the door. And if
the Lord wished to fill my cup of happiness, He
would grant me the pleasure of seeing some six or
seven of my enemies hanged on those trees. With
a heart moved to pity, I would, before their death,
forgive the injury they had done me during their
lives. Yes, we ought to forgive our enemies — but
not until they are hanged." Some would pursue
them after they are hanged. "Our measure of
rewards and punishments," says Thackeray, "is most
partial and incomplete, absurdly inadequate, utterly
worldly, and we wish to continue it into the next
world. Into that next and awful world we strive to
pursue men, and send after them our impotent party
verdicts, of condemnation or acquittal. We set up
our paltry little rods to measure Heaven immeasurable, as if, in comparison to that, Newton's mind, or
Pascal's, or Shakespeare's, was any loftier than
mine; as if the ray which travels from the sun
would reach me sooner than the man who blacks my
boots. Measured by that altitude, the tallest and
the smallest among us are so alike diminutive and
pitifully base that I say we should take no count of
the calculation, and it is a meanness to reckon the
difference."

Tertullian, according to Lecky, had written a treatise dissuading the Christians of his day from fre-

quenting the public spectacles. He had collected on
the subject many arguments, some of them very
powerful, and others extremely grotesque ; but he
perceived that to make his exhortations forcible to
the majority of his readers, he must point them to
some counter-attraction. He accordingly proceeded
— and his style assumed a richer glow and a more
impetuous eloquence as he rose to the congenial
theme — to tell them that a spectacle was reserved for
them, so fascinating and so attractive that the most
joyous festivals of earth faded in insignificance by the
comparison. That spectacle was the agonies of their
fellow-countrymen as they writhe amid the torments
of hell. " What! " he exclaimed, " shall be the
magnitude of that scene ! How shall I wonder !
How shall I laugh ! How shall I rejoice ! How shall
I triumph, when I behold so many and such illustrious kings, who were said to have mounted into
heaven, groaning with Jupiter their god in the lowest
darkness of hell ! Then shall the soldiers who had
persecuted the name of Christ burn in more cruel fire
than any they had kindled for the saints. Then shall
the tragedians pour forth in their own misfortune
more piteous cries than those with which they had
made the theatre to resound, while the comedian's
powers shall be better seen as he becomes more flex-
ible by the heat. Then shall the driver of the circus
stand forth to view, all blushing in his flaming chariot,
and the gladiators pierced, not by spears, but by darts
of fire. Compared with such spectacles, with such
subjects of triumph as these, what can prætor or
consul, quæstor or pontiff, afford ? And even now

faith can bring them near, imagination can depict
them as present!" Crabb Robinson says some one
at a party at which he was present, abusing Mahomet-
anism in a commonplace way, said: "Its heaven is
quite material." He was met with the quiet remark,
"So is the Christian's hell;" to which there was no
reply. In the time of Tertullian, "the angel in the
Last Judgment was constantly represented weighing
the souls in a literal balance, while devils clinging to
the scales endeavored to disturb the equilibrium."
"The redbreast, according to one popular legend,
was commissioned by the Deity to carry a drop of
water to the souls of unbaptized infants in hell, and
its breast was singed in piercing the flames." "A
Calvinistic divine, of the name of Petit Pierre, was
ejected from his church at Neufchatel for preaching
and publishing the doctrine that the damned would at
some future period be pardoned. A member said to
him, 'My good friend, I no more believe in the
eternity of hell than yourself; but recollect that it
may be no bad thing, perhaps, for your servant, your
tailor, and your lawyer, to believe in it.'" We are
told of a country clergyman in France, who, having
had a great number of sheep stolen from him, at
length said to his hearers, in the course of one of his
sermons, "I cannot conceive what Christ was thinking about when he died for such a set of scoundrels
as you are." This assault reminds one of the carrancha, a kind of hawk in South America, which
"picks off the scabs from the sore backs of horses
and mules. The poor animal, on the one hand, with
its ears down, and back arched, and, on the other,

the hovering bird eying at the distance of a yard the disgusting morsel, form a picture which has been described by Captain Hill with his peculiar spirit and accuracy." The carrancha also pursues the gallinazo, one of the carrion-eating tribe, "till that bird is compelled to vomit up the carrion it may have recently gorged." Mrs. Gaskell relates this of Rev. William Grimshaw, curate of Haworth for twenty years, who "was occasionally assisted by Wesley and Whitefield, and at such times the little church proved much too small to hold the throng that poured in from distant villages, or lonely moorland hamlets; and frequently they were obliged to meet in the open air; indeed there was not room enough in the church even for the communicants. Mr. Whitefield was once preaching in Haworth, and made use of some such expression, as that he 'hoped there was no need to say much to this congregation, as they had sat under so pious and godly a minister for so many years;' whereupon Mr. Grimshaw stood up in his place, and said with a loud voice, 'Oh, sir! for God's sake do not speak so. I pray you do not flatter them. I fear the greater part of them are going to hell with their eyes open.'" Cowper's friend, Newton, says this in one of his letters: "A friend of mine was desired to visit a woman in prison; he was informed of her evil habits of life, and therefore spoke strongly of the terrors of the Lord, and the curses of the law: she heard him a while, and then laughed in his face; upon this he changed his note, and spoke of the Saviour, and what he had done and suffered for sinners. He had not talked long in this strain before he saw a

tear or two in her eyes: at length she interrupted
him by saying: ' Why, sir, do you think there can be
any hope of mercy for me?' He answered, ' Yes, if
you feel your need of it, and are willing to seek it in
God's appointed way. I am sure it is as free for you
as for myself.' She replied, ' Ah, if I had thought
so, I should not have been in this prison. I long since
settled it in my mind that I was utterly lost; that
I had sinned beyond all possibility of forgiveness,
and that made me desperate.' " " The most awfully
tremendous of all metaphysical divines," wrote Robinson, " is the American ultra Calvinist, Jonathan
Edwards, whose book on Original Sin I unhappily
read when a very young man. It did me an irrepar-
able mischief."

" Soon after the accession of James I. to the throne
of England," writes Lecky, in his History of Ration-
alism in Europe, " a law was enacted which subjected
witches to death on the first conviction, even though
they should have inflicted no injury upon their neighbors. This law was passed when Coke was attorney-
general, and Bacon a member of Parliament; and
twelve bishops sat upon the commission to which it
was referred. The prosecutions were rapidly multiplied throughout the country, but especially in Lan-
cashire, and at the same time the general tone of literature was strongly tinged with the superstition. Sir
Thomas Browne declared that those who denied the
existence of witchcraft were not only ' infidels, but
also, by implication, atheists.' In Cromwell's time
there was still greater persecution. The county of
Suffolk was especially agitated, and the famous

witch-finder, Matthew Hopkins, pronounced it to be infested with witches. A commission was accordingly issued, and two distinguished Presbyterian divines were selected by the Parliament to accompany it. It would have been impossible to take any measure more calculated to stimulate the prosecutions, and we accordingly find that in Suffolk sixty persons were hung for witchcraft in a single year. In 1664 two women were hung in Suffolk, under a sentence of Sir Matthew Hale, who took the opportunity of declaring that the reality of witchcraft was unquestionable; 'for, first, the Scriptures had affirmed so much; and, secondly, the wisdom of all nations had provided laws against such persons, which is an argument of their confidence of such a crime.' Sir Thomas Browne, who was a great physician, as well as a great writer, was called as a witness, and swore 'that he was clearly of opinion that the persons were bewitched.' "

Here is a terrible story, perfectly well authenticated, taken from the official report of the proceedings by an English historian: " Towards the end of 1593 there was trouble in the family of the Earl of Orkney. His brother laid a plot to murder him, and was said to have sought the help of a notorious witch called Alison Balfour. When Alison Balfour's life was looked into, no evidence could be found connecting her either with the particular offense or with witchcraft in general; but it was enough in these matters to be accused. She swore she was innocent; but her guilt was only held to be aggravated by perjury. She was tortured again and again. Her legs

were put in the caschilaws,— an iron frame which
was gradually heated till it burned into the flesh,—
but no confession could be wrung from her. The
caschilaws failed utterly, and something else had to
be tried. She had a husband, a son, and a daughter,
a child seven years old. As her own sufferings did
not work upon her, she might be touched, perhaps,
by the sufferings of those who were dear to her.
They were brought into court, and placed at her
side, and the husband first placed in the ' long irons '
— some accursed instrument, I know not what.
Still the devil did not yield. She bore this ; and
her son was next operated on. The boy's legs were
set in ' the boot,'— the iron boot you may have heard
of. The wedges were driven in, which, when forced
home, crushed the very bone and marrow. Fifty-seven
mallet strokes were delivered upon the wedges. Yet
this, too, failed. There was no confession yet. • So,
last of all, the little daughter was taken. There was
a machine called the piniwinkies — a kind of thumb-
screw, which brought blood from under the finger-
nails, with a pain successfully terrible. These things
were applied to the poor child's hands, and the mother's constancy broke down, and she said she would
admit anything they wished. She confessed her
witchcraft, — so tried, she would have confessed to
the seven deadly sins, — and then she was burned,
recalling her confession, and with her last breath
protesting her innocence."

"In 1768 John Wesley prefaced an account of an
apparition that had been related by a girl named
Elizabeth Hobson, by some extremely remarkable

sentences on the subject. 'It is true, likewise,' he wrote, 'that the English in general, and, indeed, most of the men of learning in Europe, have given up all accounts of witches and apparitions as mere old wives' fables. I am sorry for it, and I willingly take this opportunity of entering my solemn protest against this violent compliment which so many that believe the Bible pay to those that do not believe it. I owe them no such service. I take knowledge that these are at the bottom of the outcry which has been raised, and with such insolence spread through the land, in direct opposition, not only to the Bible, but to the suffrage of the wisest and best men in all ages and nations. They well know (whether Christians know it or not) that the giving up of witchcraft is in effect giving up the Bible.' In the first year of this persecution, Cotton Mather wrote a history of the earliest of the trials. This history was introduced to the English public by Richard Baxter, who declared in his preface that 'that man must be a very obdurate Sadducee who would not believe it.' Not content with having thus given the weight of his great name to the superstition, Baxter in the following year published his treatise on The Certainty of the World of Spirits; in which he collected, with great industry, an immense number of witch cases; reverted in extremely laudatory terms to Cotton Mather and his crusade; and denounced, in unmeasured language, all who were skeptical upon the subject. This work appeared in 1691, when the panic in America had not yet reached its height; and being widely circulated there, is said to have contributed much to stimulate the persecutions. The Pilgrim Fathers had brought to America the seeds of the persecution; and at the same time when it was rapidly fading in England, it flourished with fearful vigor in Massachusetts. Cotton Mather and Parris proclaimed the frequency of the crime; and, being warmly supported by their brother divines, they succeeded in creating a panic through the whole country. A commission was issued. A judge named Stoughton, who appears to have been a perfect creature of the clergy, conducted the trials. Scourgings and tortures were added to the terrorism of the pulpit, and many confessions were obtained. The few who ventured to oppose the prosecutions were denounced as Sadducees and infidels. Multitudes were thrown into prison, others fled from the country, abandoning their property, and twenty-seven persons were executed. An old man of eighty was pressed to death — a horrible sentence, which was never afterwards executed in America. [Giles Corey was the name of the victim. He refused to plead, to save his property from confiscation. He urged the executioners, says Upham, in his History of Witchcraft and Salem Village, to increase the weight which was crushing him; he told them that it was no use to expect him to yield; that there could be but one way of ending the matter, and that they might as well pile on the stones. Calef says, that as his body yielded to the pressure, his tongue protruded from his mouth, and an official forced it back with his cane.] The ministers of Boston and Charlestown drew up an address, warmly thanking the commissioners for their zeal, and ex-

pressing their hope that it would never be relaxed."
" There is no more painful reading than this," says
Lowell, in his essay on Witchcraft, " except the
trials of the witches themselves. These awaken,
by turns, pity, indignation, disgust, and dread, —
dread at the thought of what the human mind may
be brought to believe not only probable, but proven.
But it is well to be put upon our guard by lessons of
this kind, for the wisest man is in some respects little
better than a madman in a straight-waistcoat of
habit, public opinion, prudence, or the like. Skepticism began at length to make itself felt, but it
spread slowly, and was shy of proclaiming itself.
The orthodox party was not backward to charge with
sorcery whoever doubted their facts or pitied their
victims. The mob, as it always is, was orthodox.
It was dangerous to doubt, it might be fatal to deny."

" The spirit of party," quaintly says Bayle, in his
Critical Dictionary, discoursing of Margaret, Queen
of Navarre, " the attachment to a sect, and even zeal
for orthodoxy, produce a kind of ferment in the
humors of our body ; and hence the medium through
which reason ought to behold these primitive ideas, is
clouded and obscured. These are infirmities which
will attend our reason, as long as it shall depend
upon the ministry of organs. It is the same thing
to it, as the low and middle region of the air, the
seat of vapors and meteors. There are but very
few persons who can elevate themselves above these
clouds, and place themselves in a true serenity. If
any one could do it, we must say of him what Virgil
did of Daphnis : —

   'Daphnis, the guest of Heaven, with wondering eyes,
   Views in the milky-way the starry skies ;
   And far beneath him, from the shining sphere,
   Beholds the moving clouds and rolling year.'

And he would not have so much the appearance of a man, as of an immortal Being, placed upon a mountain above the region of wind and clouds. There is almost as much necessity for being above the passions to come to a knowledge of some kind of truths, as to act virtuously." "How limited is human reason," exclaims Disraeli, the younger, " the profoundest inquirers are most conscious. We are not indebted to the reason of man for any of the great achievements which are the landmarks of human action and human progress. It was not reason that besieged Troy ; it was not reason that sent forth the Saracen from the desert to conquer the world ; that inspired the crusades ; that instituted the monastic orders ; it was not reason that produced the Jesuits ; above all, it was not reason that enacted the French Revolution. Man is only truly great when he acts from the passions ; never irresistible but when he appeals to the imagination. Even Mormon counts more votaries than Bentham." " Let us not dream," said Goethe, " that reason can ever be popular. Passions, emotions, may be made popular ; but reason remains ever the property of an elect few." " It is not from reason and prudence that people marry," said Dr. Johnson, " but from inclination. A man is poor ; he thinks it cannot be worse, and so I 'll e'en marry Peggy." " If people," says Thackeray, " only made prudent marriages, what a stop to population there would be ! "

III.

DISGUISES.

MAN, poor fellow, would be a curious object for microscopic study. If it were possible to view him through powerful glasses, what humiliating resemblances and infirmities would be discovered. He would be found to have innumerable tentacula and appendages, for protection and warning, and especially to possess unconceived of apparatus for making his way in the dark, — necessities to him, it would appear, when further inspection of the creature had shown him to be — blind. At last, he finds himself obliged to rely upon such qualities and faculties as take the place of powers and eyes. Cowardly, he is gregarious, and will not live alone ; weak, he consorts with weakness, to acquire strength ; ignorant, he contributes the least bit of reason to the common stock of intelligence, and escapes responsibility. One of many, he has the protection of the mob ; embodying others' weaknesses, he is strong in the bundle of sticks ; joining his voice with the million, it is lost in the confusion of tongues. Attacked, he is fortified by his society ; down, he will rise again with his fellows ; stupid with the rest, his shame is unfelt by being diffused. In any extremity, there is safety in counsel ; in the ranks, he cannot run ; in the crowd,

it were vain to think. Weary of stagnation or tired
by the eddies, he goes with the current; unable to
stand an individual, he joins with a party; a poor
creature of God, he is afraid to trust Him on his
Word, and flies to a sect with a creed for protection.
In the wake of thought, he may be thoughtless; vot-
ing the ticket, he is a patriot; a stiff bigot, there can
be no doubt about his religion. He submits to be
thought for as a child; to be cared for as an invalid;
to be subordinated as an idiot. Unequal to a scheme
of his own, he falls into one already devised for him;
without independent views, he relies upon his newspaper; without implicit trust in God, he leans upon
a broken reed in preference. Thus his business, his
politics, his religion, are defined for him, and are of easy
reference; indeed it may be said he knows them by
heart, so little there is of them. Of the laws of trade,
political economy, essential Christianity, he may be
as ignorant as a barbarian, at the same time be com-
placent and respectable in his ignorance. Acting for
himself, he would be set down as eccentric by his
banker; thinking for himself, he would be thought to
be too uncertain to be trustworthy; living virtuously,
walking humbly, and trusting his Creator to take care
of his creature, he would be an object of suspicion,
even if he escaped being called an infidel. His tailor
determines the cut of his coat; the street defines his
manners and morals; custom becomes his law, and
compliance his gospel. Addison, in The Spectator,
gives an account of a gentleman who determined to
live and dress according to the rules of common sense,
and was shut up in a lunatic asylum in consequence.

" Custom," says Carlyle, " doth make dotards of us
all. Philosophy complains that custom has hood-
winked us from the first; that we do everything by
custom, even believe by it; that our very axioms,
let us boast of free-thinking as we may, are oftenest
simply such beliefs as we have never heard ques-
tioned." " In this great society wide lying around
us," says Emerson, " a critical analysis would find
very few spontaneous actions. It is almost all custom
and gross sense." Nevertheless, there are a few, and
many more than appear. " Every man is conscious,"
says Lowell, " that he leads two lives, — the one
trivial and ordinary, the other sacred and recluse ; one
which he carries to society and the dinner-table, the
other in which his youth and aspirations survive for
him, and which is a confidence between himself and
God. Both may be equally sincere, and there need
be no contradiction between them, any more than in
a healthy man between soul and body." But we play
our parts so faithfully, not to say conscientiously, that
often we have difficulty in placing ourselves, whether
with the assumed or the natural. The little arts and
artifices we thrive by, become essentially a part of us ;
and in the jostle and conflict — the greater to devour
the lesser and the lesser the least — we become in a
manner stolid, and seem impelled to pursue the objects
and ends which long habit has somehow convinced us
nature particularly suited us to pursue. When an
event occurs to attract attention to our follies or baseness, it has not the effect to prompt repentance, but
to excite our cunning, and set us to work to find ex-
cuses, or to imagine some other course of conduct

which would have been more foolish or mischievous. "We keep on deceiving ourselves in regard to our faults, until we, at last, come to look upon them as virtues." Like Selwyn, the accomplished courtier and wit in the time of George III., we get to think even our vices necessities. After a night of elegant rioting and debauch, he tumbled out of his bed at ·noon the next day, and reeling with both hands upon his brain to a mirror in his apartment, gazed at himself and soliloquized : " I look and feel most villainously mean ; but it 's life — hang it, it 's life ! " Very readily our ethics are made to fortify our follies, and make them imposing and respectable. Infirmities and calamities even have been made to serve an important use in the designs of men. " It was necessary," says a writer upon Mahomet, " that the religion he proposed to establish should have a divine sanction ; and for this purpose he turned a calamity with which he was afflicted to his advantage. He was often subject to fits of epilepsy, a disease which those whom it afflicts are desirous to conceal ; Mahomet gave out, therefore, that these fits were trances, into which he was miraculously thrown by God Almighty, during which he was instructed in his will, which he was commanded to publish to the world. By this strange story, and by leading a retired, abstemious, and austere life, he easily acquired a character for superior sanctity among his acquaintances and neighbors. When he thought himself sufficiently fortified by the numbers and enthusiasm of his followers, he boldly · declared himself a prophet, sent by God into the world, not only to teach his will, but to compel mankind to obey it." The world not only seems easily deceived, but seems to delight in deception. "If you wish to be powerful," said Horne Tooke, "pretend to be powerful." If you wish to be considered wise, systematically pretend to be, and you will generally be acknowledged to be. We all know the influence of manner, as sometimes displayed by persons of great assumed personal dignity. Every neighborhood is afflicted with such characters. "Among those terms," says Whipple, indignantly, "which have long ceased to have any vital meaning, the word dignity deserves a disgraceful prominence. No word has fallen so readily into the designs of cant, imposture, and pretense ; none has played so well the part of verbal scarecrow, to frighten children of all ages and both sexes. It is at once the thinnest and most effective of all the coverings under which duncedom sneaks and skulks. Most of the men of dignity, who awe or bore their more genial brethren, are simply men who possess the art of passing off their insensibility for wisdom, their dullness for depth, and of concealing imbecility of intellect under haughtiness of manner. Their success in this small game is one of the stereotyped satires upon mankind. Once strip from these pretenders their stolen garments — once disconnect their show of dignity from their real meanness — and they would stand shivering and defenseless, — objects of the tears of pity, or targets for the arrows of scorn. . . . . Manner triumphs over matter ; and throughout society, politics, letters, and science, we are doomed to meet a swarm of dunces and wind-bags, disguised as gentlemen, statesmen, and scholars." When they open their

6

mouths, it is to expand themselves with a new inhalation of emptiness, or to depreciate or belittle what they pretend is insignificant, because beyond their capacity. They put up their heads and expectorate with a smirky haughtiness, as if everything worth knowing were known to them, when a single sensation of modesty would envelop their moony faces with blushes. Every one has seen such a character, — "an embodied tediousness, which society is apt not only to tolerate, but to worship ; a person who announces the stale commonplaces of conversation with the awful precision of one bringing down to the valleys of thought bright truths plucked on its summits ; who is so profoundly deep and painfully solid, on the weather, or some nothing of the day ; who is inexpressibly shocked if your eternal gratitude does not repay him for the trite information he consumed your hour in imparting ; and who, if you insinuate that this calm, contented, imperturbable stupidity is preying upon your patience, instantly stands upon his dignity, and puts on a face." "A certain nobleman, some years ago," says Bulwer, in his Caxtons, "was conspicuous for his success in the world. He had been employed in the highest situations, at home and abroad, without one discoverable reason for his selection, and without justifying the selection by one proof of administrative ability. Yet at each appointment the public said, 'A great gain to the government! Superior man!' And when from each office he passed away, or rather passed imperceptibly onward toward offices still more exalted, the public said, 'A great loss to the government! Superior man!' He was the most silent person I ever met. But when the first reasoners of the age would argue some knotty point in his presence, he would, from time to time, slightly elevate his eyebrows, gently shake his head, or, by a dexterous smile of significant complacency, impress on you the notion how easily he could set those babblers right if he would but condescend to give voice to the wisdom within him. I was very young when I first met this superior man; and chancing on the next day to call on the late Lord Durham, I said, in the presumption of early years, ' I passed six mortal hours last evening in company with Lord ——. I don't think there is much in him.' ' Good heavens ! ' cried Lord Durham, ' how did you find that out? Is it possible that he could have — talked ? ' " Coleridge speaks of a dignified man he once saw at a dinner-table. " He listened to me," says the poet, " and said nothing for a long time ; but he nodded his head, and I thought him intelligent. At length, toward the end of the dinner, some apple dumplings were placed on the table, and my man had no sooner seen them, than he burst forth with — ' Them 's the jockies for me ! ' I wish Spurzheim could have examined the fellow's head." The Duke of Somerset is described as one of these dignified gentlemen. His second wife was one of the most beautiful women in England. She once suddenly threw her arms around his neck, and gave him a kiss which might have gladdened the heart of an emperor. The duke, lifting his shoulders with an aristocratic square, slowly said, " Madam, my first wife was a Howard, and she never would have taken such a liberty ! " If it were practicable to expose the artifice and emptiness of such characters, the exhibition would be as amusing as the scene once unexpectedly presented on the stage of a theatre. The comedian; enveloped in a great india-rubber suit, expanded by air to give it the proper proportions to represent Falstaff, when just in the middle of one of the inimitable speeches of that inimitable character, some wag of the stock insinuated a sharp-pointed instrument into the immense windful garment : immediately the great proportions of Falstaff began to diminish, attended by an audible hissing noise ; and before the discomposed actor, overwhelmed with the laughter of the uproarious audience, could retire from the stage, he had shrunk to an insignificant one hundred and fifty pounds avoirdupois, with his deceptive covering hanging about his gaunt limbs in voluminous folds ! Such persons will generally be found with good moral habits — props they instinctively set up to sustain their pretenses. They know by intuition that an affectation of wisdom and greatness would be intolerable attended by vicious propensities and practices, and they cultivate with systematic carefulness all the forms of morality and virtue. They know that their good habits will always insure the respect of even those who detect and despise their emptiness. But they are never heard to claim anything on the score of superior virtue ; they demand to be known as Solons — as abridgments of all that is profound and wonderful known among men. Like the owl — that wise bird, sacred of old to Minerva — they make their pretensions respected by the most commendable propriety. Occasionally they may waive their conventional virtue, and lapse a little, without suffering in their trade of deception, if only the frailty be one which is indulged by the rich or the great; indeed it may advance them in proportion as they imitate their envied exemplars. Goldsmith, that sweet writer of pure English, of whom it has been said he never wrote a line which he could have wished to blot, relates this in his Citizen of the World: " The Russians, who trade with the Tartars of Koreki, carry thither a kind of mushrooms, which they exchange for furs of squirrels, ermines, sables, and foxes. These mushrooms the rich Tartars lay up in large quantities for the winter; and when a nobleman makes a mushroom-feast, all the neighbors around are invited. The mushrooms are prepared by boiling, by which the water acquires an intoxicating quality, and is the sort of drink which the Tartars prize beyond all other. When the nobility and ladies are assembled, and the ceremonies usual between people of distinction over, the mushroom-broth goes freely round; they laugh, talk double entendre, grow fuddled, and become excellent company. The poorer sort, who love mushroom-broth to distraction as well as the rich, but cannot afford it at the first hand, post themselves on these occasions round the huts of the rich, and watch the opportunity of the ladies and gentlemen as they come down to pass their liquor; and holding a wooden bowl, catch the delicious fluid, very little altered by filtration, being still strongly tinctured with the intoxicating quality. Of this they drink with the utmost satisfaction, and thus they get as drunk and jovial as their betters."

The absorbing desire for wealth — " that bad
thing, gold," that " buys all things good." — like
ambition, " often puts men upon doing the meanest
offices : as climbing is performed in the same posture
with creeping." Almost every act may be a lie
against the thought or motive which prompted it.
The great aim of the mere money-getter — to get
and get forever — involves him in false pretense and
practical falsehood. He advises to inveigle ; he con-
doles and sympathizes to ruin. He talks of liberal-
ity, and never gives. He depreciates money and the
love of it, at the same time glows and dimples with
the consciousness of his possessions. He calls life a
humbug and muck, and proves it by a hypocritical
exhibit of his gains. He puts a penny in the urn of
poverty, and sees clearly how he will get a shilling
out. He whines for wretchedness, forgetting the
number he has made wretched. He gives to religion,
and plunders her devotees. He hires an expensive
pew near the pulpit, and. cheats his woodsawyer and
washer-woman. He builds costly churches with tall
steeples, and, writing the Almighty in his list of debt-
ors, formally bargains admission to heaven. " He
falls down and worships the god of *this* world, but
will have neither its pomps, its vanities, nor its pleasures, for his trouble. He begins to accumulate treas-
ure as a mean to happiness, and by a common but
morbid association, he continues to accumulate it as
an end. He lives poor to die rich, and is the mere
jailer of his house, and the turnkey of his wealth.
Impoverished by his gold, he slaves harder to imprison
it in his chest, than his brother-slave to liberate it

from the mine." " Foote, in endeavoring to express the microscopic niggardliness of a miser of his acquaintance, expressed a belief that he would be willing to take the *beam* out of his own eye if he knew he could sell the timber. Doubtless one source of the miser's insane covetousness and parsimony is the tormenting fear of dying a beggar — that 'fine horror of poverty,' according to Lamb, ' by which he is not content to keep want from the door, or at arm's-length, but he places it, by heaping wealth upon wealth, *at a sublime distance.*' " (" All the arguments which are brought to represent poverty as no evil," impatiently exclaimed Dr. Johnson, " show it to be evidently a great evil. You never find people laboring to convince you that you may live very happily upon a plentiful fortune. So you hear people talking how miserable a king must be ; and yet they all wish to be in his place.") The hoarding habits of the miser remind one of a device of American boatmen, at an early day, before the steamboat was invented, and when the forest was infested with red men and robbers. Receiving specie at New Orleans for their produce, they deposited it in a wet buckskin belt, of sufficient length to surround the body, which, as it dried, contracted and shrunk round the coin, till no amount of shaking would cause it to jingle. So may the heart and soul of the avaricious man shrink round his little heap of gold, until all healthy circulation ceases, and his heart never jingles with a genuine, generous, manly impulse. Disraeli, in his Curiosities, gives an interesting philosophical sketch of Audley, — the great Audley, as he was called in his time,

— who concentrated all the powers of a vigorous intellect in the accumulation of wealth. He lived in England in the beginning of the seventeenth century, through the reigns of James I. and Charles I., and, beginning life with almost nothing, died worth four hundred thousand pounds sterling. He " lived to view his mortgages, his statutes, and his judgments so numerous, that it was observed, his papers would have made a good map of England. This philosophical usurer never pressed hard for his debts ; like the fowler, he never shook his nets lest he might startle, satisfied to have them, without appearing to hold them. With great fondness he compared his ' bonds to infants, which battle best by sleeping.' To battle is to be nourished, a term still retained at the University of Oxford. His familiar companions were all subordinate actors in the great piece he was performing ; he too had his part in the scene. When not taken by surprise, on his table usually laid open a great Bible, with Bishop Andrews' folio Sermons, which often gave him an opportunity of railing at the covetousness of the clergy ! declaring their religion was a ' mere preach,' and that ' the time would never be well till we had Queen Elizabeth's Protestants again in fashion.' He was aware of all the reasons arising out of a population beyond the means of subsistence, and dreaded an inundation of man, spreading like the spawn of a cod. Hence he considered marriage, with a modern political economist, as very dangerous ; bitterly censuring the clergy, whose children, he said, never thrived, and whose widows were left destitute. An apostolic life, ac-

cording to Audley, required only books, meat, and
drink, to be had for fifty pounds a year! Celibacy,
voluntary poverty, and all the mortifications of a
primitive Christian, were the virtues practiced by
this Puritan among his money-bags. Audley's was
that worldly wisdom which derives all its strength
from the weaknesses of mankind. Everything was
to be obtained by stratagem, and it was his maxim,
that to grasp our object the faster, we must go a little
round about it. His life is said to have been one of
intricacies and mysteries, using indirect means in all
things; but if he walked in a labyrinth, it was to
bewilder others; for the clew was still in his own
hand; all he sought was that his designs should not
be discovered in his actions. His word, we are told,
was his bond; his hour was punctual; and his opinions were compressed and weighty; but if he was
true to his bond-word, it was only a part of the system to give facility to the carrying on of his trade,
for he was not strict to his honor; the pride of victory, as well as the passion for acquisition, combined
in the character of Audley, as in more tremendous
conquerors. In the course of time he purchased a
position in the 'court of wards,' which enabled him
to plunder the estates of deceased persons and minors.
When asked the value of this new office, he replied
that 'it might be worth some thousands of pounds
to him who after his death would go instantly to
heaven; twice as much to him who would go to pur-
gatory, and nobody knows what to him who would
adventure to go to hell.'" What he thought of a
venture to the latter place, his four hundred thousand
pounds must speak.

Did you ever read that remarkable out-of-the-way paper of Lamb's, the Reminiscences of Juke Judkins, Esq., of Birmingham? It is a nice, microscopic, philosophic study and analysis of meanness, — as common, we dare say, in this world, as avarice, — and will make us wonder that ordinary gifts and traits can be so perverted and belittled by debasing uses. All that is good of humanity was once united with Divinity, and made the best character that ever existed on earth. Humiliating it would be, if not impious, to imagine how much worse might be the devil if he would adopt the bestial qualities and worse than Satanic traits that men are constantly exposing and cultivating in their relations with one another. " I was always," says Juke, " my father's favorite. He took a delight, to the very last, in recounting the little sagacious tricks and innocent artifices of my childhood. One manifestation thereof I never heard him repeat without tears of joy trickling down his cheeks. It seems that when I quitted the parental roof (August 27, 1788), being then six years and not quite a month old, to proceed to the Free School at Warwick, where my father was a sort of trustee, my mother — as mothers are usually provident on these occasions — had stuffed the pocket of the coach, which was to convey me and six more children of my own growth that were going to be entered along with me at the same seminary, with a prodigious quantity of gingerbread, which I remember my father said was more than was needed: and so indeed it was ; for, if I had been to eat it all myself, it would have got stale and mouldy before it had

been half spent. The consideration whereof set me
upon my contrivances how I might secure to myself
as much of the gingerbread as would keep good for
the next two or three days, and yet none of the rest
in manner be wasted. I had a little pair of pocket
compasses, which I usually carried about me for the
purpose of making draughts and measurements, at
which I was always very ingenious, of the various
engines and mechanical inventions in which such a
town as Birmingham abounded. By the means of
these, and a small penknife which my father had
given me, I cut out the one half of the cake, calcu-
lating that the remainder would reasonably serve my
turn ; and subdividing it into many little slices,
which were curious to see for the neatness and nice-
ness of their proportion, I sold it out in so many
pennyworths to my young companions as served us
all the way to Warwick, which is a distance of some
twenty miles from this town ; and very merry, I assure you, we made ourselves with it, feasting all the
way. By this honest stratagem, I put double the
prime cost of the gingerbread into my purse, and se-
cured as much as I thought would keep good and
moist for my next two or three days' eating. When
I told this to my parents on their first visit to me at
Warwick, my father (good man) patted me on the
cheek, and stroked my head, and seemed as if he
could never make enough of me ; but my mother un-
accountably burst into tears, and said ' it was a very
niggardly action,' or some such expression, and that
' she would rather it would please God to take me ' —
meaning, God help me, that I should die — ' than

that she should live to see me grow up a *mean man;*'
which shows the difference of parent from parent,
and how some mothers are more harsh and intolerant
to their children than some fathers; when we might
expect the contrary. My father, however, loaded me
with presents from that time, which made me the
envy of my school-fellows. As I felt this growing
disposition in them, I naturally sought to avert it by
all the means in my power; and from that time I
used to eat my little packages of fruit, and other
nice things, in a corner, so privately that I was
never found out. Once, I remember, I had a huge
apple sent me, of that sort which they call cats'-
heads. I concealed this all day under my pillow;
and at night, but not before I had ascertained that
my bed-fellow was sound asleep, — which I did by
pinching him rather smartly two or three times,
which he seemed to perceive no more than a dead
person, though once or twice he made a motion as he
would turn, which frightened me, — I say, when I
had made all sure, I fell to work upon my apple ; and,
though it was as big as an ordinary man's two fists, I
made shift to get through before it was time to get
up. And a more delicious feast I never made;
thinking all night what a good parent I had (I mean
my father), to send me so many nice things, when
the poor lad that lay by me had no parent or friend
in the world to send him anything nice; and, thinking of his desolate condition, I munched and munched
as silently as I could, that I might not set him
a-longing if he overheard me. And yet, for all this
considerateness and attention to other people's feel-

ings, I was never much a favorite with my school-
fellows; which I have often wondered at, seeing that
I never defrauded any one of them of the value of a
half-penny, or told stories of them to their master, as
some little lying boys would do, but was ready to do
any of them all the services in my power that were
consistent with my own well-doing. I think nobody
can be expected to go further than that." Juke, in
the course of time, was engaged to be married to a
maiden named Cleora. Hear him relate the circumstance that broke off the engagement: "I was
never," he says, " much given to theatrical entertainments; that is, at no turn of my life was I ever what
they call a regular play-goer; but on some occasion
of a benefit-night, which was expected to be very
productive, and indeed turned out so, Cleora expressing a desire to be present, I could do no less
than offer, as I did very willingly, to squire her and
her mother to the pit. At that time, it was not customary in our town for tradesfolk, except some of the
very topping ones, to sit, as they now do, in the
boxes. At the time appointed, I waited upon the
ladies, who had brought with them a young man, a
distant relation, whom it seems they had invited to
be of the party. This a little disconcerted me, as I
had about me barely silver enough to pay for our
three selves at the door, and did not at first know
that their relation had proposed paying for himself.
However, to do the young man justice, he not only
paid for himself but for the old lady besides; leaving
me only to pay for two, as it were. In our passage
to the theatre, the notice of Cleora was attracted to

some orange wenches that stood about the doors vending their commodities. She was leaning on my arm; and I could feel her every now and then giving me a nudge, as it is called, which I afterwards discovered were hints that I should buy some oranges. It seems it is a custom at Birmingham, and perhaps in other places, when a gentleman treats ladies to the play, — especially when a full night is expected, and that the house will be inconveniently warm, — to provide them with this kind of fruit, oranges being esteemed for their cooling property. But how could I guess at that, never having. treated ladies to a play before, and being, as I said, quite a novice in these kind of entertainments? At last, she spoke plain out, and begged that I would buy some of ' those oranges,' pointing to a particular barrow. But, when I came to examine the fruit, I did not think the quality of it was answerable to the price. In this way, I handled several baskets of them; but something in them all displeased me. Some had thin rinds, and some were plainly over-ripe, which is as great a fault as not being ripe enough; and I could not (what they call) make a bargain. While I stood haggling with the women, secretly determining to put off my purchase till I should get within the theatre, where I expected we should have better choice, the young man, the cousin (who it seems, had left us without my missing him), came running to us with his pockets stuffed out with oranges, inside and out, as they say. It seems, not liking the look of the barrow-fruit any more than myself, he had slipped away to an eminent fruiterer's, about three

doors distant, which I never had the sense to think
of, and had laid out a matter of two shillings in some
of the best St. Michael's, I think, I ever tasted.
What a little hinge, as I said before, the most important affairs in life may turn upon ! The mere in-
advertence to the fact that there was an eminent
fruiterer's within three doors of us, though we had
just passed it without the thought once occurring to
me, which he had taken advantage of, lost me the
affection of my Cleora. From that time she visibly
cooled towards me, and her partiality was as visibly
transferred to this cousin. I was long unable to account for this change in her behavior; when one day,
accidentally discoursing of oranges to my mother,
alone, she let drop a sort of reproach to me, as if I
had offended Cleora by my *nearness*, as she called it,
that evening. Even now, when Cleora has been
wedded some years to that same officious relation, as
I may call him, I can hardly be persuaded that such
a trifle could have been the motive to her incon-
stancy ; for could she suppose that I would sacrifice
my dearest hopes in her to the paltry sum of two
shillings, when I was going to treat her to the play,
and her mother too (an expense of more than four
times that amount), if the young man had not interfered to pay for the latter, as I mentioned ? But the
caprices of the sex are past finding out ; and I begin
to think my mother was in the right ; for doubtless
women know women better than we can pretend to
know them."

Juke would have made a good tradesman under
the rules laid down by De Foe : " A tradesman be-

hind his counter must have no flesh and blood about
him, no passions, no resentment; he must never be
angry, no, not so much as seem to be so, if a cus-
tomer tumbles him five hundred pounds' worth of
goods, and scarce bids money for anything ; nay,
though they really come to his shop with no intent
to buy, as many do, only to see what is to be sold,
and though he knows they cannot be better pleased
than they are at some other shop where they intend
to buy, 't is all one ; the tradesman must take it ; he
must place it to the account of his calling, that 't is
his business to be ill-used and resent nothing. I
could give you many examples, how and in what
manner a shopkeeper is to behave himself in the
way of business; what impertinences, what taunts,
flouts, and ridiculous things, he must bear in his
trade; and must not show the least return, or the
least signal of disgust; he must have no passions,
no fire in his temper; he must be all soft and
smooth ; nay, if his real temper be naturally fiery
and hot, he must show none of it in his shop; he
must be a perfect, complete hypocrite, if he would
be a complete tradesman. It is true, natural tem-
pers are not to be always counterfeited: the man
cannot easily be a lamb in his shop, and a lion in
himself ; but, let it be easy or hard, it must be done,
and is done. There are men who have by custom and
usage brought themselves to it, that nothing could
be meeker and milder than they when behind the
counter, and yet nothing be more furious and raging
in every other part of life ; nay, the provocations they
have met with in their shops have so irritated their

rage, that they would go up-stairs from their shop,
and fall into frenzies, and a kind of madness, and
beat their heads against the wall, and perhaps mischief themselves, if not prevented, till the violence
of it had gotten vent; and the passions abate and
cool. I heard once of a shop-keeper that behaved
himself thus to such an extreme that, when he was
provoked by the impertinence of the customers beyond what his temper could bear, he would go up-
stairs and beat his wife, kick his children about like
dogs, and be as furious for two or three minutes as a
man chained down in Bedlam; and again, when that
heat was over, would sit down and cry faster than
the children he had abused; and, after the fit, he
would go down into the shop again, and be as humble, as courteous, and as calm, as any man whatever;
so absolute a government of his passions had he in
the shop, and so little out of it: in the shop, a soul-
less animal that would resent nothing; and in the
family, a madman: in the shop, meek like a lamb;
but in the family, outrageous, like a Libyan lion.
The sum of the matter is, it is necessary for a tradesman to subject himself, by all the ways possible, to
his business; his customers are to be his idols: so far
as he may worship idols by allowance, he is to bow
down to them, and worship them; at least, he is not
in any way to displease them, or show any disgust or
distaste, whatever they may say or do. The bottom
of all is that he is intending to get money by them;
and it is not for him that gets money to offer the
least inconvenience to them by whom he gets it: he
is to consider that, as Solomon says, 'the borrower is

7

servant of the lender;' so the seller is servant to the buyer."

Poor George Dyer " commenced life, after a course of hard study, in the ' House of Pure Emanuel,' as usher to a knavish, fanatic school-master, at a salary of eight pounds per annum, with board and lodging. Of this poor stipend he never received above half in all the laborious years he served this man. He tells a pleasant anecdote, that when poverty, staring out at his ragged knees, has sometimes compelled him, against the modesty of his nature, to hint at arrears, the school-master would take no immediate notice; but after supper, when the school was called together to even-song, he would never fail to introduce some instructive homily against riches, and the corruption of the heart occasioned through the desire of them, ending with, ' Lord, keep thy servants, above all things, from the heinous sin of avarice. Having food and raiment, let us therewithal be content. Give me Agur's wish,' — and the like, — which, to the little auditory, sounded like a doctrine full of Christian prudence and simplicity, but to poor Dyer was a receipt in full for that quarter's demands at least."

" The late grand duke," said Goethe to Ecker- mann, " was very partial to Merck, so much so that he once became his security for a debt of four thou- sand dollars. Very soon Merck, to our surprise, gave him back his bond. As Merck's circumstances were not improved, we could not divine how he had been able to do this. When I saw him again, he ex- plained the enigma thus: ' The duke,' said he, ' is an excellent, generous man, who trusts and helps men whenever he can. So I thought to myself, Now if you cozen him out of his money, that will prejudice a thousand others; for he will lose his precious trustfulness, and many unfortunate but worthy men will suffer, because one was worthless. So I made a speculation, and borrowed the money from a scoundrel, whom it will be no matter if I do cheat; but if I had not paid our good lord, the duke, it would have been a pity.' "

" The greatest pleasure I know," said Lamb, " is to do a good action by stealth, and to have it found out by accident."

IV.

STANDARDS.

At a glance, it would appear that as a rule all men think all men imperfect but themselves. It follows, therefore, that all would reform all but themselves. But if every man's standard of excellence could be accounted for, what a melancholy history of human frailties and follies might be had. What sad curiosities, perhaps, would be our pet virtues — offspring, alas, too often, of sated appetites, spent passions, hairbreadth escapes, and disappointed hopes. Knowing all, with what wondrous pity must God hear our poor prayers. To seek perfect virtue or contentment " is as hopeless as to try to recover a lost limb. Those only have it who never have thought about it. The moment we feel that we wish for it, we may be certain that it is gone forever." " To know how cherries and strawberries taste, you must ask the children and the birds."

"All things," says Emerson, " work exactly according to their quality, and according to their quantity; attempt nothing they cannot do, except man." He ventures " to say that what is bad is bad," and finds himself " at war with all the world." " Do not be so vain of your one objection. Do you think there is only one ? Alas, my good friend, there is no part of society or of life better than any other part. All our things are right and wrong together. The wave of evil washes all alike." "Probably there never was," says De Quincey, "one thought, from the foundation of the earth, that has passed through the mind of man, which did not offer some blemish, some sorrowful shadow of pollution, when it came up for review before a heavenly tribunal; that is, supposing it a thought entangled at all with human interests or human passions." "All the progress which we have really made," says a writer in Blackwood, "and all the additional and fictitious progress which exists in our imagination, prompts us to the false idea that there is a remedy for everything, and that no pain is inevitable. But there *are* pains which are inevitable in spite of philosophy, and conflicting claims to which Solomon himself could do no justice. We are not complete syllogisms, to be kept in balance by intellectual regulations, we human creatures. We are of all things and creatures in the world the most incomplete; and there are conditions of our warfare, for the redress of which, in spite of all the expedients of social economy, every man and woman, thrown by whatever accident out of the course of nature, must be content to wait perhaps for years, perhaps for a life long, perhaps till the consummation of all things." "For a reasonable, voluntary being," says Sterling, "learning as he only can learn by experience, there will always be errors behind to mourn over, and a vista of unattainable good before, which inevitably lengthens as we advance." If we only *could* "grieve without affectation or imbecility, and journey on without turning aside or stopping."

"It is the conviction of the purest men, that the net amount of man and man does not much vary. Each is incomparably superior to his companion in some faculty. Each seems to have some compensation yielded to him by his infirmity, and every hinderance operates as a concentration of his force." "Everything we do has its results. But the right and prudent does not always lead to good, or contrary measures to bad; frequently the reverse takes place. Some time since," said Goethe, "I made a mistake in one of these transactions with booksellers, and was disturbed that I had done so. But, as circumstances turned out, it would have been very unfortunate if I had not made that very mistake. Such instances occur frequently in life, and it is the observation of them which enables men of the world to go to work with such freedom and boldness."

"When we see an eager assailant of one of these wrongs, a special reformer, we feel like asking him," says Emerson, "What right have you, sir, to your one virtue? Is virtue piecemeal?" "Your mode of happiness," said Coleridge, talking to such an one, "would make me miserable. To go about doing as much *good* as possible, to as many men as possible, is, indeed, an excellent object for a man to propose to himself; but then, in order that you may not sacrifice the real good and happiness of others to your particular views, which may be quite different from your neighbors', you must do *that* good to others which the reason, common to all, pronounces to be good for all." "What I object," said Sydney Smith, "to Scotch philosophers in general is, that they reason upon man as they would upon a divinity; they pursue truth without caring if it be useful truth." Michel Angelo's great picture of the Last Judgment, in the Sistine Chapel, narrowly escaped from destruction by the monastic views of Paul IV. In the commencement of his reign, we are told, he conceived a notion of reforming that picture, in which so many academical figures offended his sense of propriety. This was communicated to Michel Angelo, who desired that the pope might be told "that what he wished was very little, and might be easily effected; for if his holiness would only reform the opinions of mankind, the picture would be reformed of itself." "You must have a genius for charity as well as for anything else. As for doing-good," says Thoreau, "that is one of the professions which are full. What *good* I do," says he, "in the common sense of that word, must be aside from my main path, and for the most part wholly unintended. Men say, practically, Begin where you are and such as you are, without aiming mainly to become of more worth, and with kindness aforethought go about doing good. If I were to preach at all in this strain, I should say, rather, Set about being good. As if the sun should stop when he had kindled his fires up to the splendor of a moon, or a star of the sixth magnitude, and go about like a Robin Goodfellow, peeping in at every cottage window, inspiring lunatics, and tainting meats, and making darkness visible, instead of steadily increasing his genial heat and beneficence till he is of such brightness that no mortal can look him in the face, and then, and in the mean while too, going about the

world in his own orbit, doing it good, or rather, as
a truer philosophy has discovered, the world going
about him, getting good. When Phaeton, wishing to
prove his heavenly birth by his beneficence, had the
sun's chariot but one day, and drove out of the beaten
track, he burned several blocks of houses in the lower
streets of heaven, and scorched the surface of the
earth, and dried up every spring, and made the great
Desert of Sahara, till at length Jupiter hurled him
headlong to the earth with a thunderbolt, and the
sun, through grief at his death, did not shine for a
year."

" There is no odor so bad," continues the same de-
fiant radical, " as that which arises from goodness
tainted.   It is human, it is divine, carrion.   If I
knew for a certainty that a man was coming to my
house with the conscious design of doing me good,
I should run for my life, as from that dry and parch-
ing wind of the African deserts called the simoom,
which fills the mouth and nose and ears and eyes with
dust till you are suffocated, for fear that I should get
some of his good done to me, — some of its virus
mingled with my blood.   No ; in this case I would
rather suffer evil the natural way."

An officer of the government called one day at the
White House, and introduced a clerical friend to
Lincoln. " Mr. President," said he, " allow me to
present to you my friend, the Rev. Mr. F., of ——.
Mr. F. has expressed a desire to see you and have
some conversation with you, and I am happy to be the
means of introducing him."   The president shook
hands with Mr. F., and, desiring him to be seated,

took a seat himself. Then, his countenance having assumed an air of patient waiting, he said, "I am now
ready to hear what you have to say." "Oh, bless
you, sir," said Mr. F., "I have nothing special to say;
I merely called to pay my respects to you, and, as one
of the million, to assure you of my hearty sympathy
and support." "My dear sir," said the president,
rising promptly, his face showing instant relief, and
with both hands grasping that of his visitor, "I am
very glad to see you, indeed. I thought you had
come to preach to me!"

"My father," said the Attic Philosopher, "feared
everything that had the appearance of a lesson. He
used to say that virtue could make herself devoted
· friends, but she did not take pupils; therefore he was
not anxious to teach goodness; he contented himself
with sowing the seeds of it, certain that experience
would make them grow." "The disease of men," said
Mencius, "is this: that they neglect their own fields,
and go to weed the fields of others, and that what
they require from others is great, while what they lay
upon themselves is light."

"There are a thousand hacking at the branches of
evil," says Thoreau, again, "to one who is striking at
the root; and it may be that he who bestows the
largest amount of time and money on the needy is
doing the most by his mode of life to produce that
misery which he strives in vain to relieve. It is the
pious slave-breeder devoting the proceeds of every
tenth slave to buy a Sunday's liberty for the rest.
. . . . The philanthropist too often surrounds mankind with the remembrance of his own cast-off griefs

as an atmosphere, and calls it sympathy. We should impart our courage, and not our despair, our health and ease, and not our disease, and take care that this does not spread by contagion. . . . . If anything ail a man, so that he does not perform his functions, if he have a pain in his bowels even, for that is the seat of sympathy, he forthwith sets about reforming — the world. Being a microcosm himself, he discovers — and it is a true discovery, and he is the man to make it — that the world has been eating green apples ; to his eyes, in fact, the globe itself is a great green apple, which there is danger awful to think of that the children of men will nibble before it is ripe ; and straightway his drastic philanthropy seeks out the Esquimaux and the Patagonian, and embraces the populous Indian and Chinese villages ; and thus, by a few years of philanthropic activity, the powers in the mean while using him for their own ends, no doubt, he cures himself of his dyspepsia, the globe acquires a faint blush on one or both of its cheeks, as if it were beginning to be ripe, and life loses its crudity and is once more sweet and wholesome to live. I never dreamed of any enormity greater than I have committed. I never knew, and never shall know, a worse man than myself. . . . . My excuse for not lecturing against the use of tobacco is that I never chewed it ; that is a penalty which reformed tobacco-chewers have to pay ; though there are things enough I have chewed, which I could lecture against. If you should ever be betrayed into any of these philanthropies, do not let your left hand know what your right hand does, for it is not worth knowing.

Rescue the drowning, and tie your shoe-strings. Take your time, and set about some free labor."

It has been observed that persons who are themselves very pure are sometimes on that account blunt in their moral feelings. " Right, too rigid, hardens into wrong "— even into cruelty sometimes. A friend of one of these malicious philanthropists dined with him one day, and afterward related an anecdote illustrative of his character. While at the table, the children of the refining humanitarian, playing about the open door, were noisy and intractable, which caused him to speak to them impatiently. The disturbance, however, did not cease, and hearing one of the children cry out, he jumped spasmodically from the table, and demanded to know what was the matter. Upon being informed that one had accidentally pinched the finger of another, he immediately seized the hand of the innocent offender, and placing the forefinger at the hinge of the door, deliberately closed it — crushing the poor child's finger as a punishment. There is another authentic story of a reformer who hired his children to go to bed without their supper as a means of preserving their health, and then stole their money back again to pay them for the next abstinence.

" I have never known a trader in philanthropy," says Coleridge, " who was not wrong in head or heart somewhere or other. Individuals so distinguished are usually unhappy in their family relations : men not benevolent or beneficent to individuals, but almost hostile to them ; yet lavishing money and labor and time on the race, the abstract notion." " This is always true of those men," says Hawthorne, in his.

analysis of Hollingsworth, " who have surrendered
themselves to an overruling power. It does not so
much impel them from without, nor even operate as
a motive power from within, but grows incorporate in
all they think and feel, and finally converts them into
little else save that one principle. When such begins
to be the predicament, it is not cowardice, but wisdom, to avoid these victims. They have no heart, no
sympathy, no reason, no conscience. They will keep
no friend, unless he make himself the mirror of their
purpose ; they will smite and slay you, and trample
your dead corpse under foot, all the more readily, if
you take the first step with them, and cannot take
the second, and the third, and every other step of
their terribly straight path. They have an idol, to
which they consecrate themselves high-priest, and
deem it holy work to offer sacrifices of whatever is
most precious ; and never once seem to suspect — so
cunning has the devil been with them — that this false
deity, in whose iron features, immitigable to all the
rest of mankind, they see only benignity and love, is
but a spectrum of the very priest himself, projected
upon the surrounding darkness. And the higher and
purer the original object, and the more unselfishly it
may have been taken up, the slighter is the probability that they can be led to recognize the process by
which godlike benevolence has been debased into all-
devouring egotism."

The same writer, in one of his minor productions,
says, " When a good man has long devoted himself
to a particular kind of beneficence, to one species of
reform, he is apt to become narrowed into the limits

STANDARDS. 109

of the path wherein he treads, and to fancy that
there is no other good to be done on earth but that
self-same good to which he has put his hand, and in
the very mode that best suits his own conceptions.
All else is worthless. His scheme must be wrought
out by the united strength of the whole world's stock
of love, or the world is no longer worthy of a position
in the universe. Moreover, powerful Truth, being
the rich grape-juice expressed from the vineyard of
the ages, has an intoxicating quality when imbibed
by any save a powerful intellect, and often, as it
were, impels the quaffer to quarrel in his cups."

At a dinner-party one day, Madame de Staël said
to Lady Mackintosh, after Godwin was gone, "I am
glad to have seen this man, — it is curious to see how
naturally Jacobins become the advocates of tyrants."

"I have often blamed myself," said Boswell, "for
not feeling for others as sensibly as many say they
do." "Sir," replied Johnson, "don't be duped by
them any more. You will find these very feeling people are not very ready to do you good. They *pay*
you by *feeling*."

It has been observed that a very large proportion
of the men who during the French Revolution proved
themselves most absolutely indifferent to human suffering, were deeply attached to animals. Fournier
was devoted to a squirrel, Couthon to a spaniel,
Panis to two gold pheasants, Chaumette to an aviary,
Marat kept doves. Bacon has noticed that the
Turks, who are a most cruel people, are nevertheless
conspicuous for their kindness to animals, and he
mentions the instance of a Christian boy who was

nearly stoned to death for gagging a long-billed fowl.
Abbé Migne tells how one old Roman fed his oysters
on his slaves; how another put a slave to death that
a curious friend might see what dying was like; how
Galen's mother tore and bit her waiting-women when
she was in a passion with them. Caligula conferred
the honor of priesthood upon his horse. " The day
before the Circensian games," says Suetonius, " he
used to send his soldiers to enjoin silence in the neighborhood, that the repose of the animal might not
be disturbed. For this favorite, besides a marble stable, an ivory manger, purple housings, and a jew-
eled frontlet, he appointed a house, with a retinue of
slaves and fine furniture, for the reception of such
as were invited in the horse's name to sup with him.
It is even said that he intended to make him consul."
" In Egypt there are hospitals for superannuated cats,
and the most loathsome insects are regarded with
tenderness; but human life is treated as if it were of
no account, and human suffering scarcely elicits a
care."

Sydney Smith advised the bishop of New Zealand,
previous to his departure, to have regard to the minor
as well as to the more grave duties of his station —
to be given to hospitality, and, in order to meet the
tastes of his native guests, never to be without a
smoked little boy in the bacon-rack, and a cold clergyman on the sideboard. "And as for myself, my
lord," he concluded, "all I can say is, that when
your new parishioners *do* eat you, I sincerely hope
you will disagree with them."

Lamb once told a droll story of an India-house

clerk accused of eating man's flesh, and remarked
that " among cannibals those who rejected the favorite
dish would be called *misanthropists*."

The eternal barbarisms must not be forgotten by
the reformer while he is reforming the barbarians.
The pagan Frisians, that illustrious northern German tribe, afterward known as the "free Frisians," " whose name is synonymous with liberty, —
nearest blood-relations of the Anglo-Saxon race," —
struggled for centuries against the dominion of the
Franks, and were only eventually subjugated by
Charlemagne, who left them their name of free Frisians. " The Frisians," says their statute-book, "shall
be free as long as the wind blows out of the clouds
and the world stands." Radbod, their chief, was
first overcome by Pepin the younger, and Pepin's
bastard, Charles the Hammer, with his " tremendous blows, completed his father's work ; " he " drove
the Frisian chief into submission, and even into Christianity. A bishop's indiscretion, however, neutral-
ized the apostolic blows " of the Christian conqueror.
" The pagan Radbod had already immersed one of
his royal legs in the baptismal font, when a thought
struck him. ' Where are my dead forefathers at present?' he said, turning suddenly upon Bishop Wolfran.
'In hell, with all other unbelievers,' was the impru-
dent answer. ' Mighty well,' replied Radbod, removing his leg, ' then will I rather feast with my ancestors
in the halls of Woden, than dwell with your little
starveling band of Christians in heaven.' Entreaties and threats were unavailing. The Frisian declined positively a rite which was to cause an eter-

nal separation from his buried kindred, and he died
as he had lived, a heathen."

Tomochichi, chief of the Chickasaws, said to Wesley, " I will go up and speak to the wise men of the
nation, and I hope they will hear. But we would
not be made Christians as the Spaniards make Christians; we would be taught before we are baptized."
He felt the want unconsciously acknowledged by the
King of Siam, spoken of by John Locke in his chapter on Probability. A Dutch ambassador, when entertaining the king with the peculiarities of Holland,
amongst other things told the sovereign that the
water in Holland would sometimes in cold weather
be so hard that men walked upon it, and that it
would bear an elephant if he were there. To which
the king replied, "Hitherto I have believed the
strange things you have told me, because I looked
upon you as a sober, fair man, but now I am sure
you lie." But Tomochichi had an eye that saw the
faults of the colonists, if he did not understand their
religion. When urged to listen to the doctrines of
Christianity, he keenly replied, " Why, these are
Christians at Savannah ! these are Christians at Fred-
erica ! Christian much drunk ! Christian beat men !
Christian tell lies ! Devil Christian ! Me no Christian!" This recalls the pathetic story of the West
Indian cazique, who, " at the stake, refused life, tem-
poral or eternal, at the price of conversion, asking
where he should go to live so happily. He was told
— in heaven; and then he at once refused, on the
ground that the whites would be there; and he had
rather live anywhere, or nowhere, than dwell with such

people as he had found the white Christians to be."
Almost the first word, says Dr. Medhurst, uttered
by a Chinese, when anything is said concerning
the excellence of Christianity, is, "Why do Christians bring us opium, and bring it directly in defiance
of our laws? The vile drug has destroyed my son,
has ruined my brother, and well-nigh led me to beggar my wife and children. Surely those who import
such a deleterious substance, and injure me for the
sake of gain, cannot wish me well, or be in possession
of a religion better than my own. Go first and persuade your own countrymen to relinquish their nefa-
rious traffic; and give me a prescription to correct
this vile habit, and then I will listen to your exhortations on the subject of Christianity!" Dr. Livingstone says he found a tribe of men in the interior
of Africa so pure and simple that they seemed to
have no idea of untruthfulness and dishonesty until
they were brought into contact with Asiatics and
Europeans. Some of Dr. Kane's men, "while resting at Kalutunah's tent, had appropriated certain
fox-skins, boots, and sledges, which their condition
seemed to require. The Esquimaux complained of
the theft, and Dr. Kane, after a careful inquiry into
the case, decided in their favor. He gave to each
five needles, a file, and a stick of wood, and knives
and other extras to Kalutunah and Shanghu, and
after regaling them with a hearty supper, he returned
the stolen goods, and tried to make them believe that
his people did not steal, but only took the articles to
save their lives! In imitation of this Arctic morality the natives, on their departure, carried off a

few knives and forks, which they deemed as essential to their happiness as the fox-dresses were to the white men."

"Among the airy visions which had been generated in the teeming brain of Coleridge," says a writer in the London Quarterly, "was the project of pantisocracy — a republic to be founded in the wilds of America, of which the fundamental principles were an equality of rank and property, and where all who composed it were to be under the perpetual dominion of reason, virtue, and love. Southey was inflamed by it and converted. Through it he saw a way out of all his troubles. There he would enjoy the felicity of living in a pure democracy, where he could sit unelbowed by kings and aristocrats. ' You,' he wrote to his brother Tom, ' are unpleasantly situated, so is my mother, so were we all till this grand scheme of pantisocracy flashed upon our minds, and now all is perfectly delightful.' Coleridge, contented to have delivered a glowing description of Utopia, did nothing further, and departed on a pedestrian tour through Wales, where, as the ridiculous will sometimes mingle itself with the sublime, he feared he had caught the itch from an admiring democratical auditor at an inn, who insisted upon shaking hands with him. Some time after, Southey, having tried his panacea upon a few select pantisocratic friends, wrote, ' There was a time when I believed in the persuadability of man, and had the mania of man-mending. Experience has taught me better. The ablest physician can do little in the great lazar-house of society. He acts the wisest part who retires from the contagion.' "

"Nature goes her own way," said Goethe, "and all that to us seems an exception is really according to order." He quoted the saying of Rousseau, that you cannot hinder an earthquake by building a city near a burning mountain. Peter the Great, he said, repeated Amsterdam so dear to his youth, in locating St. Petersburg at the mouth of the Neva. The ground rises in the neighborhood, and the emperor could have had a city quite free from all the trouble arising from overflow if he had but gone a little higher up. An old shipmaster represented this to him, and prophesied that the people would be drowned every seventy years. There stood also an old tree, with various marks from times when the waters had risen to a great height. But all was in vain ; the emperor stood to his whim, and had the tree cut down, that it might not be witness against him! Sydney Smith said of a certain fanatical member of Parliament, that "he was losing his head. When he brings forward his Suckling Act, he will be considered as quite mad. No woman to be allowed to suckle her own child without medical certificates. Three classes, viz., free-sucklers, half-sucklers, and spoon-meat mothers. Mothers, whose supply is uncertain, to suckle upon affidavit ! How is it possible that an act of Parliament can supply the place of nature and natural affection ?"

"There is in nature," said Goethe to Soret, "an accessible and an inaccessible. Be careful to discriminate between the two, be circumspect, and proceed with reverence." "The sight of a primitive phenomenon," he said to Eckermann, "is generally not

enough for people; they think they must go still further; and are thus like children who, after peeping
into a mirror, turn it round directly to see what is on
the other side." "When one," said he on another
occasion, "has looked about him in the world long
enough to see how the most judicious enterprises frequently fail, and the most absurd have the good fortune to succeed, he becomes disinclined to give any
one advice. At bottom, he who asks advice shows
himself limited; he who gives it gives also proof that
he is presumptuous. If any one asks me for good
advice, I say, I will give it, but only on condition that
you will promise not to take it. . . . . Much is said
of aristocracy and democracy; but the whole affair is
simply this: in youth, when we either possess nothing, or know not how to value the tranquil possession
of anything, we are democrats; but when we, in a
long life, have come to possess something of our own,
we wish not only ourselves to be secure of it, but that
our children and grandchildren should be secure of in-
heriting it. Therefore, we always lean to aristocracy in our old age, whatever were our opinions in
youth."

Elliott, the Corn-Law Rhymer, being asked, "What
is a communist?" answered, "One who has yearn-
ings for equal division of unequal earnings. Idler or
bungler, he is willing to fork out his penny and
pocket your shilling."

"Sir," said Johnson, "your levelers wish to level
down as far as themselves; but they cannot bear lev-
eling *up* to themselves. They would all have some
people under them; why not then have some people
above them?"

Margaret Fuller, speaking of the greatest of German poets, says, "He believes more in man than men, effort than success, thought than action, nature than providence. He does not insist on my *believing* with him."

"He who would help himself and others," says Emerson, "should not be a subject of irregular and interrupted impulses of virtue, but a continent, persisting, immovable person, — such as we have seen a few scattered up and down in time for the blessing of the world; men who have in the gravity of their nature a quality which answers to the fly-wheel in a mill, which distributes the motion equally over all the wheels, and hinders it from falling unequally and suddenly in destructive shocks. It is better that joy should be spread over all the day in the form of strength, than that it should be concentrated into ecstasies, full of danger, and followed by reactions." "It only needs that a just man should walk in our streets, to make it appear how pitiful and inartificial a contrivance is our legislation. The man whose part is taken, and who does not wait for society in anything, has a power which society cannot choose but feel."

What a character was Sir Isaac Newton. He is described as modest, candid, and affable, and without any of the eccentricities of genius, suiting himself to every company, and speaking of himself and others in such a manner that he was never even suspected of vanity. "But this," says Dr. Pemberton, "I immediately discovered in him, which at once both surprised and charmed me. Neither his extreme great age, nor his universal reputation, had rendered him stiff in opinion, or in any degree elated." His modesty arose from the depth and extent of his knowledge, which showed him what a small portion of nature he had been able to examine, and how much remained to be explored in the same field in which he had himself labored. In a letter to Leibnitz, 1675, he observes, " I was so persecuted with discussions arising out of my theory of light, that I blamed my own imprudence for parting with so substantial a blessing as my quiet, to run after a shadow." Nearly a year after his complaint to Leibnitz, he uses the following remarkable expression in a communication to Oldenburg: " I see I have made myself a slave to philosophy; but if I get free of Mr. Linus's business, I will resolutely bid adieu to it eternally, excepting what I do for my private satisfaction, or leave to come out after me; for I see a man must either resolve to put out nothing new, or to become a slave to defend it." His assistant and amanuensis for five years (Humphrey Newton) never heard him laugh but once in all that time: " 'T was upon occasion of asking a friend, to whom he had lent Euclid to read, what progress he had made in that author, and how he liked him. He answered by desiring to know what use and benefit in life that study would be to him. Upon which Sir Isaac was very merry." He was once disordered with pains at the stomach, which confined him for some days to his bed, but which he bore with a great deal of patience and magnanimity, seemingly indifferent either to live or to die. " He seeing me," said his assistant, "much concerned at his illness, bid me not trouble myself; 'For if I die,' said Sir Isaac, 'I shall leave you an estate,' which he then for the first time mentioned.'' Says Bishop Atterbury, '' In the whole air of his face and make there was nothing of that penetrating sagacity which appears in his compositions. He had something rather languid in his look and manner, which did not raise any great expectations in those who did not know him.'' When Pope expressed a wish for '' some memoirs and character of Newton, as a private man,'' he did '' not doubt that his life and manners would make as great a discovery of virtue and goodness and rectitude of heart, as his works have done of penetration and the utmost stretch of human knowledge.'' When Vigani told him '' a loose story about a nun,'' he gave up his acquaintance; and when Dr. Halley ventured to say anything disrespectful to religion, he invariably checked him with the remark, '' I have studied these things, — you have not.'' When he was asked to take snuff or tobacco, he declined, remarking '' that he would make no necessities to himself.'' Bishop Burnet said that he '' valued him for something still more valuable than all his philosophy, — for having the whitest soul he ever knew.''

Slowly and modestly the great in all things is developed. '' Though the mills of God grind slowly, yet they grind exceeding small.'' Look at the Netherlands. '' Three great rivers — the Rhine, the Meuse, and the Scheldt — had deposited their slime for ages among the dunes and sand-banks heaved up by the ocean around their mouths. A delta was thus

formed, habitable at last for man. It was by nature
a wide morass, in which oozy islands and savage for-
ests were interspersed among lagoons and shallows ; a
district lying partly below the level of the ocean at
its higher tides, subject to constant overflow from the
rivers, and to frequent and terrible inundations by
the sea. Here, within a half submerged territory, a
race of wretched ichthyophagi dwelt upon mounds,
which they had raised, like beavers, above the almost
fluid soil. Here, at a later day, the same race
chained the tyrant Ocean and his mighty streams
into subserviency, forcing them to fertilize, to render
commodious, to cover with a beneficent net-work of
veins and arteries, and to bind by watery highways,
with the farthest ends of the world, a country disin-
herited by nature of its rights. A region outcast of
ocean and earth wrested at last from both domains
their richest treasures. A race engaged for generations in stubborn conflict with the angry elements
was unconsciously educating itself for its great
struggle with the still more savage despotism of
man.''

In the central part of a range of the Andes, at an
elevation of about seven thousand feet, on a bare
slope, may be observed some snow-white projecting
columns. These are petrified trees, eleven being
silicified, and from thirty to forty converted into
coarsely crystallized white calcareous spar. They are
abruptly broken off, the upright stumps projecting a
few feet above the ground. The trunks measured
from three to five feet each in circumference. They
stood a little way apart from each other, but the

whole formed one group. The volcanic sandstone in which the trees were imbedded, and from the lower part of which they must have sprung, had accumulated in successive thin layers around their trunks, and the stone yet retained the impression of the bark. " It required," says the eminent scientific man who visited the spot in 1835, " little geological practice to interpret the marvelous story which this scene at once unfolded. I saw the spot where a cluster of fine trees once reared their branches on the shores of the Atlantic, when that ocean, now driven back seven hundred miles, came to the foot of the Andes. I saw that they had sprung from a volcanic soil which had been raised above the level of the sea, and that subsequently this dry land, with its upright trees, had been let down into the depths of the ocean. In these depths, the formerly dry land was covered by sedimentary beds, and these again by enormous streams of submarine lava — one such mass attaining the thickness of a thousand feet; and these deluges of molten stone and aqueous deposits five times alternately had been spread out. The ocean which received such thick masses must have been profoundly deep; but again the subterranean forces exerted themselves, and I now beheld the bed of that ocean, forming a chain of mountains more than seven thousand feet in height. Nor had those antagonist forces been dormant which are always at work, wearing down the surface of the land; the great piles of strata had been intersected by many wide valleys, and the trees, now changed into silex, were exposed projecting from the volcanic soil, now changed into rock, whence formerly, in a green and budding state, they had raised their lofty heads."

" The world," said Goethe, " is not so framed that it can keep quiet ; the great are not so that they will not permit misuse of power ; the masses not so that, in hope of a gradual amelioration, they will keep tranquil in an inferior condition. Could we perfect human nature, we might expect perfection everywhere ; but as it is, there will always be this wavering hither and thither ; one part must suffer while the other is at ease." " It is with human things," says Froude, " as it is with the great icebergs which drift southward out of the frozen seas. They swim two thirds under water, and one third above ; and so long as the equilibrium is sustained you would think that they were as stable as the rocks. But the sea water is warmer than the air. Hundreds of fathoms down, the tepid current washes the base of the berg. Silently in those far deeps the centre of gravity is changed ; and then, in a moment, with one vast roll, the enormous mass heaves over, and the crystal peaks which had been glancing so proudly in the sunlight are buried in the ocean forever." " The secret which you would fain keep, — as soon as you go abroad, lo! there is one standing on the door-step to tell you the same." The revolution is all at once ripe, and the bottom is at the top again. Nobody and everybody is responsible. " It is seldom," says John Galt, in his life of Wolsey, " that any man can sway the current of national affairs ; but a wide and earnest system of action never fails to produce results which resemble the preëxpected effects of particular designs." At the gorgeous coronation of Napoleon, some one asked the republican general Augereau whether anything was wanting to the splendor of the scene. "Nothing," replied Augereau, "but the presence of the million of men who have died to do away with all this."

You remember the value, to the cause of civil liberty and Christianity, of the accidental epithet of "beggars," applied to the three hundred nobles who petitioned Margaret of Parma for a stay of the edicts of Philip and the Inquisition, about to be terribly executed upon the rebellious Protestants under the leadership of William of Orange. Motley, in his Dutch Republic, gives a vivid account of it. The duchess was agitated and irritated by the petition. "The Prince of Orange addressed a few words to the duchess, with the view of calming her irritation. He observed that the confederates were no seditious rebels, but loyal gentlemen, well-born, well connected, and of honorable character. They had been influenced, he said, by an honest desire to save their country from impending danger, — not by avarice or ambition. 'What, madam,' cried Berlaymont in a passion, 'is it possible that your highness can entertain fears of these beggars? Is it not obvious what manner of men they are? They have not had wisdom enough to manage their own estates, and are they now to teach the king and your highness how to govern the country? By the living God, if my advice were taken, their petition should have a cudgel for a commentary, and we would make them go down the steps of the palace a great deal faster than they

mounted them!' Afterwards, as the three hundred
gentlemen and nobles passed by the house of Berlaymont, that nobleman, standing at his window in company with Count Aremberg, repeated his jest: 'There
go our fine beggars again. Look, I pray you, with
what bravado they are passing before us!' 'They
call us beggars,' said Brederode, to the three hundred
banqueting with him in the Calemburg mansion on
that famous April night. 'Let us accept the name.
We will contend with the Inquisition, but remain
loyal to the king, even till compelled to wear the beggar's sack.' He then beckoned to one of his pages,
who brought him a leathern wallet, such as was worn
at that day by professional mendicants, together with
a large wooden bowl, which also formed part of their
regular appurtenances. Brederode immediately hung
the wallet round his neck, filled the bowl with wine,
lifted it with both hands, and drained it at a draught.
'Long live the beggars!' he cried, as he wiped his
beard and set the bowl down. 'Long live the beggars!' Then for the first time from the lips of those
reckless nobles rose the famous cry, which was so
often to ring over land and sea, amid blazing cities,
on blood-stained decks, through the smoke and car-
nage of many a stricken field. The humor of Brederode was hailed with deafening shouts of applause.
The count then threw the wallet round the neck of
his nearest neighbor, and handed him the wooden
bowl. Each guest, in turn, donned the mendicant's
knapsack. Pushing aside his golden goblet, each
filled the beggar's bowl to the brim, and drained it to
the beggar's health. Roars of laughter and shouts

of 'Long live the beggars!' shook the walls of the stately mansion, as they were doomed never to shake again. The shibboleth was invented. The conjuration which they had been anxiously seeking was found. Their enemies had provided them with a spell which was to prove, in after days, potent enough to start a spirit from palace or hovel, forest or wave, as the deeds of the 'wild beggars,' the 'wood beggars,' and the 'beggars of the sea' taught Philip at last to understand the nation which he had driven to madness."

"Johnny Appleseed," by which name Jonathan Chapman was known in every log-cabin from the Ohio River to the Northern Lakes, is an interesting character to dwell upon. Barefooted, and with scanty clothing, he traversed the wilderness for many years, planting appleseeds in the most favorable situations. His self-sacrificing life made him a favorite with the frontier settlers — men, women, and especially children ; even the savages treated him with kindness, and the rattlesnakes, it was said, hesitated to bite him. "During the war of 1812, when the frontier settlers were tortured and slaughtered by the savage allies of Great Britain, Johnny Appleseed continued his wanderings, and was never harmed by the roving bands of hostile Indians. On many occasions the impunity with which he ranged the country enabled him to give the settlers warning of approaching danger, in time to allow them to take refuge in their block-houses before the savages could attack them. An informant refers to one of these instances, when the news of Hull's surrender came like a thunderbolt upon the frontier. Large bands of Indians and British were destroying everything before them, and murdering defenseless women and children, and even the block-houses were not always a sufficient protection. At this time Johnny traveled day and night, warning the people of the impending danger. He visited every cabin and delivered this message : ' The Spirit of the Lord is upon me, and He hath anointed me to blow the trumpet in the wilderness, and sound an alarm in the forest ; for behold, the tribes of the heathen are round about your doors, and a devouring flame followeth after them ! ' The aged man who narrated this incident said that he could feel even then the thrill that was caused by this prophetic announcement of the wild-looking herald of danger, who aroused the family on a bright moonlight midnight with his piercing cry. Refusing all offers of food, and denying himself a moment's rest, he traversed the border day and night until he had warned every settler of the impending peril. Johnny also served as colporteur, systematically leaving with the settlers chapters of certain religious books, and calling for them afterwards ; and was the first to engage in the work of protecting dumb brutes. He believed it to be a sin to kill any creature for food. No Brahman could be more concerned for the preservation of insect life, and the only occasion on which he destroyed a venomous reptile was a source of long regret, to which he could never refer without manifesting sadness. He had selected a suitable place for planting apple-seeds on a small prairie, and in order to prepare the ground, he was mowing the long grass, when he was bitten by a rattlesnake. In describing the event he sighed heavily, and said, ' Poor fellow, he only just touched me, when I, in the heat of my ungodly passion, put the heel of my scythe in him, and went away. Some time afterwards I went back, and there lay the poor fellow, dead ! ' " " He was a man, after all,"— Hawthorne might have exclaimed of him, too, — " his Maker's own truest image, a philanthropic man ! — not that steel engine of the devil's contrivance — a philanthropist ! "

John Brown, when he was twelve years old, from seeing a negro slave of his own age cruelly beaten, began to hate slavery and love the slaves so intensely as " sometimes to raise the question, Is God their Father ? " At forty, " he conceived the idea of becoming a liberator of the Southern slaves ; " at the same time " determined to let them know that they had friends, and prepared himself to lead them to liberty. From the moment that he formed this resolution, he engaged in no business which he could not, without loss to his friends and family, wind up in fourteen days." His favorite texts of Scripture were, " Remember them that are in bonds as bound with them ; " " Whoso stoppeth his ear at the cry of the poor, he also shall cry himself, but shall not be heard ; " " Whoso mocketh the poor reproacheth his Maker, and he that is glad at calamities shall not be unpunished ; " " Withhold not good from them to whom it is due, when it is in the power of thine hand to do it." His favorite hymns were, " Blow ye the trumpet, blow ! " and " Why should we start and fear to die ? " " I asked him," said a child, " how he felt when he

left the eleven slaves, taken from Missouri, safe in
Canada? His answer was, 'Lord, permit now thy
servant to die in peace, for mine eyes have seen thy sal-
vation. I could not brook the idea that any ill should
befall them, or they be taken back to slavery. The
arm of Jehovah protected us.'" "Upon one occasion,
when one of the ex-governors of Kansas said to him
that he was a marked man, and that the Missourians
were determined, sooner or later, to take his scalp, the
old man straightened himself up, with a glance of enthusiasm and defiance in his gray eye. 'Sir,' said he,
'the angel of the Lord will camp round about me.'"
On leaving his family the first time he went to Kansas, he said, "If it is so painful for us to part, with
the hope of meeting again, how dreadful must be the
separation for life of hundreds of poor slaves." "He
deliberately determined, twenty years before his attack upon Harper's Ferry," says Higginson, "that at
some future period he would organize an armed party,
go into a slave State, and liberate a large number
of slaves. Soon after, surveying professionally in
the mountains of Virginia, he chose the very ground
for the purpose. He said 'God had established the
Alleghany Mountains from the foundation of the
world that they might one day be a refuge for fugitive slaves.' Visiting Europe afterward, he studied
military strategy for this purpose, even making designs for a new style of forest fortifications, simple
and ingenious, to be used by parties of fugitive slaves
when brought to bay. He knew the ground, he knew
his plans, he knew himself; but where should he find
his men? Such men as he needed are not to be *found*

ordinarily; they must be *reared*. John Brown did not merely look for men, therefore; he reared them in his sons. Mrs. Brown had been always the sharer of his plans. 'Her husband always believed,' she said, 'that he was to be an instrument in the hands of Providence, and she believed it too.' 'This plan had occupied his thoughts and prayers for twenty years.' 'Many a night he had lain awake and prayed concerning it.'" "He believed in human brotherhood, and in the God of Battles; he admired Nat Turner, the negro patriot, equally with George Washington, the white American deliverer." "He secretly despised even the ablest antislavery orators. He could see 'no use in this talking,' he said. 'Talk is a national institution; but it does no manner of good to the slave.'" The year before his attack, he uttered these sentences in conversation: "Nat Turner, with fifty men, held Virginia five weeks. The same number, well organized and armed, can shake the system out of the State." "Give a slave a pike, and you make him a man. Deprive him of the means of resistance, and you keep him down." "The land belongs to the bondsman. He has enriched it, and been robbed of its fruits." "Any resistance, however bloody, is better than the system which makes every seventh woman a concubine." "A few men in the right, and knowing they are, can overturn a king. Twenty men in the Alleghanies could break slavery to pieces in two years." "When the bondsmen stand like men, the nation will respect them. It is necessary to teach them this." About the same time he said, in another conversation, "that it was nothing

9

to die in a good cause, but an eternal disgrace to sit
still in the presence of the barbarities of American
slavery." " Providence," said he, " has made me an
actor, and slavery an outlaw." " Duty is the voice
of God, and a man is neither worthy of a good home
here, or a heaven, that is not willing to be in peril for
a good cause." He scouted the idea of rest while he
held " a commission direct from God Almighty to act
against slavery." After his capture, and while he
lay in blood upon the floor of the guard-house, he was
asked by a bystander upon what principle he justified
his acts ? " Upon the Golden Rule," he answered.
" I pity the poor in bondage that have none to help
them. That is why I am here; it is not to gratify
any personal animosity, or feeling of revenge, or vin-
dictive spirit. It is my sympathy with the oppressed
and the wronged, that are as good as you, and as precious in the sight of God. I want you to understand,
gentlemen, that I respect the rights of the poorest and
weakest of the colored people, oppressed by the slave
system, just as much as I do those of the most wealthy
and powerful. That is the idea that has moved me,
and that alone. We expected no reward except the
satisfaction of endeavoring to do for those in distress —
the greatly oppressed — as we would be done by. The
cry of distress, of the oppressed, is my reason, and the
only thing that prompted me to come here. I wish to
say, furthermore, that you had better, all you people
of the South, prepare yourselves for a settlement of
this question. It must come up for settlement sooner
than you are prepared for it, and the sooner you commence that preparation, the better for you. You may

dispose of me very easily. I am nearly disposed of now; but this question is still to be settled — this negro question, I mean. The end of that is not yet." In his "last speech," before sentence was passed upon him, he said, "This court acknowledges, as I suppose, the validity of the law of God. I see a book kissed here which I suppose to be the Bible, or, at least, the New Testament. That teaches me that all things 'whatsoever I would that men should do unto me I should do even so to them.' It teaches me further, to 'remember them that are in bonds as bound with them.' I endeavored to act up to that instruction. I say, I am yet too young to understand that God is any respecter of persons. I believe that to have interfered as I have done, as I have always freely admitted I have done, in behalf of *his* despised poor, was not wrong, but right. Now, if it is deemed necessary that I should forfeit my life for the furtherance of the ends of justice, and mingle my blood further with the blood of my children, and with the blood of millions in this slave country whose rights are disregarded by wicked, cruel, and unjust enactments — I submit: so let it be done." In a postscript to a letter to a half-brother, written in prison, he said, "Say to my poor boys never to grieve for one moment on my account; and should any of you live to see the time when you will not blush to own your relation to old John Brown, it will not be more strange than many things that have happened." In a letter to his old school-master, he said, "I have enjoyed much of life, as I was enabled to discover the secret of this somewhat early. It has been in making

the prosperity and happiness of others my own; so
that really I have had a great deal of prosperity."
To another he wrote, " I commend my poor family
to the kind remembrance of all friends, but I well understand that they are not the only poor in our world.
I ought to begin to leave off saying our world." In
his last letter to his family, he said, "I am waiting
the hour of my public murder with great composure
of mind and cheerfulness, feeling the strong assurance
that in no other possible way could I be used to so
much advantage to the cause of God and of humanity,
and that nothing that I or all my family have sacrificed or suffered will be lost. Do not feel ashamed
on my account, nor for one moment despair of the
cause, or grow weary of well-doing. I bless God I
never felt stronger confidence in the certain and near
approach of a bright morning and glorious day than
I have felt, and do now feel, since my confinement
here." In a previous letter to his family, he said,
" Never forget the poor, nor think anything you bestow on them to be lost to you, even though they may
be as black as Ebed Melech, the Ethiopian eunuch,
who cared for Jeremiah in the pit of the dungeon, or
as black as the one to whom Philip preached Christ.
' Remember them that are in bonds as bound with
them.'" As he stepped out of the jail-door, on his
way to the gallows, "a black woman, with a little
child in her arms, stood near his way. The twain
were of the despised race for whose emancipation and
elevation to the dignity of the children of God he was
about to lay down his life. His thoughts at that

moment none can know except as his acts interpret them. He stopped for a moment in his course, stooped over, and with the tenderness of one whose love is as broad as the brotherhood of man, kissed it affectionately. As he came upon an eminence near the gallows, he cast his eye over the beautiful landscape, and followed the windings of the Blue Ridge Mountains in the distance. He looked up earnestly at the sun, and sky, and all about, and then remarked, ' This is a beautiful country. I have not cast my eyes over it before.' " " You are more cheerful than I am, Captain Brown," said the undertaker, who sat with him in the wagon. " Yes," answered the old man, " I ought to be." " ' Gentlemen, good-by,' he said to two acquaintances, as he passed from the wagon to the scaffold, which he was first to mount. As he quietly awaited the necessary arrangements, he surveyed the scenery unmoved, looking principally in the direction of the people, in the far distance. ' There is no faltering in his step,' wrote one who saw him, ' but firmly and erect he stands amid the almost breathless lines of soldiery that surround him. With a graceful motion of his pinioned right arm he takes the slouched hat from his head and carelessly casts it upon the platform by his side. His elbows and ankles are pinioned, the white cap is drawn over his eyes, the hangman's rope is adjusted around his neck.' ' Captain Brown,' said the sheriff, ' you are not standing on the drop. Will you come forward ? ' ' I can't see you, gentlemen,' was the old man's answer, unfalteringly spoken ; ' you must lead me.' The sheriff led his prisoner forward to the centre of the drop. 'Shall I give you a handkerchief,' he then asked, 'and let you drop it as a signal?' 'No; I am ready at any time; but do not keep me needlessly waiting.' "

" Give the corpse a good dose of arsenic, and make sure work of it!" exclaimed a captain of Virginia militia.

" The Saint, whose martyrdom will make the gallows glorious like the Cross!" exclaimed the Massachusetts sage and seer.

Froude's reflections upon the death of John Davis, the navigator, one of England's Forgotten Worthies, may well be applied to John Brown: " A melancholy end for such a man — the end of a warrior, not dying Epaminondas-like on the field of victory, but cut off in a poor brawl or ambuscade. Life with him was no summer holiday, but a holy sacrifice offered up to duty, and what his Master sent was welcome." It was " hard, rough, and thorny, trodden with bleeding feet and aching brow; the life of which the cross is the symbol; a battle which no peace follows, this side the grave; which the grave gapes to finish, before the victory is won; and — strange that it should be so — this is the highest life of man. Look back along the great names of history; there is none whose life has been other than this. They to whom it has been given to do the really highest work in this earth, whoever they are, Jew or Gentile, Pagan or Christian, warriors, legislators, philosophers, priests, poets, kings, slaves — one and all, their fate has been the same: the same bitter cup has been given to them to drink."

> " Whether on the scaffold high,
> Or in the battle's van,
> The fittest place where man can die
> Is where he dies for man."

V.

REWARDS.

THE Bishop of Llandaff was standing in the House of Lords, in company with Lords Thurlow and Loughborough, when Lord Southampton accosted him: "I want your advice, my lord; how am I to bring up my son so as to make him get forward in the world?" "I know of but one way," replied the bishop; "give him parts and poverty." Poussin, being shown a picture by a person of rank, remarked, "You only want a little poverty, sir, to make you a good painter."

"The advantage of riches remains with him who procured them, not with the heir." Yet, says Froude, "The man who with no labor of his own has inherited a fortune, ranks higher in the world's esteem than his father who made it. We take rank by descent. Such of us as have the longest pedigree, and are therefore the furthest removed from the first who made the fortune and founded the family, we are the noblest. The nearer to the fountain, the fouler the stream; and that first ancestor, who has soiled his fingers by labor, is no better than a parvenu."

"From a very early period," says Lecky, "the existence of slavery had produced, both in Greece and

Rome, a strong contempt for commerce and for manual labor, which was openly professed by the ablest men, and which harmonized well with their disdain for the more utilitarian aspects of science. Among the Bœotians those who had defiled themselves with commerce were excluded for ten years from all offices in the state. Plato pronounced the trade of a shop-keeper to be a degradation to a freeman, and he wished it to be punished as a crime. Aristotle, who asserted so strongly the political claims of the middle classes, declared, nevertheless, that in a perfect state no citizen should exercise any mechanical art. Zenophon and Cicero were both of the same opinion. Augustus condemned a senator to death because he had debased his rank by taking part in a manufacture."

Labor, curse though we call it, as things are, seems to be life's chiefest blessing. "There is more fatigue," says Tom Brown, "and trouble in a lady than in the most laborious life ; who would not rather drive a wheelbarrow with nuts about the streets, or cry brooms, than be Arsennus ?" When Sir Horace Vere died, it was asked what had occasioned his death ; to which some one replied, " By doing nothing." " Too much idleness," said Burke, "fills up a man's time much more completely, and leaves him less his own master, than any sort of employment whatsoever." Too much leisure may be as bad as superfluous wealth, which a passage from Saadi illustrates. " I saw," he says, " an Arab sitting in a circle of jewelers of Básráh, and relating as follows : 'Once on a time, having missed my way in the des-

ert, and having no provisions left, I gave myself up
for lost: when I happened to find a bag full of pearls.
I shall never forget the relish and delight that I felt
on supposing it to be fried wheat ; nor the bitterness
and despair which I suffered on discovering that the
bag contained pearls.' "

In the executive chamber one evening, there were
present a number of gentlemen, among them Mr.
Seward. A point in the conversation suggesting the
thought, the president said, " Seward, you never
heard, did you, how I earned my first dollar ? "
" No," rejoined Mr. Seward. " Well," continued
Lincoln, " I was about eighteen years of age; I belonged, you know, to what they call down South the
' scrubs ; ' people who do not own slaves are nobody
there. But we had succeeded in raising, chiefly by
my labor, sufficient produce, as I thought, to justify
me in taking it down the river to sell. After much
persuasion, I got the consent of mother to go, and
constructed a little flat-boat, large enough to take a
barrel or two of things that we had gathered, with
myself and little bundle, down to New Orleans. A
steamer was coming down the river. We have, you
know, no wharves on the Western streams ; and the
custom was, if passengers were at any of the land-
ings, for them to go out in a boat, the steamer stopping and taking them on board. I was contemplating my new flat-boat, wondering whether I could
make it stronger or improve it in any particular,
when two men came down to the shore in carriages,
with trunks, and looking at the different boats singled
out mine, and asked, ' Who owns this ? ' I answered,

somewhat modestly, ' I do.'   ' Will you,' said one of
them, ' take us and our trunks out to the steamer ? '
' Certainly,' said I.   I was very glad to have the
chance of earning something.   I supposed that each
of them would give me two or three bits.   The
trunks were put on my flat-boat, the passengers seated
themselves on the trunks, and I sculled them out to
the steamboat.   They got on board, and I lifted up
their heavy trunks, and put them on deck.   The
steamer was about to put on steam again, when I
called out that they had forgotten to pay me.   Each
of them took from his pocket a silver half-dollar, and
threw it on the floor of my boat.   I could scarcely
believe my eyes as I picked up the money.   Gentlemen, you may think it was a very little thing, and in
these days it seems to me a trifle ; but it was a most
important incident in my life.   I could scarcely credit
that I, a poor boy, had earned a dollar in less than a
day, — that by honest work I had earned a dollar.
The world seemed wider and fairer before me.   I was
a more hopeful and confident being from that time."

 " Only such persons interest us who have stood
in the jaws of need, and have by their own wit
and might extricated themselves, and made man vic-
torious."   Young and old, all of us, have been intensely interested in knowing what Robinson Crusoe
was to do with his few small means.   Wonderful
Robert Burns !   " While his youthful mother was
still on the straw, the miserable clay cottage fell
above her and the infant bard, who both narrowly escaped, first being smothered to death, and then of
being starved by cold, as they were conveyed through

frost and snow by night to another dwelling." While
he was yet a child, the poverty of the family increased to wretchedness. The "cattle died, or were
lost by accident; the crops failed, and debts were ac-
cumulating. To these buffetings of misfortune the
family could oppose only hard labor and the most rigid
economy. They lived so sparingly that butcher-meat
was a stranger in their dwelling for years." "The
farm proved a ruinous bargain," said the poet; "and
to clench the misfortune, we fell into the hands of a
factor, who sat for the picture I have drawn of one
in my tale of Twa Dogs. My indignation yet boils
at the recollection of the scoundrel factor's insolent
letters, which used to set us all in tears. This kind
of life — the cheerless gloom of a hermit, with the.
unceasing moil of a galley-slave — brought me to my
sixteenth year; a little before which period I first
committed the sin of rhyme. . . . . My passions,
when once lighted up, raged like so many devils, till
they got vent in rhyme; and then the conning over
my verses, like a spell, soothed all into quiet."

We are told that among the companions of Reynolds, when he was studying his art at Rome, was a
fellow-pupil of the name of Astley. They made an
excursion, with some others, on a sultry day, and all
except Astley took off their coats. After several
taunts he was persuaded to do the same, and displayed on the back of his waistcoat a foaming water-
fall. Distress had compelled him to patch his clothes
with one of his own landscapes. Henderson, the
actor, after a simple reading of a newspaper, repeated
such an enormous portion of it as seemed utterly mar-

velous. "If you had been obliged, like me," he said, in reply to the surprise expressed by his auditors, "to depend during many years for your daily bread on getting words by heart, you would not be so much astonished at habit having produced the facility."

Excellence is not matured in a day, and the cost of it is an old story. The beginning of Plato's Republic, it is said, was found in his tablets written over and over in a variety of ways. Addison, we are told, wore out the patience of his printer; frequently, when nearly a whole impression of a Spectator was worked off, he would stop the press to insert a new preposition. Lamb's most sportive essays were the result of most intense brain labor; he used to spend a week at a time in elaborating a single humorous letter to a friend. Tennyson is reported to have written Come into the Garden, Maud, more than fifty times over before it pleased him; and Locksley Hall, the first draught of which was written in two days, he spent the better part of six weeks, for eight hours a day, in altering and polishing. Dickens, when he intended to write a Christmas story, shut himself up for six weeks, lived the life of a hermit, and came out looking as haggard as a murderer. Balzac, after he had thought out thoroughly one of his philosophical romances, and amassed his materials in a most laborious manner, retired to his study, and from that time until his book had gone to press, society saw him no more. When he appeared again among his friends, he looked, said his publisher, in the popular phrase, like his own ghost. The manuscript was afterward altered and copied, when it passed into the hands of the printer, from whose slips the book was re-written for the third time. Again it went into the hands of the printer, — two, three, and sometimes four separate proofs being required before the author's leave could be got to send the perpetually re-written book to press at last, and so have done with it. He was literally the terror of all printers and editors. Moore thought it quick work if he wrote seventy lines of Lalla Rookh in a week. King-lake's Eothen, we are told, was re-written five or six times, and was kept in the author's writing-desk almost as long as Wordsworth kept the White Doe of Rylstone, and kept like that to be taken out for review and correction almost every day. Buffon's Studies of Nature cost him fifty years of labor, and he re-copied it eighteen times before he sent it to the printer. "He composed in a singular manner, writing on large-sized paper, in which, as in a ledger, five distinct columns were ruled. In the first column he wrote down the first thoughts; in the second, he corrected, enlarged, and pruned it; and so on, until he had reached the fifth column, within which he finally wrote the result of his labor. But even after this, he would re-compose a sentence twenty times, and once devoted fourteen hours to finding the proper word with which to round off a period." John Foster often spent hours on a single sentence. Ten years elapsed between the first sketch of Goldsmith's Traveler and its completion. La Rochefoucauld spent fifteen years in preparing his little book of maxims, altering some of them, Segrais says, nearly thirty times. We all know how Sheridan polished his wit and finished his jokes, the same things being found on different bits of paper, differently expressed. Rogers showed Crabb Robinson a note to his Italy, which, he said, took him a fortnight to write. It consists of a very few lines.

" Fortune," says Disraeli, " has rarely condescended to be the companion of genius ; others find a hundred by-roads to her palace ; there is but one open, and that a very indifferent one, for men of letters. Cervantes, the immortal genius of Spain, is supposed to have wanted bread ; Le Sage was a victim of poverty all his life ; Camoëns, the solitary pride of Portugal, deprived of the necessaries of life, perished in an hospital at Lisbon. The Portuguese, after his death, bestowed on the man of genius they had starved the appellation of Great. Vondel, the Dutch Shakespeare, after composing a number of popular tragedies, lived in great poverty, and died at ninety years of age ; then he had his coffin carried by fourteen poets, who, without his genius, probably partook of his wretchedness. The great Tasso was reduced to such a dilemma that he was obliged to borrow a crown from a friend to subsist through the week. He alludes to his dress in a pretty sonnet, which he addresses to his cat, entreating her to assist him, during the night, with the lustre of her eyes, having no candle to see to write his verses." One day Louis the Fourteenth asked Racine what there was new in the literary world. The poet answered that he had seen a melancholy spectacle in the house of Corneille, whom he found dying, deprived even of a little broth. Spenser, the child of Fancy, lan-

guished out his life in misery. Lord Burleigh, it is
said, prevented the queen giving him a hundred
pounds, thinking the lowest clerk in his office a more
deserving person. Sydenham, who devoted his life
to a laborious version of Plato, died in a miserable
spunging-house. " You," said Goldsmith to Bob Bry-
anton, " seem placed at the centre of fortune's wheel,
and, let it revolve ever so fast, are insensible to the
motion. I seem to have been tied to the circumference, and whirled disagreeably round, as if on a
whirligig. . . . . Oh gods! gods! here in a garret,
writing for bread, and expecting to be dunned for a
milk-score." To another, about the same time, he
wrote, " I have been some years struggling with a
wretched being — with all that contempt that indi-
gence brings with it — with all those passions which
make contempt insupportable. What, then, has a
jail that is formidable? I shall at least have the
society of wretches, and such is to me true society."
Cervantes planned and commenced Don Quixote in
prison. John Bunyan wrote the first part, at least,
of Pilgrim's Progress in jail. Both of these immortal works have been the delight and solace of
reading people wherever there has been a literature.
The latter is said to have been translated into a
greater number of languages than any other book in
the world, with two exceptions, the Bible and the Imitation of Christ. Sir James Harrington, author of
Oceana, on pretense of treasonable practices, was put
into confinement, which lasted until he became de-
ranged, when he was liberated. Sir Robert L'Es-
trange was tried and condemned to death, and lay in

prison nearly four years, constantly expecting to be led forth to execution. Ben Jonson, John Selden, Jeremy Taylor, and Edmund Waller were imprisoned. Sir Walter Raleigh, during his twelve years' imprisonment, wrote his best poems and his History of the World, a work accounted vastly superior to all the English historical productions which had previously appeared. "Written," says the historian Tytler, "in prison, during the quiet evening of a tempestuous life, we feel, in its perusal, that we are the companions of a superior mind, nursed in contemplation, and chastened and improved by sorrow, in which the bitter recollection of injury, and the asperity of resentment, have passed away, leaving only the heavenly lesson, that all is vanity." Old George Wither wrote his Shepherd's Hunting during his first imprisonment. The superiority of intellectual pursuits over the gratification of sense, and all the malice of fortune, has never been more touchingly or finely illustrated, it has been well said, than in this poem.

" Can anything be so elegant," asks Emerson, " as to have few wants, and to serve them one's self? It is more elegant to answer one's own needs than to be richly served ; inelegant perhaps it may look to-day, and to a few, but it is an elegance forever and to all. . . . . Parched corn, and a house with one apartment, that I may be free of all perturbations, that I may be serene and docile to what the mind shall speak, and girt and road-ready for the lowest mission of knowledge or good-will, is frugality for gods and heroes." Said Confucius, " With coarse rice to eat, with water to drink, and my bended arm for a pillow, — I have still joy in the midst of these things." " For my own private satisfaction," said Bishop Berkeley, " I had rather be master of my own time than wear a diadem." " I would rather," said Thoreau, " sit on a pumpkin and have it all to myself, than to be crowded on a velvet cushion. . . . . If you have any enterprise before you, try it in your old clothes. All men want, not something *to do with*, but something *to do*, or rather something *to be*. Perhaps we should never procure a new suit, however ragged or dirty the old, until we have so conducted, so enterprised or sailed in some way, that we feel like new men in the old, and that to retain it would be like keeping new wine in old bottles. Our moulting season, like that of fowls, must be a crisis in our lives. The loon retires to solitary ponds to spend it. Thus also the snake casts its slough, and the caterpillar its wormy coat, by an internal industry and expansion ; for clothes are but our outmost cuticle and mortal coil. . . . . It is desirable that a man be clad so simply that he can lay his hands on himself in the dark, and that he live in all respects so compactly and preparedly, that, if an enemy take the town, he can, like the old philosopher, walk out the gate empty-handed without anxiety."

" You see in my chamber," said Goethe, near the close of his life, " no sofa ; I sit always in my old wooden chair, and never, till a few weeks ago, have permitted even a leaning-place for my head to be added. If surrounded by tasteful furniture, my thoughts are arrested, and I am placed in an agreeable, but passive state. Unless we are accustomed to them from early youth, splendid chambers and elegant furniture had best be left to people who neither have nor can have any thoughts."

Rogers, the banker poet, once said to Wordsworth, " If you would let me edit your poems, and give me leave to omit some half-dozen, and make a few trifling alterations, I would engage that you should be as popular a poet as any living." Wordsworth's answer is said to have been, " I am much obliged to you, Mr. Rogers ; I am a poor man, but I would rather remain as I am."

Thomson solicited Burns to supply him with twenty or thirty songs for the musical work in which he was engaged, with an understanding distinctly specified, that the bard should receive a regular pecuniary remuneration for his contributions. With the first part of the proposal Burns instantly complied, but peremptorily rejected the last. " As to any remuneration, you may think my songs either above or below price ; for they shall absolutely be the one or the other. In the honest enthusiasm with which I embark in your undertaking, to talk of money, wages, fee, hire, etc., would be downright prostitution of soul." Thomson, some time after, notwithstanding the prohibition, ventured to acknowledge his services by a small pecuniary present, which the poet with some difficulty restrained himself from returning. " I assure you, my dear sir," he wrote to Thomson, " that you truly hurt me with your pecuniary parcel. It degrades me in my own eyes. However, to return it would savor of affectation ; but as to any more traffic of that debtor and creditor kind, I swear by that honor which crowns the upright statue of Robert

Burns' integrity — on the least motion of it, I will indignantly spurn the by-past transaction, and from
that moment commence entire stranger to you!
Burns' character for generosity of sentiment and independence of mind will, I trust, long outlive any of
his wants which the cold, unfeeling ore can supply ; at
least, I will take care that such a character he shall
deserve." His sensitive nature inclined him to reject
the present, as proud old Sam Johnson threw away
with indignation the new shoes which had been placed
at his chamber door. " I ought not," says Emerson,
" to allow any man, because he has broad lands, to
feel that he is rich in my presence. I ought to make
him feel that I can do without his riches, that I cannot be bought, — neither by comfort, neither by
pride, — and though I be utterly penniless, and receiving bread from him, that he is the poor man be-
side me."

Foote's mother had been heiress to a large fortune, spent it all, and was at length imprisoned for
debt. In this condition she wrote to Sam, who had
been allowing her a hundred a year out of the proceeds of his acting, " Dear Sam, I am in prison for
debt ; come and assist your loving mother, E. Foote."
To which her son characteristically replied, " Dear
Mother, so am I ; which prevents his duty being paid
to his loving mother by her affectionate son, Sam
Foote."

Isaac Disraeli, when a young man, was informed
that a place in the establishment of a great mer-
chant was prepared for him ; he replied that he had
written and intended to publish a poem of consider-

able length against commerce, which was the cor-
rupter of man; and he at once inclosed his poem to
Dr. Johnson, who, however, was in his last illness,
and was unable to read it. Coleridge, on being offered a half share in the Morning Post and Courier,
with a prospect of two thousand pounds a year, announced that he would not give up country life, and
the lazy reading of old folios, for two thousand times
that income. "In short," he added, "beyond three
hundred and fifty pounds a year, I regard money as
a real evil." Professor Agassiz, when once invited to
lecture in Portland, Maine, replied to the munificent
lecture association that he was very sorry, but he was
just then busy with some researches that left him no
time to make money.

Sir John Hawkins one day met Oliver Goldsmith;
his lordship told him he had read his poem, The
Traveler, and was much delighted with it; that he
was going lord lieutenant to Ireland, and that hearing that he was a native of that country, he should
be glad to do him any kindness. The honest poor
man and sincere lover of literature replied that he
"had a brother there, a clergyman, that stood in
need of help. As for myself, I have no dependence
upon the promises of great men; I look to the booksellers for support; they are my best friends, and
I am not inclined to forsake them for others." For
this frank expression of magnanimity and manly self-
dependence, the pricked Hawkins, and the envious
Boswell, speaking of the incident afterward, called
Goldsmith an "idiot."

Dr. Johnson "contracted an inveterate dislike to

sustained intellectual exertion, and wondered how any one could write except for money, and never, or very rarely, wrote from any more elevated impulse than the stern pressure of want." " Who will say," says Richard Cumberland, " that Johnson himself would have been such a champion in literature, such a front-rank soldier in the fields of fame, if he had not been pressed into the service, and driven on to glory with the bayonet of sharp necessity pointed at his back ? If fortune had turned him into a field of clover, he would have laid down and rolled in it. The mere manual labor of writing would not have allowed his lassitude and love of ease to have taken the pen out of the inkhorn, unless the cravings of hunger had reminded him that he must fill the sheet before he saw the table-cloth. . . . . He would have put up prayers for early rising, and laid in bed all day, and with the most active resolutions possible, been the most indolent mortal living. . . . . I have heard that illustrious scholar assert that he subsisted himself for a considerable space of time upon the scanty pittance of four-pence half-penny per day. How melancholy to reflect that his vast trunk and stimulating appetite were to be supported by what will barely feed the weaned infant ! " No wonder he so often screened himself when he ate, or, later in life, lost his temper with Mrs. Thrale when she made a jest of hunger !

We are told that soon after the publication of the Life of Savage, which was anonymous, Mr. Walter Harte, dining with Mr. Cave, the proprietor of The Gentleman's Magazine, at St. John's Gate, took oc-

casion to speak very handsomely of the work. The
next time Cave met Harte, he told him that he had
made a man happy the other day at his home, by the
encomiums he bestowed on Savage's Life. "How
could that be?" said Harte; "none were present but
you [and I." Cave replied, "You might observe I
sent a plate of victuals behind the screen. There
skulked the biographer, *one* Johnson, whose dress
was so shabby that he durst not make his appearance. He overheard our conversation; and your ap-
plauding his performance delighted him exceedingly."

"Man," said Goethe, "recognizes and praises only
that which he himself is capable of doing; and those
who by nature are mediocre have the trick of depreciating productions which, if they have faults,
have also good points, so as to elevate the mediocre
productions which they are fitted to praise." "While
it is so undesirable that any man should receive what
he has not examined, a far more frequent danger is
that of flippant irreverence. Not all the heavens
contain is obvious to the unassisted eye of the care-
less spectator. Few men are great, almost as few
able to appreciate greatness. The critics have written little upon the Iliad in all these ages, which Alexander would have thought worth keeping with it
in his golden box. Nor Shakespeare, nor Dante, nor
Calderon, have as yet found a sufficient critic, though
Coleridge and the Schlegels have lived since they
did. Meantime," continues Margaret Fuller, "it is
safer to take off the hat and shout *Vivat!* to the conqueror, who may become a permanent sovereign, than

to throw stones and mud from the gutter. The star
shines, and that it is with no borrowed light, his foes
are his voucher. And every planet is a portent to
the world; but whether for good or ill, only he can
know who has science for many calculations. Not he
who runs can read these books, or any books of any
worth."

Homer was called a plagiarist by some of the earlier critics, and was accused of having stolen from
older poets all that was remarkable in the Iliad and
Odyssey. Sophocles was brought to trial by his children as a lunatic. Socrates, considered as the wisest and the most moral of men, Cicero treated as
an usurer, and the pedant Athenæus as illiterate.
Plato was accused of envy, lying, avarice, robbery,
incontinence, and impiety. Some of the old writers
wrote to prove Aristotle vain, ambitious, and ignorant. Plato is said to have preferred the burning of
all of the works of Democritus. Pliny and Seneca
thought Virgil destitute of invention, and Quintilian
was alike severe upon Seneca. It was a long time,
says Seneca, that Democritus was taken for a madman, and before Socrates had any esteem in the
world. How long was it before Cato could be understood? Nay, he was affronted, contemned, and
rejected; and people never knew the value of him
until they had lost him. "The Northern Highlanders,"
said Wilson, " do not admire Waverley, so I presume
the Southern Highlanders despise Guy Mannering.
The Westmoreland peasants think Wordsworth a fool.
In Borrowdale, Southey is not known to exist. I met
ten men at Hawick who did not think Hogg a poet,

and the whole city of Glasgow think me a madman.
So much for the voice of the people being the voice
of God."

Goldsmith tells us, speaking of Waller's Ode on
the Death of Cromwell, that English poetry was not
then " quite harmonized : so that this, which would
now be looked upon as a slovenly sort of versifica-
tion, was in the times in which it was written almost
a prodigy of harmony." At the same time, after
praising the harmony of the Rape of the Lock, he
observes that the irregular measure at the opening of
the Allegro and Penseroso " hurts our English ear."
Gray "loved intellectual ease and luxury, and wished
as a sort of Mohammedan paradise to ' lie on a sofa,
and read eternal new romances of Mirivaux and Cré-
billon.' Yet all he could say of Thomson's Castle of
Indolence, when it was first published, was, that
there were some good verses in it. Akenside, too,
whom he was so well fitted to appreciate, he thought
' often obscure, and even unintelligible.' " Horace
Walpole marveled at the dullness of people who can
admire anything so stupidly extravagant and barbarous as the Divina Commedia. " The long-continued
contempt for Bunyan and De Foe was merely an expression of the ordinary feeling of the cultivated
classes towards anything which was identified with
Grub Street ; but it is curious to observe the incapac-
ity of such a man as Johnson to understand Gray or
Sterne, and the contempt which Walpole expressed
for Johnson and Goldsmith, while he sincerely believed that the poems of Mason were destined to
immortality." The poet Rogers tells us that Henry

Mackenzie advised Burns to take for his model in
song-writing Mrs. John Hunter! " Byron believed
that Rogers and Moore were the truest poets among
his contemporaries; that Pope was the first of all
English, if not of all existing poets, and that Wordsworth was nothing but a namby-pamby driveler.   De
Quincey speaks of ' Mr. Goethe ' as an immoral and
second-rate author, who owes his reputation chiefly to
the fact of his long life and his position at the court
of Weimar, and Charles Lamb expressed a decided
preference of Marlowe's Dr. Faustus to Goethe's immortal Faust."   Dr. Johnson's opinion of Milton's
sonnets is pretty well known — " those soul-animat-
ing strains, alas! too few," as Wordsworth estimated
them.   Hannah More wondered that Milton could
write " such poor sonnets."   Johnson said, " Milton,
madam, was a genius that could cut a Colossus from
a rock, but could not carve heads upon cherry-stones."
He attacked Swift on all occasions.   He said, speaking of Gulliver's Travels, " When once you have
thought of big men and little men, it is very easy
to do all the rest."   He called Gray " a dull fellow."
" Sir, he was dull in company, dull in his closet, dull
everywhere.   He was dull in a new way, and that
made many people call him great."   Talking of
Sterne, he said, " Nothing odd will last long.   Tristram Shandy did not last."   See how Horace Walpole disposes of some of the gods of literature.   " Tire-
some Tristram Shandy, of which I could never get
through three volumes."   " I have read Sheridan's
Critic ; it appeared wondrously flat and old, and a
poor imitation."   He speaks of wading through Spen-

ser's "allegories and drawling stanzas." Chaucer's
Canterbury Tales, he said, are "a lump of mineral
from which Dryden extracted all the gold, and converted it into beautiful medals." "Dante was extravagant, absurd, disgusting: in short, a Meth-
odist parson in Bedlam." "Montaigne's Travels I
have been reading; if I was tired of the Essays, what
must one be of these? What signifies what a man
thought who never thought of anything but himself?
and what signifies what a man did who never did anything?" "Boswell's book," he said, "is the story
of a mountebank and his zany." Coleridge, talking of
Goethe's Faust, said, "There is no whole in the poem;
the scenes are mere magic-lantern pictures, and a
large part of the work is to me very flat. Moreover,
much of it is vulgar, licentious, and blasphemous."
"Coleridge's Ancient Mariner, is, I think," says
Southey, "the clumsiest attempt at German sublimity I ever saw." Johnson told Anna Seward that
"he would hang a dog that read the Lycidas of
Milton twice." Waller wrote of Paradise Lost on
its first appearance, "The old blind school-master,
John Milton, hath published a tedious poem on the
fall of man; if its length be not considered a merit,
it has no other." Curran declared Paradise Lost to
be the "worst poem in the language." When Harvey's book on the circulation of the blood came out,
"he fell mightily in his practice. It was believed by
the vulgar that he was crack-brained, and all the
physicians were against him." Schiller's nearest
friends decided against the Indian Death Song,
which Goethe afterward pronounced one of his

best poems. Scott tells us that one of his nearest
friends predicted the failure of Waverley. Herder,
one of the most comprehensive thinkers and versatile authors of Germany, we are told, adjured Goethe not to take so unpromising a subject as Faust.
Hume, it is said, tried to dissuade Robertson from
writing the History of Charles V. Montesquieu,
upon the completion of The Spirit of Laws, which
had cost him twenty years of labor, and which ran
through twenty-two editions in less than as many
months after its publication, submitted the manuscript to Helvetius and Saurin, who returned it with
the advice not to spoil a great reputation by publishing it. Wordsworth told Robinson that before his
ballads were published, Tobin implored him to leave
out We are Seven, as a poem that would damn the
book. It turned out to be one of the most popular.
That charming and once popular Scottish story, The
Annals of the Parish, by John Galt, was written ten or
twelve years before the date of its publication, and
anterior to the appearance of Waverley and Guy
Mannering, and was rejected, we are told, by the
publishers of those works, with the assurance that a
novel or work of fiction entirely Scottish would not take
with the public. St. Pierre submitted his delightful
tale, Paul and Virginia, to the criticisms of a circle
of his learned friends. They told him that it was a
failure; that to publish it would be a piece of fool-
ishness; that nobody would read it. St. Pierre appealed from his learned critics to his unlearned but
sympathetic and sensible housekeeper. He read —
she listened, admired, and wept. He accepted her

verdict, and will be remembered by one little story
longer than his contemporaries by their weary tomes.

" On my walk with Lamb," notes Crabb Robinson, " he spoke with enthusiasm of Manning, declaring that he is the most wonderful man he ever knew,
more extraordinary than Wordsworth or Coleridge.
Yet he does nothing. He has traveled even in
China, and has been by land from India through Thibet, yet, as far as is known, he has written nothing."
(" It is to be lamented," says Dr. Johnson, " that
those who are most capable of improving mankind
very frequently neglect to communicate their knowledge; either because it is more pleasing to gather
ideas than to impart them, or because to minds naturally great, few things appear of so much importance
as to deserve the notice of the public." " Great con-
stitutions," says Sir Thomas Browne, " and such as
are constellated unto knowledge, do nothing till
they outdo all; they come short of themselves, if
they go not beyond others, and must not sit down
under the degree of worthies. God expects no
lustre from the minor stars ; but if the the sun should
not illuminate all, it were a sin in nature.") Robinson also makes this memorandum in his Diary :
" A party at Miss Rogers' in the evening. Among
those present were Milman, Lyell, and Sydney Smith.
With the last-named I chatted for the first time.
His faun-like face is a sort of promise of a good
thing when he does but open his lips. He says nothing that from an indifferent person would be recol-
lected." Rogers said of Sydney Smith (of whose
death he had just heard), in answer to the question,

" How came it that he did not publicly show his powers? " " He had too fastidious a taste, and too high an *idea* of what ought to be." The same complaint or curiosity has often been expressed of Coleridge by those who have heard so much of his superhuman powers. How could he have done more? His was one of those great, homeless souls which fly between heaven and earth ; his language was only partly understood in this world, if wholly in another. His utterances were but mutterings in the human ears that heard them. The means he desperately made use of, to adapt himself, only spoiled his wings for flight and his voice for intelligible expression. Stupid John Chester understood him as well as any. Landor says, " Vast objects of remote altitude must be looked at a long while before they are ascertained. Ages are the telescope tubes that must be lengthened out for Shakespeare ; and generations of men serve but as single witnesses to his claims." " Shakespeare," said Coleridge, " is of no age — nor, I may add, of any religion, or party, or profession. The body and substance of his works came out of the unfathomable depths of his own oceanic mind ; his observation and reading supplied him with the drapery of his figures." " It was really Voltaire," said Goethe, " who excited such minds as Diderot, D'Alembert, and Beaumarchais ; for to be somewhat near him a man needed to be much, and could take no holidays." " Nature," said Heine, " wanted to see how she looked, and she created Goethe." " Were Byron now alive, and Burns," said Hawthorne, " the first

would come from his ancestral abbey, flinging aside,
although unwillingly, the inherited honors of a
thousand years, to take the arm of the mighty
peasant who grew immortal while he stooped behind
his plow." Landor, in his Imaginary Conversa-
tions, makes Marvell thus to address Marten : " Hast
thou not sat convivially with Oliver Cromwell ?
Hast thou not conversed familiarly with the only man
greater than he, John Milton ? One was ambitious
of perishable power, the other of imperishable glory ;
both have attained their aim." On one occasion
when Hazlitt and Coleridge were together, some
comparison was introduced between Shakespeare and
Milton. Coleridge said " he hardly knew which to
prefer. Shakespeare seemed to him a mere stripling
in the art ; he was as tall and as strong, with infinitely
more activity than Milton, but he never appeared to
have come to man's estate ; or if he had, he would
not have been a man, but a monster." " A rib of
Shakespeare," said Landor, " would have made a
Milton ; the same portion of Milton, all poets born
ever since." Said Goethe, " Would you see Shakespeare's intellect unfettered, read Troilus and Cressida, and see how he uses the materials of the Iliad
in his fashion." Said Coleridge, " Compare Nestor,
Ajax, Achilles, etc., in the Troilus and Cressida of
Shakespeare, with their namesakes in the Iliad. The
old heroes seem all to have been at school ever since."
" Young," he said, " was not a poet to be read
through at once. His love of point and wit had
often put an end to his pathos and sublimity ; but
there were parts in him which must be immortal."

He loved to read a page of Young, and walk out to think of him.

"It is natural to man," said Goethe, "to regard himself as the object of the creation, and to think of all things in relation to himself, and the degree in which they can serve and be useful to him. He takes possession of the animal and vegetable world, and while he swallows other creatures as his proper food, he acknowledges his God, and thanks the paternal kindness which has made such provision for him. . . . . Generally, the personal character of the writer influences the public, rather than his talents as an artist. Napoleon said of Corneille, 'If he were living now, I would make him a prince,' yet he never read him."

Lowell, in his essay upon Rousseau and the Sentimentalists, says, "In proportion as solitude and communion with self lead the sentimentalist to exaggerate the importance of his own personality, he comes to think the least event connected with it is of consequence to his fellow-men. If he change his shirt, he would have mankind aware of it. Victor Hugo, the greatest living representative of the class, considers it necessary to let the world know by letter from time to time his opinions on every conceivable subject about which it is not asked nor is of the least value unless we concede to him an immediate inspiration. We men of colder blood, in whom self-consciousness takes the form of pride, and who have deified *mauvaise honte* as if our defect were our virtue, find it especially hard to understand that artistic impulse of more southern races to *pose* themselves properly on every occasion, and not even to die without some tribute of deference to the taste of the world they are leaving. Was not even mighty Cæsar's last thought of his drapery? Petrarch, seeking a solitude at Vaucluse because it made him more likely to be in demand at Avignon, praising philosophic poverty with a sharp eye to the next rich benefice in the gift of his patron, commending a good life, but careful first of a good living, happy only in seclusion, but making a dangerous journey to enjoy the theatrical show of a coronation in the capital, cherishing a fruitless passion which broke his heart three or four times a year and yet could not make an end of him till he had reached the ripe age of seventy, and survived his mistress a quarter of a century, — surely a more exquisite perfection of inconsistency would be hard to find. When he returned from his journey into the north of Europe, he balanced the books of his unrequited passion, and, finding that he had now been in love seven years, thought the time had at last come to call deliberately on Death. Had Death taken him at his word, he would have protested that he was only in fun. For we find him always taking good care of an excellent constitution, avoiding the plague with commendable assiduity, and in the very year when he declares it absolutely essential to his peace of mind to die for good and all, taking refuge in the fortress of Capranica, from a wholesome dread of having his throat cut by robbers. There is such a difference between dying in a sonnet with a cambric handkerchief at one's eyes, and the prosaic reality of

11

demise certified in the parish register! Practically, it is inconvenient to be dead. Among other things, it puts an end to the manufacture of sonnets."

" Lamartine, after passing round the hat in Europe and America, takes to his bed from wounded pride when the French senate votes him a subsidy, and sheds tears of humiliation."

" There can be no doubt," says Macaulay, " that Byron owed the vast influence which he exercised over his contemporaries, at least as much to his gloomy egotism as to the real power of his poetry. We never could very clearly understand how it is that egotism, so unpopular in conversation, should be so popular in writing; or how it is that men who affect in their compositions qualities and feelings which they have not, impose so much more easily on their contemporaries than on posterity. The interest which the loves of Petrarch excited in his own time, and the pitying fondness with which half Europe looked upon Rousseau, are well known. To readers of our time, the love of Petrarch seems to have been love of that kind which breaks no hearts; and the sufferings of Rousseau to have deserved laughter rather than pity — to have been partly counterfeited, and purely the consequence of his own perverseness and vanity."

Byron, we are told by one of his friends, had a morbid love of a bad reputation. There was hardly an offense of which he would not, with perfect indifference, accuse himself. An old school-fellow, who met him on the Continent, said that he would continually write paragraphs against himself in the foreign journals, and delighted in their republication by the English newspapers, as in the success of a practical joke. " The best thing left by Byron with Lady Blessington is a copy of a letter written by him in the name of Fletcher, giving an account of his own death, and of his abuse of his friends; humor and irony mingled with unusual grace." He had an impression that he was the offspring of a demon. No wonder. " If a man's conduct," said Coleridge, " cannot be ascribed to the angelic, nor to the bestial within him, what is there left for us to refer it to but the fiendish? Passion, without any appetite, is fiendish." " My journal of Switzerland," says Crabb Robinson, " does not mention what I well recollect, and Wordsworth has made the subject of a sonnet, the continued barking of a dog, irritated by the echo of his own voice. In human life this is perpetually occurring. It is said that a dog has been known to contract an illness by the continued labor of barking at his own echo, and finally to be *killed* by it."

VI.

LIMITS.

MINDS, like some seed-plants, delight in sporting; there is great variety in thinking, but the few great ideas remain the same. They are constantly re-appearing in all ages and in all literatures, modified by new circumstances and new uses; though in new dresses, they are still the old originals. Like the virtues, they have great and endless services to perform in this world. Now they appear in philosophy, now in fiction; the moralist uses them, and the buffoon; dissociate them, analyze them, strip them of their innumerable dresses, and they are recognized and identified — the same from the foundation and forever. If a discriminating general reader for forty years had noted their continual reappearance in the tons of books he has perused upon all subjects, he would be astonished at their varied and multiplied uses. Thinkers he would perhaps find more numerous than thoughts; yet of the former how few. The original thought of one age diffuses itself through the next, and expires in commonplace — to be born again when occasion necessitates and God wills. At each birth it is a new creation — to the brain it springs from and to the creatures it is to enlighten and serve. If the writer or speaker could know how

often it has done even hack-service in the ages before
him, he would repentantly blot it out, or choke in its
utterance. In the unpleasant discovery, that indispensable and inspiring quality, self-conceit, would
suffer a wound beyond healing.

" The number of those writers who can, with any
justness of expression," says Melmoth, " be termed
thinking authors, would not form a very copious
library, though one were to take in all of that kind
which both ancient and modern times have produced.
Epicurus, we are told, left behind him three hundred
volumes of his own works, wherein he had not inserted a single quotation; and we have it upon the
authority of Varro's own works, that he himself
composed four hundred and ninety books. Seneca
assures us that Didymus, the grammarian, wrote no
less than four thousand; but Origen, it seems, was
yet more prolific, and extended his performances even
to six thousand treatises. It is obvious to imagine
with what sort of materials the productions of such
expeditious workmen were wrought up: sound
thought and well-matured reflections could have no
share, we may be sure, in these hasty performances.
Thus are books multiplied, whilst authors are scarce;
and so much easier is it to write than to think."
" The same man," said Publius Syrus, " can rarely
say a great deal and say it to the purpose."

To ridicule the pervading absence of thought in
common conversation, the author of Lothair makes
Pinto exclaim, " English is an expressive language,
but not difficult to master. Its range is limited. It
consists, as far as I observe, of four words : ' nice,'

'jolly,' 'charming,' and 'bore;' and some gramma-
rians add, ' fond.' "

Proverbs, old as they are, seem always new, and
are always smartly uttered. Sancho Panza is but
one of an immortal type, and the proverbs and maxims he was always using are older than the pyramids
— as old as spoken language. Pascal conceived that
every possible maxim of conduct existed in the world,
though no individual can be conversant with the entire series. "There is a certain list of vices committed in all ages, and declaimed against by all authors, which," says Sir Thomas Browne, " will last as
long as human nature ; which, digested into commonplaces, may serve for any theme, and never be out of
date until doomsday." A proverb Lord John Russell
has defined to be "the wisdom of the many in the
wit of one." "The various humors of mankind,"
says the elder Disraeli, " in the mutability of human
affairs, has given birth to every species ; and men
were wise, or merry, or satirical, and mourned or re-
joiced in proverbs. Nations held an universal intercourse of proverbs, from the eastern to the western
world ; for we discover among those which appear
strictly national many which are common to them all.
Of our own familiar ones several may be tracked
among the snows of the Latins and the Greeks, and
have sometimes been drawn from The Mines of the
East; like decayed families which remain in obscurity,
they may boast of a high lineal descent whenever
they recover their lost title-deeds. The vulgar proverb, ' To carry coals to Newcastle,' local and idio-
matic as it appears, however, has been borrowed and

applied by ourselves; it may be found among the
Persians; in the Bustan of Saadi we have ' To carry
pepper to Hindostan ; ' among the Hebrews, ' To carry
oil to a city of olives ; ' a similar proverb occurs in
Greek; and in Galland's Maxims of the East we may
discover how many of the most common proverbs
among us, as well as some of Joe Miller's jests, are of
Oriental origin. The resemblance of certain proverbs
in different nations must, however, be often ascribed
to the identity of human nature; similar situations
and similar objects have unquestionably made men
think and act and express themselves alike. All nations are parallels of each other. Hence all collectors
of proverbs complain of the difficulty of separating
their own national proverbs from those which had
crept into the language from others, particularly when
nations have held much intercourse together. We
have a copious collection of Scottish proverbs by
Kelly ; but this learned man was mortified at discovering that many, which he had long believed to have
been genuine Scottish, were not only English, but
French, Italian, Spanish, Latin, and Greek ones ;
many of his Scottish proverbs are almost literally expressed among the fragments of remote antiquity. It
would have surprised him further had he been aware
that his Greek originals were themselves but copies,
and might have been found in D'Herbelot, Erpenius,
and Golius, and in many Asiatic works, which have
been more recently introduced to the enlarged knowledge of the European student, who formerly found
his most extended researches limited by Hellenistic
lore."

The author of The Eclipse of Faith, in one of his intellectual visions, saw suddenly expunged – " remorselessly expunged"—from literature "every text, every phrase, which had been quoted from the Bible, not only in the books of devotion and theology, but in those of poetry and fiction.   Never before," he says, " had I any adequate idea of the extent to which the Bible had moulded the intellectual and moral life of the last eighteen centuries, nor how intimately it had interfused itself with the habits of thought and modes of expression ; nor how naturally and extensively its comprehensive imagery and language had been introduced into human writings, and most of all where there had been most of genius.   A vast portion of literature became instantly worthless, and was transformed into so much waste paper.   It was almost impossible to look into any book of merit, and read ten pages together, without coming to some provoking erasures and mutilations, which made whole passages perfectly unintelligible.   Many of the sweetest passages of Shakespeare were converted into unmeaning nonsense, from the absence of those words which his own all but divine genius had appropriated from a still diviner source.   As to Milton, he was nearly ruined, as might naturally be supposed.   Walter Scott's novels were filled with *lacunœ*.   I hoped it might be otherwise with the philosophers, and so it was ; but even here it was curious to see what strange ravages the visitation had wrought.   Some of the most beautiful and comprehensive of Bacon's Aphorisms were reduced to enigmatical nonsense."

A scholarly article upon Homeric Characters in and

out of Homer, published in The London Quarterly, 1857, opens with this passage: " To one only among the countless millions of human beings has it been given to draw characters, by the strength of his own individual hand, in lines of such force and vigor that they have become from his day to our own the common inheritance of civilized man. That one is Homer. Ever since his time, besides finding his way even into the impenetrable East, he has found literary capital and available stock in trade for reciters and hearers, for authors and readers of all times and of all places within the limits of the western world. Like the sun, which furnishes with its light the courts and alleys of London, while himself unseen by their inhabitants, he has supplied with the illumination of his ideas millions of minds never brought into direct contact with his works, and even millions hardly aware of his existence."

One of the most eminent platform orators of the time has treated the habit of borrowing, in literature, in a most striking manner. " Take," he said, " the stories of Shakespeare, who has, perhaps, written his forty-odd plays. Some are historical. The rest, two thirds of them, he did not stop to invent, but he found them. These he clutched, ready-made to his hand, from the Italian novelists, who had taken them before from the East. Cinderella and her Slipper is older than all history, like half a dozen other baby legends. The annals of the world do not go back far enough to tell us from where they first came. Bulwer borrowed the incidents of his Roman stories from legends of a thousand years before. Indeed, Dunloch, who has

grouped the history of the novels of all Europe into
one essay, says that in the nations of modern Europe
there have been two hundred and fifty or three hundred distinct stories. He says at least two hundred
of these may be traced, before Christianity, to the
other side of the Black Sea. Even our newspaper
jokes are enjoying a very respectable old age. Take
Maria Edgeworth's essay on Irish bulls and the
laughable mistakes of the Irish. The tale which Maria Edgeworth or her father thought the best is that
famous story of a man writing a letter as follows:
' My dear friend, I would write you more in detail,
more minutely, if there was not an impudent fellow
looking over my shoulder reading every word.' (' No,
you lie; I 've not read a word you have written !')
This is an Irish bull, still it is a very old one.
It is only two hundred and fifty years older than the
New Testament. Horace Walpole dissented from
Richard Lovell Edgeworth, and thought the other
Irish bull was the best — of the man who said,
' I would have been a very handsome man, but
they changed me in the cradle.' That comes from
Don Quixote, and is Spanish ; but Cervantes borrowed it from the Greek in the fourth century, and
the Greeks stole it from the Egyptians hundreds of
years back. There is one story which it is said
Washington has related of a man who went into an
inn and asked for a glass of drink from the landlord,
who pushed forward a wine-glass about half the usual
size. The landlord said, ' That glass out of which
you are drinking is forty years old.' ' Well,' said the
thirsty traveler, contemplating its minute propor-

tions, 'I think it is the smallest thing I ever saw.'
[The same story is told of Foote. Dining while in
Paris with Lord Stormont, that thrifty Scotch peer,
then ambassador, as usual produced his wine in the
smallest of decanters, and dispensed it in the smallest
of glasses, enlarging all the time on its exquisite
growth and enormous age. "It is very little of its
age," said Foote, holding up his diminutive glass.]
That story as told is given as a story of Athens three
hundred and seventy-five years before Christ was
born. Why, all these Irish bulls are Greek — every
one of them. Take the Irishman who carried around
a brick as a specimen of the house he had to sell;
take the Irishman who shut his eyes and looked into
the glass to see how he would look when he was
dead; take the Irishman that bought a crow, alleg-
ing that crows were reported to live two hundred
years, and he meant to set out and try it; take the
Irishman that met a friend who said to him, 'Why,
sir, I heard you were dead.' 'Well,' says the man,
'I suppose you see I am not.' 'Oh, no,' says he, 'I
would believe the man who told me a great deal
quicker than I would you.' Well, those are all Greek.
A score or more of them, of the parallel character,
come from Athens." ・

On the other hand, the critics and scholiasts are
determined that much of ancient story which has
passed into history shall be considered only fiction,
with hardly the slightest basis of foundation in truth.
They would have us believe that "we have no very
credible account of Rome or the Romans for more
than four hundred years after the foundation of the

city; and that the first book of Livy, containing the
regal period, can lay claim, when severely tested, to
no higher authority than Lord Macaulay's Lays.
Livy states that whatever records existed prior to the
burning of Rome by the Gauls — three hundred and
sixty-five years after its foundation — were then
burnt or lost. We are left, therefore, in the most
embarrassing uncertainty whether Tarquin outraged
Lucretia; or Brutus shammed idiotcy, and condemned
his sons to death; or Mutius Scævola thrust his hand
into the fire; or Curtius jumped into the gulf — if
there was one; or Clœlia swam the Tiber; or Cocles
defended a bridge against an army. We could fill
pages with skeptical doubts of scholiasts, who would
fain deprive Diogenes of his lantern and his tub,
Æsop of his hump, Sappho of her leap, Rhodes of its
Colossus, and Dionysius the First of his ear; nay,
who pretend that Cadmus did not come from Phœni-
cia, that Belisarius was not blind, that Portia did not
swallow burning coals, and that Dionysius the Second never kept a school at Corinth. Modern chemists have been unable to discover how Hannibal could
have leveled rocks, or Cleopatra dissolved pearls with
vinegar. A German pedant has actually ventured to
question the purity of Lucretia."

Hayward (translator of Faust), in his article on
Pearls and Mock Pearls of History, says, " We are
gravely told, on historical authority, by Moore, in a
note to one of his Irish Melodies, that during the
reign of Bryan, King of Munster, a young lady of
great beauty, richly dressed, and adorned with jewels, undertook a journey from one end of the king-

dom to another, with a wand in her hand, at the top of which was a ring of exceeding great value; and such was the perfection of the laws and the government that no attempt was made upon her honor, nor was she robbed of her clothes and jewels. Precisely the same story is told of Alfred, of Frothi, King of Denmark, and of Rollo, Duke of Normandy. Another romantic anecdote, fluctuating between two or more sets of actors, is an episode in the amours of Emma, the alleged daughter of Charlemagne, who, finding that the snow had fallen thickly during a nightly interview with her lover, Eginhard, took him upon her shoulders, and carried him some distance from her bower, to prevent his footsteps from being traced. Unluckily, Charlemagne had no daughter named Emma or Imma ; and a hundred years before the appearance of the chronicle which records the adventure, it had been related in print of a German emperor and a damsel unknown. The story of Canute commanding the waves to roll back rests on the authority of Henry of Huntingdon, who wrote about a hundred years after the Danish monarch. ' As for the greater number of the stories with which the *ana* are stuffed,' says Voltaire, ' including all those humorous replies attributed to Charles the Fifth and Henry the Fourth, to a hundred modern princes, you find them in Athenæus and in our old authors.' Dionysius the tyrant, we are told by Diogenes of Laërte, treated his friends like vases full of good liquors, which he broke when he had emptied them. This is precisely what Cardinal Retz says of Madame de Chevreuse's treatment of her lovers. There is a story

of Sully's meeting a young lady, veiled, and dressed
in green, on the back stairs leading to Henry's apartment, and being asked by the king whether he had
not been told that his majesty had a fever and could
not receive that morning, replied, ' Yes, sire, but the
fever is gone; I have just met it on the staircase,
dressed in green.' This story is told of Demetrius
and his father. The lesson of perseverance in adversity taught by the spider to Robert Bruce is said to
have been taught by the same insect to Tamerlane.
' When Columbus,' says Voltaire, ' promised a new
hemisphere, people maintained that it did not exist;
and when he had discovered it, that it had been known
a long time.' It was to confute such detractors that
he resorted to the illustration of the egg, already employed by Brunelleschi when his merit in raising the
cupola of the cathedral of Florence was contested.
The anecdote of Northampton reading The Faery
Queen, whilst Spenser was waiting in the ante-
chamber, may pair off with one of Louis XIV. As
this munificent monarch was going over the improve-
ments of Versailles with Le Notre, the sight of each
fresh beauty or capability tempts him to some fresh
extravagance, till the architect cries out that if their
promenade is continued in this fashion, it will end in
the bankruptcy of the state. Southampton, after
sending first twenty, and then fifty guineas, on coming to one fine passage after another, exclaims, ' Turn
the fellow out of the house, or I shall be ruined.' On
the morning of his execution, Charles I. said to his
groom of the chambers, ' Let me have a shirt on more
than ordinary, by reason the season is so sharp as

probably may make me shake, which some observers will imagine proceeds from fear. I would have no such imputation; I fear not death.' As Bailly was waiting to be guillotined, one of the executioners accused him of trembling. 'I am cold,' was the reply. Frederick the Great is reported to have said, in reference to a troublesome assailant, 'This man wants me to make a martyr of him, but he shall not have that satisfaction.' Vespasian told Demetrius the Cynic, 'You do all you can to get me to put you to death, but I do not kill a dog for barking at me.' This Demetrius was a man of real spirit and honesty. When Caligula tried to conciliate his good word by a large gift in money, he sent it back with the message, 'If you wish to bribe me, you must send me your crown.' George III. ironically asked an eminent divine, who was just returned from Rome, whether he had converted the pope. 'No, sire, I had nothing better to offer him.' Cardinal Ximenes, upon a muster which was taken against the Moors, was spoken to by a servant of his to stand a little out of the smoke of the harquebuse, but he said again that 'that was his incense.' The first time Charles XII. of Sweden was under fire, he inquired what the hissing he heard about his ears was, and being told that it was caused by the musket-balls, 'Good,' he exclaimed, 'this henceforth shall be my music.' Pope Julius II., like many a would-be connoisseur, was apt to exhibit his taste by fault-finding. On his objecting that one of Michel Angelo's statues might be improved by a few touches of the chisel, the artist, with the aid of a few pinches of marble dust, which he dropped adroitly, conveyed an impression that he had acted on the hint. When Halifax found fault with some passages in Pope's translation of Homer, the poet, by the advice of Garth, left them as they stood, but told the peer that they had been retouched, and had the satisfaction of finding him as easily satisfied as his holiness. When Lycurgus was to reform and alter the state of Sparta, in the consultation one advised that it should be reduced to an absolute popular equality; but Lycurgus said to him, 'Sir, begin it in your own house.' Had Dr. Johnson forgotten this among Bacon's Apothegms when he told Mrs. Macaulay, 'Madam, I am now become a convert to your way of thinking. I am convinced that all mankind are upon an equal footing, and to give you an unquestionable proof, madam, that I am in earnest, here is a very sensible, civil, well-behaved fellow-citizen, your footman; I desire that he may be allowed to sit down and dine with us'?" Boswell once said, "A man is reckoned a wise man, rather for what he does not say, than for what he says: perhaps upon the whole Limbertongue speaks a greater quantity of good sense than Manly does, but Limbertongue gives you such floods of frivolous nonsense that his sense is quite drowned. Manly gives you unmixed good sense only. Manly will always be thought the wisest man of the two." Corwin, a brilliant wit and humorist of the Sydney Smith stamp, and in his time the greatest of American stump-orators, was often heard to say that his life was a failure, because he had not been, with the public, more successful in serious veins. A friend relates that he was riding with him one day, when

Corwin remarked of a speech made the evening before, "It was very good indeed, but in bad style. Never make the people laugh. I see that you cultivate that. It is easy and captivating, but death in the long run to the speaker." "Why, Mr. Corwin, you are the last man living I expected such an opinion from." "Certainly, because you have not lived so long as I have. Do you know, my young friend, that the world has a contempt for the man that entertains it? One must be solemn — solemn as an ass — never say anything that is not uttered with the greatest gravity, to win respect. The world looks up to the teacher and down at the clown; yet, nine cases out of ten, the clown is the better fellow of the two." Sydney Smith is reported to have said to his eldest brother, a grave and prosperous gentleman: "Brother, you and I are exceptions to the laws of nature. You have risen by your gravity, and I have sunk by my levity." In one of Steele's Tatlers, Sancroft asked the question, why it was that actors, speaking of things imaginary, affected audiences as if they were real; whilst preachers, speaking of things real, could only affect their congregations as with things imaginary. Bickerstaff answered, "Why, indeed, I don't know; unless it is that we actors speak of things imaginary as if they were real, while you in the pulpit speak of things real as if they were imaginary." This anwer, besides being borrowed by Betterton, has been credited to every famous actor since Steele printed it. Every reader of Charles Lamb remembers his amusing essay on the Origin of Roast Pig. The legend of the first act of oyster-eating is enough

12

like it to remind one of it. It is related that a man, walking one day by the shore of the sea, picked up one of those savory bivalves, just as it was in the act of gaping. Observing the extreme smoothness of the interior of the shells, he insinuated his finger that he might feel the shining surface, when suddenly they closed upon the exploring digit, causing a sensation less pleasurable than he anticipated. The prompt withdrawal of his finger was scarcely a more natural movement than its transfer to his mouth, when he tasted oyster-juice for the first time, as the Chinaman in Elia's essay, having burnt his finger, first tasted cracklin. The savor was delicious, — he had made a great discovery ; so he picked up the oyster, forced open the shells, banqueted upon the contents, and soon brought oyster-eating into fashion. Nothing, it is said, puzzled Bonaparte more than to meet an honest man of good sense ; " He did not know what to make of him. He would offer a man money ; if that failed, he would talk of glory, or promise him rank and power ; but if all these temptations failed, he set him down for an idiot, or a half-mad dreamer. Conscience was a thing he could not understand." Rulhière, who was at St. Petersburg in 1762, when Catherine caused her husband, Peter III., to be murdered, wrote a history of the transaction on his return to France, which was handed about in manuscript. The empress was informed of it, and endeavored to procure the destruction of the work. Madame Geoffrin was sent to Rulhière to offer him a considerable bribe to throw it into the fire. He eloquently remonstrated that it would be a base and cowardly action, which honor and virtue forbade. She heard him patiently to the end, and then calmly replied, " What! is n't it enough ? " Lord Orrery related as an unquestionable occurrence that Swift once commenced the service, when nobody except the clerk attended his church, with, " Dearly beloved Roger, the Scripture moveth you and me in sundry places." Mr. Theophilus Swift afterward discovered the anecdote in a jest-book which was published before his great kinsman was born. " We all remember," says Mrs. Jameson, in her Commonplace Book of Thoughts, " the famous *bon mot* of Talleyrand. When seated between Madame de Staël and Madame Récamier, and pouring forth gallantry, first at the feet of one, then of the other, Madame de Staël suddenly asked him if she and Madame Récamier fell into the river, which of the two he would save first ? ' Madame,' replied Talleyrand, ' *you* could swim ! ' Now we will match this pretty *bon mot* with one far prettier, and founded on it. Prince S., whom I knew formerly, was one day loitering on the banks of the Isar, in the English garden at Munich, by the side of the beautiful Madame de V., then the object of his devoted admiration. For a while he had been speaking to her of his mother, for whom, *vaurien* as he was, he had ever shown the strongest filial love and respect. Afterward, as they wandered on, he began to pour forth his soul to the lady of his love with all the eloquence of passion. Suddenly she turned and said to him, ' If your mother and myself were both to fall into this river, whom would you save first ? ' ' My mother,' he instantly replied ; and then, looking at

her expressively, immediately added, ' To save *you*
first, would be as if I were to save *myself* first.'"
Jones tells a story of Scott, of whom he once made a
bust. Having a fine subject to start with, he succeeded in giving great satisfaction. At the last
sitting he attempted to refine and elaborate the lines
and markings of the face. The general sat patiently;
but when he came to see the result, his countenance
indicated decided displeasure. " Why, Jones, what
have you been doing ? " he asked. " Oh," answered
the sculptor, " not much, I confess; I have been
working out the details of the face a little more,
this morning." " Details ? " exclaimed the general
warmly; " —— the details ! Why, man, you are
spoiling the bust ! " Sir Joshua Reynolds, we are
told, once went with one of his pupils to see a
celebrated painting. After viewing it for a while,
the young man gave it as his deliberate opinion
that the picture " needed finishing." " Finishing ? "
exclaimed Sir Joshua, a little impatiently; " finishing would only spoil the painting." Judge Rodgers
once related a death-bed incident of a neighbor of
his, — a poor honest Scotsman, a wood-sawyer, —
whose admiration and solace, all through his hard
life, had been Scotia's great poet. The good man,
worn out and weary, was told by his physician that
his last hour had come — that he must soon die.
He received the announcement philosophically, and
after naming a few things for which he expressed a
desire to live, he said to the judge — about the last
thing he said on earth, " Yes; for these things I
should like to live ; but — but — judge [they had

many a time read the poet together] — I shall see — *Burns!*" Socrates, upon receiving sentence of death, said, amongst other things, to his judges, "Is this, do you think, no happy journey? Do you think it nothing to speak with Orpheus, Musæus, Homer, and Hesiod?" "Shakespeare's Joan of Arc," says Hayward, "is a mere embodiment of English prejudice; yet it is not much further from the truth than Schiller's transcendental and exquisitely poetical character of the maid. The German dramatist has also idealized Don Carlos to an extent that renders recognition difficult; and he has flung a halo round William Tell which will cling to the name while Switzerland is a country or patriotism any better than a name. Yet more than a hundred years ago the eldest son of Haller undertook to prove that the legend, in its main features, is the revival or imitation of a Danish one, to be found in Saxo Grammaticus. The canton of Uri, to which Tell belonged, ordered the book to be publicly burnt, and appealed to the other cantons to coöperate in its suppression, thereby giving additional interest and vitality to the question, which has been at length pretty well exhausted by German writers. The upshot is that the episode of the apple is relegated to the domain of the fable; and that Tell himself is grudgingly allowed a commonplace share in the exploits of the early Swiss patriots. Strange to say, his name is not mentioned by any contemporary chronicler of the struggle for independence. Sir A. Callcott's picture of Milton and his Daughters, one of whom holds a pen as if writing to his dictation, is in open defiance of Dr. Johnson's statement that the

daughters were never taught to write. There is the
story of Poussin impatiently dashing his sponge
against his canvas, and producing the precise effect
(the foam on a horse's mouth) which he had been
long and vainly laboring for; and there is a similar
one told of Haydn, the musical composer, when required to imitate a storm at sea. 'He kept trying all
sorts of passages, ran up and down the scale, and exhausted his ingenuity in heaping together chromatic
intervals and strange discords. Still Curtz (the author of the *libretto*) was not satisfied. At last the
musician, out of all patience, extended his hands to
the two extremities of the keys, and, bringing them
rapidly together, exclaimed, " The deuce take the
tempest; I can make nothing of it." " That is the
very thing," exclaimed Curtz, delighted with the *truth*
of the representation.' Neither Haydn nor Curtz,
adds the author from whom we quote, had ever seen
the sea. Sir David Brewster, in his life of Newton,
says that neither Pemberton nor Whiston, who received from Newton himself the history of his first
ideas of gravity, records the story of the falling apple. It was mentioned, however, to Voltaire by Catherine Barton, Newton's niece, and to Mr. Green by
Mr. Martin Folkes, the President of the Royal Society. ' We saw the apple-tree in 1814, and brought
away a portion of one of its roots.' The concluding
remark reminds us of Washington Irving's hero, who
boasted of having parried a musket bullet with a small
sword, in proof of which he exhibited the sword a
little bent in the hilt. The apple is supposed to have
fallen in 1665. Father Prout (Mahony) translated

several of the Irish Melodies into Greek and Latin verse, and then jocularly insinuated a charge of plagiarism against the author. Moore was exceedingly annoyed, and remarked to a friend who made light of the trick, ' This is all very well for your London critics ; but, let me tell you, my reputation for originality has been gravely impeached in the provincial newspapers on the strength of these very imitations.'" Dr. Johnson's Latin translation of the Messiah was published in 1731, and Pope is reported to have said, " The writer of this poem will leave it a question for posterity, whether his or mine be the original." Trench, in a note to one of his Hulsean lectures, says, " There is a curious account of a fraud which was played off on Voltaire, connecting itself with a singular piece of literary forgery. A Jesuit missionary, whose zeal led him to assume the appearance of an Indian fakir, in the beginning of the last century forged a Veda, of which the purport was secretly to undermine the religion which it professed to support, and so to facilitate the introduction of Christianity — to advance, that is, the kingdom of truth with a lie. This forged Veda is full of every kind of error or ignorance in regard to the Indian religion. After lying, however, long in a Romanist missionary college at Pondicherry, it found its way to Europe, and a transcript of it came into the hands of Voltaire, who eagerly used it for the purpose of depreciating the Christian books, and showing how many of their doctrines had been anticipated by the wisdom of the East. The book had thus an end worthy of its beginning."

Wendell Phillips, in his lecture upon the Lost
Arts, made some remarkable statements, to prove the
superiority of the ancients in many things. "In
every matter," he said, "that relates to invention —
to use, or beauty, or form — we are borrowers. You
may glance around the furniture of the palaces of
Europe, and you may gather all these utensils of art
or use, and when you have fixed the shape and forms
in your mind, I will take you into the Museum of
Naples, which gathers all remains of the domestic
life of the Romans, and you shall not find a single
one of these modern forms of art, or beauty, or use,
that was not anticipated there. We have hardly
added one single line or sweep of beauty to the antique. . . . . I had heard that nothing had been observed in ancient times which could be called by the
name of glass; that there had been merely attempts
to imitate it. In Pompeii, a dozen miles south of
Naples, which was covered with ashes eighteen hundred years ago, they broke into a room full of glass;
there was ground glass, window glass, cut glass, and
colored glass of every variety. It was undoubtedly
a glass-maker's factory. . . . . Their imitations of
gems deceived not only the lay people, but the con-
noisseurs were also cheated. Some of these imitations in later years have been discovered. The
celebrated vase of the Geneva Cathedral was considered a solid emerald. The Roman Catholic legend of it was that it was one of the treasures that
the Queen of Sheba gave to Solomon, and that it was
the identical cup out of which the Saviour ate the
Last Supper. Columbus must have admired it. It

was venerable in his day; it was death at that time
for anybody to touch it but a Catholic priest. And
when Napoleon besieged Genoa it was offered by the
Jews to loan the senate three millions of dollars on
that single article as security. Napoleon took it and
carried it to France, and gave it to the Institute. In
a fool's night, somewhat reluctantly, the scholars said,
' It is not a stone; we hardly know what it is.'
Cicero said he had seen the entire Iliad, which is a
poem as large as the New Testament, written on skin
so that it could be rolled up in the compass of a nut-
shell. Now this is imperceptible to the ordinary eye.
You have seen the Declaration of Independence in
the compass of a quarter of a dollar, written with
glasses. I have to-day a paper at home as long as
half my hand, on which was photographed the whole
contents of a London newspaper. It was put under
a dove's wing and sent into Paris, where they enlarged it and read the news. That copy of the Iliad
must have been made by some such process. . . . . .
You may visit Dr. Abbott's Museum, where you will
see the ring of Cheops. Bunsen puts him at five
hundred years before Christ. The signet of the ring
is about the size of a quarter of a dollar, and the engraving is invisible without the aid of glasses. No
man was ever shown into the cabinet of gems in
Italy without being furnished with a microscope to
look at them. It would be idle for him to look at
them without one. He could n't appreciate the delicate lines and the expression of the faces. If you go
to Parma, they will show you a gem once worn on
the finger of Michel Angelo, of which the engraving

is two thousand years old, on which there are the figures of seven women. You must have the aid of a glass in order to distinguish the forms at all. I have a friend who has a ring, perhaps three quarters of an inch in diameter, and on it is the naked figure of the god Hercules. By the aid of glasses you can distinguish the interlacing muscles, and count every separate hair on the eyebrows. Layard says he would be unable to read the engravings on Nineveh without strong spectacles, they are so extremely small. Rawlinson brought home a stone about twenty inches long and ten inches wide, containing an entire treatise on mathematics. It would be perfectly illegible without glasses. Now, if we are unable to read it without the aid of glasses, you may suppose the man who engraved it had pretty good spectacles. So the microscope, instead of dating from our time, finds its brothers in the Books of Moses — and these are infant brothers." Speaking of colors, he said, "The burned city of Pompeii was a city of stucco. All the houses are stucco outside, and it is stained with Tyrian purple — the royal color of antiquity. But you can never rely on the name of a color after a thousand years, so the Tyrian purple is almost a red. This is a city of all red. It had been buried seventeen hundred years, and, if you take a shovel now and clear away the ashes, this color flames up upon you a great deal richer than anything we can produce. You can go down into the narrow vault which Nero built him as a retreat from the great heat, and you will find the walls painted all over with fanciful designs in arabesque, which have been buried beneath the earth fifteen hundred years ; but when the peasants light it up with their torches, the colors flash out before you as fresh as they were in the days of St. Paul. Page, the artist, spent twelve years in Venice, studying Titian's method of mixing his colors, and he thinks he has got it. Yet come down from Titian, whose colors are wonderfully and perfectly fresh, to Sir Joshua Reynolds, and, although his colors are not yet a hundred years old, they are fading ; the color on his lips is dying out, and the cheeks are losing their tints. He did not know how to mix well. And his mastery of color is as yet unequaled. . . . . The French have a theory that there is a certain delicate shade of blue that Europeans cannot see. In one of his lectures to his students, Ruskin opened his Catholic mass-book and said, ' Gentlemen, we are the best chemists in the world. No Englishman ever could doubt that. But we cannot make such a scarlet as that, and even if we could, it would not last for twenty years. Yet this is five hundred years old.' The Frenchman says, ' I am the best dyer in Europe ;·nobody can equal me, and nobody can surpass Lyons.' Yet in Cashmere, where the girls make shawls worth thirty thousand dollars, they will show him three hundred distinct colors which he not only cannot make but cannot even distinguish. . . . . Mr. Colton, of the Boston Journal, the first week he landed in Asia, found that his chronometer was out of order from the steel of the works having become rusted. The London Medical and Surgical Journal advises surgeons not to venture to carry any lancets to Calcutta ; to have

them gilded, because English steel could not bear the
atmosphere of India. Yet the Damascus blades of
the Crusades were not gilded, and they are as perfect
as they were eight centuries ago. . . . . If a London
chronometer-maker wants the best steel to use in his
chronometer, he does not send to Sheffield, the centre
of all science, but to the Punjaub, the empire of the
five rivers, where there is no science at all. . . . .
Scott, in his Crusaders, describes a meeting between
Richard Cœur de Lion and Saladin. Saladin asks
Richard to show him the wonderful strength for
which he is famous, and the Norman monarch re-
sponds by severing a bar of iron which lies on the
floor of the tent. Saladin says, ' I cannot do that ; '
but he takes an eider-down pillow from the sofa, and
drawing his keen blade across it, it falls in two pieces.
Richard says, ' This is the black art ; it is magic ; it
is the devil ; you cannot cut that which has no resistance ; ' and Saladin, to show him that such is not
the case, takes a scarf from his shoulders, which is so
light that it almost floats in the air, and tossing it up,
severs it before it can descend. George Thompson
saw a man in Calcutta throw a handful of floss silk
into the air, and a Hindoo sever it into pieces with
his sabre. . . . . Mr. Batterson, of Hartford, walking
with Brunel, the architect of the Thames Tunnel, in
Egypt, asked him what he thought of the mechanical
power of the Egyptians, and he said, ' There is Pompey's Pillar ; it is one hundred feet high, and the
capital weighs two thousand pounds. It is something
of a feat to hang two thousand pounds at that height
in the air, and the few men that can do it would

better discuss Egyptian mechanics.' . . . . We have only just begun to understand ventilation properly for our houses, yet late experiments at the pyramids in Egypt show that those Egyptian tombs were ventilated in the most perfect and scientific manner. Again, cement is modern, for the ancients dressed and jointed their stones so closely that in buildings thousands of years old, the thin blade of a penknife cannot be forced between them. The railroad dates back to Egypt. Arago has claimed that they had a knowledge of steam. Bramah acknowledges that he took the idea of his celebrated lock from an ancient Egyptian pattern. De Tocqueville says there was no social question that was not discussed to rags in Egypt."

Humboldt, in his Cosmos, states that the Chinese had magnetic carriages with which to guide themselves across the great plains of Tartary, one thousand years before our era, on the principle of the compass. The Romans used movable types to mark their pottery and indorse their books. Layard found in Nineveh a magnifying lens of rock crystal, which Sir David Brewster considers a true optical lens, and the origin of the microscope. Experiments foreshadowing photography, giving remarkable results, began to be made more than three centuries ago, and more than two and a half centuries before Daguerre. The principle of the stereoscope, invented by Professor Wheatstone, was known to Euclid, described by Galen fifteen hundred years ago, and more fully long afterward in the works of Giambattista Porta. The Thames Tunnel, thought such a novelty, was anticipated by that under the Euphrates at Babylon.

The so-called modern manifestations of spiritualism, as table-turning and direct spirit-writing, have
been practiced in China from time immemorial; they
have been known there at least from the days of
Laou-tse, and he was an aged man when Confucius
was a youth, between five and six centuries before
the Christian era. Those who have read the travels
in Thibet of the two Lazarite monks, Huc and Ga-
bet, will recall many illustrations of spiritualism from
their pages; and here, too, as in China, these practices date from a very remote time. M. Tscherpanoff
published, in 1858, at St. Petersburg, the results of
his investigations with the Lamas of Thibet. He at-
tests (having been a witness in one or two cases)
" that the Lamas, when applied to for the recovery of
stolen or hidden things, take a little table, put one
hand on it, and after nearly half an hour the table is
lifted up by an invisible power, and is (with the
hand of the Lama always on it) carried to the place
where the thing in question is to be found, whether
in or out of doors, where it drops, generally indicat-.
ing exactly the spot where the article is to be found."
Mesmerism is not new. Amongst Egyptian sculpt-
ures are people in the various attitudes which mesmerism in modern times induces. The Hebrews knew
something of this science, for Baalam manifestly consulted a clairvoyant — a man in a " trance with his
eyes open." The Greeks also had a knowledge of it.
In Taylor's Plato it is said a man appeared before
Aristotle in the Lyceum, who could read on one side
of a brazen shield what was written on the other.
The Romans were not ignorant of it, for Plautus, in

one of his plays, asks, " What, and although I were by my continual slow touch to make him as if asleep ? "

As to social science, here is the germ of Fourierism, in the Confessions of Augustine, Bishop of Hippo, fifteen hundred years before Fourier: " And many of us friends, conferring about and detesting the turbulent turmoil of human life, had debated and now almost resolved on living apart from business and the bustle of men ; and this was to be thus obtained: we were to bring whatever we might severally possess, and make one household of all ; so that through the truth of our friendship nothing should belong especially to any, but the whole, thus derived from all, should as a whole belong to each, and all to all. We thought there might be some ten persons in this society; some of us very rich, especially Romanianus, our townsman, from childhood a very familiar friend of mine, whom the grievous perplexities of his affairs had brought up to court. He was the most earnest for this project; and his voice was of great weight, because his ample estate far exceeded any of the rest. We had settled, also, that two annual officers, as it were, should provide all things necessary, the rest being undisturbed. But when we began to consider whether the wives, which some of us already had, and others hoped to have, would allow this, all that plan, which was being so well moulded, fell to pieces in our hands, and was utterly dashed and cast aside. Thence we betook us to sighs and groans, and to follow the broad and beaten ways of the world."

In this beautiful passage from the Gulistan, or Rose Garden, of Saadi, written more than seven centuries ago, will be found an incomparable recipe for a famous hot-weather drink, much affected by Americans. Heliogabalus would have given a slice of his empire for that one immortal cobbler. " I recollect," says the poet, " that in my youth, as I was passing through a street, I cast my eyes on a beautiful girl. It was in the autumn, when the heat dried up all moisture from the mouth, and the sultry wind made the marrow boil in the bones; so that, being unable to support the sun's powerful beams, I was obliged to take shelter under the shade of a wall in hopes that some one would relieve me from the distressing heat of summer, and quench my thirst with a draught of water. Suddenly from the shade of the portico of a house I beheld a female form, whose beauty it is impossible for the tongue of eloquence to describe; insomuch that it seemed as if the dawn was rising in the obscurity of night, or as if the water of immortality was issuing from the land of darkness. She held in her hand a cup of snow-water, into which she sprinkled sugar, and mixed it with the juice of the grape. I know not whether what I perceived was the fragrance of rose-water, or that she had infused into it a few drops from the blossom of her cheek. In short, I received the cup from her beauteous hand, and drinking the contents, found myself restored to new life. The thirst of my heart is not such that it can be allayed with a drop of pure water; the streams of whole rivers would not satisfy it. How happy is that fortunate person whose eyes every morning may behold such a countenance. He who is intoxicated with wine will be sober again in the course of the night; but he who is intoxicated by the cup-bearer will not recover his senses until the day of judgment."

Cicero maintained the doctrine of universal brotherhood as distinctly as it was afterward maintained by the Christian Church. "Men were born," he says, "for the sake of men, that each should assist the others. . . . . Nature ordains that a man should wish the good of every man, whoever he may be, for this very reason, that he is a man. . . . . Nature has inclined us to love men, and this is the foundation of the law." Marcus Aurelius crystallized the "idea" of free government in one remarkable passage: " The idea of a polity in which there is the same law for all, a polity administered with regard to equal rights and equal freedom of speech, and the idea of a kingly government which respects most of all the freedom of the governed." And here is the idea of forgiveness of injuries, by Epictetus : " Every man has two handles, one of which will bear taking hold of, the other not. If thy brother sin against thee, lay not hold of the matter by this, that he sins against thee: for by this handle the matter will not bear taking hold of. But rather lay hold of it by this, that he is thy brother, thy born mate ; and thou wilt take hold of it by what will bear handling." Here too is the idea of the Golden Rule, by Confucius, five hundred years before our era: " To have enough empire over one's self, in order to judge of others by comparison with ourselves, and to act towards them as we would wish that one should act towards us — that is what we can call the doctrine of humanity. There is

13

nothing beyond it." And this is the prayer claimed
to have been in use by religious Jews for nearly four
thousand years, found by our Lord, improved by
Him, and adopted for the use of Christians in all
time: " Our Father who art in Heaven, be gracious
unto us! O Lord our God, hallowed be thy name,
and let the remembrance of Thee be glorified in
heaven above and in the earth here below! Let thy
kingdom rule over us now and forever! Remit and
forgive unto all men whatever they have done against
me! And lead us not into the power (hands) of temptation, but deliver us from the evil. For thine is the
kingdom, and Thou shalt reign in glory forever and
ever more." Now hear the saying of King Solomon
— wiser than Confucius, or Cicero, or Marcus Aurelius, or Epictetus, or any rabbi: " The thing that
hath been is that which shall be, and there is no new
thing under the sun."

VII

INCONGRUITY.

" How contradictory it seems," remarked Washington Irving, writing of Oliver Goldsmith, " that one
of the most delightful pictures of home and homefelt
happiness should be drawn by a homeless man ; that
the most amiable picture of domestic virtue and
all the endearments of the married state should be
drawn by a bachelor, who had been severed from
domestic life almost from boyhood ; that one of the
most tender, touching, and affecting appeals on behalf of female loveliness should have been made by
a man whose deficiencies in all the graces of person
and manner seemed to mark him out for a cynical
disparager of the sex." Byron thought it contradictory that the ancients, in their mythology, should
have represented Wisdom by a woman, and Love by
a boy. " Don't you know," urged Sydney Smith,
" as the French say, there are three sexes — men,
women, and clergymen ? " In the old church at
Hatfield, in England, amongst the antiquities, there
is a recumbent statue, which every one believed was
a woman, till Flaxman, the sculptor, examined it, and
satisfied himself that it was a priest ! A lady, speaking of the works of the poet Thomson, observed that
she could gather from his writings three parts of his

character: that he was an ardent lover, a great swimmer, and rigorously abstinent. Savage, to whom the remark was addressed, assured her that, in regard to the first, she was altogether mistaken; for the second, his friend was perhaps never in cold water in his life; and as to the third, he indulged in every luxury that came within his reach. It was, we are told, the joke of the season, fifty years ago, when Lord Lansdowne and Sydney Smith, with a companion or two, went incognito to Deville, the phrenologist in the Strand, to have their characters read from their skulls, and were most perversely interpreted. Lord Lansdowne was pronounced to be so absorbed in generalization as to fail in all practical matters, and Sydney Smith to be a great naturalist — " never so happy as when arranging his birds and fishes." " Sir," said the divine, with a stare of comical stupidity, " I don't know a fish from a bird ; " and the chancellor of the exchequer was conscious that " all the fiddle-faddle of the cabinet " was committed to him on account of his love of what he called practical business. Crabb Robinson, on one of his visits to the British Gallery, where a collection of English portraits was exhibited, was displeased to see the name of the hated Jeffreys put to a " dignified and sweet countenance, that might have conferred new grace on some delightful character." Consistently enough with the delineation of the portrait, Evelyn recorded in his Memoirs that he " saw the Chief Justice Jeffreys in a large company the night before, and that he thought he laughed, drank, and danced too much for a man who had that day condemned Algernon Sidney to the block." Lavater, in his Physiognomy, says that Lord Anson, from his countenance, must have been a very wise man. Horace Walpole, who knew Lord Anson well, said he was the most stupid man he ever knew. Until a few years ago, it is stated, a portrait at Holland House was prescriptively'reverenced as a speaking likeness of Addison, and a bust was designed after it by a distinguished sculptor. It turns out to · be the copy of a portrait of a quite different person from the " great Mr. Addison." Men's judgments of themselves and their own achievements 'are often just as mistaken. " Many a famous name has been indebted for its brightest lustre to things which were flung off as a pastime, or composed as an irksome duty, whilst the performances on which the author most relied or prided himself have fallen stillborn or been neglected by posterity. Thus Petrarch, who trusted to his Latin poems for immortality, mainly owes it to the Sonnets, which he regarded as ephemeral displays of feeling or fancy of the hour. Thus Chesterfield, the orator, the statesman, the Mæcenas and Petronius of his age, and (above all) the first viceroy who ventured on ' justice to Ireland,' is floated down to our times by his familiar Letters to his Son. Thus Johnson, the Colossus of Literature, were he to look up or *down* (to adopt the more polite hypothesis), would hardly believe his eyes or ears, on finding that Bozzy, the snubbed and suppressed, yet ever elastic and rebounding Bozzy, is the prop, the bulwark, the key-stone of his fame ; ' the salt which keeps it sweet, the vitality which preserves it from putrefaction.' " We have it upon authority

that " when a French printer complained that he was
utterly undone by printing a solid, serious book of
Rabelais concerning physic, Rabelais, to make him
recompense, made that his jesting, scurrilous work,
which repaired the printer's loss with advantage."
Cervantes, who was fifty-eight when he published
the first part of Don Quixote, had, like Fielding,
' " written a considerable number of indifferent dramas
which gave no indication of the immortal work which
afterward astonished and delighted the world. He
was the author of several tales, for which even his
subsequent fame can procure very few readers, and
which would certainly have been forgotten if the
lustre of his masterpiece had not shed its light upon
everything which belonged to him. It was not till
he was verging upon three-score that he hit upon the
happy plan which was to exhibit his genius, and
which nothing previously sufficed to display. Fielding was equally ignorant of his province. Writing
for a subsistence, trying everything by turns, having
the strongest interest in discovering how he could lay
out his powers to the best advantage, he mistook his
road, and only found it by chance. If Pamela had
never existed, it is more than possible that English
literature might have wanted Joseph Andrews, Tom
Jones, and Amelia." The manuscript of Robinson
Crusoe ran through the whole trade, nor would any
one print it, though the writer, De Foe, was in good
repute as an author. The bookseller who risked the
publication was a speculator, not remarkable for discernment. The Vicar of Wakefield lay unpublished
for two years after the publisher, Newberry, was im-

portuned by Dr. Johnson to pay sixty pounds for it
to save the author from distress. Paradise Lost made
a narrow escape. Sterne found it hard to find a publisher for Tristram Shandy. The sermon in it, he
says in the preface to his Sermons, was printed by
itself some years before, but could find neither pur-
chasers nor readers. When it was inserted in his
eccentric work, with the advantage of Trim's fine
reading, it met with a most favorable reception, and
occasioned the others to be collected. One is tempted
to speculate upon the books that never *were* published. As some of the best books have been written
in prison or captivity, so some of like quality may
have perished with their unfortunate authors. If so
many great authors, like Dryden, and Cervantes, and
Le Sage, and Spenser, almost starved, barely pro-
curing a pittance for their published works, how
many good works may not, in despair, have been
destroyed by their authors. If so many great works
were accidentally discovered in manuscript, how many
as great may have perished in that form. " The
Romans wrote their books either on parchment or on
paper made of the Egyptian papyrus. The latter,
being the cheapest, was, of course, the most commonly used. But after the communication between
Europe and Egypt was broken off, on account of the
latter having been seized upon by the Saracens, the
papyrus was no longer in use in Italy or in other
European countries. They were obliged, on that account, to write all their books upon parchment, and
as its price was high, books became extremely rare,
and of great value. We may judge of the scarcity of

materials for writing them from one circumstance.
There still remain several manuscripts of the eighth,
ninth, and following centuries, written on parchment,
from which some former writing had been erased, in
order to substitute a new composition in its place.
In this manner, it is probable, several books of the
ancients perished. A book of Livy, or of Tacitus,
might be erased, to make room for the legendary tale
of a saint, or the superstitious prayers of a missal."
Truly, a resurrection of the unpublished, to say the
least, would expose an interesting mass of intellectual
novelties. The book-tasters, wise as they think themselves, are very far from being unerring in their esti-
mates of brain values, and better things than they
have approved may have gone into the basket. The
weather or bad chirography may have damned many
a production of genius. The rejection of an article
for a quarterly may have snuffed out the most promising talents. Who knows but some charitable reformer may have discovered a way to fuse sects and
harmonize Christians, but was prevented from showing it to the world by the stupidity of printers? The
most wonderful and sublime things in nature and art
are rarely appreciated at first view. Every visitor is
disappointed at the first sight of Niagara. Mountains
are not appreciated till we have dwelt long among
them. Goethe was at first disturbed and confused
by the impression which Switzerland produced on
him. Only after repeated visits, he said, only in
later years, when he visited those mountains as a
mineralogist merely, could he converse with them
at his ease. The sea is but a dead, monotonous waste,

till we come to feel its immensity and power. London is but a great town till we have wandered in it, lost ourselves in it, studied it, in fine, till we have found it too great to be comprehended, when its marvelous proportions are expanded into a nation, and it is accepted as one of the great powers of the world. Sir Joshua Reynolds says he was informed by the keeper of the Vatican that many of those whom he had conducted through the various apartments of that edifice, when about to be dismissed, had asked for the works of Raphael, and would not believe that they had already passed through the rooms where they are preserved. " I remember very well," he says, " my own disappointment when I first visited the Vatican. All the indigested notions of painting which I had brought with me from England were to be totally done away with and eradicated from my mind. It was necessary, as it is expressed on a very solemn occasion, that I should become as a little child. Nor does painting in this respect differ from other arts. A just and poetical taste, and the acquisition of a nice, discriminative musical ear, are equally the work of time. Even the eye, however perfect in itself, is often unable to distinguish between the brilliancy of two diamonds, though the experienced jeweler will be amazed at its blindness." " The musician by profession," said Goethe, " hears, in an orchestral performance, every instrument, and every single tone, whilst one unacquainted with the art is wrapped up in the massive effect of the whole. A man merely bent upon enjoyment sees in a green or flowery meadow only a pleasant plain, whilst the eye of a botanist discovers an endless detail of the most varied plants and grasses." Gainsborough says that an artist knows an original from a copy, by observing the touch of the pencil; for there will be the same individuality in the strokes of the brush as in the strokes of a pen. "Those who can at once distinguish between different sorts of handwriting are yet often astonished at the possession of the faculty when it is exercised upon pictures. No engraver, in like manner, can counterfeit the style of another. His brethren of the craft would not only immediately detect the forgery, but would recognize the distinctive strokes of the forger." Hogarth and Reynolds, we are told, could not do each other justice. Hogarth ranked Reynolds very low as a painter. It does seem, as has been often said, that an exact estimate of genius is never arrived at till the possessor is gone from the world. Johnson said "Tristram Shandy did not last;" and Goldsmith noticed the faults of Sterne only. They may each have looked with some feeling of envy to the far greater immediate success than either of themselves had enjoyed; but it does not follow that Hogarth, Johnson, and Goldsmith were so dishonest as to deny the existence of the excellences they saw. Unfortunately, persons engaged in the same departments of literature or art generally dislike one another. It is one of the drawbacks of genius. Voltaire and Rousseau hated each other; Fielding despised Richardson; Petrarch, Dante; Michel Angelo sneered at Raphael; but fortunately their reputations did not depend upon one another. Envy and hatred aside, it was impossible for them to judge one another justly; they were too near. A painter once confessed to Dr. Johnson that no professor of the art ever loved a person who pursued the same craft. " The whole class of underlings who fed at the table of Smollett, and existed by his patronage, traduced his character and abused his works, and, as they were no less treacherous to one another than to their benefactor, each was eager to betray the rest to him." At the beginning of the last century, says Southey, " books which are now justly regarded as among the treasures of English literature, which are the delight of the old and the young, the learned and the unlearned, the high and the low, were then spoken of with contempt; the Pilgrim's Progress as fit only for the ignorant and the vulgar, Robinson Crusoe for children; if any one but an angler condescended to look into Izaak Walton, it must be for the sake of finding something to laugh at. It will never be forgotten, in the history of English poetry, that with a generous and a just though impatient sense of indignation, Collins, as soon as his means enabled him, repaid the publisher of his poems the price which he had received for their copyright, indemnified him for the loss in the adventure, and committed the remainder, which was by far the greater part of the impression, to the flames. But it should also be remembered that in the course of one generation these poems, without any adventitious aids to bring them into notice, were acknowledged to be the best of their kind in the language." Tom Taylor's anecdote of Bott, the barrister, illustrates the uncertainty of literary fame. Bott occupied the rooms opposite to Goldsmith's in Brick Court; he lent the needy author money, drove him in his gig to the Shoemakers' Paradise, eight miles down the Edgeware Road, and occasionally periled both their necks in a ditch. Reynolds painted this good-natured barrister, who runs a better chance of reaching posterity in that gig of his alongside of Goldsmith, than by virtue of the Treatise on the Poor Laws which Goldsmith is said to have written up for him. And as if the uncertainty of fame were not great enough, authors sometimes increase it by most extraordinary means. You remember Southey's attempt to hoax Theodore Hook regarding the authorship of The Doctor. At Mr. Hook's death a packet of letters was found addressed to him, as the author of The Doctor, and acknowledging presentation copies — one from Southey among the rest. They had been forwarded from the publisher, and were intended, it is presumed, if they were intended for anything, as a trap for Hook's vanity. Sydney Smith positively denied all connection with the Plymley Letters in one edition, and published them in a collection of his acknowledged works some months after. Sir Walter Scott, being taxed at a dinner-table as the author of Old Mortality, not only denied being the author, but said to Murray, the publisher, who was present, " In order to convince you that I am not the author, I will review the book for you in the Quarterly," — which he actually did, and Murray retained the manuscript after Sir Walter's death. The novelty of a real work of genius is sufficient to decry it with the incredulous public. All new things, much out of the ordinary

way, must make a struggle for existence. It is but
the way of the world. The Jesuits of Peru introduced into Protestant England the Peruvian bark;
but being a remedy used by Jesuits, the Protestant
English at once rejected the drug as the invention of
the devil. Paracelsus introduced antimony as a valuable medicine; he was prosecuted for the innovation,
and the French Parliament passed an act making it a
penal offense to prescribe it. Lady Mary Wortley
Montagu first introduced into England the practice
of inoculation for the small-pox, by which malady
she had lost an only brother and her own fine eye-
lashes. She applied the process, after earnest exam-
ination, to her only son, five years old; and on her
return to England the experiment was tried, at her
suggestion, on five persons under sentence of death.
The success of the trial did not prevent the most
violent clamors against the innovation. " The faculty
predicted unknown disastrous consequences, the clergy
regarded it as an interference with Divine Providence, and the common people were taught to look
upon her as an unnatural mother, who had imperiled
the safety of her own child. Although she soon gained
influential supporters, the obloquy which she endured
was such as to make her sometimes repent her philanthropy." Jenner, who introduced the still greater discovery of vaccination, was treated with ridicule and
contempt, and was persecuted, prosecuted, and oppressed by the Royal College of Physicians. After
nearly twenty years of patient and sagacious study
and experiment, " he went to London to communicate the process to the profession, and to endeavor to

procure its general adoption.   His reception was dis-
heartening in the extreme.   Not only did the doctors
refuse to make trial of the process, but the discoverer
was accused of an attempt to ' bestialize ' his species
by introducing into the system diseased matter from
a cow's udder; vaccination was denounced from the
pulpit as ' diabolical,' and the most monstrous statements respecting its effects upon the human system
were disseminated and believed."   " On the invention
of scissors," says Voltaire, " what was not said of
those who pared their nails and cut off some of their
hair that was hanging down over their noses?   They
were undoubtedly considered as prodigals and cox-
combs, who bought at an extravagant price an instrument just calculated to spoil the work of the Creator.
What an enormous sin to pare the horn which God
himself made to grow at our fingers' ends !   It was
absolutely an insult to the Divine Being himself.
When shirts and socks were invented, it was far
worse.   It is well known with what warmth and
indignation the old counselors, who had never worn
socks, exclaimed against the youthful magistrates who
encouraged so dreadful and fatal a luxury."   When
threshing - machines were first introduced into England, there was such an opposition to them, and arson
became so common in consequence, that such farmers
as had them were obliged to surrender them, or expose them broken on the high-road.   The fashion of
wearing boots with pointed toes was supposed to have
been peculiarly offensive to the Almighty, and was
believed by many to have been the cause of the black
death, which carried off, it is estimated, in six years,

twenty-five millions, or a fourth part of the population of Europe. Amongst the curiosities of literature
is "a narrative extracted from Luther's writings, of
the dialogue related by Luther himself to have been
carried on between him and the devil, who, Luther
declares, was the first who pointed out to him the
absurdity and evil of private mass. Of course it is
strongly pressed upon the pious reader that even
Luther himself confesses that the Father of Lies was
the author of the Reformation; and a pretty good
story is made out for the Catholics." John Galt,
in his Life of Wolsey, says, "Those pious Presby-
terians, who inveigh against cards as the devil's
books, are little aware that they were an instrument
in the great work of the Reformation. The vulgar
game about that time was the devil and the priest;
and the skill of the players consisted in preserving
the priest from the devil; but the devil in the end
always got hold of him." Mighty means indeed trifles
have sometimes proved. The foolish ballad of Lilli
Burlero, treating the Papists, and chiefly the Irish, in
a very ridiculous manner, slight and insignificant as
it now seems, had once a more powerful effect than
the Philippics of either Demosthenes or Cicero; it
contributed not a little towards the great revolution
in 1688; the whole army and the people in country
and city caught it up, and "sang a deluded prince
out of three kingdoms." Percy has preserved the
ballad in his Reliques, but who remembers the air?
My Uncle Toby, it seems, was about the last to whistle
it. The most popular song ever written in the British
Islands, that of Auld Lang Syne, is anonymous, and

we know no more of the author of the music than we do of the author of the words. Much of Burns' great fame rests upon this song, in which his share amounts only to a few emendations. The Last Rose of Summer, by Bishop, is said to be made up in great part of an old Sicilian air, originating nobody knows when. Old Hundred, they say, was constructed out of fragments as old as music itself — strains that are as immortal as the instinct of music. Home, Sweet Home was written " in a garret in the Palais Royal, Paris, when poor Payne was so utterly destitute and friendless that he knew not where the next day's dinner was to come from. It appeared originally in a diminutive opera called Clari, the Maid of Milan. The opera is seldom seen or heard of now, but the song grows nearer and dearer as the years roll away, for ' it is not of an age, but for all time.' More than once the unfortunate author, walking the lonely streets of London or Paris amid the storm and darkness, hungry, houseless, and penniless, saw the cheerful light gleaming through the windows of happy homes, and heard the music of his own song drifting out upon the gloomy night to mock the wanderer's heart with visions of comfort and of joy, whose blessed reality was forever denied to him. Home, Sweet Home was written by a homeless man." Lamartine, in his History of the Girondists, has given an account of the origin of the French national air, the Marseillaise. In the garrison of Strasburg was quartered a young artillery officer, named Rouget de Lisle. He had a great taste for music and poetry, and often entertained his comrades during their long and tedious hours in the garrison. Sought after for his musical and poetical talent, he was a frequent and familiar guest at the house of one Dietrich, an Alsacian patriot, mayor of Strasburg. The winter of 1792 was a period. of great scarcity at Strasburg. The house of Dietrich was poor, his table was frugal, but a seat was always open for Rouget de Lisle. One day there was nothing but bread and some slices of smoked ham on the table. Dietrich, regarding the young officer, said to him with sad serenity, "Abundance fails at our boards; but what matters that, if enthusiasm fails not at our civic fêtes, nor courage in the hearts of our soldiers. I have still a last bottle of wine in my cellar. Bring it," said he to one of his daughters, "and let us drink France and Liberty! Strasburg should have its patriotic solemnity. De Lisle must draw from these last drops one of those hymns which raise the soul of the people." The wine was brought and drank, after which the officer departed. The night was cold. De Lisle was thoughtful. His heart was moved, his head heated. He returned, staggering, to his solitary room, and slowly sought inspiration, sometimes in the fervor of his citizen soul, and anon on the keys of his instrument, composing now the air before the words, and then the words before the air. He sang all and wrote nothing, and at last, exhausted, fell asleep, with his head resting on his instrument, and woke not till day-break. The music of the night returned to his mind like the impression of a dream. He wrote it, and ran to Dietrich, whom he found in the garden, engaged with his winter lettuces. The wife

14

and daughters of the old man were not up. Dietrich
awoke them, and called in some friends, all as passionate as himself for music, and able to execute the
composition of De Lisle.   At the first stanza, cheeks
grew pale ; at the second, tears flowed ; and at last,
the delirium of enthusiasm burst forth.   The wife of
Dietrich, his daughters, himself, and the young officer
threw themselves, crying, into each other's arms.
The hymn of the country was found.   Executed some
days afterward in Strasburg, the new song flew from
city to city, and was played by all the popular or-
chestras.   Marseilles adopted it to be sung at the
commencement of the sittings of the clubs, and the
Marseillaise spread it through France, singing it
along the public roads.   From this came the name of
Marseillaise.   It was the song for excited men under
the fiery impulse of liberty.   Those melodies for little
children, just as immortal, owe their existence to circumstances just as accidental.   We mean the melodies
of Mother Goose.   The story of this Iliad of the nursery is told by William L. Stone in the old Providence Journal.   The mother-in-law of Thomas Fleet,
the editor, in 1731, of the Boston Weekly Rehearsal,
was the original Mother Goose — the Mother Goose
of the world-famous melodies.   Mother Goose belonged to a wealthy family in Boston, where her
eldest daughter, Elizabeth Goose, was married by
Cotton Mather, in 1715, to Fleet, and in due time
gave birth to a son.   Like most mothers-in-law in
our own day, the importance of Mrs. Goose increased
with the appearance of her grandchild, and poor Mr.
Fleet, half distracted with her endless nursery ditties,

finding all other means fail, tried what ridicule could effect, and actually printed a book, with the title " Songs for the Nursery, or Mother Goose's Melodies for Children, printed by T. Fleet, at his printing house, Pudding Lane, Boston. Price, ten coppers." Mother Goose was the mother of nineteen children, and hence we may easily trace the origin of that famous classic, " There was an old woman who lived in a shoe; she had so many children she did n't know what to do." Now, as to the plays of the stage, we all know how some of them have gradually, in the long years, grown to be there, from additions by actors and managers, so wholly different from what they are in literature, that in important parts they would hardly be recognized as the same. Sheridan's Critic, with the numerous " gags " by Jack Bannister, King, Miss Pope, Richard Jones, Liston, Mrs. Gibbs, Charles Mathews, and other great actors, is a famous instance of the kind. By the way, speaking of plays, Mathews says it is possible for a man, absurd as it may seem, to obtain favor with the public by merely attending to the mechanical portion of the profession, without any exertion of his intellect beyond committing his words to memory, and speaking to his " cues " at the right moment and with the proper emphasis. He gives a remarkable illustration of this strange possibility. When Douglas Jerrold's play of the Bubbles of the Day was produced at Covent Garden Theatre, there was a long-experienced actor, standing exceedingly well with the public, and an undoubted favorite, who played one of the parts so admirably that he met with unqualified success with the audience, and was a prominent feature in the piece, highly praised by the press, and complimented by the author himself, as having perfectly embodied his conception. After the play had run for some ten or fifteen nights, he one day came to Mathews and asked him as a favor that he would let him have the manuscript of the piece for a short time. Certainly, said Mathews; but what do you want it for? Why, said he, I was unfortunately absent from the reading; and I have n't the slightest idea what it is about, or who and what I am in it. He had literally, according to Mathews, played his part admirably for many nights to the gratification of the public, the press, and the author; and he had never even had the curiosity to inquire in what way he was mixed up with the plot. He had seized the instructions given him by Jerrold during the rehearsals, and adopted his suggestions so correctly that he was able to fulfill all the requirements of the character assigned to him without the least idea of what he was doing, or of the person whom he represented. Why, it does seem that in some things ignorance is the foundation of knowledge. Take the wise doctor's remedies. They are adopted for the number that recover who use them, not for the numbers that die, who used them also. " The sun gives light to their success, and the earth covers their failures." " If your physician," says Montaigne, " does not think it good for you to sleep, to drink wine, or to eat such and such meats, never trouble yourself; I will find you another that shall not be of his opinion." Heine, during the eight years he lay bed-ridden with a kind of paralysis, read all the medical books which treated of his complaint. " But," said he to some one who found him thus engaged, " what good this reading is to do me I don't know, except that it will qualify me to give lectures in heaven on the ignorance of doctors on earth about diseases of the spinal marrow." What is often accepted as high moral truth is only a small part of what the philosopher has thought — the result less of faith than of skepticism ; the two being in about the proportion of Falstaff's bread to his sack. To get away from the ideal to the physical, what can at first blush be so absurd as the climatic changes believed by some to be produced by railroads ? The desert of Western America has been transformed into a fertile plain : the railroad, they say, has brought rain. No element, we are told, was wanting in the earth itself, nor was aught in excess to enforce sterility, but everywhere there was drought. In the hot dust nothing grew but stunted hardy grass and sage brush. All seemed desolation and utter hopelessness. Wherever irrigation was tried, its success exceeded expectation in developing an almost miraculous productiveness in the soil. No enthusiast dared, however, to dream of the possibility of artificial irrigation over all that enormous expanse. Rivers entering there would soon have been drunk up by the thirsty earth and sky. Yet man's work, it would seem, has irrigated that whole desert by an unexpected means. The railroad brought rain. Year by year, since the Union Pacific Railroad has been operated through, the rain-fall had steadily increased until the summer of 1873, when it became, to the operators of the road, a positive

nuisance. Now, somehow, treating thus of the production of water, we are led to speak of one of its
products — *icicles*. They are formed, science tells
us, by the process of freezing in sunshine hot enough
to melt snow, blister the human skin, and even,
when concentrated, to burn up the human body
itself. They result from the fact that air is all but
completely transparent to the heat rays emitted by
the sun — that is, such rays pass through the air
without warming it. Only the scanty fraction of
rays to which air is not transparent expend their
force in raising its temperature. In the Alps, Tyn-
dall tells us, when the liquefaction is copious and the
cold intense, icicles grow to an enormous size. Over
the edges (mostly the southern edges) of the chasms
hangs a coping of snow, and from this depend, like
stalactites, rows of transparent icicles, ten, twenty,
thirty feet long, constituting one of the most beautiful features of the higher crevasses. An icicle would
be incomprehensible if we did not know that the solar
beams may pass through the air, and still leave it at
an icy temperature. Speaking of icicles, one of the
contradictions of *ice* is that, formed at a temperature
of twenty-five to thirty degrees Fahrenheit, it is as
different from that which is formed when the temperature has ranged for some time between ten degrees and one degree, as chalk is from granite. The
ice at the lower temperature is dense and hard as
flint. It strikes fire at the prick of a skate. In
St. Petersburg, in 1740, when masses of it were
turned and bored for cannon, though but four inches
thick, they were loaded with iron cannon-balls and a

charge of a quarter of a pound of powder, and fired
without explosion. But ice is a cold subject to
handle. The warm-blooded, fur-covered cat is just
as absurdly contradictory — in one peculiarity at
least. Gilbert White says, "There is a propensity
belonging to common house-cats that is very remarkable; that is, their violent fondness for fish, which
appears to be their most favorite food: and yet
nature in this instance seems to have planted in them
an appetite that, unassisted, they know not how to
gratify; for of all quadrupeds cats are the least disposed towards water; and will not, when they can
avoid it, deign to wet a foot, much less to plunge into
that element." And there is the tortoise. The same
ingenious naturalist we have quoted had a pet one, of
whose habits he made many curious notes. He says
no part of its behavior ever struck him more than the
"extreme timidity it always expressed with regard
to rain; for though it had a shell that would secure
it against the wheel of a loaded cart, yet did it discover as much solicitude about rain as a lady dressed
in all her best attire, shuffling away on the first
sprinklings, and running its head up in a corner."
But man, at last, is the creature fullest of contradictions, and his vanity is at the bottom of most of them.
"What a sensible and agreeable companion is that
gentleman who has just left us," said the famous
Charles Townshend to the worthy and sensible Fitzherbert; "I never passed an evening with a more
entertaining acquaintance in my life." "What could
entertain you? the gentleman never opened his lips."
"I grant you, my dear Fitz, but he listened faithfully

to what I said, and always laughed in the right
place." Darwin, speaking of one of his walks in
New Zealand, says, " I should have enjoyed it more,
if my companion, the chief, had not possessed extraordinary conversational powers. I knew only three
words — ' good,' ' bad,' and ' yes ; ' and with these I
answered all his remarks, without, of course, having
understood one word he said. This, however, was
quite sufficient; I was a good listener, an agreeable
person, and he never ceased talking to me." John
Chester was a delightful companion to Coleridge, on
the same principle. This Chester, says Hazlitt, was
one of those who was attracted to. Coleridge's discourse as flies are to honey, or bees in swarming-time
to the sound of a brass pan. He gave Hazlitt his
private opinion, though he rarely opened his lips,
that Coleridge was a wonderful man! " He followed Coleridge into Germany, where the Kantian
philosophers were puzzled how to bring him under
any of their categories. When he sat down at
table with his idol, John's felicity was complete ;
Sir Walter Scott's, or Blackwood's, when they sat
down at the table with the king, was not more so.
Once he was astonished," continues Hazlitt, " that
I should be able to suggest anything to Coleridge
that he did not already know." " Demosthenes Taylor, as he was called (that is, the editor of Demosthenes), was the most silent man," said Dr. Johnson
to Boswell, " the merest statue of a man, that I have
ever seen. I once dined in company with him, and
all he said during the whole time was not more than
Richard. How a man should say only Richard, it is

not easy to imagine. But it was thus: Dr. Douglass was talking of Dr. Zachary Grey, and was ascribing to him something that was written by Dr. Richard Grey. So, to correct him, Taylor said (imitating his affected sententious emphasis and nod) ' Richard.' " "Demosthenes" must have been "a sensible and agreeable companion." That one word was to the point, and was more effective than a dozen would have been to a man like Johnson. Two words, however, if we are to believe the story chronicled by John of Brompton of the mother of Thomas à Becket, performed a still more memorable service. "His father, Gilbert à Becket, was taken prisoner during one of the Crusades by a Syrian emir, and held for a considerable period in a kind of honorable captivity. A daughter of the emir saw him at her father's table, heard him converse, fell in love with him, and offered to arrange the means by which both might escape to Europe. The project only partly succeeded; he escaped, but she was left behind. Soon afterward, however, she contrived to elude her attendants, and after many marvelous adventures by sea and land arrived in England, knowing but two English words, ' London' and ' Gilbert.' By constantly repeating the first, she was directed to the city; and there, followed by a mob, she walked for months from street to street, crying as she went, ' Gilbert! Gilbert!' She at last came to the street in which her lover lived. The mob and the name attracted the attention of a servant in the house; Gilbert recognized her; and they were married!" But there remains one to be spoken of who gained immortal reputation for his sayings, who may be said to have never said anything at all of his own. Joe Miller, whose name as a wit is now current wherever the English language is spoken, was, when living, himself a jest for dullness. According to report, Miller, who was " an excellent comic actor, but taciturn and saturnine, was in the habit of spending his afternoons at the Black Jack, a well-known public-house in London, which at that time was frequented by the most respectable tradesmen in the neighborhood, who from Joe's imperturbable gravity, whenever any risible saying was recounted, ironically ascribed it to him. After his death, having left his family unprovided for, advantage was taken of this badinage. A Mr. Motley, a well-known dramatist of that day, was employed to collect all the stray jests then current on the town. Joe Miller's name was affixed to them, and from that day to this the man who never uttered a jest has been the reputed author of every jest."

VIII.

MUTATIONS.

SWIFT left some thoughts on various subjects —
acute and profound — which it would appear were
jotted down at different periods of life, and in different humors. In his most prosperous days, when he
dreamed of becoming a bishop, he might have written hopefully, "No wise man ever wished to be
younger." At a much later time in life he might
have written, sagely and sadly, " Every man desireth
to live long, but no man would be old." We can
imagine he wrote the former just after he received the
deanery of St. Patrick, and the latter just after he
returned from the walk recorded by the author of
Night Thoughts. He was walking with some friends
in the neighborhood of Dublin. " Perceiving he did
not follow us," says Young, " I went back, and found
him fixed as a statue, and earnestly gazing upward
at a noble elm, which in its uppermost branches was
much decayed. Pointing at it, he said, 'I shall be
like that tree ; I shall die at the top.'"

Bolingbroke, writing to Swift, says, " It is now
six in the morning; I recall the time — and am glad
it is over — when about this hour I used to be going
to bed surfeited with pleasure, or jaded with business ;
my head often full of schemes, and my heart as often

full of anxiety. Is it a misfortune, think you, that I rise at this hour refreshed, serene, and calm; that the past and even the present affairs of life stand like objects at a distance from me, where I can keep off the disagreeable, so as not to be strongly affected by them, and from whence I can draw the others nearer to me ? "

De Foe moralizes in this remarkable manner: " I know too much of the world to expect good in it, and have learned to value it too little to be concerned at the evil. I have gone through a life of wonders, and am the subject of a vast variety of providences. I have been fed more by miracles than Elijah when the ravens were his purveyors. I have some time ago summed up the scenes of my life in this distich : —

> ' No man has tasted differing fortunes more ;
>   And thirteen times I have been rich and poor.'

In the school of affliction I have learnt more philosophy than at the academy, and more divinity than from the pulpit. In prison I have learnt that liberty does not consist in open doors and the egress and regress of locomotion. I have seen the rough side of the world as well as the smooth ; and have in less than half a year tasted the difference between the closet of a king and the dungeon of Newgate. I have suffered deeply for cleaving to principles, of which integrity I have lived to say, none but those I suffered for ever reproached me with."

We are told by Middleton that " before Cicero left Sicily, at the end of his term as quæstor, he made the tour of the island, to see everything in it that was curious, and especially the city of Syracuse, which had always made the principal figure in its history. Here his first request to the magistrates, who were showing him the curiosities of the place, was to let him see the tomb of Archimedes, whose name had done so much honor to it; but to his surprise, he perceived that they knew nothing at all of the matter, and even denied that there was any such tomb remaining; yet as he was assured of it beyond all doubt, by the concurrent testimony of writers, and remembered the verses inscribed, and that there was a sphere with a cylinder engraved on some part of it, he would not be dissuaded from the pains of searching it out. When they had carried him, therefore, to the gate where the greatest number of their old sepulchres stood, he observed, in a spot overgrown with shrubs and briers, a small column, whose head just appeared above the bushes, 'with the figure of a sphere and a cylinder upon it; this, he presently told the company, was the thing they were looking for; and sending in some men to clear the ground of the brambles and rubbish, he found the inscription also which he expected, though the latter part of all the verses was effaced. Thus,' says he, ' one of the noblest cities of Greece, and once likewise the most learned, had known nothing of the monument of its most deserving and ingenious citizen, if it had not been discovered to them by a native of Arpinum.' "

Anaxagoras knew the short memory of the people, and chose a happy way to lengthen it, and at the same time to perpetuate himself. When the chief persons of the city paid him a visit, and asked him

whether he had any commands for them, he answered
that he only desired that children might be permitted
to play every year during the month in which he died.
His request was respected, and the custom continued
for ages.

" Ruins," in the impressive language of Alger,
" symbolize the wishes and fate of man; the weakness of his works, the fleetingness of his existence.
Who can visit Thebes, in whose crowded crypts, as
he enters, a flight of bats chokes him with the dust
of disintegrating priests and kings; see the sheep
nibbling herbage between the fallen cromlechs of
Stonehenge; or confront a dilapidated stronghold of
the Middle Age, where the fox looks out of the window and the thistle nods on the wall, without thinking of these things? They feelingly persuade him
what he is. . . . . Tyre was situated of old at the
entry of the sea, the beautiful mistress of the earth,
haughty in her purple garments, the tiara of commerce on her brow. Now the dust has been scraped
from her till she has become a blistered rock, whereon
the solitary fisher spreads his nets. A few tattered
huts stand among shapeless masses of masonry where
glorious Carthage stood; the homes of a few hus-
bandmen where voluptuous Corinth once lifted her
splendid array of marble palaces and golden towers.
Many a nation, proud and populous in the elder days
of history, like Elephanta, or Memphis, is now merely
a tomb and a shadowy name. Pompeii and Hercu-
laneum are empty sepulchres, which that fatal flight
before the storm of ashes and lava cheated of their
occupants; the traveler sees poppies blooming in the

streets where chariots once flashed. . . . . Tigers foray in the palace yards of Persepolis, and camels browse in Babylon on the site of Belshazzar's throne; at Baalbec, lizards overrun the altars of the Temple of the Sun, and in the sculptured friezes, here the nests of obscene birds, there the webs of spiders."

St. Austin, with his mother Monica, was led one day by a Roman prætor to see the tomb of Cæsar. Himself thus describes the corpse: "It looked of a blue mould, the bone of the nose laid bare, the flesh of the nether lip quite fallen off, his mouth full of worms, and in his eye-pit a hungry toad, feasting upon the remnant portion of flesh and moisture: and so he dwelt in his house of darkness."

A traveler in Ceylon, who visited the ruins of ancient Mahagam, says that one of the ruined buildings had apparently rested upon seventy-two pillars. These were still erect, standing in six lines of twelve columns. This building must have formed an oblong of three hundred feet by two hundred and fifty. The stone causeway which passed through the ruins was about two miles in length, being for the most part overgrown with low jungle and prickly cactus. The first we hear of this city is 286 B. C.; but we have no account of the era or cause of its destruction. The records of Ceylon give no satisfactory account of it. The wild elephants come out of the jungles and rub their backs against the columns of this forgotten temple, as the naked Indians gamble with forked sticks on the desolate ruins of Central America.

But a few years sometimes change the whole face of a country. Sir Woodbine Parish informed Dar-

win that during the three years' drought in Buenos
Ayres, beginning in 1827, the ground being so long
dry, such quantities of dust were blown about that in
the open country the landmarks became obliterated,
and people could not tell the limits of their estates.

But what shall we say of the instability of human
greatness ?   The career and end of Pompey furnish
a striking example.   " He who a few days before
commanded kings and consuls, and all the noblest of
Rome, was sentenced to die by a council of slaves ;
murdered by a base deserter; cast out naked and
headless on the Egyptian strand ; and when the whole
earth, as Velleius says, had scarce been sufficient for
his victories, could not find a spot upon it at last for
a grave.   His body was burnt on the shore by one of
his freedmen, with the planks of an old fishing-boat ;
and his ashes, being conveyed to Rome, were deposited
privately by his wife Cornelia in a vault of his Alban
Villa."

" Aristotle, that prince of all true thinkers, loaded
with immortal glory, was compelled to flee suddenly
and by stealth to Chalcis, in order to save his life, and
spare, as he said, the Athenians a new crime against
philosophy.   There, it is believed, the great man, in
his old age, wearied with persecutions, poisoned himself."

" The venerable Hildebrand, the greatest of all the
popes, after the herculean labors of his self-devoted
and mighty career, crushed by an accumulation of
hardships, said, ' I have loved justice and hated iniquity ; therefore I die in exile.' "

"The ceremony of Galileo's abjuration," says Sir

David Brewster in his biography of that great man, " was one of exciting interest and of awful formality. Clothed in the sackcloth of a repentant criminal, the venerable sage fell upon his knees before the assembled cardinals ; and, laying his hands upon the Holy Evangelists, he invoked the divine aid in abjuring and detesting, and vowing never again to teach, the doctrine of the earth's motion and of the sun's stability. He pledged himself that he would never again, either in words or in writing, propagate such heresies ; and he swore that he would fulfill and observe the penances which had been inflicted upon him. At the conclusion of this ceremony, in which he recited his abjuration word for word, and then signed it, he was conveyed, in conformity with his sentence, to the prison of the Inquisition." All because it had been said that the " sun runneth about from one end of heaven to the other," and that " the foundations of the earth are so firmly fixed that they cannot be moved."

Think of this in connection with the fact that " in five years Charles II. touched twenty-three thousand six hundred and one of his subjects for the evil ; that the bishops invented a sort of heathen service for the occasion ; that the unchristianlike, superstitious ceremony was performed in public ; and that, as soon as prayers were ended, the Duke of Buckingham brought a towel, and the Earl of Pembroke a basin and ewer, who, after they had made obeisance to his majesty, kneeled down till his majesty had washed." Dr. Wiseman, an eminent surgeon of that period, in writing on scrofula, says, " However, I must needs pro-

15

fess that his majesty (Charles II.) cureth more in any one year than all the chirurgeons of London have done in an age."

And think at the same time of the trial of a mother and her daughter, eleven years old, before "the great and good Sir Matthew Hale," then Lord Chief Baron, for witchcraft; their conviction and execution at Bury St. Edmunds, principally on the evidence of Sir Thomas Browne, one of the first physicians and scholars of his day.

In Fuller's Church History may be found this curious fact, illustrating the power of superstition over even such a man as Wolsey. The great cardinal " in his life-time was informed by some fortune-tellers that he should have his end at Kingston. This his credulity interpreted of Kingston-on-Thames; which made him always to avoid the riding through that town, though the nearest way from his house to the court. Afterwards, understanding that he was to be committed by the king's express orders to the charge of Sir Anthony Kingston, it struck to his heart; too late perceiving himself deceived by that father of lies in his homonymous prediction."

But credulity seems to have had a foundation place in the characters of some of the world's greatest men. There, for instance, is Hooker, author of that great work, Ecclesiastical Polity, — according to Hallam " the finest as well as the most philosophical writer of the Elizabethan period; " according to Lecky " the most majestic of English writers." Being appointed to preach a sermon at St. Paul's Cross, London, he lodged at the Shunamite's house, a dwelling appropriated to preachers, and was skillfully persuaded by the landlady "that it was best for him to have a wife that might prove a nurse to him, such an one as might prolong his life, and make it more comfortable, and such an one as she could and would provide for him if he thought fit to marry." The unsuspecting young divine agreed to abide by her choice, which fell upon her own daughter, who proved to be not only " a silly, clownish woman," but a Xantippe. Old Izaak Walton, in his biography of Hooker, thus philosophizes upon that remarkable marriage: " This choice of Mr. H. (if it were his choice) may be wondered at; but let us consider that the prophet Ezekiel says, ' There is a wheel within a wheel;' a secret, sacred wheel of Providence (not visible in marriages), guided by his hand, that ' allows not the race to the swift,' nor ' bread to the wise,' nor good wives to good men; and He that can bring good out of evil (for mortals are blind to this reason) only knows why this blessing was denied to patient Job, to meek Moses, and to our as meek and patient Mr. Hooker." Further on, by way of analysis and apology, old Izaak quaintly says, " God and nature blessed him with so blessed a bashfulness, that as in his younger days his pupils might easily look him out of countenance; so neither then, nor in his age, did he ever willingly look any man in the face: and was of so mild and humble a nature, that his poor parish clerk and he did never talk but with both their hats on or both off at the same time : and to this may be added, that though he was not purblind, yet he was short or weak sighted; and where he fixed his eyes at the beginning of his sermon, there they continued till it was ended : and the reader has a liberty to believe, that his modesty and dim sight were some of the reasons why he trusted Mrs. Churchman to choose his wife." His anger is said to have been like a vial of clear water, which, when shook, beads at the top, but instantly subsides, without any soil or sediment of uncharitableness.

Nobody knows, to say truth, how much the great, modest Hooker was benefited by what appeared to his friends his calamitous marriage. " There is no great evil," said Publius Syrus, " which does not bring with it some advantage." Calamities, we know, have often proved blessings. There are cases where blows on the head have benefited the brain, and produced extraordinary changes for the better. Mabillon was almost an idiot at the age of twenty-six. He fell down a stone staircase, fractured his skull, and was trepanned. From that moment he became a genius. Dr. Prichard mentioned a case of three brothers, who were all nearly idiots. One of them was injured on the head, and from that time he brightened up, and became a successful barrister. Wallenstein, too, they say, was a mere fool, till he fell out of a window, and awoke with enlarged capabilities. Here is an instance noted by Robinson in his Diary : " After dinner called on the Flaxmans. Mrs. Flaxman — wife of the sculptor — admitted me to her room. She had about a fortnight before broken her leg, and sprained it besides, by falling downstairs. This misfortune, however, instead of occasioning a repetition of the paralytic stroke which she had a year ago, seemed to have improved her health. She had actually recovered the use of her hand in some degree, and her friends expect that she will be benefited by the accident."

There is Cowper. But for his mental malady the world would have had much less of good poetry and fewer perfect letters. The thought of a clerkship in the House of Lords made him insane! " Innocent, pious, and confiding, he lived in perpetual dread of everlasting punishment: he could only see between him and heaven a high wall which he despaired of ever being able to scale; yet his intellectual vigor was not subdued by affliction. What he wrote for amusement or relief in the midst of 'supreme distress,' surpasses the elaborate efforts of others made under the most favorable circumstances; and in the very winter of his days, his fancy was as fresh and blooming as in the spring and morning of his existence." The Diverting History of John Gilpin, the production of a single night, was, to repeat, written by a man who lived in perpetual dread of eternal punishment; and while it was being read by Henderson, the actor, to large audiences in London, its author was raving mad. Southey, in his fine biography of the poet, says that Henderson read to crowded audiences in London, all through Lent, John Gilpin, at high prices. " The ballad, which had become the town talk, was reprinted from the newspaper, wherein it had lain three years dormant. Gilpin, passing at full stretch by the Bell at Edmonton, was to be seen at all print-shops. One print-seller sold six thousand. What had succeeded so well in London was repeated with inferior ability, but with equal success, on provincial stages, and the ballad became in the highest degree popular before the author's name became known." The last reading to which Cowper listened appears to have been that of his own works. Beginning with the first volume, Mr. Johnson went through them, and he listened to them in silence till he came to John Gilpin, which he begged not to hear. It reminded him of cheerful days, and of those of whom he could not bear to think. "The grinners at John Gilpin," he said, "little dream what the author sometimes suffers. How I hated myself yesterday for having ever wrote it!" On his deathbed, when the clergyman told him to confide in the love of the Redeemer, who desired to save all men, Cowper gave a passionate cry, begging him not to give him such consolations. To our ignorant eyes it looks strange that the author of our best and most popular hymns should have thought his sins unpardonable; should have believed himself already damned.

One of Cowper's visitors and pensioners at Olney was a poor school-master (Teedon) who thought himself specially favored by Providence, and to whom Cowper communicated his waking dreams, and consulted, as a person whom the Lord was pleased to answer in prayer. This recalls a similar superstitious belief of the illustrious Tycho Brahe. When he lived in Uraniberg he maintained an idiot of the name of Lep, who lay at his feet whenever he sat down to dinner, and whom he fed with his own hand. Persuaded that his mind, when moved, was capable of foretelling future events, Tycho carefully marked everything he said.

It is pathetic to think, says Alger, how many great men have, like Homer and Milton, had the windows of their souls closed. Galileo, in his seventy-third year, wrote to one of his correspondents, "Alas! your dear friend has become irreparably blind. These heavens, this earth, this universe, which by wonderful observation I had enlarged a thousand times past the belief of past ages, are henceforth shrunk into the narrow space which I myself occupy. So it pleases God; it shall, therefore, please me also." Händel passed the last seven years of his life in total blindness, in the gloom of the porch of death. How he and the spectators must have felt when the great composer, in 1753, stood pale and tremulous, with his sightless eyeballs turned towards a tearful concourse of people, while his sad song from Samson, "Total eclipse, no sun, no moon," was delivered!

Beethoven was afflicted with "dense and incurable deafness" long before he had composed his greatest works. He said, "I was nigh taking my life with my own hands. But art held me back. I could not leave the world until I had revealed what lay within me." He occupied for a long time a room in a remote house on a hill, and was called the Solitary of the Mountain, where he heard, no doubt, more distinctly "the voices," than if he had been blest with the best of ears. "When he produced his mighty opera, Fidelio, it failed. In vain he again modeled and remodeled it. He went himself into the orchestra and attempted to lead it; and the pitiless public of Vienna laughed." His works so far surpassed the appreciation of many of his contemporaries as to be condemned as the va-

garies of a madman. Haydn and Mozart, as was
said, had perfected instrumental music in form; it
remained for deaf Beethoven to touch it, so that it
became a living soul.

It does seem that God in his mystery has sometimes put out the eyes of poets and stopped the ears
of musicians to admit them to glimpses of his own
glories, and whisper to them his own harmonies.
Homer and Milton had inward poetic visions which
light and sight alone never gave to man. Beethoven,
unable from defective hearing to conduct an orchestra,
produced celestial harmonies out of the silence of divine meditation.

The philanthropy of John Howard was so prodigious that it rendered him incapable of ordinary enjoyments. His faculties were so absorbed by his great
humanity that he was voted a bore by the liveliest
and cleverest of his contemporaries. "But the mere
men of taste," says John Foster, " ought to be silent
respecting such a man as Howard; he is above their
sphere of judgment. The invisible spirits, who fulfill
their commissions of philanthropy among mortals, do
not care about pictures, statues, and public buildings;
and no more did he, when the time in which he must
have inspected and admired them would have been
taken from the work to which he had consecrated his
life. The curiosity which he might feel was reduced
to wait till the hour should arrive when its gratification should be presented by conscience, which kept a
scrupulous charge of all his time, as the most sacred
duty of that hour. If he was still at every hour, when
it came, fated to feel the attractions of the fine arts

but the second claim, they might be sure of their revenge ; for no other man will ever visit Rome under
such a despotic consciousness of duty as to refuse
himself time for surveying the magnifience of its ruins.
Such a sin against taste is far beyond the reach of
common saintship to commit. It implied an inconceivable severity of conviction, that he had *one thing
to do*, and that he who would do some great thing in
this short life must apply himself to the work with
such a concentration of his forces as to idle spectators,
who live only to amuse themselves, looks like insanity." Look a little over his wonderful life, by the
aid of a few facts set down by the encyclopedist :
At about the age of twenty-five he experienced a
severe attack of illness, and upon his recovery testi-
fied his gratitude to the woman who had nursed him,
and who was nearly thirty years his senior, by marrying her. Moved by the accounts of the horrors of
the earthquake at Lisbon, he embarked for that place
with a view of doing something to alleviate the calamity. On the voyage he was taken prisoner by a
French privateer and carried into Brest, where he
became a witness of the inhuman treatment to which
prisoners of war were subjected. Designing to visit
the new lazaretto of Marseilles, he endeavored in vain
to procure a passport from the French government,
which was incensed against him for having published
a translation of a suppressed French account of the
interior of the Bastile. He therefore traveled
through the country in various disguises, and after
a series of romantic adventures and several narrow
escapes from the police, who were constantly on his

track, succeeded in his purpose. He proceeded thence
to Malta, Zante, Smyrna, and Constantinople, visiting
prisons, pest-houses, and hospitals, and in the two
latter cities gratuitously dispensing his medical services, often with great benefit to the poor. The freedom with which he exposed his person in infected
places, whither his attendants refused to follow him,
was characteristic of his fearless and self-sacrificing
character ; but as if by a miracle he escaped all contagion. His most daring act, however, has yet to be
recorded. Feeling that he could not speak with authority on the subject of pest-houses until he had
experienced the discipline of one, he went to Smyrna,
sought out a foul ship, and sailed in her for Venice.
After a voyage of sixty days, during which by his
energy and bravery he assisted the crew in beating off
an attack of pirates, he arrived at his destination, and
was subjected to a rigorous confinement in the Vene-
tian lazaretto, under which his health suffered severely. In the preface to one of his numerous works,
he announced his intention to pursue his work, observing, "Should it please God to cut off my life in
the prosecution of this design, let not my conduct be
imputed to rashness or enthusiasm, but to a serious
conviction that I am pursuing the path of duty." He
died of camp-fever, which he contracted from a patient at Kherson, Russia, on the Black Sea, having
expended nearly the whole of his large fortune in
various benefactions. In a speech to the electors of
Bristol, Edmund Burke thus eloquently sums up the
public services of Howard : " He has visited all
Europe, not to survey the sumptuousness of palaces,

or the stateliness of temples; not to make accurate measurement of the remains of ancient grandeur, nor to form a scale of the curiosity of modern art; not to collect medals or collect manuscripts; but to dive into the depths of dungeons; to plunge into the infections of hospitals; to survey the mansions of sorrow and pain; to take the gauge and dimensions of misery, depression, and contempt; to remember the forgotten, to attend to the neglected, to visit the forsaken, and to compare and collate the distresses of all men in all countries."

In persons of genius, defects often appear to take the place of merits, and weaknesses to act the part of auxiliaries. The "plastic nature of the versatile faculty" is such that common laws do not govern it, nor common standards judge it. " Men of genius," says an acute historian and critic of literature and literary men, " have often resisted the indulgence of one talent to exercise another with equal power; some, who have solely composed sermons, could have touched on the foibles of society with the spirit of Horace or Juvenal; Blackstone and Sir William Jones directed that genius to the austere studies of law and philology which might have excelled in the poetical and historical character. So versatile is this faculty of genius, that its possessors are sometimes uncertain of the manner in which they shall treat their subject, whether to be grave or ludicrous. When Brébeuf, the French translator of the Pharsalia of Lucan, had completed the first book as it now appears, he at the same time composed a burlesque version, and sent both to the great arbiter of taste in that day, to decide which the poet should continue. The decision proved to be difficult." For that and other reasons, men of genius and their productions are often enigmas to the world. " The hero," says Carlyle, " can be poet, prophet, king, priest, or what you will, according to the kind of world he finds himself born into. I confess I have no notion of a truly great man that could not be *all* sorts of men. The poet who could merely sit on a chair, and compose stanzas, would never make a stanza worth much. He could not sing the heroic warrior, unless he himself were at least a heroic warrior too. I fancy there is in him the politician, the thinker, legislator, philosopher; in one or the other degree, he could have been, he is, all these. . . . . Shakespeare, — one knows not what *he* could not have made in the supreme degree."

" It is notorious," says Macaulay, " that Niccolo Machiavelli, out of whose surname they have coined an epithet for a knave, and out of his Christian name a synonym for the devil, was through life a zealous republican. In the same year in which he composed his manual of king-craft, he suffered imprisonment and torture in the cause of public liberty. It seems inconceivable that the martyr of freedom should have designedly acted as the apostle of tyranny." But the real object and meaning of his celebrated book, The Prince, have been subjects of dispute for centuries. One old critic says, " Machiavel is a strenuous defender of democracy ; he was born, educated, and respected under that form of government, and was a great enemy to tyranny. Hence it is that he does not favor a tyrant : it is not his design to instruct a tyrant, but to detect his secret attempts, and expose him naked and conspicuous to the poor people. Do we not know there have been many princes such as he describes? Why are such princes angry at being immortalized by his means? This excellent author's design was, under the show of instructing the prince, to inform the people." Another says, " I must say that Machiavel, who passed everywhere for a teacher of tyranny, detested it more than any man of his time ; as may easily appear by the tenth chapter of the first book of his Discourses, in which he expresses himself very strongly against tyrants." Nardi, his contemporary, calls his works " panegyrics upon liberty." Bayle says, " The Jesuit Porsevin, who had not read The Prince, was nevertheless the cause of its being condemned by the Inquisition. He charges Machiavel with such things as are not in The Prince. His charges were made upon passages from a work, published anonymously, entitled Anti-Machiavel, and not from The Prince. The Prince was published about the year 1515, and dedicated to Lorenzo de' Medici, nephew to Leo X. It did not prejudice the author with this pope, who nevertheless was the first who threatened those with excommunication that read a prohibited book ! "

Sir John Denham, according to Count Grammont, " was one of the brightest geniuses England ever produced for wit and humor, and for brilliancy of composition ; satirical and free in his poems, he spared neither frigid writers nor jealous husbands, nor even their wives ; every part abounded with the most poign-. ant wit, and the most entertaining stories ; but his most delicate and spirited raillery turned generally against matrimony ; and as if he wished to confirm, by his own example, the truth of what he had written in his youth," he married, at the age of seventy-nine, Miss Brook, aged eighteen, a favorite of King Charles II., and mistress of his brother, the Duke of York, afterwards King James II. "As no person entertained any doubt of his having poisoned her (on account of jealousy), the populace of his neighborhood had a design of tearing him in pieces as soon as he should come abroad ; but he shut himself up to bewail her death, until their fury was appeased by a magnificent funeral, at which he distributed four times more burnt wine than had ever been drank at any burial in England."

(You remember the plea Denham urged in behalf of old George Wither, the Puritan poet, when he was taken prisoner by the Cavaliers, and a general disposition was displayed to hang him at once. Sir John saved his life by saying to Charles, "I hope your majesty will not hang poor George Wither, for as long as he lives it can't be said that I am the worst poet in England.")

Literature is full of such facts as at first blush appear incredible. Consider, that " although the soil of Sweden is not rich in either plants or insects, and many of its feathered tribes are but temporary visitants, leaving it at stated periods in quest of milder climes, nevertheless it was amidst this physical barrenness that the taste of Linnæus for his favorite pursuit broke out almost from his earliest infancy, and found the means not only of its gratification, but of laying a basis of a system which soon spread its dominion over the whole world of science. Almost within the Arctic circle, this enthusiast of nature felt all those inspirations which are generally supposed to be the peculiar offspring of warmer regions. He traveled over the greater part of Lapland, skirting the boundaries of Norway, and returning to Upsala by the Gulf of Bothnia, having passed over an extent of about four thousand miles. Nothing but the enthusiasm of genius would have made him, night and day, wade the cold creeks and treacherous bogs, and climb the bleak mountains of Lapland — eating little but fish, unsalted, and crawling with vermin. He considered his labor amply remunerated by the information he had gained, and the discovery of new plants in the higher mountains, with the payment of his expenses, amounting to about ten pounds!"

Or reflect, that "on a bulk, in a cellar, or in a glass-house, among thieves and beggars, was to be found the author of the Wanderer, the man of exalted sentiments, extensive views, and curious observations; the man whose remarks on life might have assisted the statesman, whose ideas of virtue might have enlightened the moralist, whose eloquence might have influenced senates, and whose delicacy might have polished courts."

And see what Bishop Burnet, in his History of his Own Times, says of the vile Lord Rochester: " In the last year of his life I was much with him, and have writ a book of what passed between him and me : I do verily believe he was then so changed that if he had recovered he would have made good all his resolutions." Of this book, mentioned by the bishop, Dr. Johnson said, It is one " which the critic ought to read for its eloquence, the philosopher for its arguments, and the saint for its piety."

Soame Jenyns, a friend of Johnson and Goldsmith and Reynolds, is thus spoken of by Cumberland : " He came into your house at the very moment you had put upon your card ; he dressed himself to do your party honor in all the colors of the jay ; his lace indeed had long since lost its lustre, but his coat had faithfully retained its cut since the days when gentlemen wore embroidered figured velvet, with short sleeves, boot-cuffs, and buckram skirts ; as nature had cast him in the exact mould of an ill-made pair of stiff stays, he followed her so close in the fashion of his coat that it was doubted if he did not wear them : because he had a protuberant wen just under his poll, he wore a wig, that did not cover above half his head. His eyes were protruded like the eyes of the lobster, who wears them at the end of his feelers, and yet there was room between one of these and his nose for another wen that added nothing to his beauty ; yet I heard this good man very innocently remark, when Gibbon published his history, that he wondered anybody so ugly could write a book ! ' "

It has been remarked as an interesting fact, that " Wilberforce at the age of twenty-five, and Wendell Phillips at the same age, were the two persons who seemed the least likely of all their respective contemporaries to become world-renowned as advocates of the cause of antislavery. Wilberforce was returned to parliament at twenty-one, when, according to his biographer, 'he became the idol of the fashionable world, dancing at Almack's, and singing before the Prince of Wales.' At twenty-five, he abandoned his gayeties, entered upon a new life, and took up the great cause which he advocated during the remainder of his long career. Wendell Phillips at the age of twenty-two was a Boston lawyer, aristocratic, wealthy, handsome, polished, and sought after; colonel of a city militia company, and a lover of blooded horses, of fencing and boxing. He was born on Beacon Street, and his father was one of the most popular mayors Boston ever had. At Harvard University, where he graduated, he was president of the 'exclusive society' known as the Gentleman's Club, and in fact he was the leader of the aristocratic party among the students. At twenty-five he abandoned his practice of law, gave up the fashionable world, and espoused the cause of the slave."

Robespierre, anarchist and philanthropist, and Frederick of Prussia, despot and philosopher, were both bitter and vitriolic natures; yet both, in their youth, exceeded Exeter Hall itself in their professions of universal beneficence. Frederick indeed wrote early in life a treatise called the Anti-Machiavel, which was, says his biographer, "an edifying homily against rapacity, perfidy, arbitrary government, unjust war; in short, against almost everything for which its author is now remembered among men."

Hazlitt, in his essay on the Shyness of Scholars, makes some striking remarks upon the poet Gray. His "diffidence, or fastidiousness, was such as to prevent his associating with his fellow-collegians, or

16

mingling with the herd, till at length, like the owl, shutting himself up from society and daylight, he was hunted and hooted at like the owl whenever he chanced to appear, and was even assailed and disturbed in the haunts in which 'he held his solitary reign.' He was driven from college to college, and was subjected to a persecution the more harassing to a person of his indolent and retired habits. But he only shrunk the more within himself in consequence, read over his favorite authors, corresponded with his distant friends, was terrified out of his wits at the bare idea of having his portrait prefixed to his works, and probably died from nervous agitation at the publicity into which his name had been forced by his learning, taste, and genius." Such was the author of the immortal Elegy, which Daniel Webster died repeating, and of which Wolfe said he would rather be the author than be conqueror of Quebec.

Washington Irving's modesty and diffidence did not make him shut "himself up from society and daylight," but it made him a stranger to many of his neighbors, and even to the boys about Sunnyside. It will be a surprise to many to know that one morning he was ordered out of a field he was crossing — belonging to a neighbor of his, a liquor dealer, who threatened, if he found the "old vagabond" on his premises again, he would set his dogs on him! It will also be a surprise to know that the distinguished author of the Sketch Book was a confessed orchard thief. Once, when picking up an apple under a tree in his own orchard, he was accosted by an urchin of the neighborhood, who, not recognizing him as the proprietor, offered to show him a tree where he could "get better apples than those." "But," urged the boy, "we must take care that the old man don't see us." "I went with him," said Irving, "and we stole a dozen of my own apples!"

IX

PARADOXES.

Is there anything more curious or strange in fiction than the simple fact expressed by Thucydides, that ignorance is bold and knowledge reserved? or that by Thomas Fuller, that learning has gained most by those books by which the printers have lost? or that by Pascal, that it is wonderful a thing so obvious as the vanity of the world is so little known, and that it is a strange and surprising thing to say that seeking its honors is a folly? or that by John Selden, that of all actions of a man's life, his marriage does least concern other people, yet of all actions of his life 't is most meddled with by other people? or that by Goldsmith, that the most delicate friendships are always most sensible of the slightest invasion, and the strongest jealousy is ever attendant on the warmest regard? And what is more remarkable than that labor should be so scarce in China that vast tracts of land lie waste because there are no laborers to reclaim them? That in the pontifical army, not long before Victor Emanuel, Spain — "the bones of whose children for centuries had whitened every battle-field where she found it necessary to defend her religion" — should have been represented by but thirty-eight soldiers; while Holland, "which protected the Reformation by its Princes of Orange, and introduced liberty of religious opinion into the modern world," was represented by hundreds and hundreds of volunteers? That the best building in Iceland should be the jail at Reikiavik (the capital), and that during the many years since its erection it should never have contained a prisoner? That in the Arctic region a smaller proportion of fuel should be consumed than in any other habitable part of the globe? That in the next voyage of the Mayflower after carrying the pilgrims (as Monckton Milnes told Hawthorne), she should have been engaged in transporting a cargo of slaves to the West Indies? That the plant papyrus, which gave its name to our word paper, — first used for writing between three and four thousand years ago, of more importance in history than cotton and silver and gold, — once so common in Egypt, should have become so scarce there that Emerson in his late visit searched in vain for it? That house-building, which ought to be among the most perfect of the arts, after the experience and efforts of myriads in every generation, should have produced no stereotyped models of taste and convenience? That the founder and editor of one of the great London periodicals should never have written a line for his journal? or that when he died the review which he had built up by his individual ability should not have made the slightest mention of the event? That those three books which have been so widely read, and which have exercised incalculable influence upon morals and politics, — the Imitation of Christ, the Whole Duty of Man, and the Letters of

Junius, — should be of unknown or disputed authorship? That the Bible — the incomparably wisest
and best book, the Book of books, the guide of life,
the solace in death, the way to heaven — should be
so little read by the many and so little understood
by the few? How difficult it is to realize that Dr.
Johnson, the great Cham of English literature, spent
more than one half of his days in penury; that the
" moral, pious Johnson," and the " gay, dissipated
Beauclerc," were companions; or that they should
ever have spent a whole day together, " half-seas
over," wandering through the markets, cracking jokes
with the fruit and fish women, on their way to
Billingsgate. It is hard to believe that that great
moralist ever wandered whole nights through the
streets of London, with the unfortunate, gifted Savage,
too miserably poor to hire lodgings. And it is still
harder to believe that the best biography of that great
man, and the best biography in our language, was
written by a gossiping literary bore — the " bear-
leader to the Ursa Major," as Irving calls him —
whom Johnson pretended to despise, and of whom he
once said, " if he thought Boswell intended to write
his (Johnson's) life he would take Boswell's." We
wonder that the great, strong-minded Luther ever
flung an inkstand at the devil's head. We cannot
conceive that Wesley and Johnson and Addison believed in ghosts. It looks strange to us that Socrates,
who taught the doctrines of the one Supreme Being
and the immortality of the soul, should have bowed
down to a multiplicity of idols; and after he had
swallowed the fatal hemlock, should have directed

the sacrifice of a cock to Esculapius. We cannot
credit the fact that Marlborough, at the moment he
was the terror of France and the glory of Germany,
was held under the finger of his wife by the meanest
of passions, avarice. We utterly refuse to believe the
complaint of Burns, the greatest of lyric poets, that
he " could never get the art of commanding respect."
It seems impossible that Goldsmith should ever have
" talked like poor Poll," when he " wrote like an
angel." It appears strange enough that Sir George
Makenzie should have written an elegant and eloquent treatise in favor of solitude, while living a most
active life; and still more strange that his arguments should have been triumphantly answered by
Evelyn, who passed his days in tranquillity and solitude. We believe only when we are compelled by
authority, that Tycho Brahe, the illustrious astrono-
mer, changed color, and his legs shook under him, on
meeting with a hare or a fox. That Dr. Johnson
would never enter a room with his left foot foremost. That Cæsar Augustus was almost convulsed
by the sound of thunder, and always wanted to get
into a cellar, or under-ground, to escape the dreadful
noise. That Talleyrand trembled when the word
death was pronounced. That Marshal Saxe ever
screamed in terror at the sight of a cat. That Peter
the Great could never be persuaded to cross a bridge;
and though he tried to master the terror, he failed to
do so. That Byron would never help any one to salt
at the table, nor be helped himself. That an air
that was beneficial to Schiller should have acted upon
Goethe like poison. (" I called on him one day,"

said Goethe to Soret, " and as I did not find him at home, and his wife told me that he would soon return, I seated myself at his work-table to note down various matters. I had not been seated long before I felt a strange indisposition steal over me, which gradually increased, until at last I nearly fainted. At first I did not know to what cause I should ascribe this wretched and, to me, unusual state, until I discovered that a dreadful odor issued from a drawer near me. When I opened it, I found to my astonishment that it was full of rotten apples. I immediately went to the window and inhaled the fresh air, by which I felt myself instantly restored. In the mean time his wife had reëntered, and told me that the drawer was always filled with rotten apples, because the scent was beneficial to Schiller, and he could not live or work without it.") That Queen Elizabeth should have issued proclamations against excessive apparel, leaving, as she did, three thousand changes of dress in the royal wardrobe. That Bayle, the faithful compiler of impurities, should have " resisted the corruption of the senses as much as Newton." That Smollett, who has so grossly offended decency in his novels, should have had so immaculate a private character. That Cowley, who boasts with so much gayety of the versatility of his passion amongst so many sweethearts, should have wanted the confidence even to address one. That Seneca should have philosophized so wisely and eloquently upon the blessings of poverty and moderate desires, while usuriously lending his seven millions, and writing his homilies on a table of solid gold. That Sir Thomas

More, who, in his Utopia, declares that no man should be punished for his religion, should have been a fierce persecutor, racking and burning men at the stake for heresy. That Young, the author of the sombre Night Thoughts, was known as the gayest of his circle of acquaintance. That Molière, the famous French humorist and writer of comedies, bore himself with habitual seriousness and melancholy. That he should have married an actress, who made him experience all those bitter disgusts and embarrassments which he himself played off at the theatre. That the cynicism and bitterness exhibited in the writings of Rousseau were in consequence of an unfortunate marriage to an ill-bred, illiterate woman, who ruled him as with a rod of iron. That Addison's fine taste in morals and in life could suffer the ambition of a courtier to prevail with himself to seek a countess, who drove him, we are told, contemptuously into solitude, and shortened his days. That the impulsive and genial Steele should have married a cold, precise Miss Prue, as he called her, from whom he never parted without bickerings. That Shenstone, while surrounding himself with the floral beauties of Paradise, exciting the envy and admiration and imitation of persons of taste throughout England, should have lived in utter wretchedness and misery. That Swift, with all his resources of wit and wisdom, should have died, to use his own language, "in a rage, like a poisoned rat in a hole." That the thoughtful, cast-iron essays of John Foster should have been originally written as love epistles to the lady who afterward became his wife. That the only person who could

make grave George Washington laugh was an officer
in the army so obscure in rank and character as not
to be even mentioned in popular history. That the
man whom Daniel Webster pronounced the best con-
versationist he ever knew should be utterly unknown
or forgotten outside of his neighborhood. That the
pious Cowper should have attempted suicide; or that
he should have had as an intimate associate the
swearing Lord Chancellor Thurlow — with whom, he
confesses, he spent three years, " giggling and making
giggle." That Lord Chancellor Eldon, who, while
simple John Scott, son of a Newcastle coal-fitter, ran
away with Bessy Surtees, daughter of a prosperous
banker of the same town, and who was so proud of
the exploit that he never tired of referring to it,
when his eldest daughter, Lady Elizabeth, gave her
hand, without his consent, to an ardent lover of respectable character and good education, but not of
much wealth, should have permitted years to roll
away before he would forgive her. That not long
after the elopement referred to, while a law student
at Oxford, having been appointed to read to the class,
at a small salary, the lectures of one of the professors
who was then absent in the East Indies, it should
have happened that the first lecture he had to read
was upon the statute (4 & 5 P. M. c. 8) " Of young
men running away with maidens." (" Fancy me," he
said, " reading, with a hundred and forty boys and
young men all giggling.") That Lord Chancellor
Thurlow, who was never married at all, should have
been so outraged at the love marriage, against his consent, of his third and favorite daughter, that, though

he became reconciled to her, he never would consent to see her husband. That, according to John Lord Campbell, so many of the most important points in the law of real property should have been settled in suits upon the construction of the wills of eminent judges. That "the religious, the moral, the immaculate" Sir Matthew Hale, when chief justice of the king's bench, should have allowed the infamous Jeffreys, who "was not redeemed from his vices by one single solid virtue," to gain, in the opinion of Roger North, "as great an ascendant over him as ever counsel had over a judge." That the gentle Charles Lamb and Mary Lamb should have been confined in a mad-house, and the latter have cut the throat of her mother at the dinner-table. That Tasso should have lamented the publication of Jerusalem Delivered, and that its publication should have been the one great cause of his insanity. That Thomson, the poet of the Seasons, should have composed so much classic and vigorous verse in bed ; or that he should have been seen in Lord Burlington's garden, with his hands in his waistcoat pockets, biting off the sunny sides of the peaches. That King Solomon, who wrote so wisely of training children, should have had so wicked a son as Rehoboam. That the good stoic, Marcus Aurelius, of proverbial purity, should have had so doubtful a wife as Faustiana, and so vicious a son as Commodus. That that good old Roman emperor, whose Meditations rank with the best works of the greatest moralists, breathing and inculcating the spirit of Christianity, should have been the bitter persecutor of the Christians in Gaul. That his graceless heir,

Commodus, should have left the Christians wholly
untroubled, through the influence of his mistress,
Marcia. That the English-reading world should be
directly indebted to the Reign of Terror — the horrors of Robespierre's tyranny — for the most popular
translation of St. Pierre's sweet story of Paul and
Virginia. That the author of the Marseillaise
should have first heard of the great fame of his piece
in the mountains of Piedmont, when fleeing from
France as a political refugee. That that ode to temperance, The Old Oaken Bucket, should have been
written by Woodworth, a journeyman printer, under
the inspiration of brandy. That we should owe all
that remains of Tacitus to a single copy discovered in
a monastery of Westphalia. That so many of the exquisite letters of Lady Mary Wortley Montagu should
have been destroyed by her mother, who " did not approve that she should disgrace her family by adding
to it literary honors." That the famous speech of
Pitt, in reply to Walpole's taunt of being " a young
man," should be the composition of Dr. Johnson. That
Johnson, looking at Dilly's edition of Lord Chesterfield's miscellaneous works, should have laughed and
said, " Here are now two speeches ascribed to him,
both of which were written by me : and the best of
it is, they have found out that one is like Demosthenes, and the other like Cicero." That many of
the sermons of famous contemporaneous clergymen
were the productions' of the same laborious Grub
Street drudge, forty or more of which have been re-
claimed and published, now conceded to have been
written by the inexhaustible Johnson. That the

only paper of the Rambler which had a prosperous sale, and may be said to have been popular, was one which Johnson did not write — No. 97, written by Richardson. That the Ramblers of Dr. Johnson, elaborate as they appear, should have been " written rapidly, seldom undergoing revision, whilst the simple language of Rousseau, which seems to come flowing from the heart, was the slow production of painful toil, pausing on every word, and balancing every sentence." That Burke's Reflections on the Revolution in France, which has the free and easy flow of extemporaneous eloquence, should have been polished with extraordinary care, — more than a dozen proofs being worked off and destroyed, according to Dodsley's account, before he could please himself. That the winged passages in Curran's speeches, which seem born of the moment, should have been the results of painstaking, protracted labor. (" My dear fellow," said he to Phillips, " the day of inspiration has gone by. Everything I ever said which was worth remembering, my *de bene esses*, my white horses, as I call them, were all carefully prepared.") That the Essay on Man, according to Lord Bathurst, " was originally composed by Lord Bolingbroke, in prose, and Pope did no more than to put it into verse." That those brilliant wits and prolific dramatists, Peele, Greene, and Marlowe, the associates of Shakespeare, to whom the great dramatist was so much indebted, should all have been wretched and unsuccessful, — the first dying in utter want, the second of excessive pickled herring, at the point nearly of starvation, the third being stabbed in the head in a

drunken brawl at a tavern by his own dagger in his
own hand. That Shakespeare should have married
at eighteen, had three children at twenty, removed
to London at twenty-three, begun writing plays at
twenty-seven, and, a little more than twenty years
after, returned to his native town, rich and immortal.
That but a few signatures — differently spelled —
should be all of his handwriting that has been preserved. That so many critics should believe, and
some ingenious books have been printed to prove,
that the authorship of the plays of Shakespeare
belongs to Bacon — the only man then living, they
claim, who knew enough to write them. That the
great Bacon should have been unable to grasp the
great discoveries of his time — rejecting the Coper-
nican system to the last, and treating not only with
incredulity, but with the most arrogant contempt,
the important discoveries of Gilbert about the mag-
net. That Apuleius, author of the Metamorphosis of
the Golden Ass (a paraphrase, according to Bayle,
of what he had taken from Lucian, as Lucian had
taken it from Lucius, one of the episodes of which —
Psyche — furnished Molière with matter for one of
his dramas, and La Fontaine materials for a romance), who did not, to use his own language,
"make the least scruple of expending his whole
fortune in acquiring what he believed to be more
valuable, a contempt of it," should have afterward
married a woman more than twice his own age, thirteen years a widow, to procure for himself, as he
acknowledged, "a large settlement, and an easy condition of life." That Pythagoras, the first of the

ancient sages who took the name of philosopher; who made himself so illustrious by his learning and virtue; who proved so useful in reforming and instructing the world; whose eloquence moved the inhabitants of a great city, plunged in debauchery, to avoid luxury and good cheer, and to live according to the rules of virtue; who prevailed upon the ladies to part with their fine clothes, and all their ornaments, and to make a sacrifice of them to the chief deity of the place; who engaged his disciples to practice the most difficult things, making them undergo a noviciate of silence for at least two years, and extending it to five years for those whom he knew to be more inclined to speak, — should have peremptorily ordered his disciples to abstain from eating beans, choosing himself rather, as some authorities have it, to be killed by those that pursued him, than to make his escape through a field of beans, so great was his respect or abhorrence of that plant. That Luther, the greatest of the reformers, and Baxter, the greatest of the Puritans, and Wesley, the greatest religious leader of the last century, should have believed in witchcraft. That Dr. Johnson should have thought Swift's reputation greater than he deserved, questioning his humor, and denying him the authorship of the Tale of a Tub, at the same time taking to his confidence, and reverencing for his piety, George Psalmanazar, who deceived the world for some time by pretending to be a native of the island of Formosa, to support which he invented an alphabet and a grammar. ("I should," said Johnson, "as soon think of contradicting a bishop.") That Coleridge should have been able, according to Freiligrath, to depict Mont Blanc and the Vale of Chamouni at sunrise in such an overpowering manner, though he had never seen the Alps; while half-Oriental Malta and classical Italy, both of which he had seen, gave him no fruits of poetry. That Schiller should have written his William Tell without ever seeing any of the glories of Lake Lucerne. That Vathek, that splendid Oriental tale, should have been written by a young man of twenty-two who had never visited the countries whose manners he so vividly described; and that " of all the glories and prodigalities of the English Sardanapalus, his slender romance, the work of three days, is the only durable memorial." That Beckford's father, while Lord Mayor of London, should have become especially famous for a speech that was never delivered — the speech in reply to the king, written after the event by Horne Tooke, and engraved on the pedestal of a statue of Beckford erected in Guildhall. That Michel Angelo, unexpectedly, should have laid the first stone of the Reformation. (History tells us that Julius II. gave him an unlimited commission to make a mausoleum, in which their mutual interests should be combined. The artist's plan was a parallelogram, and the superstructure was to consist of forty statues, many of which were to be colossal, and interspersed with ornamental figures and bronze basso-rilievos, besides the necessary architecture, with appropriate decorations to unite the composition into one stupendous whole. To make a fitting place for it, the pope determined to rebuild St. Peter's itself; and this is the origin of that edifice, which took a hundred and fifty years to complete, and is now the grandest display of architectural splendor that ornaments the Christian world. " To prosecute the undertaking, money was wanted, and indulgences were sold to supply the deficiency of the treasury; and a monk of Saxony, opposing the authority of the church, produced this singular event, that whilst the most splendid edifice which the world had ever seen was building for the Catholic faith, the religion to which it was consecrated was shaken to its foundation.") That Bruce, the traveler, after all his perils by flood and by field, from wars, from wild beasts, from deserts, from savage natives, should have broken his neck down his own staircase at home, owing to a slip of the foot, while seeing some visitors out whom he had been entertaining. That Diogenes, who was so fond of expressing his contempt for money, should, in his younger days, have been driven out of the kingdom of Pontus for counterfeiting the coin. That the mighty Dr. Johnson should at times have been so languid as not to be able to distinguish the hour upon the clock; or that the ready and voluminous De Quincey, during the four years he was " under the Circean spells of opium," seldom could prevail on himself, he said, to write even a letter; an answer of a few words to any that he received was the utmost that he could accomplish; and that, often, not until the letter had lain weeks, or even months, on his writing-desk. That out of the name of Epicurus should have been coined a synonym for indulgence and sensuality, when that virtuous philosopher " placed his felicity

17

not in the pleasures of the body, but the mind, and tranquillity thereof;" who "was contented with bread and water;" and when he would feast with Jove, "desired no other addition than a piece of Cytheridian cheese." That Phidias should have made his sitting statue of Jupiter so large "that if he had risen up he had borne up the top of the temple." That Canova, whenever the conversation turned upon sculpture, should have exhibited "a freshly-bedaubed tablet," "with a smile of paternal pride." That Goethe should have undervalued himself as a poet, claiming only superiority over his "century" in "the difficult science of colors." That Jerrold should have been ambitious to write a treatise on natural philosophy. That Paul Jones, the "hero of desperate sea-fights," should have been enamored of Thomson's Seasons. That Bonaparte, who "over-ran Europe with his armies," should have "recreated himself with the wild rhapsodies of Ossian." That John Wesley, who "set all in motion," should have been himself (as described by Robert Hall) "perfectly calm and phlegmatic"—"the quiescence of turbulence." That Persius, whose satires are most licentious, sharp, and full of bitterness, should be described as "very chaste, though a beautiful young man: sober, as meek as a lamb, and as modest as a young virgin." That Luis de Camoëns, the greatest of the Portuguese poets, author of The Lusiad, or Os Lusiadas, should for a long time have been supported by a devoted Javanese servant, Antonio, who collected alms for him during the night, and nursed him during the day. That Paulo Borghese, pronounced almost as good a poet as Tasso, should have known fourteen different trades, yet have died because he could get employment in none. That Bentivoglio, " whose comedies will last with the Italian language," having dissipated a noble fortune in acts of charity and benevolence, and fallen into misery in his old age, should have been refused admittance into a hospital which he himself had erected. That Demosthenes should have thrown " down his arms when he came within sight of the enemy, and lost that credit in the camp which he gained in the pulpit." That " Socrates, by the oracle adjudged to be the wisest of mortals, when he appeared in the attempt of some public performance before the people," should have " faltered in the first onset ; " he " did not recover himself, but was hooted and hissed home again." That Plato, the famous philosopher, should have been " so dashed out of countenance by an illiterate rabble as to demur, and hawk, and hesitate, before he could get to the end of one short sentence." That Theophrastus should have been " such another coward, who beginning to make an oration was presently struck down with fear, as if he had seen some ghost or hobgoblin." That Isocrates should have been " so bashful and timorous, that though he taught rhetoric, yet he could never have the confidence to speak in public." That Cicero, that master of Roman eloquence, should have " begun his speeches with a low, quivering voice, just like a school-boy afraid of not saying his lesson perfect enough to escape whipping." That Pope, who had the courage in his Dunciad to attack a whole generation of scholars and wits, should have acknowledged his inability to face a half-dozen persons to make a statement or relate an incident of considerable length. That Plutarch, the great biographer, should be without a biography, — none of the eminent Roman writers who were his contemporaries even mention his name. That of Correggio, who delineated the features of others so well, there should not exist an authentic portrait. That of Romanianus, whom Augustine speaks of as the greatest genius that ever lived, there should be nothing known but his name. That though the epitaph of Gordianus was written in five languages, it proved insufficient to save him from oblivion. That Domitian, after he had possessed himself of the Roman Empire, should have turned his desires upon catching flies. That Robert Burns, the sweetest of all the Scottish song-writers, should in early life have been thought to be insensible to music. (Murdock, the teacher of Burns and his brother Gilbert, says that he "tried to teach them a little sacred music, but found this impracticable, there being no music in either of their souls. As for Robert, his ear was so completely dull that he could not distinguish one tune from another, and his voice was so untunable that he could not frame a note, and was left behind by all the boys and girls of the school.") That Sir Isaac Newton, according to Spence, though so deep in algebra and fluxions, could not readily make up a common account, and whilst he was master of the mint, used to get somebody to make up the account for him. That Socrates, according to Plato, should have given occasion of laughter, at the expense of his own reputation, to the Athenians, for having never been able to sum up the votes of his tribe to deliver it to the council. That Prime Minister Gladstone, upon being asked how he employed his mind when duty compelled him to sit on the bench of the ministers while a tory was delivering himself of a dull three hours' harangue, should have made answer, " Last evening, when Mr. —— was speaking, I turned Rock of Ages into the Greek, and had half an hour to spare." That the great and wise and pious Chalmers should so far have adopted and become impressed with the views of Malthus as to urge the expediency of a restraint upon marriage, and that the same be "inculcated upon the people as the very essence of morality and religion by every pastor and instructor throughout England." That The Admirable Crichton, master of a dozen languages, after disputing for six hours with eminent doctors of Padua on topics of science, delighting the assembly as much by his modesty as by his wonderful learning and judgment, should, at the conclusion, have given an extemporaneous oration in praise of ignorance with so much ingenuity that he reconciled his audience to their inferiority. That the Duke of Marlborough, who, while an ensign of guards, received from the Duchess of Cleveland, then favorite mistress of Charles II., five thousand pounds, with which he bought an annuity for his life of five hundred pounds,—the foundation of his subsequent fortune, — should afterward, when he was famous as well as rich, and the duchess was poor and necessitous, have " refused the common civility of lending

her twenty guineas." That although Sir Isaac Newton told Mr. Conduit that he "excelled particularly
in making verses," no authentic specimen of his
poetry has been preserved. That the first public
speech of John Randolph, three hours in length, and
which established his reputation as an orator, should
have been made in reply to the last ever delivered by
the venerable Patrick Henry, — the former in his
twenty-sixth year, a self-announced candidate for
Congress, and the latter in his sixty-third year, the
candidate of George Washington for a place in the
Virginia legislature. That but a few years after
John Brown's defeat and execution in Virginia,
Congress should have enacted a law and the president approved it, by which a portion of the Harper's
Ferry buildings, including the famous engine-house,
so nobly defended by the old hero, and to capture
which from his little garrison Robert E. Lee and the
United States marines had to be sent for, was presented by the government as a free gift to the Storer
College, an institution expressly designed for the
education of colored men. That Henry A. Wise,
who, as governor of Virginia, hung John Brown,
should a few years after have fled Richmond, the
capital of Virginia, at the head of a Confederate division of white troops, closely followed by a division of
loyal black troops, singing, " John Brown's body lies
mouldering in the grave, but his soul is marching
on." That a daughter of John Brown should have
taught a free school of emancipated slave children in
the deserted drawing-room of Henry A. Wise. That
about the same time, at Lumpkin's Jail, which was

the slave-market, there should have been established
a theological seminary for colored young men. That
at the same time, also, Richard Realf, one of John
Brown's trusted men, should have been appointed
assessor of internal revenue for the district of
Edgefield, South Carolina. That the first Confederate officer in South Carolina who officially met an
officer of colored troops under a flag of truce should
have been Captain John C. Calhoun. That one
of Jefferson Davis's old slaves should have become a
lessee of Jefferson Davis's old plantation. That
Foote, the celebrated actor, should have died with
the dropsy, never in his life, as he said, having drank
a drop of water. That the great Neander, sometimes called the "second John," — "the son of thunder and the son of love," — should have had his mind
first turned in the direction in which he afterward
found truth and peace, by a passage in Plutarch's
Pedagogue. That Plutarch, who wrote so volumi-
nously and excellently upon morals, great personages,
and great influences, should have made no mention
in any of his books of Christ or Christianity. ("If
we place his birth," says Archbishop Trench, "at
about the year A. D. 50, then long before he began
to write, St. Peter and St. Paul must have finished
their course. All around him — at Rome, where he
dwelt so long; in that Greece where the best part of
his life was spent; in Asia Minor, with which Greece
was in constant communication; in Macedonia — there
were flourishing churches. Christianity was everywhere in the air, so that men unconsciously inhaled
some of its influences, even where they did not sub-

mit themselves to its positive teaching. But for all this, no word, no allusion of Plutarch's testifies to his knowledge of the existence of these churches, or to the slightest acquaintance on his part with the Christian books." Suetonius, a contemporary of Plutarch, calls the Christians "a sort of people who held a new and impious superstition." Pliny, another contemporary, pronounces the Christian religion "a depraved, wicked, and outrageous superstition;" Tacitus, "a foreign and deadly superstition.") That John Stuart Mill, who found time and space in his autobiography to make careful lists of the incredible number of books he read between the ages of three and fourteen, to note the languages and sciences he acquired in the same time, as well as his associations and relations with his father, his brothers, and his sisters; who accepted his wife, during her life-time, as his divinity, and, after her death, confessed her memory to have been his religion, — should have omitted to say one word about his mother. That Jonathan Edwards, the great theologian and thinker, should never have had the degree of doctor of divinity or doctor of laws conferred on him, while they were showered on scores of his commonplace contemporaries. That Sir John Suckling and Richard Lovelace, so famous as courtiers and poet cavaliers, the pets of the king and the people, the much admired and adored by the female sex, should have died in wretchedness and despair, — the former taking poison, and the latter dying in rags in a miserable alley in London. That Milton, advanced in years, blind, and in misfortune, should have entered upon the composition of his immortal epic, achieving it in six years; and that Scott, at nearly the same age, his private affairs in ruin, should have undertaken to liquidate, by intellectual labors alone, a debt of more than half a million of dollars, nearly accomplishing it in the same time. That Dr. Lardner, who published a treatise to prove that a steamboat could never cross the Atlantic (the steamship Sirius, which crossed soon after, carrying over his pamphlet), should also have staked his reputation as a man of science to a committee of the House of Commons that no railway train could ever be propelled faster than ten miles in an hour, and that the slightest curve would infallibly throw it off the rails. That Babinet, the French calculator, should also have risked his reputation upon the declaration that no telegram would ever be transmitted through the Atlantic to America. That Renous, a German collector in natural history, having left in a house in San Fernandino, Chili, some caterpillars under charge of a girl to feed that they might turn into butterflies, should have been arrested upon returning to the house, his extraordinary conduct having been rumored through the town till it reached the padres and governor, who consulted together and determined to punish the pernicious heresy. That Socrates should have learned music, Cato the Greek language, Plutarch Latin, and Dr. Johnson Dutch, after they were seventy years old. That Robert Hall should have sought relief in Dante from the racking pains of spinal disease; and that Sydney Smith should have resorted to the same poet for comfort and solace in his old age. That De Foe, the author of two hundred and ten books and pamphlets, should have died

insolvent. That Sheridan should have got Woodfall to
insert in his paper a calumnious article, and neglected
to answer it afterward, as he intended — expending,
according to Moore, all his activity in assisting the
circulation of the poison, and not having industry
enough left to supply the antidote. That Hugh
Miller, who had such healthy views of life, as shown
in his autobiography, should have voluntarily left it
by means of a pistol. That Lloyd, one of the early
friends and literary associates of Lamb and Coleridge,
should have taken lodgings at a working brazier's
shop in Fetter Lane, to distract his mind from melancholy and postpone his madness. That Hazlitt
should have said that Mary Lamb was the wisest and
most rational woman he had ever known. That Professor Wilson, soon after he was selected to fill the
moral philosophy chair at Edinburgh, and the poet
Campbell, should have been seen one morning leaving a tavern in that city, both "haggard and red-
eyed, hoarse and exhausted, having sat tête-à-tête for
twenty-four hours discussing poetry and wine to the
top of their bent." That Richard Baxter, the stern
Calvinist, and author of one hundred and sixty-eight
works upon theology, should have written at the end
of his long life, "I now see more good and more
evil in all men than heretofore I did. I see that
good men are not so good as I once thought they
were, and I find that few are so bad as either malicious enemies or censorious separating professors do
imagine." That Theodore de Beza, the apostle of
John Calvin, should have put to press at the same
time his coarse amorous poems (Juvenilia) and his
intolerant apology for the trial and execution of Ser-

vetus. That " the mighty Dr. Hill, who was not a
very delicate feeder, could not make a dinner out of
the press till by a happy transformation into Hannah
Glass he turned himself into a cook, and sold receipts
for made dishes to all the savory readers in the kingdom — the press then acknowledging him second in
favor only to John Bunyan ; his feasts kept pace in
sale with Nelson's fasts, and when his own name was
fairly written out of credit, he wrote himself into immortality under an alias." That Madame de Montespan, who found it " for her interest and vanity to
live in habitual violation of the seventh commandment," should have been so rigorous in her devotions
as to weigh her bread in Lent. That Cardinal Bernis,
" the most worthless of abbés," who owed his ad-
vancement in the church to Madame de Pompadour,
the most worthless of women, should have refused
" to communicate in the dignity of the purple with a
woman of so unsanctimonious a character." That
Rousseau, " whose preaching made it fashionable for
women of rank to nurse their own children," should
have " sent his own, as soon as born, to the foundling
hospital." That Coleridge and Goldsmith should
have written The House that Jack Built and Goody
Two Shoes : more than all it is curious, and wonderful, that these two simple trifles seem destined to
outlive their more elaborate productions — the Ancient Mariner and the Vicar of Wakefield. Christa-
bel and the Deserted Village may hardly be preserved
amongst the curiosities of literature, when the famous
nursery rhymes — joyously ringing upon the tongues
of silver-voiced children — will be immortally fresh
and new.

X.

CONTRASTS.

THE world will never be tired reading and talking of the peculiarities and struggles of some of its literary worthies, they seem so incredible. Poor Goldsmith, for example: every incident relating to him is interesting, even if colored by envy — as most of the contemporaneous gossip about him was. "I first met Goldsmith," says Cumberland, "at the British Coffee House. He dined with us as a visitor, introduced by Sir Joshua Reynolds, and we held a consultation upon the naming of his comedy, which some of the company had read, and which he detailed to the rest after his manner with a great deal of good-humor. Somebody suggested She Stoops to Conquer, and that title was agreed upon. . . . . 'You and I,' said he, 'have very different motives for resorting to the stage. I write for money, and care little about fame.' . . . . The whole company pledged themselves to the support of the poet, and faithfully kept their promise to him. In fact, he needed all that could be done for him, as Mr. Colman, then manager of Covent Garden Theatre, protested against the comedy, when as yet he had not struck upon a name for it. Johnson at length stood forth in all his terror, as champion for the piece, and backed by us, his

clients and retainers, demanded a fair trial. Colman
again protested, but, with that salvo for his own reputation, liberally lent his stage to one of the most
eccentric productions that ever found its way to it,
and She Stoops to Conquer was put into rehearsal.
We were not over-sanguine of success, but perfectly
determined to struggle hard for our author; we accordingly assembled our strength at the Shakespeare
Tavern in a considerable body for an early dinner,
where Samuel Johnson took the chair at the head of
a long table, and was the life and soul of the corps :
the poet took post silently by his side, with the
Burkes, Sir Joshua Reynolds, Fitzherbert, Caleb
Whitefoord, and a phalanx of North British prede-
termined applauders, under the banner of Major
Mills, all good men and true. Our illustrious president was in inimitable glee, and poor Goldsmith
that day took all his raillery as patiently and com-
placently as my friend Boswell would have done any
day or every day of his life. In the mean time, we
did not forget our duty, and though we had a better
comedy going, in which Johnson was chief actor, we
betook ourselves in good time to our separate and
allotted posts, and waited the awful drawing up of
the curtain. As our stations were preconcerted, so
were our signals for plaudits arranged and determined upon in a manner that gave every one his
cue where to look for them and how to follow them
up. We had amongst us a very worthy and sufficient
member, long since lost to his friends and the world
at large, Adam Drummond, of amiable memory, who
was gifted by nature with the most sonorous, and, at

the same time, the most contagious, laugh that ever
echoed from the human lungs.   The neighing of the
horse of the son of Hystaspes was a whisper to it;
the whole thunder of the theatre could not drown it.
This kind and ingenuous friend fairly forewarned us
that he knew no more when to give his fire than the
cannon did that was planted on a battery.   He desired, therefore, to have a flapper at his elbow, and I
had the honor to be deputed to that office.   I planted
him in an upper box, pretty nearly over the stage, in
full view of the pit and galleries, and perfectly well
situated to give the echo all its play through the hol-
lows and recesses of the theatre.   The success of our
manœuvres was complete.   All eyes were upon Johnson, who sat in a front row of a side box, and when
he laughed everybody thought themselves warranted
to roar.   In the mean time, my friend followed signals with a rattle so irresistibly comic that, when he
had repeated it several times, the attention of the
spectators was so engrossed by his person and performances that the progress of the play seemed likely
to become a secondary object, and I found it prudent
to insinuate to him that he might halt his music without any prejudice to the author ; but, alas, it was
now too late to rein him in ; he had laughed upon
my signal where he found no joke, and now unluckily
he fancied that he found a joke in almost everything
that was said ; so that nothing in nature could be
more malapropos than some of his bursts every now
and then were.   These were dangerous moments, for
the pit began to take umbrage ; but we carried our
play through, and triumphed not only over Colman's

judgment, but our own." It is related that Goldsmith, during the performance of the comedy, walked
all the time in St. James's Park, in great uneasiness;
and when he thought it must be over, he hastened to
the theatre. His ears were assailed with hisses as he
entered the green-room, when he eagerly inquired of
Mr. Colman the cause. "Psha! psha!" said Colman, "don't be afraid of squibs, when we have been
sitting on a barrel of gunpowder these two hours."
The fact was, that the comedy had been completely
successful, and that it was the farce which had excited those sounds so terrific to Goldsmith.

A scene very different from that occurred at another "first acting"—as remarkable if not as famous. It was on the occasion of the first presentation
of Lamb's farce of Mr. H., thirty years later, at Drury
Lane. That acute dramatic scholar and critic had
written a tragedy, — John Woodvil, — the fate of
which his friend Procter has pleasantly narrated:
"It had been in Mr. Kemble's hands for about a
year, and Lamb naturally became urgent to hear his
decision upon it. Upon applying for this he found
that his play was—lost! This was at once acknowledged, and a 'courteous request made for another
copy, if I had one by me.' Luckily, another copy
existed. The 'first runnings' of a genius were not,
therefore, altogether lost, by having been cast, without a care, into the dusty limbo of the theatre. The
other copy was at once supplied, and the play very
speedily rejected. It was afterwards facetiously
brought forward in one of the early numbers of
the Edinburgh Review, and there noticed as a rude

specimen of the earliest age of the drama, 'older than
Æschylus.'" But the condemnation of his tragedy
did not discourage him; he now tried his genius upon
a farce. Its acceptance, Talfourd says, gave Lamb
some of the happiest moments he ever spent. He
wrote joyously to Wordsworth about it, even carrying his humorous anticipations so far as to indulge in
a draft of the "orders" he should send out to his
friends after it had had a successful run: "Admit
to Boxes. Mr. H. Ninth Night. Charles Lamb."
Hear what he says about it to his friend Manning,
then in China: "The title is Mr. H., no more; how
simple, how taking! A great H— sprawling over
the play-bill, and attracting eyes at every corner.
The story is a coxcomb appearing at Bath, vastly
rich — all the ladies dying for him — all bursting
to know who he is — but he goes by no other
name than Mr. H.; a curiosity like that of the
dames of Strasburg about the man with the great
nose. But I won't tell you any more about it.
Yes, I will; but I can't give you any idea how
I have done it. I'll just tell you that after much
vehement admiration, when his true name comes
out, — 'Hogsflesh' — all the women shun him,
avoid him, and not one can be found to change her
name for him — that's the idea: how flat it is
here, but how whimsical in the farce! And only
think, how hard upon me it is that the ship is dis-
patched to-morrow, and my triumph cannot be ascertained till the Wednesday after; but all China
will ring of it by and by. . . . . I shall get two
hundred pounds from the theatre if Mr. H. has a

good run, and I hope one hundred pounds for the copyright. . . . . Mary and I are to sit next the orchestra in the pit, next the dweedle dees." The Wednesday came, the wished-for evening, which decided the fate of Mr. H. " Great curiosity," says Talfourd, "was excited by the announcement ; the house was crowded to the ceiling, and the audience impatiently awaited the conclusion of the long, intolerable opera by which it was preceded. At length the hero of the farce entered, gayly dressed, and in happiest spirits, — enough, not too much, elated, — and delivered the prologue with great vivacity and success. The farce began ; at first it was much applauded ; but the wit seemed wire-drawn ; and when the curtain fell on the first act, the friends of the author began to fear. The second act dragged heavily on, as second acts of farces will do; a rout at Bath, peopled with ill-dressed and over-dressed actors and actresses, increased the disposition to yawn ; and when the moment of disclosure came, and nothing worse than the name Hogsflesh was heard, the audience resented the long play on their curiosity, and would hear no more. Lamb, with his sister, sat, as he anticipated, in the front of the pit ; and having joined in encoring the epilogue, the brilliancy of which injured the farce, he gave way with equal pliancy to the common feeling, and hissed and hooted as loudly as any of his neighbors ! " Away went the poet's fame, and the hoped-for three hundred pounds ! Not even the autocratic countenance of Johnson, and the big, contagious laugh of Drummond, could have saved them. The next morning's

18

play-bill contained a veracious announcement, that
" the new farce of Mr. H., performed for the first
time last night, was received by an overflowing audience with universal applause, and will be repeated for
the second time to-morrow; " but the stage lamps
never that morrow saw ! An amusing, sad spectacle
the whole thing was ; Lamb, especially, — the dramatic scholar, critic, and wit, the theatre-goer, the associate of playwrights and actors, — hissing and hoot-
ing his own bantling ! In a letter afterward to Manning, he labors to be amusing over the catastrophe
in this ghastly and extravagant manner : " So I go
creeping on since I was lamed by that cursed fall from
off the top of Drury Lane Theatre into the pit, something more than a year ago. However, I have been
free of the house ever since, and the house was pretty
free with me upon that occasion. Hang 'em, how
they hissed ! It was not a hiss neither, but a sort of
a frantic yell, like a congregation of mad geese ; with
roaring sometimes like bears ; mows and mops like
apes ; sometimes snakes, that hissed me into madness. 'T was like St. Anthony's temptations. Mercy
on us ! that God should give his favorite children,
men, mouths to speak with, to discourse rationally, to
promise smoothly, to flatter agreeably, to encourage
warmly, to counsel wisely, to sing with, to drink with,
and to kiss with, and that they should turn them
into mouths of adders, bears, wolves, hyenas, and
whistle like tempests, and emit breath through them
like distillations of aspic poison, to asperse and vilify
the innocent labors of their fellow-creatures who are
desirous to please them ! Heaven be pleased to make

the teeth rot out of them all, therefore ! Make them a reproach, and all that pass by them to loll out their tongues at them! Blind mouths ! as Milton somewhere calls them."

Poor Elia! Of crazy stock, himself in a madhouse for six weeks at the end of his twentieth year, his sister insane at intervals throughout her life, his mother hopelessly bed-ridden till killed by her daughter in a fit of frenzy, his father pitifully imbecile, his old maiden aunt home from a rich relation's to be nursed till she died — all dependent upon him, his more prosperous brother declining to bear any part of the burden ; his work for more than thirty years monotonous, and most of it performed at the same desk in the same back office, pinched all the time by poverty, with no ear for music, the list of his few friends, to use his own words, " in the world's eye, a ragged regiment," — including the poet Lloyd, who died insane, and the scholar Dyer, who was so absent-minded as at one time to empty the contents of his snuff-box into the tea-pot when he was preparing breakfast for a hungry friend, at another, ' with staff in hand, and at noonday," to walk straight into the river, — the humor, we say, of dear, wretched, gentle Charles Lamb must stand a wonder in English literature.

Not less incredible was the steady growth of the prodigious genius of Charlotte Brontë, under circumstances hardly less awfully depressing. Think of the woful life of that suffering prodigy, in that cheerless village of forbidding stone houses, whose grim architecture illustrated the rigid hardness of their inhab-

itants. Above, below, all around, were rocks and
moors, "where neither flowers nor vegetables would
flourish, and where even a tree of moderate dimensions might be hunted far and wide; where the snow
lay long and late; and where often, on autumnal and
winter nights, the four winds of heaven seemed to
meet and rage together, tearing round the houses as
if they were wild beasts striving to find an entrance."
Stone dikes were used in place of hedges. The cold
parsonage, at the top of the one desolate street, with
its stone stairs and stone floors in the passages and
parlors, was surrounded on three sides by the " great
old church-yard," which was " terribly full of upright
tombstones," and which poisoned the water-springs of
the pumps. The funeral bells, tolling, tolling, and
the "chip, chip " of the mason, as he cut the grave-
stones in a shed close by, were habitual sounds. The
pews in the old church " were of black oak, with high
divisions, with the names of the owners painted in
white letters on the doors." Her father, the clergyman, harsh, hard, and unsocial; at all times denying
flesh food to his puny children; at dinner permitting
them only potatoes, and rarely or never taking his
meals with them; with a temper so violent and distrustful as to cause him always to carry a pistol, which
he was in the habit of discharging from an upper
window whenever in a fit of passion; who burned the
little colored shoes of his children, presented by their
mother's cousin, lest they should foster a love of
dress; who cut in strips the silk gown of his wife because its color was not suited to his puritanical taste
— at the time, too, when she was slowly dying of an

internal cancer. Sent from home to be educated at a miserable school provided for the daughters of clergymen, where were bad air and bad food, an experience which caused the speedy death of both her elder sisters. So short-sighted that " she always seemed to be seeking something, moving her head from side to side to catch a sight of it." Having no visitors ; visiting, during her childhood, but at one house, and that for but a short time. Her only intimate associates her two younger sisters. Wonderful trio! "At nine o'clock they put away their work, and began to pace the room backward and forward, up and down, over the stone floors, — as often with the candles extinguished, for economy's sake, as not, — their figures glancing in the firelight, and out into the shadow, perpetually. At this time they talked over past cares and troubles ; they planned for the future, and consulted each other as to their plans. In after years, this was the time for discussing together the plots of their novels. And again, still later, this was the time for the last surviving sister (Charlotte) to walk alone, from old accustomed habit, round and round the desolate room, thinking sadly upon the ' days that were no more.' " Is there anything in books more sad and touching? Her only pet was a fierce bull-dog, and her only male associate her brilliant, drunken brother (who willfully died upon his feet, in an upright position, to fulfill an oft-declared purpose), a continual disgrace and terror as long as he lived. And much of the time, poor thing, in an agony about the fate of her soul ! How the little, pinched victim of all this misery and wretchedness could have written a narra-

tive which at once took its place, in spite of faithless
and unsympathizing critics, and securely kept it, too,
amongst the highest and best productions of the age,
is a startling marvel in literature. Out of her own
life she wrought her wonderful works. " The fiery
imagination that at times eats me up," she wrote to
her friend. In her stories she but told her own agonies, as Cowper noted the progress of his insanity, or
the French physiologist his ebbing pulse under the
deadly influence of burning charcoal.

But, recurring to Lamb and his set, what impossible, incomprehensible characters it included : Elton
Hammond, for instance, a contemporary if not an
associate. He inherited his father's tea business in
Milk Street. In order, he said, to set an example to
the world how a business should be carried on, and
that he might not be interfered with in his plans, he
turned off the clerks and every servant in the establishment, which soon wound up the business altogether. For a while he had no other society than a
little child, which he taught its letters, and a mouse,
that fed out of his hands. He journalized his food,
his sleep, his dreams. He had a conviction that he
was to have been, and ought to have been, the greatest of men, but was conscious in fact that he was not.
The reason assigned by him for putting an end to his
life was that he could not condescend to live without
fulfilling his proper vocation. He said to one of his
friends that he was on the point of making a discovery which would put an end to physical and moral
evil in the world. He quarreled with another of his
friends for not being willing to join him in carrying a

heavy box through the streets of London for a poor woman. He refused a private secretaryship to Rough, a colonial chief justice, on the ground of the obligation involved to tell a lie and write a lie every day, subscribing himself the humble servant of people he did not serve, and toward whom he felt no humility. Here are a few things he wrote : " When I was about eight or ten I promised marriage to a wrinkled cook we had, aged about sixty-five. I was convinced of the insignificance of beauty, but really felt some considerable ease at hearing of her death, about four years after, when I began to repent of my vow." . . . . " I always said that I would do anything to make another happy, and told a boy I would give him a shilling if it would make him happy ; he said it would, so I gave it to him. It is not to be wondered at that I had plenty of such applications, and soon emptied my purse. It is true I rather grudged the money, because the boys laughed rather more than I wished them. But it would have been inconsistent to have appeared dissatisfied. Some of them were generous enough to return the money, and I was prudent enough to take it, though I declared that if it would make them happy I should be sorry to have it back." . . . . " It is not pain, it is not death, that I dread, it is the hatred of a man ; there is something in it so shocking that I would rather submit to any injury than incur or increase the hatred of a man by revenging it." . . . . " The chief philosophical value of my papers I conceive to be that they record something of a mind that was very near taking a station far above all that have hitherto appeared in the world." . . . . " It is provoking that the secret of rendering man perfect in wisdom, power, virtue, and happiness should die with me. I never till this moment doubted that some other person would discover it; but I now recollect that when I have relied on others I have always been disappointed. Perhaps none may ever discover it, and the human race has lost its only chance of eternal happiness." . . . . "I believe that man requires religion. I believe that there is no true religion now existing. I believe that there will be one. It will not, after eighteen hundred years of existence, be of questionable truth and utility, but perhaps in eighteen years be entirely spread over the earth, an effectual remedy for all human suffering, and a source of perpetual joy. It will not need immense learning to be understood, it will be subject to no controversy." . . . . "Another sufficient reason for suicide is that I was this morning out of temper with Mrs. Douglas (for no fault of hers). I did not betray myself in the least, but I reflected to be exposed to the possibility of such an event once a year was evil enough to render life intolerable. The disgrace of using an impatient word is to me overpowering." . . . . "I am stupefied with writing, and yet I cannot go my long journey without taking leave of one from whom I have received so much kindness, and from whose society so much delight. My place is booked in Charon's boat to-night at twelve. Diana kindly consents to be of the party. This is handsome of her. She was not looked for on my part. Perhaps she is willing to acknowledge my obedience to her laws by a genteel compliment. Good. The gods, then, are grateful." To the coroner and his jury he wrote, "Let me suggest the following verdict, as combining literal truth with justice: 'Died by his own hand, but not feloniously.' If I have offended God, it is for God, not you, to inquire. Especial public duties I have none. If I have deserted any engagement in society, let the parties aggrieved consign my name to obloquy. I have for nearly seven years been disentangling myself from all my engagements, that I might at last be free to retire from life. I am free to-day, and avail myself of my liberty. I cannot be a good man, and prefer death to being a bad one, — as bad as I have been and as others are."

And George Dyer — a pet associate of Lamb's — what a character was he! A bundle of contradictions if ever there was one. Poor and always struggling, but never envious, and utterly without hatred of the rich. A poet whose poetry was to himself "as good as anybody's, and anybody's as good as his own." A bachelor, his life was solitary, but he never thought of his solitude, till it was suggested to him by an observing, sympathizing widow, who kindly and generously consented to share it with him — her fourth husband! He is characterized by one of his literary friends as "one of the best creatures morally that ever breathed." He was a ripe scholar, but to the end of his days (and he lived to be eighty-five) he was a bookseller's drudge. He made indexes, corrected the press, and occasionally gave lessons in Greek and Latin. Simple and kind, he repeatedly gave away his last guinea. He was the author of the Life and Writings of Robert Robinson, which was

pronounced by Wordsworth and Samuel Parr one of
the best biographies in the language. The charm of
the book is that Robinson's peculiar humor was wholly
unappreciated by the simple-minded biographer. Robinson was a fine humorist; Dyer had absolutely no
sense of humor. It was when he was on his way from
Lamb's to Mrs. Barbauld's, that, in his absent-mind-
edness, he walked straight into New River, and was
with difficulty saved from drowning. (Young, who
sat for the portrait of Parson Adams, was another
such character. He also "supported an uncom-
fortable existence by translating for the booksellers
from the Greek," overflowed with benevolence and
learning, and was noted for his absence of mind. He
had been chaplain of a regiment during Marlborough's
wars; and "meditating one evening upon the glories
of nature, and the goodness of Providence, he walked
straight into the camp of the enemy; nor was he
aroused from his reverie till the hostile sentinel
shouted, 'Who goes there?' The commanding officer, finding that he had come among them in simplicity and not in guile, allowed him to return, and lose
himself, if he pleased, in meditations on his danger
and deliverance.") It is said that certain roguish
young ladies, Dyer's cousins, lacking due reverence
for learning and poetry, were wont to heap all sorts
of meats upon the worthy gentleman's plate at dinner, he being lost in conversation until near the close
of the repast, when he would suddenly recollect himself and fall to till he had finished the whole. Talfourd, speaking of Lamb and Dyer, says, "No contrast could be more vivid than that presented by the

relations of each to the literature they both loved,—
one divining its inmost essences, plucking out the
heart of its mysteries, shedding light on its dimmest
recesses; the other devoted with equal assiduity to
its externals. Books, to Dyer, 'were a real world,
both pure and good;' among them he passed, uncon-
scious of time, from youth to extreme old age, vege-
tating on their dates and forms, and 'trivial fond
records,' in the learned air of great libraries, or the
dusty confusion of his own, with the least possible
apprehension of any human interest vital in their
pages, or of any spirit of wit or fancy glancing across
them. His life was an academic pastoral. Methinks
I see his gaunt, awkward form, set off by trousers
too short, like those outgrown by a gawky lad, and a
rusty coat as much too large for the wearer, hanging
about him like those garments which the aristocratic
Milesian peasantry prefer to the most comfortable
rustic dress; his long head silvered over with short
yet straggling hair, and his dark gray eyes glisten-
ing with faith and wonder, as Lamb satisfies the curiosity which has gently disturbed his studies as to the
authorship of the Waverley Novels, by telling him, in
the strictest confidence, that they are the works of
Lord Castlereagh, just returned from the Congress of
Sovereigns at Vienna. Off he runs, with animated
stride and shambling enthusiasm, nor stops till he
reaches Maida Hill, and breathes his news into the
startled ear of Leigh Hunt, who, 'as a public writer,'
ought to be possessed of the great fact with which
George is laden! Or shall I endeavor to revive the
bewildered look with which just after he had been

announced as one of Lord Stanhope's executors and residuary legatees, he received Lamb's grave inquiry whether it was true, as commonly reported, that he was to be made a lord? 'Oh dear, no, Mr. Lamb,' responded he with earnest seriousness, but not without a moment's quivering vanity. 'I could not think of such a thing; it is not true, I assure you.' 'I thought not,' said Lamb, 'and I contradict it wherever I go. But the government will not ask your consent; they may raise you to the peerage without your ever knowing it.' 'I hope not, Mr. Lamb; indeed — indeed, I hope not. It would not suit me at all,' responded Dyer, and went his way musing on the possibility of a strange honor descending on his reluctant brow. Or shall I recall the visible presentment of his bland unconsciousness of evil when his sportive friend taxed it to the utmost by suddenly asking what he thought of the murderer Williams, who, after destroying two families in Ratcliffe Highway, had broken prison by suicide, and whose body had just before been conveyed in shocking procession to its cross-road grave? The desperate attempt to compel the gentle optimist to speak ill of a mortal creature produced no happier success than the answer, 'Why, I should think, Mr. Lamb, he must have been rather an eccentric character.'" Honest, simple soul! My Uncle Toby over again, for all the world.

What a contrast with all these ailing souls was the magnificent Christopher North! You remember the scene of his triumph on the occasion of his first lecture to the moral philosophy class in the University of Edinburgh. It deserves to be thought of along with the "trial scenes" we have been reviewing. The contest for the professorship had been bitterly fought over a period of four months, with Sir William Hamilton for competitor, — Sir James Mackintosh and Mr. Malthus being only possible candidates. Abuse and prejudice — essential and saintly elements in all good Scotsmen — skillfully combined against him, and inveterately pursued him. "When it was found useless to gainsay his mental qualifications for the office, or to excite odium on the ground of his literary offenses, the attack was directed against his moral character, and it was broadly insinuated that this candidate for the chair of ethics was himself a man of more than doubtful morality; that he was, in fact, not merely a 'reveler,' and a 'blasphemer,' but a bad husband, a bad father; a person not fit to be trusted as a teacher of youth." A "bad husband" to the good woman he thus memorably characterized in a letter to one of his friends: "I was this morning married to Jane Penney, and doubt not of receiving your blessing, which, from your brotherly heart, will delight me, and doubtless not be unheard by the Almighty. She is gentleness, innocence, sense, and feeling, surpassed by no woman, and has remained pure, as from her Maker's hands;" the mother of all those children he loved so, — the death of whom, in his ripe manhood and in the bloom of his fame, nearly broke his heart! Sir Walter and other powerful friends repelled the slanders. Wilson triumphed. Still he was pursued; his enemies determined he should be put down, humiliated, even in his own class-room. An eye-witness thus describes the scene on the occa-

sion of the delivery of the professor's first lecture:
"There was a furious bitterness of feeling against
him among the classes of which probably most of his
pupils would consist, and although I had no prospect
of being among them, I went to his first lecture, prepared to join in a cabal, which I understood was
formed to put him down. The lecture-room was
crowded to the ceiling. Such a collection of hard-
browed, scowling Scotsmen, muttering over their
knobsticks, I never saw. The professor entered with
a bold step, amid profound silence. Every one expected some deprecatory or propitiatory introduction
of himself and his subject, upon which the mass was
to decide against him, reason or no reason; but he
began in a voice of thunder right into *the matter* of
his lecture, kept up unflinchingly and unhesitatingly,
without a pause, a flow of rhetoric such as Dugald
Stewart or Thomas Brown, his predecessors, never
delivered in the same place. Not a word, not a mur-
mur escaped his captivated, I ought to say his conquered audience, and at the end they gave him a downright unanimous burst of applause. Those who came
to scoff remained to praise." The ruling classes in
educational matters could not conceive of the fitness
of a man like Wilson for the moral philosophy chair
in a university. The giant he was physically, with
appetites and passions to match, he was a reproach to
the feeble, a terror to the timid, and a horror to the
"unco guid, or the rigidly righteous." The truth of
him was such an exaggeration of the average man
that the scholars and pedagogues and parsons could
only look upon him as a monster, with a character as

monstrous as his nature. He is described as " long-
maned and mighty, whose eyes were ' as the light-
nings of fiery flame,' and his voice like an organ bass ;
who laid about him, when the fit was on, like a Titan,
breaking small men's bones ; who was loose and care-
less in his apparel, even as in all things he seemed
too strong and primitive to heed much the niceties of
custom." In his youth, he " ran three miles for a
wager against a chaise," and came out ahead. Somewhat later he "gained a bet by walking, toe and heel,
six miles in two minutes within the hour." When he
was twenty-one, height five feet eleven inches, weight
eleven stone, he leaped, with a run, twenty-three feet
"on a slightly inclined plane, perhaps an inch to a
yard," and " was admitted to be (Ireland excepted)
the best far leaper of his day in England." He could
jump twelve yards in three jumps, with a great stone
in each hand. " With him the angler's silent trade
was a ruling passion. He did not exaggerate to the
Shepherd in the Noctes, when he said that he had
taken ' a hundred and thirty in one·day out of Loch
Aire,' as we see by his letters that even larger numbers were taken by him." Of his pugilistic skill, it
is said by De Quincey that " there was no man who
had any talents, real or fancied, for thumping or being thumped, but he had experienced some *preeing* of
his merits from Mr. Wilson." " Meeting one day
with a rough and unruly wayfarer, who showed inclination to pick a quarrel concerning right of passage
across a certain bridge, the fellow obstructed the way,
and making himself decidedly obnoxious, Wilson lost
all patience, and offered to fight him. The man

made no objection to the proposal, but replied that
he had better not fight with *him*, as he was so and so,
mentioning the name of a (then not unknown) pu-
gilist. This statement had, as may be supposed, no
effect in dampening the belligerent intentions of the
Oxonian; he knew his own strength, and his skill too.
In one moment off went his coat, and he set to upon
his antagonist in splendid style. The astonished and
punished rival, on recovering from his blows and surprise, accosted him thus: ' You can only be one of the
two: you are either Jack Wilson or the devil.' "
His pedestrian feats were marvelous. " On one occasion," writes an old classmate of Wilson's at Oxford, " having been absent a day or two, we asked
him, on his return to the common room, where he
had been. He said, In London. When did you return? This morning. How did you come? On
foot. As we all expressed surprise, he said, ' Why,
the fact is, I dined yesterday with a friend in Gros-
venor (I think it was) Square, and as I quitted the
house, a fellow who was passing was impertinent and
insulted me, upon which I knocked him down ; and
as I did not choose to have myself called in question
for a street row, I at once started, as I was, in my
dinner dress, and never stopped until I got to the
college gate this morning, as it was being opened.'
Now this was a walk of fifty-eight miles at least,
which he must have got over in eight or nine hours
at most, supposing him to have left the dinner-party
at nine in the evening." Some years later, he walked
— *his wife accompanying him* — " three hundred and
fifty miles in the Highlands, between the 5th of July

and the 26th of August, sojourning in divers glens
from Sabbath unto Sabbath, fishing, eating, and staring." Mrs. Wilson returned from this wonderful
tour " bonnier than ever," and Wilson himself, to
use his own phrase, " strong as an eagle." One of
their resting-places was at the school-master's house
in Glenorchy. While there " his time was much occupied by fishing, and distance was not considered
an obstacle. He started one morning at an early
hour to fish in a loch which at that time abounded
in trout, in the Braes of Glenorchy, called Loch Toilà.
Its nearest point was thirteen miles distant from
his lodgings at the school-house. On reaching it,
and unscrewing the butt-end of his fishing-rod to
get the top, he found he had it not. Nothing
daunted, he walked back, breakfasted, got his fishing-rod, made all complete, and off again to Loch
Toilà. He could not resist fishing on the river when
a pool looked inviting, but he went always onwards,
reaching the loch a second time, fished round it, and
found that the long summer day had come to an end.
He set off for his home again with his fishing-basket
full, and confessing somewhat to weariness. Passing
near a farm-house whose inmates he knew (for he had
formed acquaintance with all), he went to get some
food. They were in bed, for it was eleven o'clock at
night, and after rousing them, the hostess hastened
to supply him ; but he requested her to get him some
whisky and milk. She came with a bottle full, and
a can of milk, with a tumbler. Instead of a tumbler,
he requested a bowl, and poured the half of the whisky
in, along with half the milk. He drank the mixture
19

at a draught, and while his kind hostess was looking
on with amazement, he poured the remainder of the
whisky and milk into the bowl, and drank that also.
He then proceeded homeward, performing a journey
of not less than seventy miles." Prodigious! It beat
the achievement of Phidippides, who, according to
tradition, ran from Athens to Sparta, one hundred
and twenty miles, in two days. But here is a street
scene, related to his daughter by a lady who saw it,
which illustrates the tremendous professor of moral
philosophy still further. "One summer afternoon,
as she was about to sit down to dinner, her servant
requested her to look out of the window, to see a
man cruelly beating his horse. The sight not being a
very gratifying one, she declined, and proceeded to take
her seat at table. It was quite evident that the servant had discovered something more than the ill-usage
of the horse to divert his attention, for he kept his
eyes fixed on the window, again suggesting to his
mistress that she ought to look out. Her interest was
at length excited, and she rose to see what was going
on. In front of her house (Moray Place) stood a
cart of coals, which the poor victim of the carter was
unable to drag along. He had been beating the beast
most unmercifully, when at that moment Professor
Wilson, walking past, had seen the outrage and immediately interfered. The lady said that from the
expression of his face, and vehemence of his manner,
the man was evidently 'getting it,' though she was
unable to hear what was said. The carter, exas-
perated at this interference, took up his whip in a
threatening way, as if with the intent to strike the

professor. In an instant that well-nerved hand twisted it from the coarse fist of the man as if it had been a straw, and walking quietly up to the cart he unfastened its trams, and hurled the whole weight of coals into the street. The rapidity with which this was done left the driver of the cart speechless. Meanwhile, poor Rosinante, freed from his burden, crept slowly away, and the professor, still clutching the whip in one hand, and leading the horse in the other, proceeded through Moray Place to deposit the wretched animal in better keeping than that of his driver." Another of his "interferences" occurred during vacation time, in the south of Scotland, when the professor had exchanged the gown for the old "sporting jacket." "On his return to Edinburgh, he was obliged to pass through Hawick, where, on his arrival, finding it to be fair-day, he readily availed himself of the opportunity to witness the amusements going on. These happened to include a ' little mill ' between two members of the local ' fancy.' His interest in pugilism attracted him to the spot, where he soon discovered something very wrong, and a degree of injustice being perpetrated which he could not stand. It was the work of a moment to espouse the weaker side, a proceeding which naturally drew down upon him the hostility of the opposite party. This result was to him, however, of little consequence. There was nothing for it but to beat or be beaten. He was soon ' in position ; ' and, before his unknown adversary well knew what was coming, the skilled fist of the professor had planted such a ' facer ' as did not require repetition. Another ' round ' was not

called for ; and leaving the discomfited champion to
recover at his leisure, the professor walked coolly
away to take his seat in the stage-coach, about to
start for Edinburgh." Is it any wonder that such a
gigantic specimen of human nature was thought by
the steady-going and saintly Edinburghers, who tried
men only by mathematics and the catechism, to be
preposterously unfit for the chair of ethics in their
hallowed university ? They did not know then that
the monster they hunted was capable of producing a
description of *a fairy's funeral* — one of the most exquisite bits of prose composition in literature, which
is said to have so impressed Lord Jeffrey's mind that
he never was tired of repeating it. Read it, and say
you if anybody but Christopher North *could* have
written it : " There it was, on a little river island,
that once, whether sleeping or waking we know not,
we saw celebrated a fairy's funeral. First we heard
small pipes playing, as if no bigger than hollow
rushes that whisper to the night winds ; and more
piteous than aught that trills from earthly instrument
was the scarce audible dirge ! It seemed to float over
the stream, every foam-bell emitting a plaintive note,
till the fairy anthem came floating over our couch,
and then alighting without footsteps among the
heather. The pattering of little feet was then heard,
as if living creatures were arranging themselves in
order, and then there was nothing but a more ordered
hymn. The harmony was like the melting of musical dew-drops, and sang, without words, of sorrow
and death. We opened our eyes, or rather sight
came to them when closed, and dream was vision.

Hundreds of creatures, no taller than the crest of the lapwing, and all hanging down their veiled heads, stood in a circle on a green plat among the rocks ; and in the midst was a bier, framed as it seemed of flowers unknown to the Highland hills ; and on the bier a fairy lying with uncovered face, pale as a lily, and motionless as the snow. The dirge grew fainter and fainter, and then died quite away ; when two of the creatures came from the circle, and took their station, one at the head, the other at the foot of the bier. They sang alternate measures, not louder than the twitter of the awakened woodlark before it goes up the dewy air, but dolorous and full of the desolation of death. The flower-bier stirred ; for the spot on which it lay sank slowly down, and in a few moments the greensward was smooth as ever, the very dews glittering above the buried fairy. A cloud passed over the moon ; and, with a choral lament, the funeral troop sailed duskily away, heard afar off, so still was the midnight solitude of the glen. Then the disenthralled Orchy began to rejoice as before, through all her streams and falls ; and at the sudden leaping of the waters and outbursting of the moon, we awoke."

XI.

TYPES.

"It never rains but it pours," is the pat proverb of all the world to express its belief in the inevitableness and omnipotence of extremes. Carlyle has enlarged upon it significantly, in that famous passage in which he likens men collectively to sheep. Like sheep, he says, are we seen ever running in torrents and mobs, if we ever run at all. "Neither know we, except by blind habit, where the good pastures lie : solely when the sweet grass is between our teeth, we know it, and chew it ; also when the grass is bitter and scant, we know it, — and bleat and butt : these last two facts we know of a truth, and in very deed. Thus do men and sheep play their parts on this nether earth ; wandering restlessly in large masses, they know not whither ; for most part, each following his neighbor, and his own nose. Nevertheless, not always ; look better, you shall find certain that do, in some small degree, know whither. Sheep have their bell-wether, some ram of the folds, endued with more valor, with clearer vision than other sheep ; he leads them through the wolds, by height and hollow, to the woods and water-courses, for covert or for pleasant provender ; courageously marching, and if need be leaping, and with hoof and horn doing battle, in the van : him they courageously, and with assured heart, follow. Touching it is, as every herdsman will inform you, with what chivalrous devotedness these woolly hosts adhere to their wether; and rush after him, through good report and through bad report, were it into safe shelters and green thymy nooks, or into asphaltic lakes and the jaws of devouring lions. Even also must we recall that fact which we owe Jean Paul's quick eye: ' If you hold a stick before the wether, so that he, by necessity, leaps in passing you, and then withdraw your stick, the flock will nevertheless all leap as he did; and the thousandth sheep shall be found impetuously vaulting over air, as the first did over an otherwise impassable barrier.' "

Society is always swaying, backward and forward — vibrating, like the pendulum, from one extreme to another; for a moment only, now and then, is it upright, and governed by reason. " In the grove of Gotama lived a Brahman, who, having bought a sheep in another village, and carrying it home on his shoulder to sacrifice, was seen by three rogues, who resolved to take the animal from him by the following stratagem : Having separated, they agreed to encounter the Brahman on his road as if coming from different parts. One of them called out, ' O Brahman! why dost thou carry that dog on thy shoulder? ' ' It is not a dog,' replied the Brahman; ' it is a sheep for sacrifice.' As he went on, the second knave met him, and put the same question; whereupon the Brahman, throwing the sheep on the ground, looked at it again and again. Having replaced it on his shoulder, the good man went with mind waving like a string. But when the third rogue met him and said, ' Father, where art thou taking that dog ? ' the Brahman, believing his eyes bewitched, threw down the sheep and hurried home, leaving the thieves to feast on that which he had provided for the gods." Traveling through Switzerland, Napoleon was greeted with such enthusiasm that Bourrienne said to him, " It must be delightful to be greeted with such demonstrations of enthusiastic admiration." " Bah ! " replied Napoleon, " this same unthinking crowd, under a slight change of circumstances, would follow me just as eagerly to the scaffold." Madame Roland wrote from her prison-cell to Robespierre, " It is not, Robespierre, to excite your compassion, that I present you with a picture less melancholy than the truth. I am above asking your pity ; and, were it offered, I should, perhaps, deem it an insult. I write for your instruction. Fortune is fickle ; and popular power is liable to change." " Society," said Macaulay, writing of Byron, " capricious in its indignation, as it had been capricious in its fondness, flew into a rage with its froward and petted darling. He had been worshiped with an irrational idolatry. He was persecuted with an irrational fury." Junius, in the celebrated letter, warns the king that " while he plumes himself upon the security of his title to the crown, he should remember that, as it was acquired by one revolution, it may be lost by another." " The Jews," said Luther, " have various stories about a king of Bashan, whom they call Og ; they say he had lifted a great rock to throw at his enemies, but God made a hole in the middle, so that it slipped down upon the giant's neck, and he could never rid himself of it."

Causes of good or evil seem to accumulate, when a very slight thing is the beginning of a succession of blessings or curses. All things conspire, till the recipients of blessings are smothered, or the victims of curses are crushed. Till the cup is full, overflowing; till the burden is unbearable, merciless; till good becomes satiety, or evil cruelty, — all the world seems to delight in contributing or robbing, deifying or anathematizing.

> " Never stoops the soaring vulture
> On his quarry in the desert,
> On the sick or wounded bison,
> But another vulture, watching
> From his high aerial lookout,
> Sees the downward plunge and follows;
> And a third pursues the second,
> Coming from the invisible ether,
> First a speck, and then a vulture,
> Till the air is dark with pinions.
> So disasters come not singly;
> But as if they watched and waited,
> Scanning one another's motions,
> When the first descends, the others
> Follow, follow, gathering flock-wise
> Round their victim, sick and wounded,
> First a shadow, then a sorrow,
> Till the air is dark with anguish."

" What a noise out-of-doors!" exclaimed Souvestre's Philosopher from his attic in Paris. " What is the meaning of all these shouts and cries? Ah! I recollect: this is the last day of the carnival, and the maskers are passing. Christianity has not been able to abolish the noisy bacchanalian festivals of the pagan times, but it has changed the names. That

which it has given to these 'days of liberty' announces the ending of the feasts, and the month of
fasting which should follow ; ' carn-a-val' means literally ' down with flesh meat ! ' It is a forty days'
farewell to the ' blessed pullets and fat hams,' so celebrated by Pantagruel's minstrel. Man prepares for
privation by satiety, and finishes his sins thoroughly
before he begins to repent. Why, in all ages and
among every people, do we meet with some one of
these mad festivals ? Must we believe that it requires
such an effort for men to be reasonable, that the
weaker ones have need of rest at intervals. The
monks of La Trappe, who are condemned to silence
by their rule, are allowed to speak once in a month,
and on this day, they all talk at once from the rising
to the setting of the sun."

It is reported of Scaramouche, the first famous
Italian comedian, that being in Paris, and in great
want, he bethought himself of constantly plying near
the door of a noted perfumer in that city, and when
any one came out who had been buying snuff, never
failed to desire a taste of them : when he had by this
means got together a quantity made up of several
different sorts, he sold it again at a lower rate to the
same perfumer, who, finding out the trick, called it
" snuff of a thousand flowers." The story further
tells us that by this means he got a very comfortable
subsistence, until, making too great haste to grow
rich, he one day took such an unreasonable pinch out
of the box of a Swiss officer as engaged him in a
quarrel, and obliged him to quit this ingenious way
of life.

"I remember," says Cumberland, in his Memoirs, "the predicament of an ingenious mechanic and artist, who, when Rich the harlequin was the great dramatic author of his time, and wrote successfully for the stage, contrived and executed a most delicious serpent for one of those inimitable productions, in which Mr. Rich, justly disdaining the weak aid of language, had selected the classical fable, if I rightly recollect, of Orpheus and Eurydice, and, having conceived a very capital part for the serpent, was justly anxious to provide himself with a performer who could support a character of that consequence with credit to himself and his author. The event answered his most ardent hopes; nothing could be more perfect than his entrances and exits; nothing ever crawled across the stage with more accomplished sinuosity than this enchanting serpent; every one was charmed with its performance; it twirled and twisted, and wriggled itself about in so divine a manner, that the whole world was ravished by the lovely snake; nobles and non-nobles, rich and poor, old and young, reps and demi-reps, flocked to see it and admire it. The artist, who had been the master of the movement, was intoxicated with his success; he turned his hand and head to nothing else but serpents; he made them of all sizes; they crawled about his shop as if he had been chief snake-catcher to the furies; the public curiosity was satisfied with one serpent, and he had nests of them yet unsold; his stock lay dead upon his hands, his trade was lost, and the man was ruined, bankrupt, and undone."

Lecky observes that when, after long years of ob-

stinate disbelief, the reality of the great discovery of
Harvey dawned upon the medical world, the first
result was a school of medicine which regarded man
simply as an hydraulic machine, and found the principle of every malady in imperfections of circulation.

In 'the Arctic region, says Lieutenant Kane, the
frost is so intense as to burn. In Arabia, travelers
declare, the silence of the desert is so profound that
it soon ceases to be soothing or solemn, and becomes
absolutely painful, if not appalling. In Java, that
magnificent and fearful clime, the most lovely flowers
are found to conceal hidden reptiles ; the most tempt-
ing fruits are tinct with subtle poisons; there grow
those splendid trees whose shadow is death ; there the
vampire, an enormous bat, sucks the blood of the victims whose sleep he prolongs, by wafting over them
an air full of freshness and perfume. Darwin, in his
Voyage, speaks of the strange mixture of sound and
silence which pervades the shady parts of the wood
on the shore of Brazil. The noise from the insects is
so loud that it may be heard even in a vessel an-
chored several hundred yards from the shore; yet
within the recesses of the forest a universal silence
appears to reign. " A dunghill at a distance," says
Coleridge, " sometimes smells like musk, and a dead
dog like elder-flowers." Scargill declared that an
Englishman is never happy but when he is miserable ; a Scotchman is never at home but when he is
abroad ; an Irishman is at peace only when he is fighting. " The melancholy," says Horace, " hate the
merry, the jocose the melancholy; the volatile dislike the sedate, the indolent the stirring and vivacious ;

the modest man generally carries the look of a churl."
Meyer, in conversation with Goethe, said he saw a
shoemaker in Italy who hammered his leather upon
the antique marble head of a Roman emperor. The
lark, that sings out of the sky, purifies himself, like
the pious Mussulman, in the dust of the ground. The
elephant, that no quadruped has the temerity to attack, is said to be the favorite victim of a worm that
bores into his foot and slowly tortures him to death.
" The impious Nimrod," according to a tradition of
the Arabs, " enraged at the destruction of his gods by
Abraham, sought to slay him, and waged war against
him. But the prophet prayed to God, and said,
' Deliver me, O God, from this man, who worships
stones, and boasts himself to be the lord of all beings ; ' and God said to him, ' How shall I punish
him ? ' And the prophet answered, ' To Thee armies
are as nothing, and the strength and power of men
likewise. Before the smallest of thy creatures will
they perish.' And God was pleased at the faith of
the prophet, and he sent a gnat, which vexed Nimrod
night and day, so that he built a room of glass in his
palace, that he might dwell therein, and shut out the
insect. But the gnat entered also, and passed by his
ear into his brain, upon which it fed, and increased in
size day by day, so that the servants of Nimrod beat
his head with a hammer continually, that he might
have some ease from his pain ; but he died, after
suffering these torments for four hundred years."

" The grandiose statues of Michel Angelo," said a
traveler, descanting upon the art and architecture of
old Rome, " appear to the greatest advantage under

the bold arches of Bramante. There — between those broad lines, under those prodigious curves — placed in one of those courts, or near one of the great temples where the perspective is incomplete — the statues of Michel Angelo display their tragic attitudes, their gigantic members, which seem animated by a ray from the divinity, and struggling to mount from earth to heaven. Bramante and Michel Angelo detested but completed each other. Thus it is often in human nature. Those two men knew not that they were laborers in the same work. And history is silent on such points till death has passed over her heroes. Armies have fought until they have been almost annihilated on the field of battle ; men have hated and injured one another by their calumnies; the learned and powerful persecute and seek to blot their fellows from the earth, as if there was not air and space for all; they know not, blinded by their passions, and warped by the prejudices of envy, that the future will blend them in the same glory, that to posterity they will represent but one sentiment. Bramante and Michel Angelo, enemies during life, are reconciled in immortality."

See how the extremes in morals and legislation met during the few years of English history covering the Protectorate and the Restoration. Puritanism and liberty of conscience, whose exponents were Cromwell and Milton, met licentiousness and corrupted loyalty, with Charles II. and Wycherley for representatives. Cromwell was " Puritanism armed and in power ; " Milton was its apostle and poet. Charles II. was kingcraft besotted; Wycherley its jester and pimp.

Cromwell — farmer, preacher, soldier, party leader, prince — radical, stern, hopeful ; Charles — debauchee, persecuting skeptic, faithless ruler ; Milton — lofty in his Paradise ; Wycherley — nasty in his Love in a Wood, and Country Wife. " A larger soul never dwelt in a house of clay," said one who had been much about Cromwell, after his death, when flattery was mute. " Old Goat " was the name given to Charles by one who knew him best. Cromwell, " after all his battles and storms, and all the plots of assassins against his life, died of grief at the loss of his favorite daughter, and of watching at her side." Charles went out of life in a fit, the result of his horrible excesses, if not of poison, — as said and believed by many, administered by one of his own numerous mistresses.

First, " the Puritans," says Macaulay, " interdicted, under heavy penalties, the use of the Book of Common Prayer, not only in churches but in private houses. It was a crime in a child to read by the bedside of a sick parent one of those beautiful collects which had soothed the griefs of forty generations of Christians. Severe punishments were denounced against such as should presume to blame the Calvinistic mode of worship. Clergymen of respectable character were not only ejected from their benefices by thousands, but were frequently exposed to the outrages of a fanatical rabble. Churches and sepulchres, fine works of art and curious remains of antiquity, were brutally defaced. The Parliament resolved that all pictures in the royal collection which contained representations of Jesus or of the Virgin Mother should be burned. Sculpture fared as ill as painting. Nymphs and graces, the work of Ionian chisels, were delivered over to Puritan stone-masons to be made decent. Against the lighter vices the ruling faction waged war with a zeal little tempered by humanity or by common-sense. Public amusements, from the masques which were exhibited at the mansions of the great down to the wrestling matches and grinning matches on village greens, were vigorously attacked. One ordinance directed that all the May-poles in England should forthwith be hewn down. One of the first resolutions adopted by Barebone's Parliament was that no person should be admitted into the public service till the house should be satisfied with his real godliness."

Suddenly the wheel turned. " The same people who, by a solemn objurgation, had excluded even the posterity of their lawful sovereign, exhausted themselves in festivals and rejoicings for his return." Restored royalty " made it a crime to attend a dissenting place of worship. A single justice of the peace might convict without a jury, and might, for a third offense, pass sentence of transportation beyond the sea, or for seven years. The whole soul of the restored church was in the work of crushing the Puritans, and of teaching her disciples to give unto Cæsar the things which were Cæsar's. She had been pillaged and oppressed by the party which preached an austere morality. She had been restored to opulence and honor by libertines. Little as the men of mirth and fashion were disposed to shape their lives according to her precepts, they were yet ready to fight knee-deep in blood for her cathedrals and palaces, for every line of her rubric and every thread of her vestments. If the debauched cavalier haunted brothels and gambling-houses, he at least avoided conventicles. If he ever spoke without uttering ribaldry and blasphemy, he made some amends by his eagerness to send Baxter and Howe to jail for preaching and praying. The ribaldry of Etherege and Wycherley was, in the presence and under the special sanction of the head of the church, publicly recited by female lips in female ears, while the author of the Pilgrim's Progress languished in a dungeon for the crime of proclaiming the gospel to the poor. Then came those days never to be recalled without a blush — the days of servitude without loyalty, and sensuality without love, of dwarfish talents and gigantic vices, the paradise of cold hearts and narrow minds, the golden age of the coward, the bigot, and the slave. The caresses of harlots and the jests of buffoons regulated the manners of a government which had just ability enough to deceive, and just religion enough to persecute. The principles of liberty were the scoff of every grinning courtier, and the Anathema Maranatha of every fawning dean. Crime succeeded to crime, and disgrace to disgrace, till the race, accursed of God and man, was a second time driven forth, to wander on the face of the earth, and be a by-word and a shaking of the head to the nations."

The morality of the time was illustrated in the character of the sovereign, according to whom " every person was to be bought; but some people haggled more about their price than others ; and when this haggling was very obstinate and very skillful, it was called by some fine name. The chief trick by which clever men kept up the price of their abilities was called integrity. The chief trick by which handsome women kept up the price of their beauty was called modesty. The love of God, the love of country, the love of family, the love of friends, were phrases of the same sort, delicate and convenient synonyms for the love of self."

"Puritanism," in the opinion of Taine, "had brought on an orgie, and fanatics had talked down the virtues."

"To what a place you come in search of knowledge!" exclaimed a bitter republican to Castelar, in the streets of Rome, during the reign of the pope, not long before Victor Emanuel. "Here everybody is interested about lottery tickets; no one for an idea of the human brain. The commemoration of the anniversary of Shakespeare has been prohibited in this city of the arts. Her censorship is so wise that when a certain writer wished to publish a book on the discoveries of Volta, she let loose on him the thunders of the Index, thinking it treated of Voltairianism — a philosophy which leaves neither repose nor digestion to our cardinals. On the other hand, a cabalistic and astrological book, professing to divine the caprices of the lottery, has been printed and published under the pontifical seal, as containing nothing contrary to religion, morals, or sovereign authority. Rabelais knew this city — Rabelais. On arriving, in place of writing a dissertation on dogmas, he penned one on lettuces, the only good and fresh articles in this cursed dungeon. And priest though he was, a priest of the sixteenth century, more religious than our generation, he had a long correspondence with the pious Bishop of Maillerais on the children of the pope; for the reverend prelate had especially charged him to ascertain whether the Cavaliere Pietro Luis Farnese was the lawful or illegitimate son of his holiness. Believe me, Rabelais knew Rome."

An old letter-writer, inditing from Paris, says, " Nakedness is so innocent here ! In a refined city, one gets back to the first chapter of Genesis ; the extremes meet, and Paradise and Paris get together."

See what opposite characters were the leaders in the Reformation. The monks said the egg was laid by Erasmus, hatched by Luther. " On the other hand," in the words of Motley, " he was reviled for not taking side manfully with the reformer. The moderate man received much denunciation from zealots on either side. He soon clears himself, however, from all suspicions of Lutheranism. He is appalled by the fierce conflict which rages far and wide. He becomes querulous as the mighty besom sweeps away sacred dust and consecrated cobwebs. ' Men should not attempt everything at once,' he writes, ' but rather step by step. That which men cannot approve they must look at through the fingers. If the godlessness of mankind requires such fierce physicians as Luther, if man cannot be healed with soothing ointments and cooling drinks, let us hope that God will comfort, as repentant, those whom he has punished as rebellious. If the dove of Christ — not the owl of Minerva — would only fly to us, some measure might be put to the madness of mankind.' Meantime, the man whose talk is not of doves and owls, the fierce physician, who deals not with ointments and cooling draughts, strides past the crowd of gentle quacks to smite the foul disease. Devils, thicker than tiles on house-tops, scare him not from his work. Bans and bulls, excommunications and decrees, are rained upon his head. The paternal emperor sends down dire edicts, thicker than hail upon the earth. The Holy Father blasts and raves from Rome. Louvain doctors denounce, Louvain hangmen burn, the bitter, blasphemous books. The immoderate man stands firm in the storm, demanding argument instead of illogical thunder; shows the hangmen and the people, too, outside the Elster gate at Wittenberg, that papal bulls will blaze as merrily as heretic scrolls."

Erasmus was a philosophical thinker; Luther a bold actor. The former would reform by the slow processes of education; the latter by revolution. " Without Erasmus," says Froude, " Luther would have been impossible ; and Erasmus really succeeded — so much of him as deserved to succeed — in Luther's victory." Erasmus said, " There is no hope for any good. It is all over with quiet learning, thought, piety, and progress ; violence is on one side and folly on the other ; and they accuse me of having caused it all. If I joined Luther I could only perish with him, and I do not mean to run my neck into the halter. Popes and emperors must decide matters. I will accept what is good, and do as I can with the rest. Peace on any terms is better than the justest war." Luther said, " I take Erasmus to be the worst enemy that Christ has had for a thousand years. Intellect does not understand religion, and when it comes to the things of God it laughs at them." " Whenever I pray," he said, " I pray for a curse upon Erasmus."

Melancthon was as different from Luther as Erasmus. He was the theologian of the three, — so much so that the scholars were all jealous of him. Sir Thomas More wrote to Erasmus that Tyndale had seen Melancthon in Paris; that Tyndale was afraid "if France should receive the word of God by him, it would be confirmed in the faith of the Eucharist contrary to the sect of the Wickliffites." Melancthon was not only the envied theologian, but he was the saintliest of all in character. He was amiable to a fault, and as timid and pure as a woman. When Melancthon arose to preach on one occasion, he took this for a text: "I am the good shepherd." In looking round upon his numerous and respectable audience, his natural timidity entirely overcame him, and he could only repeat the text over and over again. Luther, who was in the pulpit with him, at length impatiently exclaimed, " You are a very good sheep! " and telling him to sit down, took the same text, and preached an excellent discourse from it.

Coming down to later times, and to characters more purely literary, what could more beautifully illustrate the harmony of opposites, so often observable in literature and life, than the intimacy which existed between Professor Wilson and Dr. Blair? The course and habit of Dr. Blair's life " were like the smooth, deep water; serene, undisturbed to outer eye; and the very repose that was about him had a charm for the restless, active energy of his friend, who turned to this gentle and meek nature for mental rest. I have often seen them sitting together," says Mrs. Gordon, "in the quiet retirement of the study, perfectly absorbed in each other's presence, like school-boys in the abandonment of their love for each other, occupying one seat between them, my father, with his arm lovingly embracing 'the dear doctor's' shoulders, playfully pulling the somewhat silvered locks to draw his attention to something in the tome spread out on their knees, from which they were both reading. Such discussions as they had together hour upon hour! Shakespeare, Milton — always the loftiest themes — never weary in doing honor to the great souls from whom they had learnt so much. Their voices were different, too: Dr. Blair's soft and sweet as that of a woman; the professor's sonorous, sad, with a nervous tremor: each revealing the peculiar character of the man."

In the same character opposite faculties and qualities are sometimes so blended as to give very mysterious results. Every reader knows how difficult it often is to determine the irony or seriousness of Swift and De Foe, so very nicely they run together. Pure imagination is so realistic as to appear indubitable truth. Take De Foe's history of the Plague. What boy ever doubted the truth of Robinson Crusoe? or, while he was reading them, the adventures of Lemuel Gulliver, grotesque and extravagant as they are? You remember the story of the peasant and the Vicar of Wakefield. The dull rustic was a slow reader, and could get through but a few pages in a long evening; yet he was absorbed by the story, and read it as if it were a veritable history. A wag in the family, discerning the situation, thought to amuse himself by putting back the book-mark each morning nearly to the point the man had read from the previous evening, so that it turned out he was all winter getting through the little volume. When he had finished it, the wag asked him his opinion of it. He answered that it was good, — that he had no doubt every word of it was true, — but it did seem to him there was some repetition in it!

The author of Six Months at the White House relates an incident which illustrates how ignorance and superstition sometimes give birth to the sublimest eloquence. Colonel McKaye had been speaking of the ideas of power entertained by the poor negro slaves. He said they had an idea of God, as the Almighty, and they had realized in their former condition the power of their masters. Up to the time of the arrival among them of the Union forces, they had no knowledge of any other power. Their masters fled upon the approach of our soldiers, and this gave the negroes a conception of a power greater than that exercised by them. This power they called " Massa Linkum." Their place of worship was a large building which they called " the praise house; " and the leader of the meeting, a venerable black man, was known as " the praise man." On a certain day, when there was quite a large gathering of the people, considerable confusion was created by different persons attempting to tell who and what " Massa Linkum " was. In the midst of the excitement the white-headed leader commanded silence. " Brederin," said he, " you don't know nosein' what you 're talkin' 'bout. Now, you just listen to me. Massa Linkum, he eberywhar. He know eberyting." Then, solemnly looking up, he added, " He walk de earf like de Lord ! "

Curran, who was so merry and charming in conversation, was also very melancholy. He said he never went to bed in Ireland without wishing not to rise again. It seems to be a law of our nature that " as high as we have mounted in delight, in our dejection do we sink as low." Burns expresses it, " Chords that vibrate sweetest pleasure thrill the deepest notes of woe ; " and Hood, " There 's not a string attuned to mirth, but has its chord in melancholy ; " and Burton, " Naught so sweet as melancholy," naught " so damned as melancholy ; " and King Solomon, " I said of laughter that it is mad."

It is narrated that one day Philip III., King of Spain, was standing in one of the balconies of his palace observing a young Spanish student, who was sitting in the sun and reading a book, while he was bursting out into fits of laughter. The further the student read, the more his gayety increased, until at last he was so violently excited that he let the book fall from his hands, and rolled on the ground in a state of intense hilarity. The king turned to his courtiers and said, " That young man is either mad, or he is reading Don Quixote." One of the guards of the palace went to pick up the book, and found that his majesty had guessed rightly. Yet Miguel Cervantes, the author of this book which is so amusing, had dragged on the most wretched and melancholy existence. He was groaning and weeping while all Spain was laughing at the numerous adventures of the Knight of La Mancha and the wise sayings of Sancho Panza.

The biographer of Grimaldi speaks of the devouring melancholy which pursued the celebrated actor whenever he was off the stage, or left to his own resources; and it is well known that Liston, whose face was sufficient to set an audience in a good humor, was a confirmed hypochondriac. It is said he used to sit up after midnight to read Young's Night Thoughts, delighting in its monotonous solemnity.

"The gravest nations," says Landor, "have been the wittiest; and in those nations some of the gravest men. In England, Swift and Addison; in Spain, Cervantes. Rabelais and La Fontaine are recorded by their countrymen to have been *rêveurs*. Few men have been graver than Pascal; few have been wittier." Robert Chambers tells in one of his essays of a person residing near London, who could make one's sides ache at any time with his comic songs, yet had so rueful, woe-begone a face that his friends addressed him by the name of Mr. Dismal. Nothing remains of Butler's private history but the record of his miseries; and Swift, we are told, was never known to smile. Burns confessed in one of his letters that his design in seeking society was to fly from constitutional melancholy. "Even in the hour of social mirth," he tells us, "my gayety is the madness of an intoxicated criminal under the hands of the executioner." The most facetious of all Lamb's letters was written to Barton in a fit of the deepest melancholy.

Jerrold, it has been said, was a little ashamed of

the immense success of the Caudle Lectures, which,
as social drolleries, set nations laughing. He took
their celebrity rather sulkily. He did not like to be
talked of as a funny man. His mixture of satire
and kindliness reminded one of his friends of those
lanes near Beyrout, in which you ride with the prickly-
pear bristling alongside of you, and yet can pluck the
grapes which force themselves among it from the
fields.

There is an account of a singer and his wife who
were to sing a number of humorous couplets at a restaurant in Leipsic. The wife made her appearance
there at the appointed hour, but, owing to the unex-
plained absence of her husband, she was compelled
to amuse the visitors by singing couplets alone.
While her droll performance was eliciting shouts of
laughter, her husband hung himself in the court-yard
of the restaurant.

Some one said to Dr. Johnson that it seemed strange
that he, who so often delighted his company by his
lively conversation, should say he was miserable,
" Alas ! it is all outside," replied the sage ; " I may
be cracking my joke and cursing the sun : sun, how
I hate thy beams ! " " Are we to think Pope was
happy," said he, on another occasion, " because he
says so in his writings ? We see in his writings
what he wished the state of his mind to appear. Dr.
Young, who pined for preferment, talks with contempt of it in his writings, and affects to despise everything he did not despise." The author of John
Gilpin said of himself and his humorous poetry,
" Strange as it may seem, the most ludicrous lines I

ever wrote have been when in the saddest mood, and but for that saddest mood, perhaps, would never have been written at all." Sir Walter Scott, in the height of his ill fortune, was ever giving vent in his diary or elsewhere to some whimsical outburst or humorous sally, and after an extra gay entry in his journal just before leaving his dingy Edinburgh lodgings for Abbotsford, he follows it up next day with this bit of self-portraiture : " Anybody would think from the fal-de-ral conclusion of my journal of yesterday that I left town in a very good humor. But nature has given me a kind of buoyancy — I know not what to call it — that mingles with my deepest afflictions and most gloomy hours. I have a secret pride — I fancy it will be most truly termed — which impels me to mix with my distress strange snatches of mirth which have no mirth in them."

" There have been times in my life," said Goethe, " when I have fallen asleep in tears ; but in my dreams the most charming forms have come to console and to cheer me."

We are told that after Scott began the Bride of Lammermoor, he had one of his terrible seizures of cramp, yet during his torment he dictated that fine novel ; and when he rose from his bed, and the published book was placed in his hands, " he did not," James Ballantyne explicitly assured Lockhart, " recollect one single incident, character, or conversation it contained."

Jean Paul wrote a great part of his comic romance (Nicholas Margraf) in an agony of heart-break from the death of his promising son Max. He could not,

one of his biographers says, bear the sight of any
book his son had touched; and the word philology
(the science in which Max excelled) went through
his heart like a bolt of ice. He had such wonderful
power over himself as to go on with his comic romance while his eyes continually dropped tears. He
wept so much in secret that his eyes became impaired,
and he trembled for the total loss of sight. Wine,
that had previously, after long-sustained labor, been
a cordial to him, he could not bear to touch ; and after
employing the morning in writing, he spent the whole
afternoon lying on the sofa in his wife's apartment,
his head supported by her arm.

Washington Irving completed that most extrava-
gantly humorous of all his works — the History of
New York — while he was suffering from the death
of his sweetheart, Matilda Hoffman, which nearly
broke his heart. He says, in a memorandum found
amongst his private papers after his death, " She was
but about seventeen years old when she died. I cannot tell what a horrid state of mind I was in for a
long time. I seemed to care for nothing ; the world
was a blank to me. I went into the country, but
could not bear solitude, yet could not enjoy society.
There was a dismal horror continually in my mind,
that made me fear to be alone. I had often to get
up in the night, and seek the bedroom of my brother,
as if the having a human being by me would relieve
me from the frightful gloom of my own thoughts.
. . . . When I became more calm and collected, I applied myself, by way of occupation, to the finishing
of my work. I brought it to a close, as well as I

could, and published it; but the time and circumstances in which it was produced rendered me almost unable to look upon it with satisfaction. Still it took with the public, and gave me celebrity, as an original work was something remarkable and uncommon in America. . . . . I seemed to drift about without aim or object, at the mercy of every breeze; my heart wanted anchorage. I was naturally susceptible, and tried to form other attachments, but my heart would not hold on; it would continually roam to what it had lost; and whenever there was a pause in the hurry of novelty and excitement, I would sink into dismal dejection. For years I could not talk on the subject of this hopeless regret; I could not even mention her name; but her image was continually before me, and I dreamt of her incessantly."

Many of Hood's most humorous productions were dictated to his wife, while he himself was in bed, from distressing and protracted sickness. His own family was the only one which was not delighted with the Comic Annual, so well thumbed in every house. "We, ourselves," writes his son, "did not enjoy it till the lapse of many years had mercifully softened down some of the sad recollections connected with it." Fun and suffering seemed to be natural to him, and to be constantly helping each other. When a boy, he drew the figure of a demon with the smoke of a candle on the staircase ceiling near his bed room door, to frighten his brother. Unfortunately he forgot that he had done so, and, when he went to bed, succeeded in terrifying himself into fits almost — while his brother had not observed the picture. Joke

he would, suffering as he might be. It is recorded of
him, that upon a mustard plaster being applied to his
attenuated feet, as he lay in the direst extremity, he
was heard feebly to remark that there was "very
little meat for the mustard." But if his wit was
marvelous, so was his pathos — tender beyond comparison. His first child scarcely survived its birth.
" In looking over some old papers," says his son, " I
found a few tiny curls of golden hair, as soft as the
finest silk, wrapped in a yellow and time-worn paper,
inscribed in my father's handwriting : —

> " ' Little eyes that scarce did see,
> Little lips that never smiled ;
> Alas ! my little dear dead child,
> Death is thy father, and not me;
> I but embraced thee soon as he ! ' "

Here are a few sentences from the long letters
which the author of the Bridge of Sighs wrote to the
children of his friend, Dr. Elliot, then residing at
Sandgate, almost from his death-bed : " My dear
Jeanie, — So you are at Sandgate ! Of course,
wishing for your old playfellow to help you to make
little puddles in the sand, and swing on the gate.
But perhaps there are no sand and gate at Sandgate,
which, in that case, nominally tells us a fib. I
have heard that you bathe in the sea, which is very
refreshing, but it requires care ; for if you stay under
water too long, you may come up a mermaid, who is
only half a lady, with a fish's tail—which she can
boil if she likes. You had better try this with your
doll, whether it turns her into half a ' doll-fin.' . . . .
I hope you like the sea. I always did when I was a

child, which was about two years ago. Sometimes it
makes such a fizzing and foaming, I wonder some of
our London cheats do not bottle it up, and sell it for
ginger-pop. When the sea is too rough, if you pour
the sweet oil out of the cruet *all over it*, and wait for
a calm, it will be quite smooth — much smoother than
a dressed salad. . . . . Do you ever see any boats or
vessels? And don't you wish, when you see a ship,
that somebody was a sea-captain instead of a doctor,
that he might bring you home a pet lion, or calf-
elephant, ever so many parrots, or a monkey from
foreign parts? I knew a little girl who was promised
a baby-whale by her sailor-brother, and who *blubbered*
because he did not bring it. I suppose there are no
whales at Sandgate, but you might find a seal about
the beach; or at least a stone for one. The sea-stones
are not pretty when they are dry, but look beautiful
when they are wet — and we can *always* keep sucking
them!" To Jeanie's brother, among other things he
writes, "I used to catch flat-fish with a very long
string line. It was like swimming a kite. Once I
caught a plaice, and seeing it all over red spots, thought
I had caught the measles." To Mary Elliot, a still
more youthful correspondent, he says, "I remember
that when I saw the sea, it used sometimes to be very
fussy and fidgety, and did not always wash itself quite
clean; but it was very fond of fun. Have the waves
ever run after you yet, and turned your little two
shoes into pumps, full of water? Have you been
bathed yet in the sea, and were you afraid? I was
the first time, and the time before that; and, dear
me, how I kicked and screamed — or, at least, meant

to scream; but the sea, ships and all, began to run into my mouth, and so I shut it up. I think I see you being dipped into the sea, screwing your eyes up, and putting your nose, like a button, into your mouth, like a button-hole, for fear of getting another smell and taste. Did you ever try, like a little crab, to run two ways at once? See if you can do it, for it is good fun; never mind tumbling over yourself a little at first. . . . . And now good-by; Fanny has made my tea, and I must drink it before it gets too hot, as we *all* were last Sunday week. They say the glass was eighty-eight in the shade, which is a great age. The last fair breeze I blew dozens of kisses for you, but the wind changed, and, I am afraid, took them all to Miss H——, or somebody that it should n't."

You remember the anecdote Southey repeats in his Doctor, of a physician who, being called in to an unknown patient, found him suffering under the deepest depression of mind, without any discoverable disease, or other assignable cause. The physician advised him to seek for cheerful objects, and recommended him especially to go to the theatre and see a famous actor then in the meridian of his powers, whose comic talents were unrivaled. Alas! the comedian who kept crowded theatres in a roar was this poor hypochondriac himself!

XII.

CONDUCT.

HAZLITT, in one of his discursive essays, says, "I stopped these two days at Bridgewater, and when I was tired of sauntering on the banks of its muddy river, returned to the inn and read Camilla. So have I loitered my life away, reading books, looking at pictures, going to plays, hearing, thinking, writing on what pleased me best. I have wanted only one thing to make me happy; but wanting that, have wanted everything." Alas, who has not wanted one thing? Fortunatus had a cap, which when he put on, and wished himself anywhere, behold he was there. Aladdin had a lamp, which if he rubbed, and desired anything, immediately it was his. If we each had both, there would still be something wanting — one thing more. Donatello's matchless statue of St. George "wanted one thing," in the opinion of Michel Angelo; it wanted "the gift of speech." The poor widow in Holland that Pepys tells us about in his Diary, who survived twenty-five husbands, wanted one thing more, no doubt — perhaps one more husband. We never are, but always to be, blest. "A child," said the good Berthold Sachs, "thinks the stars blossom on the trees; when he climbs to the tree-tops, he fancies they cluster on the spire; when

21

he climbs the spire, he finds, to reach them, he must leave the earth and go to heaven." There is an old German engraving, in the manner of Holbein, which represents an aged man near a grave, wringing his hands. Death, behind, directs his attention to heaven. What we have is nothing, what we want, everything. "All worldly things," says Baxter, "appear most vain and unsatisfactory, when we have tried them most." The prize we struggled for, which filled our imagination, when attained was not much; worthless in grasp, priceless in expectation. The one thing we want is one thing we have not — that we have not had.

> "I saw the little boy;
>   I thought how oft that he
> Did wish of God, to scape the rod,
>   A tall young man to be.
>
> "The young man eke that feels
>   His bones with pain opprest,
> How he would be a rich old man,
>   To live and lie at rest.
>
> "The rich old man that sees
>   His end draw on so sore,
> How he would be a boy again,
>   To live so much the more."

This hunger, this hope, this longing, is our best possession at last, and fades not away, unsubstantial as it may seem. It builds for each one of us magnificent castles. "All the years of our youth and the hopes of our manhood are stored away, like precious stones, in the vaults; and we know that we shall find everything convenient, elegant, and splendid, when

we come into possession." Curtis, in one of his exquisite sketches, treats this element of us as no other
author has. He calls it his Spanish property. " I
am the owner," he says, " of great estates ; but the
greater part are in Spain. It is a country famously
romantic, and my castles are all of perfect proportions,
and appropriately set in the most picturesque situations. I have never been to Spain myself, but I have,
naturally, conversed much with travelers to that
country, although, I must allow, without deriving
from them much substantial information about my
property there. The wisest of them told me that
there were more holders of real estate in Spain than
in any other region he had ever heard of, and they
are all great proprietors. Every one of them pos-
sesses a multitude of the stateliest castles. From conversation with them you easily gather that each one
considers his own castles much the largest and in the
loveliest positions. . . . . It is remarkable that none
of the proprietors have ever been to Spain to take
possession and report to the rest of us the state of
our property there. I, of course, cannot go, I am too
much engaged. So is Titbottom. And I find that
it is the case with all the proprietors. We have so
much to detain us at home that we cannot get away.
It is always so with rich men. . . . . It is not easy
for me to say how I know so much as I certainly
do about my castles in Spain. The sun always shines
upon them. They stand large and fair in a luminous,
golden atmosphere, a little hazy and dreamy, perhaps,
like the Indian summer, but in which no gales blow
and there are no tempests. All the sublime mount-

ains, and beautiful valleys, and soft landscapes, that I have not yet seen, are to be found in the grounds. They command a noble view of the Alps ; so fine, indeed, that I should be quite content with the prospect of them from the highest tower of my castle, and not care to go to Switzerland. The neighboring ruins, too, are as picturesque as those of Italy, and my desire of standing in the Coliseum and of seeing the shattered arches of the aqueducts, stretching along the Campagna and melting into the Alban Mount, is entirely quenched. The rich gloom of my orange groves is gilded by fruit as brilliant of complexion and exquisite of flavor as any that ever dark-eyed Sorrento girls, looking over the high plastered walls of Southern Italy, hand to the youthful travelers, climbing on donkeys up the narrow lane beneath. The Nile flows through my grounds. The Desert lies upon their edge, and Damascus stands in my garden. I am given to understand, also, that the Parthenon has been removed to my Spanish possessions. The Golden Horn is my fish-preserve ; my flocks of golden fleece are pastured on the plain of Marathon, and the honey of Hymettus is distilled from the flowers that grow in the vale of Enna — all in my Spanish domains. From the windows of these castles look the beautiful women whom I have never seen, whose portraits the poets have painted. They wait for me there, and chiefly the fair-haired child, lost to my eye so long ago, now bloomed into an impossible beauty. The lights that never shone glance at evening in the vaulted halls, upon banquets that were never spread. The bands I have never collected play all night long, and enchant the brill-

iant company, that was never assembled, into silence.
In the long summer mornings the children that I
never had, play in the gardens that I never planted.
. . . . I have often wondered how I shall ever reach
my castles. The desire of going comes over me very
strongly sometimes, and I endeavor to see how I can
arrange my affairs so as to get away. To tell the
truth, I am not quite sure of the route, — I mean, to
that particular part of Spain in which my estates lie.
I have inquired very particularly, but nobody seems
to know precisely. . . . . 'Will you tell me what
you consider the shortest and safest route thither,
Mr. Bourne? for, of course, a man who drives such
an immense trade with all parts of the world will
know all that I have come to inquire.' 'My dear
sir,' answered he, wearily, 'I have been trying, all
my life, to discover it; but none of my ships have
ever been there — none of my captains have any report to make. They bring me, as they brought my
father, gold-dust from Guinea; ivory, pearls, and
precious stones from every part of the earth; but not
a fruit, not a solitary flower, from one of my castles
in Spain. I have sent clerks, agents, and travelers
of all kinds; philosophers, pleasure-hunters, and in-
valids, in all sorts of ships, to all sorts of places,
but none of them ever saw or heard of my castles,
except one young poet, and he died in a mad-house.'
. . . . At length I resolved to ask Titbottom if he
had ever heard of the best route to our estates. He
said that he owned castles, and sometimes there was
an expression in his face as if he saw them. . . . .
'I have never known but two men who reached

their estates in Spain.' 'Indeed,' said I, 'how did
they go?' 'One went over the side of a ship, and
the other out of a third story window,' answered
Titbottom. 'And I know one man that resides upon
his estates constantly,' continued he. 'Who is that?'
'Our old friend Slug, whom you may see any day
at the asylum, just coming in from the hunt, or
going to call upon his friend the Grand Lama, or
dressing for the wedding of the Man in the Moon,
or receiving an embassador from Timbuctoo. Whenever I go to see him, Slug insists that I am the
pope, disguised as a journeyman carpenter, and he
entertains me in the most distinguished manner. He
always insists upon kissing my foot, and I bestow
upon him, kneeling, the apostolic benediction. This
is the only Spanish proprietor in possession, with
whom I am acquainted.' .... Ah! if the true
history of Spain could be written, what a book were
there!"

"Gayly bedight,
    A gallant knight,
In sunshine and in shadow,
    Had journeyed long,
    Singing a song,
In search of Eldorado.

"But he grew old,
    This knight so bold,
And o'er his heart a shadow
    Fell as he found
    No spot of ground
That looked like Eldorado.

"And as his strength
    Failed him at length,

He met a pilgrim shadow :
'Shadow,' said he,
'Where can it be —
This land of Eldorado ? '

" ' Over the mountains
Of the moon,
Down the valley of shadow,
Ride, boldly ride,'
The shade replied,
' If you seek for Eldorado I ' "

Steele, in a paper of The Spectator, dilates in this vein. " I am," he says, " one of that species of men who are properly denominated castle-builders, who scorn to be beholden to the earth for a foundation, or dig in the bowels of it for materials ; but erect their structures in the most unstable of elements, the air ; fancy alone laying the line, marking the extent, and shaping the model. It would be difficult to enumerate what august palaces and stately porticoes have grown under my forming imagination, or what verdant meadows and shady groves have started into being by the powerful feat of a warm fancy. A castle-builder is ever just what he pleases, and as such I have grasped imaginary sceptres, and delivered uncontrollable edicts, from a throne to which conquered nations yielded obeisance. There is no art or profession, whose most celebrated masters I have not eclipsed. Wherever I have afforded my salutary presence, fevers have ceased to burn and agues to shake the human fabric. When an eloquent fit has been upon me, an apt gesture and proper cadence has animated each sentence, and gazing crowds have found their passions worked up into a rage, or soothed into a calm. I am short, and not very well made; yet upon sight of a fine woman, I have stretched into proper stature, and killed with a good air and mien. These are the gay phantoms that dance before my waking eyes, and compose my day-dreams. I should be the most contented happy man alive, were the chimerical happiness which springs from the paintings of fancy less fleeting and transitory. But alas! it is with grief of mind I tell you, the least breath of wind has often demolished my magnificent edifices, swept away my groves, and left no more trace of them than if they had never been. My exchequer has sunk and vanished by a rap on my door, the salutation of a friend has cost me a whole continent, and in the same moment I have been pulled by the sleeve, my crown has fallen from my head. The ill consequence of these reveries is inconceivably great, seeing the loss of imaginary possessions makes impressions of real woe. Besides, bad economy is visible and apparent in builders of invisible mansions. My tenants' advertisements of ruins and dilapidations often cast a damp on my spirits, even in the instant when the sun, in all his splendor, gilds my Eastern palaces."

"When I look around me," said Goethe, "and see how few of the companions of earlier years are left to me, I think of a summer residence at a bathing-place. When you arrive, you first become acquainted with those who have already been there some weeks, and who leave you in a few days. This separation is painful. Then you turn to the second generation, with which you live a good while, and become really intimate. But this goes also, and leaves us lonely with the third, which comes just as we are going away, and with which we have, properly, nothing to do. . . . . I have ever been considered one of Fortune's chiefest favorites; nor can I complain of the course my life has taken. Yet, truly, there has been nothing but toil and care; and in my seventy-fifth year, I may say that I have never had four weeks of genuine pleasure. The stone was ever to be rolled up anew."

, "What a multitude of past friends can I number amongst the dead!" exclaimed another venerable worthy in literature. "It is the melancholy consequence of old age; if we outlive our feelings we are nothing worth; if they remain in force, a thousand sad occurrences remind us that we live too long." It was Sir William Temple's opinion that "life is like wine; who would drink it pure must not draw it to the dregs." Dr. Sherlock thought "the greatest part of mankind have great reason to be contented with the shortness of life, because they have no temptation to wish it longer."

The following authentic memorial was found in the closet of the most illustrious of the caliphs, after his decease, who, during his life, enjoyed thousands of wives, millions upon millions of wealth, and was the object of universal admiration and envy: "I have now reigned above fifty years in victory or peace; beloved by my subjects, dreaded by my enemies, and respected by my allies. Riches and honor, power and pleasure, have waited on my call, nor does any earthly blessing appear to have been wanting to my felicity. In this situation I have diligently numbered the days of pure and genuine happiness which have fallen to my lot : they amount to fourteen. O man, place not thy confidence in this present world!"

Voltaire makes Candide sit down to supper at Venice with six strangers who were staying at the same hotel with himself, and as the servants, to his astonishment, addressed each of them by the title of "your majesty," he asked for an explanation of the pleasantry. "I am not jesting," said the first, "I am Achmet III.; I was sultan several years; I dethroned my brother, and my nephew dethroned me. They have cut off the heads of my viziers; I shall pass the remainder of my days in the old seraglio; my nephew, the Sultan Mahmoud, sometimes permits me to travel for my health, and I have come to pass the Carnival at Venice." A young man who was close to Achmet spoke next, and said, "My name is Ivan; I have been Emperor of all the Russias; I was dethroned when I was in my cradle; my father and my mother have been incarcerated; I was brought up in prison; I have sometimes permission to travel, attended by my keepers, and I have come to pass the Carnival at Venice." The third said, "I am Charles Edward, King of England; my father has surrendered his rights to me; I have fought to sustain them; my vanquishers have torn out the hearts of eight hundred of my partisans; I have been put into prison; I am going to Rome to pay a visit to my father, dethroned like my grandfather and myself, and I have come to pass the Carnival at Venice." The fourth then spoke, and said, "I am King of Poland; the fortune of war has deprived me of my hereditary states; my father experienced the same reverses; I resign myself to the will of Providence, like the Sultan Achmet, the Emperor Ivan, and the King Charles Edward, to whom God grant a long life; and I have come to pass the Carnival at Venice." The fifth said, " I am also King of Poland ; I have lost my kingdom twice, but Providence has given me another in which I have done more good than all the kings of Sarmatia put together have ever done on the banks of the Vistula. I also resign myself to the will of Providence, and I have come to pass the Carnival at Venice." There remained a sixth monarch to speak. " Gentlemen," he said, " I am not as great a sovereign as the rest, but I, too, have been a king. I am Theodore, who was elected King of Corsica; I was called ' your majesty,' and at present am hardly called ' sir ;' I have caused money to be coined, and do not now possess a penny ; I have had two secretaries of state, and have now scarcely a servant ; I have sat upon a throne, and was long in a prison in London, upon straw, and am afraid of being treated in the same manner here, although I have come, like your majesties, to pass the Carnival at Venice." The other five kings heard this confession with a noble compassion. Each of them gave King Theodore twenty sequins to buy some clothes and shirts. Candide presented him with a diamond worth two thousand sequins. " Who," said the five kings, " is this man who can afford to give a hundred times as much as any of us ? Are you, sir, also a king ? " " No, your majesties, and I have no desire to be."

Bacon's contemporary and cousin, Sir Robert Cecil, who was principal secretary of state to Queen Elizabeth and James I., and ultimately lord high treasurer, when he was acknowledged to be the ablest, as he appeared the most enviable, statesman of his time, wrote to a friend, " Give heed to one that hath sorrowed in the bright lustre of a court and gone heavily over the best seeming fair ground. It is a great task to prove one's honesty, and yet not spoil one's fortune. . . . . I am pushed from the shore of comfort, and know not where the winds and waves of a court will bear me ; I know it bringeth little comfort on earth ; and he is, I reckon, no wise man that looketh this way to heaven." Bacon himself says, in one of his Essays, " Certainly great persons have need to borrow other men's opinions to think themselves happy ; for if they judge by their own feeling they cannot find it ; but if they think with themselves what others think of them, and that other men would fain be as they are, then they are happy as it were by report, when, perhaps, they find the contrary within ; for they are the first that find their own griefs, though they be the last that find their own faults."

Madame de Staël, surrounded by the most brilliant men of genius, beloved by a host of faithful and devoted friends, the centre of a circle of unsurpassed attractions, was yet doomed to mourn " the solitude of life." A short time before her death, she said to Chateaubriand, " I am now what I have always been — lively and sad."

The illustrious Madame Récamier, "after forty years of unchallenged queenship in French society, constantly enveloped in an intoxicating incense of admiration and love won not less by her goodness and purity than by her beauty and grace," writes thus from Dieppe to her niece: " I am here in the centre of fêtes, princesses, illuminations, spectacles. Two of my windows face the ball-room, the other two front the theatre. Amidst this clatter I am in a perfect solitude. I sit and muse on the shore of the ocean. I go over all the sad and joyous circumstances of my life. I hope you will be more happy than I have been."

Madame de Pompadour, recalling her follies, serious matters they were to her, said to the Prince de Soubise, " It is like reading a strange book ; my life is an improbable romance ; I do not believe it." " Gray hairs," to quote Thackeray, " had come on like daylight streaming in, — daylight and a headache with it. Pleasure had gone to bed with the rouge on her cheeks."

" Ah ! " wrote also Madame de Maintenon to her niece, " alas that I cannot give you my experience ; that I could only show you the weariness of soul by which the great are devoured — the difficulty which they find in getting through their days ! Do you not see how they die of sadness in the midst of that fortune which has been a burden to them ? I have been young and beautiful ; I have tasted many pleasures ; I have been universally beloved. At a more advanced age, I have passed years in the intercourse of talent and wit, and I solemnly protest to you that all conditions leave a frightful void."

Coleridge sums up all more wisely. " I have

known," he says, " what the enjoyments and ad-
vantages of this life are, and what the more refined
pleasures which learning and intellectual power can
bestow ; and with all the experience that more than
three-score years can give, I now, on the eve of my
departure, declare to you that health is a great blessing, — competence obtained by honorable industry a
great blessing, — and a great blessing it is to have
kind, faithful, and loving friends and relatives ; but
that the greatest of all blessings, as it is the most en-
nobling of all privileges, is to be indeed a Christian."

" We are born and we live so unhappily that the
accomplishment of a desire appears to us a falsehood,
the realization of hope a deception, as if our sad experience had taught us the bitter lesson that in the
world nothing is true but sorrow." " Who ordered
toil," said Thackeray, " as the condition of life, ordered weariness, ordered sickness, ordered poverty,
failure, success, — to this man a foremost place, to the
other a nameless struggle with the crowd ; to that a
shameful fall, or paralyzed limb, or sudden accident ;
to each some work upon the ground he stands on,
until he is laid beneath it." "Nature," says Pliny,
" makes us buy her presents at the price of so many
sufferings, that it is dubious whether she deserves
most the name of a parent or a step-mother." " Solomon and Job judged the best and spake the truest,"
thought Pascal, "of human misery ; the former the
most happy, the latter the most unfortunate of mankind ; the one acquainted by long experience with the
vanity of pleasure, the other with the reality of affliction and pain."

"Let a man examine his own thoughts," said the same profound Christian philosopher, "and he will always find them employed about the time past or to come. We scarce bestow a glance upon the present; or, if we do, 't is only to borrow light from hence to manage and direct the future. The present is never the mark of our designs. We use both past and present as our means and instruments, but the future only as our object and aim. Thus we never live, but we ever hope to live; and under this continual disposition and preparation to happiness, 't is certain we can never be actually happy, if our hopes are terminated with the scene of this life."

The Thracians, according to Pliny, estimated their lives mathematically, making careful study and count of each day before any event of it was forgotten. "Every day they put into an urn either a black or a white pebble, to denote the good or bad fortune of that day; at last they separated these pebbles, and upon comparing the two numbers together, they formed their judgment of the whole of their lives." But time, past or present, — time, what is it? " Who can readily and briefly explain this?" inquired St. Augustine. " Who can even in thought comprehend it, so as to utter a word about it? But what in discourse do we mention more familiarly and knowingly, than time? And we understand, when we speak of it; we understand, also, when we hear it spoken of by another. What then is time? If no one asks me, I know; if I explain it to one that asketh, I know not; yet I say boldly, that I know that if nothing passed away, time passed were not; and if nothing were coming, a time to come were not; and if nothing were, time present were not. Those two times then, past and to come, how are they, seeing the past now is not, and that to come is not yet? But the present, should it always be present, and never pass into time past, verily it should not be time, but eternity. If, therefore, time present, in order to be time at all, comes into existence only because it passes into time past, how can we say that that is in existence, whose cause of being is that it shall not be? How is it that we cannot truly say that time is, but because it is tending not to be?" Comprehend this, and you see how easy a thing it was for the Thracians to "form a judgment of the whole of their lives" — to strike a nice balance between their happiness and misery.

But happiness is as illusive as time, and is proved as perspicuously to be but a thing of memory, by the same venerable saint. "Where, then, and when," he says in his famous Confessions, "did I experience my happy life, that I should remember and love and long for it? Nor is it I alone, or some few besides, but we all would fain be happy; which, unless by some certain knowledge we knew, we should not with so certain a will desire. But how is this, that if two men be asked whether they would go to the wars, one, perchance, would answer that he would, the other that he would not; but if they were asked whether they would be happy, both would instantly, without any doubting, say they would; and for no other reason would the one go to the wars, and the other not, but to be happy. Is it, perchance, that as one looks for his joy in this thing, another in that, all agree in their desire of being happy, as they would agree, if they were asked, that they wished to have joy, and this joy they call a happy life? Although, then, one obtains the joy by one means, another by another, all have one end, which they strive to attain, namely, joy. Which being a thing which all must say they have experienced, it is, therefore, found in the memory, and recognized whenever the name of a happy life is mentioned." Now do you know, perhaps, what happiness is.

Coming down from Augustine to Helps, — "The wonder is that we live on from day to day learning so little the art of life. We are constantly victims of every sort of worry and petty misery, which it would seem a little bit of reflection and sensible conduct would remove. We constantly hang together when association only produces unhappiness. We know it, but do not remedy it. . . . . We have no right to expect to meet many sympathetic people in the course of our lives. ["To get human beings together who ought to be together," said Sydney Smith, "is a dream."] . . . . The pleasant man to you is the man you can rely upon; who is tolerant, forbearing, and faithful. . . . . Again, the habit of over-criticism is another hinderance to pleasantness. We are not fond of living always with our judges; and daily life will not bear the unwholesome scrutiny of an over-critical person." The petty annoyances and wanton bitternesses of life make us, in our impatience, sometimes wish to fly from all companionship; they contributed, no doubt, — he himself could

22

not tell how much, — to make the author of the
Genius of Solitude exclaim, with so much feeling,
" Happy is he who, free from the iron visages that
hurt him as they pass in the street, free from the
vapid smiles and sneers of frivolous people, draws his
sufficingness from inexhaustible sources always at his
command when he is alone. Blest is he who, when
disappointed, can turn from the affectations of an
empty world and find solace in the generous sinceri-
ties of a full heart. To roam apart by the tinkling
rill, to crouch in the grass where the crocus grows, to
lie amid the clover where the honey-bee hums, gaze
off into the still deeps of summer blue, and feel that
your harmless life is gliding over the field of time as
noiselessly as the shadow of a cloud ; or, snuggled in
furs, to trudge through the drifts amidst the un-
spotted scenery of winter, when storm unfurls his
dark banner in the sky, and snow has camped on the
hills and clad every stone and twig with his ermine,
is pleasure surpassing any to be won in shallowly con-
sorting with mobs of men."

" The longer I live," said Maurice de Guérin,
" and the clearer I discern between true and false in
society, the more does the inclination to live, not as a
savage or a misanthrope, but as a solitary man on the
frontiers of society, on the outskirts of the world,
gain strength and grow in me. The birds come and
go, and make nests around our habitations ; they are
fellow-citizens of our farms and hamlets with us : but
they take their flight in a heaven which is boundless ;
but the hand of God alone gives and measures to
them their daily food ; but they build their nests in

the heart of the thick bushes, and hang them in the height of the trees. So would I, too, live, hovering round society, and having always at my back a field of liberty vast as the sky."

A strange instance of abandonment of the world for a solitary life is given in the history of Henry Welby, the Hermit of Grub Street, who died in 1638, at the age of eighty-four. This example affords " an eccentric illustration of one of those phases of human nature out of which the anchoretic life has sprung. When forty years old, Welby was assailed, in a moment of anger, by a younger brother with a loaded pistol. It flashed in the pan. ' Thinking of the danger he had escaped, he fell into many deep considerations, on the which he grounded an irrevocable resolution to live alone.' He had wealth and position, and was of a social temper ; but the shock he had undergone had made him distrustful and meditative, not malignant nor wretched, and engendered in him a purpose of surprising tenacity. He had three chambers, one within another, prepared for his solitude ; the first for his diet, the second for his lodging, the third for his study. While his food was set on the table by one of his servants, he retired into his sleeping-room ; and, while his bed was making, into his study ; and so on, until all was clear. ' There he set up his rest, and, in forty-four years, never upon any occasion issued out of those chambers till he was borne thence upon men's shoulders. Neither, in all that time, did any human being — save, on some rare necessity, his ancient maid-servant — look upon his face.' Supplied with the best new books in various

languages, he devoted himself unto prayers and reading. He inquired out objects of charity and sent
them relief. He would spy from his chamber, by a
private prospect into the street, any sick, lame, or
weak passing by, and send comforts and money to
them. ' His hair, by reason no barber came near
him for the space of so many years, was so much
overgrown at the time of his death, that he appeared
rather like an eremite of the wilderness than an in-
habitant of a city.' "

Welby must have possessed the jewel which this
incident, related by Izaak Walton in his Angler, discovers to be so indispensable. " I knew a man," he
says, " that had health and riches and several houses,
all beautiful and ready furnished, and would often
trouble himself and family to be removing from one
house to another : and, being asked by a friend why
he removed so often from one house to another, replied, ' It was to find content in some one of them.'
' Content,' said his friend, ' ever dwells in a meek and
quiet soul.' "

> " It 's no in titles nor in rank ;
> It 's no in wealth, like Lon'on bank,
>   To purchase peace and rest ;
> It 's no in making muckle mair:
> It 's no in books ; it 's no in lear,
>   To make us truly blest :
> If happiness ha'e not her seat
>   And centre in the breast,
> We may be wise, or rich, or great,
>   But never can be blest:
> Nae treasures, nor pleasures,
>   Could make us happy lang;
> The heart ay 's the part ay,
>   That makes us right or wrang."

" Out of mud springs the lotus flower ; out of clay comes gold and many precious things; out of oysters the pearls ; brightest silks, to robe fairest forms, are spun by a worm ; bezoar from the bull, musk from the deer, are produced ; from a stick is born flame ; from the jungle comes sweetest honey. As from sources of little worth come the precious things of earth, even so is it with hearts that hold their fortune within. They need not lofty birth or noble kin. Their victory is recorded."

" By two things," says the author of the Imitation, " a man is lifted up from things earthly, namely, by simplicity and purity. A pure heart penetrateth heaven and hell. Such as every one is inwardly, so he judgeth outwardly. If there be joy in the world, surely a man of a pure heart possesseth it. . . . . Let not thy peace depend on the tongues of·men ; for whether they judge well of thee or ill, thou art not on that account other than thyself. He that careth not to please men, nor feareth to displease them, shall enjoy much peace. . . . . He enjoyeth great tranquillity of heart, that careth neither for the praise nor dispraise of men. If thou consider what thou art in thyself, thou wilt not care what men say of thee. Man looketh on the countenance, but God on the heart. Man considereth the deeds, but God weigheth the intentions." " One night, Gabriel, from his seat in paradise, heard the voice of God sweetly responding to a human heart. The angel said, ' Surely this must be an eminent servant of the Most High, whose spirit is dead to lust and lives on high.' The angel hastened over land and sea to find this man, but could not find him in the earth or heavens. At last he exclaimed, ' O Lord, show me the way to the object of thy love!' God answered, 'Turn thy steps to yon village, and in that pagoda thou shalt behold him.' The angel sped to the pagoda, and therein found a solitary man kneeling before an idol. Returning, he cried, ' O master of the world! hast thou looked with love on a man who invokes an idol in a pagoda?' God said, ' I consider not the error of ignorance: this heart, amid its darkness, hath the highest place.'"

Anaxagoras, whose disciples were Socrates, and Pericles, and Euripides, in reply to a question, said he believed those to be most happy who seem least to be so; and that we must not look among the rich and great for persons who taste true happiness, but among those who till a small piece of ground, or apply themselves to the sciences, without ambition. " The fairest lives, in my opinion," says Montaigne, " are those which regularly accommodate themselves to the common and human model, without miracle, without extravagance." " If some great men," said Mandeville, " had not a superlative pride, and everybody understood the enjoyment of life, who would be a lord chancellor, a prime minister, or a grand pensionary?" There is in existence a precious old album containing the handwriting of many renowned men, such as Luther, Erasmus, Mosheim, and others. The last-mentioned has written, in Latin, the following remarkable words: " Renown is a source of toil and sorrow; obscurity is a source of happiness." " Does he not drink more sweetly that takes his beverage in an earthen vessel," asks Jeremy Taylor, "than he that looks and searches into his golden chalices, for fear of poison, and looks pale at every sudden noise, and sleeps in armor, and trusts nobody, and does not trust God for safety ? "

" The world," said Goethe, " could not exist, if it were not so simple. This ground has been tilled a thousand years, yet its powers remain ever the same ; a little rain, a little sun, and each spring it grows green again."

" Everything has its own limits," says Hazlitt, " a little centre of its own, round which it moves ; so that our true wisdom lies in our keeping in our own walk in life, however humble or obscure, and being satisfied if we can succeed in it. The best of us can do no more, and we shall only become ridiculous or unhappy by attempting it. We are ashamed because we are at a loss in things to which we have no pretensions, and try to remedy our mistakes by committing greater. An overweening vanity or self-opinion is, in truth, often at the bottom of this weakness ; and we shall be most likely to conquer the one by eradicating the other, or restricting it within due and moderate bounds."

" From my tutor," said the good emperor Marcus Aurelius, " I learnt endurance of labor, and to want little, and to work with my own hands, and not to meddle with other people's affairs, and not to be ready to listen to slander."

" Ah ! " exclaimed the Attic Philosopher, " if men but knew in what a small dwelling joy can live, and how little it costs to furnish it ! . . . . Does a man drink more when he drinks from a large glass ? From whence comes that universal dread of mediocrity, the fruitful mother of peace and liberty? Ah! there is the evil which, above every other, it should be the aim of both public and private education to antici- pate! If that were got rid of, what treasons would be spared, what baseness avoided, what a chain of excess and crime would be forever broken! We award the palm to charity, and to self-sacrifice : but, above all, let us award it to moderation, for it is the great social virtue. Even when it does not create the others, it stands instead of them." Socrates used to say that the man who ate with the greatest appetite had the least need of delicacies ; and that he who drank with the greatest appetite was the least in- clined to look for a draught which is not at hand ; and that those who want fewest things are nearest to the gods. Michel Angelo seldom partook of the enjoy- ments of the table, and used to say, "However rich I may have been, I have always lived as a poor man." Epicurus said, "I feed sweetly upon bread and water, those sweet and easy provisions of the body, and I defy the pleasures of costly provisions." "No man needs to flatter," says Jeremy Taylor, "if he can live as nature did intend. He need not swell his accounts, and intricate his spirit with arts of subtlety and contrivance ; he can be free from fears, and the chances of the world cannot concern him. All our trouble is from within us ; and if a dish of lettuce and a clear fountain can cool all my heats, so that I shall have neither thirst nor pride, lust nor re- venge, envy nor ambition, I am lodged in the bosom of felicity."

" I should rather say," says Froude, "that the Scots had been an unusually happy people. Intelligent industry, the honest doing of daily work, with a sense that it must be done well, under penalties ; the necessaries of life moderately provided for ; and a sensible content with the situation of life in which men are born — this through the week, and at the end of it the Cotter's Saturday Night — the homely family, gathered reverently and peacefully together, and irradiated with a sacred presence. Happiness ! such happiness as we human creatures are likely to know upon this world will be found there, if anywhere."

" On the Simplon," says a German traveler, "amid the desert of snow and mist, in the vicinity of a refuge, a boy and his little sister were journeying up the mountain by the side of our carriage. Both had on their backs little baskets filled with wood, which they had gathered in the lower mountains, where there is still some vegetation. The boy gave us some specimens of rock crystal and other stone, for which we gave him some small coins. The delight with which he cast stolen glances at his money, as he passed by our carriage, made upon me an indelible impression. Never before had I seen such a heavenly expression of felicity. I could not but reflect that God had placed all sources and capabilities for happiness in the human heart ; and that, with respect to happiness, it is perfectly indifferent how and where one dwells."

" A man who is gifted with worldly qualities and accommodations is armed with hands, as a ship with grappling-irons, ready to catch hold of, and make himself fast to everything he comes in contact with,

and such a man, with all these properties of adhesion,
has also the property, like the polypus, of a most miraculous and convenient indivisibility; cut off his hold
— nay, cut him how you will, he is still a polypus,
whole and entire. Men of this sort still work their
way out of their obscurity like cockroaches out of the
hold of a ship, and crawl into notice, nay, even into
kings' palaces, as the frogs did into Pharaoh's; the
happy faculty of noting times and seasons, and a lucky
promptitude to avail themselves of moments with address and boldness, are alone such all-sufficient requi-
sites, such marketable stores of worldly knowledge,
that, although the minds of those who own them shall
be, as to all the liberal sciences, a *rasa tabula*, yet,
knowing these things needful to be known, let their
difficulties and distresses be what they may, though
the storm of adversity threatens to overwhelm them,
they are in a life-boat, buoyed up by corks, and cannot sink. These are the stray children turned loose
upon the world, whom fortune, in her charity, takes
charge of, and for whose guidance in the by-ways and
cross-roads of their pilgrimage she sets up fairy finger-
posts, discoverable by those whose eyes are near the
ground, but unperceived by such whose looks are
raised above it."

Wordsworth's man-servant, James, was brought up
in a work-house, and at nine years of age was turned
out of the house with two shillings in his pocket.
When without a sixpence, he was picked up by a
farmer, who took him into his service on condition that
all his clothes should be burnt (they were so filthy);
and he was to pay for his new clothes out of his

wages of two pounds ten shillings per annum. Here he stayed as long as he was wanted. " I have been so lucky," said James, " that I was never out of a place a day in my life, for I was always taken into service immediately. I never got into a scrape, or was drunk in my life, for I never taste any liquor. So that I have often said, I consider myself as a favorite of fortune ! " This is like Goldsmith's cripple in the park, who, remarking upon his appealing wretchedness, said, " 'T is not every man that can be born with a golden spoon in his mouth."

" Arrogance," said Goethe, " is natural to youth. A man believes, in his youth, that the world properly began with him, and that all exists for his sake. In the East, there was a man who, every morning, collected his people about him, and never would go to work till he had commanded the sun to arise. But he was wise enough not to speak his command till the sun of its own accord was ready to appear." " At the outset of life," says Hazlitt, " our imagination has a body to it. We are in a state between sleeping and waking, and have indistinct but glorious glimpses of strange shapes, and there is always something to come better than what we see. As in our dreams the fullness of the blood gives warmth and reality to the coinage of the brain, so in youth our ideas are clothed, and fed, and pampered with our good spirits ; we breathe thick with thoughtless happiness, the weight of future years presses on the strong pulses of the heart, and we repose with undisturbed faith in truth and good. As we advance, we exhaust our fund of enjoyment and of hope. We are no longer wrapped

in lamb's-wool, lulled in Elysium. As we taste the
pleasures of life, their spirit evaporates, the sense palls,
and nothing is left but the phantoms, the lifeless
shadows of what has been!"

> " There was a time when meadow, grove, and stream,
>   The earth, and every common sight,
>   To me did seem
>   Apparel'd in celestial light,
>   The glory and the freshness of a dream.
>   It is not now as it has been of yore;
>   Turn wheresoe'er I may,
>   By night or day,
>   The things which I have seen I now can see no more.

> " The rainbow comes and goes,
>   And lovely is the rose;
>   The moon doth with delight
>   Look round her when the heavens are bare;
>   Waters on a starry night
>   Are beautiful and fair;
>   The sunshine is a glorious birth;
>   But yet I know, where'er I go,
>   That there hath passed away a glory from the earth."

" Why," asks Souvestre, " is there so much confidence at first, so much doubt at last? Has, then, the
knowledge of life no other end but to make it unfit
for happiness? Must we condemn ourselves to ignorance if we would preserve hope? Is the world, and
is the individual man, intended, after all, to find rest
only in an eternal childhood? "

" If the world does improve on the whole, yet youth
must always begin anew, and go through the stages of
culture from the beginning." Yet, " 't is a great ad-

vantage of rank," says Pascal, "that a man at eighteen or twenty shall be allowed the same esteem and deference which another purchaseth by his merit at fifty. Here are thirty years gained at a stroke."

"The whole employment of men's lives," said the same thinker, "is to improve their fortunes; and yet the title by which they hold all, if traced to its origin, is no more than the pure fancy of the legislators: but their possession is still more precarious than their right, and at the mercy of a thousand accidents: nor are the treasures of the mind better insured; while a fall, or a fit of sickness may bankrupt the ablest understanding. . . . . Cæsar was too old, in my opinion, to amuse himself with projecting the conquest of the world. Such an imagination was excusable in Alexander, a prince full of youth and fire, and not easy to be checked in his hopes. But Cæsar ought to have been more grave."

"Knowledge has two extremities, which meet and touch each other," says Pascal, again. "The first of them is pure, natural ignorance, such as attends every man at his birth. The other is the perfection attained by great souls, who, having run through the circle of all that mankind can know, find at length that they know nothing, and are contented to return to that ignorance from which they set out. Ignorance that thus knows itself is a wise and learned ignorance."

"That is ever the difference," said Emerson, "between the wise and the unwise: the latter wonders at what is unusual, the wise man wonders at the usual."

It has been said that the visitor, climbing the white

roof of the Milan cathedral, and gazing on the forest
of statues, " feels as though a flight of angels had
alighted there and been struck to marble."   " At the
top of his mind," says Alger, " the devout scholar
has a holy of holies, a little pantheon set round with
altars and the images of the greatest men. Every
day, putting on a priestly robe, he retires into this
temple and passes before its shrines and shapes.
Here he feels a thrill of awe ; there he lays a burning aspiration ; further on he swings a censer of reverence. To one he lifts a look of love ; at the feet
of another he drops a grateful tear ; and before another still, a flush of pride and joy suffuses him.
They smile on him : sometimes they speak and wave
their solemn hands. Always they look up to the
Highest. Purified and hallowed, he gathers his soul
together, and comes away from the worshipful intercourse, serious, serene, glad, and strong."

Hear this lofty strain of the old heathen emperor
Marcus Aurelius : " Short is the little which remains
to thee of life. Live as on a mountain. Let men
see, let them know, a real man, who lives as he was
meant to live. If they cannot endure him, let them
kill him. For that is better than to live as men do."

" As soon as a man," says Max Müller, " becomes
conscious of himself as distinct from all other things
and persons, he at the same moment becomes conscious of a Higher Self, a higher power, without
which he feels that neither he nor anything else would
have any life or reality."

" To live, indeed," says Sir Thomas Browne, " is to
be again ourselves, which being not only a hope but

an evidence in noble believers, 't is all one to lie in St. Innocent's church-yard, as in the sands of Egypt ; ready to be anything, in the ecstasy of being ever, and as content with six feet as the moles of Adrianus."

"At the age of seventy-five," says Goethe, "one must, of course, think frequently of death. But this thought never gives me the least uneasiness, I am so fully convinced that the soul is indestructible, and that its activity will continue through eternity. It is like the sun, which seems to our earthly eyes to set in night, but is in reality gone to diffuse its light elsewhere."

> " The soul's dark cottage, battered and decayed,
> Lets in new light thro' chinks that time has made;
> Stronger by weakness, wiser men become
> As they draw near to their eternal home.
> Leaving the old, both worlds at once they view
> That stand upon the threshold of the new."

Among the poems of Mrs. Barbauld is a stanza on Life, written in extreme old age. Madame D'Arblay told the poet Rogers that she repeated it every night. Wordsworth once said to a visitor, " Repeat me that stanza by Mrs. Barbauld." His friend did so. Wordsworth made him repeat it again. And so he learned it by heart. He was at the time walking in his sitting-room at Rydal, with his hands behind him, and was heard to mutter to himself, " I am not in the habit of grudging people their good things, but I wish I had written those lines."

> " Life ! we 've been long together,
> Thro' pleasant and thro' cloudy weather:

'T is hard to part when friends are dear,
Perhaps 't will cost a sigh, a tear:
Then steal away, give little warning,
　　Choose thine own time;
Say not good night, but in some brighter clime
Bid me good morning."

XIII.

RELIGION.

" Ah !" sighed Shelley to Leigh Hunt, as the organ was playing in the cathedral at Pisa, " what a divine religion might be found out if charity were really made the principle of it instead of faith."

" In the seventeenth century," says Dean Stanley, in one of his Lectures on the Church of Scotland, " the minister of the parish of Anworth was the famous Samuel Rutherford, the great religious oracle of the Covenanters and their adherents. It was, as all readers of his letters will remember, the spot which he most loved on earth. The very swallows and sparrows which found their nests in the church of Anworth were, when far away, the objects of his affectionate envy. Its hills and valleys were the witnesses of his ardent devotion when living ; they still retain his memory with unshaken fidelity. It is one of the traditions thus cherished on the spot, that on a Saturday evening, at one of those family gatherings whence, in the language of the good Scottish poet,

' Old Scotia's grandeur springs,'

when Rutherford was catechising his children and servants, that a stranger knocked at the door of the manse, and begged shelter for the night. The minister kindly received him, and asked him to take his

23

place amongst the family and assist at their religious
exercises. It so happened that the question in the
catechism which came to the stranger's turn was that
which asks, 'How many commandments are there?'
He answered, 'Eleven.' 'Eleven!' exclaimed Rutherford; 'I am surprised that a man of your age and
appearance should not know better. What do you
mean?' And he answered, 'A new commandment I
give unto you, that ye love one another; as I have
loved you, that ye also love one another. By this
shall all men know that ye are my disciples, if ye
have love one to another.' Rutherford was much impressed by the answer, and they retired to rest. The
next morning he rose early to meditate on the services of the day. The old manse of Anworth stood, —
its place is still pointed out, — in the corner of a field,
under the hill-side, and thence a long, winding, wooded
path, still called Rutherford's Walk, leads to the
church. Through this glen he passed, and, as he
threaded his way through the thicket, he heard
amongst the trees the voice of the stranger at his
morning devotions. The elevation of the sentiments
and of the expressions convinced him that it was no
common man. He accosted him, and the traveler
confessed to him that he was no other than the great
divine and scholar, Archbishop Usher, the Primate
of the Church of Ireland, one of the best and most
learned men of his age, who well fulfilled that new
commandment in the love which he won and which
he bore to others; one of the few links of Christian
charity between the fierce contending factions of that
time, devoted to King Charles I. in his life-time, and

honored in his grave by the Protector Cromwell. He
it was who, attracted by Rutherford's fame, had thus
come in disguise to see him in the privacy of his own
home. The stern Covenanter welcomed the stranger
prelate; side by side they pursued their way along
Rutherford's Walk to the little church, of which the
ruins still remain; and in that small Presbyterian
sanctuary, from Rutherford's rustic pulpit, the archbishop preached to the people of Anworth on the
words which had so startled his host the evening
before: 'A new commandment I give unto you, that
ye love one another; as I have loved you, that ye also
love one another.' "

In a legend which St. Jerome has recorded, and
which, says the same writer, in his Essays on the
Apostolic Age, is " not the less impressive because so
familiar to us, we see the aged Apostle (John) borne
in the arms of his disciples into the Ephesian assembly, and there repeating over and over again the same
saying, ' Little children, love one another ; ' till, when
asked why he said this and nothing else, he replied in
those well-known words, fit indeed to be the farewell
speech of the beloved disciple, ' Because this is our
Lord's command, and if you fulfill this, nothing else
is needed.' "

"An acceptance of the sentiment of love throughout Christendom for a season," says Emerson, " would
bring the felon and the outcast to our side in tears,
with the devotion of his faculties to our service. Love
would put a new face on this weary old world, in
which we dwell as pagans and enemies too long, and
it would warm the heart to see how fast the vain di-

plomacy of statesmen, the impotence of armies and
navies and lines of defense, would be superseded by
this unarmed child." We do not believe, or we forget, that "the Holy Ghost came down, not in the
shape of a vulture, but in the form of a dove."

"'Tell me, gentle traveler, who hast wandered
through the world, and seen the sweetest roses blow,
and brightest gliding rivers, of all thine eyes have
seen, which is the fairest land?' 'Child, shall I tell
thee where nature is most blest and fair? It is where
those we love abide. Though that space be small,
ample is it above kingdoms; though it be a desert,
through it runs the river of paradise, and there are
the enchanted bowers.'"

"We ought," says the author of Ecce Homo, " to
be just as tolerant of an imperfect creed as we are of
an imperfect practice. Everything which can be
urged in excuse for the latter may also be pleaded for
the former. If the way to Christian action is beset
by corrupt habits and misleading passions, the path
to Christian truth is overgrown with prejudices, and
strewn with fallen theories and rotting systems which
hide it from our view. It is quite as hard to think
rightly as to act rightly, or even to feel rightly. And
as all allow that an error is a less culpable thing than
a crime or a vicious passion, it is monstrous that it
should be more severely punished; it is monstrous
that Christ, who was called the friend of publicans
and sinners, should be represented as the pitiless enemy of bewildered seekers of truth. How could men
have been guilty of such an inconsistency? By speaking of what they do not understand. Men in gen-

eral do not understand or appreciate the difficulty of finding truth. All men must act, and therefore all men learn in some degree how difficult it is to act rightly. The consequence is that all men can make excuse for those who fail to act rightly. But all men are not compelled to make an independent search for truth, and those who voluntarily undertake to do so are always few. To the world at large it seems quite easy to find truth, and inexcusable to miss it. And no wonder! For by finding truth they mean only learning by rote the maxims current among them." " Maxims and first principles," says Pascal, " are subject to revolutions ; and we are to go to chronology for the epochas of right and wrong. A very humorsome justice this, which is bounded by a river or a mountain : orthodoxy on one side of the Pyrenees may be heresy on the other." " Let there," begs the Spanish President Castelar, " be no more accursed races on the earth. Let every one act according to his conscience, and communicate freely with his God. Let thought be only corrected by the contradiction of thought. Let error be an infirmity, and not a crime. Let us agree in acknowledging that opinions sometimes take possession of our understandings quite independent of our will or desire. Let us be so just as to be enabled to see even to what degree each race has contributed to the universal education of humanity."

" The truth," said Goethe, " must be repeated over and over again, because error is repeatedly preached among us, not only by individuals, but by the masses. In periodicals and cyclopedias, in schools and universities, everywhere, in fact, error prevails, and is quite easy in the feeling that it has quite a majority on its side." "Public opinion, of which we hear so much," said a writer in Blackwood, long ago, "is never anything else than the reëcho of the thought of a few great men half a century before. It takes that time for ideas to flow down from the elevated to the inferior level. The great never adopt, they only originate. Their chief efforts are always made in opposition to the prevailing opinions by which they are surrounded. Thence it is that a powerful mind is always uneasy when it is not in the minority on any subject which excites general attention." "If you discover a truth," says an unknown author, "you are persecuted by an infinite number of people who gain their living from the error you oppose, saying that this error itself is the truth, and that the greatest error is that which tends to destroy it." "There arose no small stir" at Ephesus on account of Paul's preaching. "For a certain man named Demetrius, a silversmith, which made silver shrines for Diana, brought no small gain unto the craftsmen; whom he called together with the workmen of like occupation, and said, Sirs, ye know that by this craft we have our wealth: moreover, ye see and hear, that not alone at Ephesus, but almost throughout all Asia, this Paul hath persuaded and turned away much people, saying that they be no gods which are made with hands. So that not only this our craft is in danger to be set at nought; but also that the temple of the great goddess Diana should be despised, and her magnificence should be destroyed, whom all Asia and the world worshipeth. And when they heard these sayings, they were full of wrath, and cried out, saying, Great is Diana of the Ephesians."

"Thomas Aikenhead, a student of eighteen, was hanged at Edinburgh, in 1697, for having uttered," says Macaulay, in his History, "free opinions about the trinity and some of the books of the Bible. His offense was construed as blasphemy under an old Scotch statute, which was strained for the purpose of convicting him. After his sentence he recanted, and begged a short respite to make his peace with God. This the privy council declined to grant, unless the Edinburgh clergy would intercede for him; but so far were they from seconding his petition, that they actually demanded that his execution should not be delayed." "Imagine, if you can," says Froude, in one of his essays, "a person being now put to death for a speculative theological opinion. You feel at once that, in the most bigoted country in the world, such a thing has become impossible; and the impossibility is the measure of the alteration which we have all undergone. The formulas remain as they were, on either side, — the very same formulas which were once supposed to require these detestable murders. But we have learned to know each other better. The cords which bind together the brotherhood of mankind are woven of a thousand strands. We do not any more fly apart or become enemies because, here and there, in one strand out of so many, there are still unsound places."

"There is a violent zeal," says Fénelon, "that we must correct; it thinks it can change the whole world, it would reform everything, it would subject every one to its laws. The origin of this zeal is disgraceful. The defects of our neighbor interfere with our own;

our vanity is wounded by that of another; our own haughtiness finds our neighbor's ridiculous and insupportable; our restlessness is rebuked by the sluggishness and indolence of this person; our gloom is disturbed by the gayety and frivolities of that person, and our heedlessness by the shrewdness and address of another. If we were faultless, we should not be so much annoyed by the defects of those with whom we associate. If we were to acknowledge honestly that we have not virtue enough to bear patiently with our neighbors' weaknesses, we should show our own imperfection, and this alarms our vanity. We therefore make our weakness pass for strength, elevate it to a virtue and call it zeal; an imaginary and often hypocritical zeal. For is it not surprising to see how tranquil we are about the errors of others when they do not trouble us, and how soon this wonderful zeal kindles against those who excite our jealousy, or weary our patience?" "We reprove our friends' faults," said Wycherley, "more out of pride than love or charity; not so much to correct them, as to make them believe we are ourselves without them." It was Dean Swift who said, "We have just enough of religion to make us hate, but not enough to make us love, one another." "Your business," said Hunt, "is to preach love to your neighbor, to kick him to bits, and to thank God for the contradiction." "The falsehood that the tongue commits," said Landor, "is slight in comparison with what is conceived by the heart, and executed by the whole man, throughout life. If, professing love and charity to the human race at large, I quarrel day after day with my next

neighbor ; if, professing that the rich can never see
God, I spend in the luxuries of my household a
talent monthly ; if, professing to place so much confidence in his word, that, in regard to wordly weal,
I need take no care for to-morrow, I accumulate
stores even beyond what would be necessary though
I quite distrusted both his providence and his ve-
racity ; if, professing that 'he who giveth to the
poor lendeth to the Lord,' I question the Lord's
security, and haggle with him about the amount
of the loan ; if, professing that I am their stew-
ard, I keep ninety-nine parts in the hundred as
the emolument of my stewardship : how, when God
hates liars, and punishes defrauders, shall I, and other
such thieves and hypocrites, fare hereafter ? " In one
of his chapters on the Study of Sociology, Herbert
Spencer remarks that "it would clear up our ideas
about many things, if we distinctly recognized the
truth that we have two religions." These two religions Mr. Spencer designates as the " religion of amity " and the " religion of enmity." " Of course,"
he says, " I don't mean that these are both called
religions. Here I am not speaking of names ; I am
speaking simply of things. Nowadays men do not
pay the same nominal homage to the religion of enmity that they do to the religion of amity — the
religion of amity occupies the place of honor. But
the real homage is paid in large measure, if not in the
larger measure, to the religion of enmity. The religion of enmity nearly all men actually believe. The
religion of amity most of them merely believe they
believe." " The Church of Rome," said F. W. Rob-

ertson, in his sermon on The Tongue, "hurls her
thunders against Protestants of every denomination;
the Calvinist scarcely recognizes the Arminian as a
Christian; he who considers himself as the true An-
glican excludes from the church of Christ all but the
adherents of his own orthodoxy; every minister and
congregation has its small circle, beyond which all are
heretics; nay, even among that sect which is most lax
as to the dogmatic forms of truth, we find the Uni-
tarian of the old school denouncing the spiritualism of
the new and rising school.   Sisters of Charity refuse
to permit an act of charity to be done by a Samari-
tan; ministers of the gospel fling the thunder-bolts of
the Lord; ignorant hearers catch and exaggerate the
spirit; boys, girls, and women shudder as one goes
by, perhaps more holy than themselves, who adores
the same God, believes in the same Redeemer, struggles in the same life-battle — and all this because they
have been taught to look upon him as an enemy of
God." "Particular churches and sects," says Sir
Thomas Browne, "usurp the gates of heaven, and
turn the keys against each other; and thus we go to
heaven against each others' wills, conceits, and opinions." "The church of the future," in the opinion of
Father Hyacinthe, "will know nothing of such divisions, such discordances, and she will uphold the
freedom of theologies and the diversity of rites in the
unity of one faith and of one worship." "As soon,"
said Goethe, "as the pure doctrine and love of Christ
are comprehended in their true nature, and have become a vital principle, we shall feel ourselves as human
beings, great and free, and not attach especial impor-

tance to a degree more or less in the outward forms
of religion : besides, we shall all gradually advance
from a Christianity of words and faith to a Christianity of feeling and action." " Could we," said
Dean Young, " but once descend from our high pretenses of religion to the humility that only makes
men religious, could we but once prefer Christianity
itself before the several factions that bear its name,
our differences would sink of themselves ; and it
would appear to us that there is more religion in not
contending than there is in the matter we contend
about." " Do you remember," asks the author of
The Eclipse of Faith, " the passage in Woodstock,
in which our old favorite represents the Episcopalian
Rochecliffe and the Presbyterian Holdenough meeting unexpectedly in prison, after many years of separation, during which one had thought the other dead ?
How sincerely glad they were, and how pleasantly
they talked ; when, lo ! an unhappy reference to 'the
bishopric of Titus' gradually abated the fervor of
their charity, and inflamed that of their zeal, even
till they at last separated in mutual dudgeon, and sat
glowering at each other in their distant corners with
looks in which the ' Episcopalian ' and ' Presbyterian '
were much more evident than the ' Christian : ' and
so they persevered till the sudden summons to them
and their fellow-prisoners, to prepare for instant execution, dissolved as with a charm the anger they had
felt, and ' Forgive me, O my brother,' and 'I have
sinned against thee, my brother,' broke from their
lips as they took what they thought would be a last
farewell." " I sometimes," says Froude, " in impa-

tient moments, wish the laity would treat their controversial divines as two gentlemen once treated their seconds, when they found themselves forced into a duel without knowing what they were quarreling about. As the principals were being led up to their places, one of them whispered to the other, ‘If you will shoot your second, I will shoot mine.’ ”

“ Man,” says Harrington, in his Political Aphorisms, “ may rather be defined a religious than a rational creature, in regard that in other creatures there may be something of reason, but there is nothing of religion.” “ If you travel through the world well,” says Plutarch, “you may find cities without walls, without literature, without kings, moneyless, and such as desire no coin ; which know not what theatres or public halls of bodily exercise mean ; but never was there, nor ever shall there be, any one city seen without temple, church or chapel ; without some god or other ; which useth no prayers nor oaths, no prophecies and divinations, no sacrifices, either to obtain good blessings or to avert heavy curses and calamities. Nay, methinks a man should sooner find a city built in the air, without any plot of ground whereon it is seated, than that any commonwealth altogether void of religion and the opinion of the gods should either be first established, or afterwards preserved and maintained in that estate. This is that containeth and holdeth together all human society ; this is the foundation, prop, and stay of all.” “ How striking a proof is it,” says a writer on The Religions of India, “ of the strength of the adoring principle in human nature — what an illustration of mankind’s sense of dependence upon an unseen Supreme — that the grandest works which the nations have reared are those connected with religion ! Were a spirit from some distant world to look down upon the surface of our planet as it spins round in the solar rays, his eye would be most attracted, as the morning light passed onward, by the glittering and painted pagodas of China, Borneo, and Japan; the richly ornamented temples and stupendous rock shrines of India ; the dome-topped mosques and tall, slender minarets of Western Asia ; the pyramids and vast temples of Egypt, with their mile-long avenues of gigantic statues and sphinxes; the graceful shrines of classic Greece ; the basilicas of Rome and Byzantium ; the semi-Oriental church-domes of Moscow; the Gothic cathedrals of Western Europe: and as the day closed, the light would fall dimly upon the ruins of the grand sun-temples of Mexico and Peru, where, in the infancy of reason and humanity, human sacrifices were offered up, as if the All-Father were pleased with the agony of his creatures ! "

" Moral rules," says Matthew Arnold, in his Essay on Marcus Aurelius, " apprehended as ideas first, and then rigorously followed as laws, are and must be for the sage only. The mass of mankind have neither force of intellect enough to apprehend them clearly as ideas, nor force of character enough to follow them strictly as laws. The mass of mankind can be carried along a course full of hardships for the natural man, can be borne over the thousand impediments of the narrow way, only by the tide of a joyful and bounding emotion. It is impossible to rise from reading

Epictetus or Marcus Aurelius without a sense of constraint and melancholy, without feeling that the burden laid upon man is well-nigh greater than he can bear. Honor to the sages who have felt this, and yet have borne it ! . . . . For the ordinary man, this sense of labor and sorrow constitutes an absolute disqualification ; it paralyzes him ; under the weight of it he cannot make way towards the goal at all. The paramount virtue of religion is that it has lighted up morality ; that it has supplied the emotion and inspiration needful for carrying the sage along the narrow way perfectly, for carrying the ordinary man along it at all. Even the religions with most dross in them have had something of this virtue ; but the Christian religion manifests it with unexampled splendor." The Duke de Chaulnes once said to Dr. Johnson that " every religion had a certain degree of morality in it." " Ay, my lord," answered he, " but the Christian religion alone puts it on its proper basis." " It is Christianity alone," said Max Müller, " which, as the religion of humanity, as the religion of no caste, of no chosen people, has taught us to respect the history of humanity as a whole, to discover the traces of a divine wisdom and love in the government of all the races of mankind, and to recognize, if possible, even in the lowest and crudest forms of religious belief, not the work of demoniacal agencies, but something that indicates a divine guidance, something that makes us perceive, with St. Peter, ' that God is no respecter of persons, but that in every nation he that feareth Him and worketh righteousness is accepted with Him.' " " The turning-point," remarks Frances

Power Cobbe, "between the old world and the new
was the beginning of the Christian movement. The
action upon human nature, which started on its new
course, was the teaching and example of Christ.
Christ was he who opened the age of endless progress. The old world grew from without, and was
outwardly symmetric. The new one grows from
within, and is not symmetric, nor ever will be; bear-
ing in its heart the germ of an everlasting, un-
resting progress. The old world built its temples,
hewed its statues, framed its philosophies, and wrote
its glorious epics and dramas, so that nothing might
evermore be added to them. The new world made
its art, its philosophy, its poetry, all imperfect, yet
instinct with a living spirit beyond the old. To the
Parthenon not a stone could be added from the hour
of its completion. To Milan and Cologne altar and
chapel, statue and spire, will be added through the
ages. Christ was not merely a moral reformer, inculcating pure ethics; not merely a religious reformer,
clearing away old theological errors and teaching
higher ideas of God. These things He was; but He
might, for all we can tell, have been them both as
fully, and yet have failed to be what He has actually
been to our race. He might have taught the world
better ethics and better theology, and yet have failed
to infuse into it that new tide which has ever since
coursed through its arteries and penetrated its minut-
est veins. What Christ has really done is beyond
the kingdom of the intellect and its theologies; nay,
even beyond the kingdom of the conscience and its
recognition of duty. His work has been in that of

the heart. He has transformed the law into the gospel. He has changed the bondage of the alien for
the liberty of the sons of God. He has glorified
virtue into holiness, religion into piety, and duty
into love." His was "a religion," says Jeremy Taylor, " that taught men to be meek and humble, apt
to receive injuries, but unapt to do any ; a religion
that gave countenance to the poor and pitiful, in a
time when riches were adored, and ambition and
pleasure had possessed the heart of all mankind ; a
religion that would change the face of things and the
hearts of men, and break vile habits into gentleness
and counsel." " Great and multiform," says Lecky,
in his History of European Morals, — summing up
some of the results of Christianity, — " great and
multiform have been the influences of Christian
philanthropy. The high conception that has been
formed of the sanctity of human life, the protection
of infancy, the elevation and final emancipation of
the slave classes, the suppression of barbarous games,
the creation of a vast and multifarious organization
of charity, and the education of the imagination by
the Christian type, constituted together a movement
of philanthropy which has never been paralleled or
approached in the pagan world."

" If there be any good in thee," says the author of
the Imitation, " believe that there is much more in
others, that so thou mayest preserve humility. It
hurteth thee not to submit to all men ; but it hurteth
thee most of all to prefer thyself even to one." " Be
assured," said Dean Young, " there can be but little
honesty without thinking as well as possible of oth-

ers ; and there can be no safety without thinking humbly and distrustfully of ourselves." " The character of a wise man consists in three things : to do himself what he tells others to do ; to act on no occasion contrary to justice ; and to bear with the weaknesses of those around him. Treat inferiors as if you might one day be in the hands of a master." " I recollect," says Saadi, " the verse which the elephant-driver rehearsed on the banks of the river Nile : ' If you are ignorant of the state of the ant under your foot, know that it resembles your own condition under the foot of the elephant.' " The stable of Confucius being burned down, when he was at court, on his return he said, " Has any man been hurt? " He did not ask about the horses. Fénelon had a habit of bringing into his palace the wretched inhabitants of the country, whom the war had driven from their homes, and taking care of them, and feeding them at his own table. Seeing one day that one of these peasants ate nothing, he asked him the reason of his abstinence. "Alas ! my lord," said the poor man, " in making my escape from my cottage, I had not time to bring off my cow, which was the support of my family. The enemy will drive her away, and I shall never find another so good." Fénelon, availing himself of his privilege of safe-conduct, immediately set out, accompanied by a servant, and drove the cow back himself to the peasant. A literary man, whose library was destroyed by fire, has been deservedly admired for saying, " I should have profited but little by my books, if they had not taught me how to bear the loss of them." The remark of

24

Fénelon, who lost his in a similar way, is still more simple and touching. " I would much rather they were burnt than the cottage of a poor peasant." Lord Peterborough said of Fénelon, " He was a delicious creature. I was obliged to get away from him, or he would have made me pious." The influence of such a character brings to mind a passage from Saadi. " One day," he says, " as I was in the bath, a friend of mine put into my hand a piece of scented clay. I took it, and said to it, ' Art thou of heaven or earth ? for I am charmed with thy delightful scent.' It answered, ' I was a despicable piece of clay ; but I was some time in company of the rose : the sweet quality of my companion was communicated to me ; otherwise I should have remained only what I appear to be, a bit of earth.' "

" If thou canst not make thyself such an one as thou wouldst," quoting the Imitation of Christ, " how canst thou expect to have another in all things to thy liking ? We would willingly have others perfect, and yet we amend not our own faults. We would have others severely corrected, and will not be corrected ourselves. The large liberty of others displeaseth us ; and yet we will not have our own desires denied us. We will have others kept under by strict laws ; but in no sort will ourselves be restrained. And thus it appeareth how seldom we weigh our neighbor in the same balance with ourselves." Addison, in one of the papers of The Spectator, enlarges upon the celebrated thought of Socrates, that if all the misfortunes of mankind were cast into a public stock, in order to be equally distributed among the whole spe-

cies, those who now think themselves the most unhappy would prefer the share they are already possessed of before that which would fall to them by such
a division — by imagining a proclamation made by
Jupiter, that every mortal should bring in his griefs
and calamities, and throw them in a heap. There
was a large plain appointed for this purpose. He took
his stand in the centre of it, and saw the whole human species marching one after another, and throwing
down their several loads, which immediately grew up
into a prodigious mountain, that seemed to rise above
the clouds. He observed one bringing in a bundle
very carefully concealed under an old embroidered
cloak, which, upon his throwing into the heap, he
discovered to be poverty. Another, after a great deal
of puffing, threw down his luggage, which, upon ex-
amining, he found to be his wife. He saw multitudes
of old women throw down their wrinkles, and several
young ones strip themselves of their tawny skins.
There were very great heaps of red noses, large lips,
and rusty teeth, — in truth, he was surprised to see
the greatest part of the mountain made up of bodily
deformities. Observing one advancing towards the
heap with a larger cargo than ordinary upon his back,
he found upon his near approach that·it was only a
natural hump, which he disposed of with great joy of
heart among the collection of human miseries. But
what most surprised him of all was that there was
not a single vice or folly thrown into the whole heap ;
at which he was very much astonished, having concluded with himself that every one would take this
opportunity of getting rid of his passions, prejudices,
and frailties.

" Passions, prejudices, and frailties ! " " There is
no man so good," says Montaigne, " who, were he to
submit all his thoughts and actions to the laws, would
not deserve hanging ten times in his life. [Talley-
rand, when Rulhière said he had been guilty of only
one wickedness in his life, asked, " When will it
end?"] We are so far from being good men, according to the laws of God, that we cannot be so according
to our own ; human wisdom never yet arrived at the
duty that it had itself prescribed ; and could it arrive
there, it would still prescribe itself others beyond it,
to which it would ever aspire and pretend ; so great
an enemy of consistency is our human condition."
Of prejudice it has been truly said by Basil Montagu,
in a note to one of his publications, that " it has the
singular ability of accommodating itself to all the
possible varieties of the human mind. Some passions
and vices are but thinly scattered among mankind,
and find only here and there a fitness of reception.
But prejudice, like the spider, makes everywhere its
home. It has neither taste nor choice of place, and all
that it requires is room. There is scarcely a situation,
except fire and water, in which a spider will not live.
So let the mind be as naked as the walls of an empty
and forsaken tenement, gloomy as a dungeon, or ornamented with the richest abilities of thinking ; let it be
hot, cold, dark or light, lonely or inhabited, still prejudice, if undisturbed, will fill it with cobwebs, and
live, like the spider, where there seems nothing to live
on. If the one prepares her food by poisoning it to
her palate and her use, the other does the same ; and
as several of our passions are strongly characterized

by the animal world, prejudice may be denominated the spider of the mind." "We are all frail, but do thou esteem none more frail than thyself." "Those many that need pity," says Jeremy Taylor, "and those infinities of people that refuse to pity, are miserable upon a several charge, but yet they almost make up all mankind."

"The most important thing in life," says Pascal, "is the choice of a profession; and yet this is a thing purely in the disposal of chance." But we take no account of the effect of occupation upon body and mind, holding all alike responsible for opinions and conduct. In an article in the Journal of Psychological Medicine on Baron Feuchtersleben's Principles of Medical Psychology, showing how the mind is influenced by a mechanical calling, there is this remarkable sentence: "Rösch and Esquirol affirm from observation that indigo-dyers become melancholy; and those who dye scarlet, choleric."

Shaftesbury, in his Characteristics, inquires, "What stranger pleasure is there with mankind, or what do they earlier learn or longer retain, than the love of hearing and relating things strange and incredible? How wonderful a thing is the love of wondering, and of raising wonder! 'T is the delight of children to hear tales they shiver at, and the vice of old age to abound in strange stories of times past. We come into the world wondering at everything; and when our wonder about common things is over, we seek something new to wonder at. Our last scene is to tell wonders of our own, to all who will believe 'em. And, amidst all this, 't is well if truth comes off but

moderately tainted." " Curiosity," says Pascal, " is
little better than mere vanity. For the most part,
we desire to know things purely that we may talk of
them. Few would undertake so dangerous voyages
and travels for the bare pleasure of entertaining their
sight, if they were bound to secresy at their return,
or forever cloistered from conversation."

Some persons need much time to know a little
truth ; others seem to know, at a glance, all that they
can. Cumberland said Bubb Doddington was in
nothing more remarkable than in ready perspicuity
and discernment of a subject thrown before him on
a sudden. " Take his first thoughts then, and he
would charm you; give him time to ponder and refine, you would perceive the spirit of his sentiments
and the vigor of his genius evaporate by the process,
for though his first view of the question would be a
wide one, and clear withal, when he came to exercise
the subtlety of his disquisitional powers upon it, he
would so ingeniously dissect and break it into fractions,
that as an object, when looked upon too intently for
a length of time, grows misty and confused, so would
the question under his discussion when the humor
took him to be hypercritical." Coleridge said Horne
Tooke " had that clearness which is founded on shal-
lowness. He doubted nothing, and therefore gave
you all that he himself knew, or meant, with great
completeness." Thucydides said of Themistocles that
" he had the best judgment in actual circumstances,
and he formed his judgment with the least delibera-
tion." Quick or deliberate, shallow or profound, all
are apt to assume to know all, when they may be

little wiser, in truth, than Æsop's two travelers, who had visited Arabia, and were conversing together about the chameleon. "A very singular animal," said one, "I never saw one at all like it in my life. It has the head of a fish, its body is as thin as that of a lizard, its pace is slow, its color blue." "Stop there," said the other, "you are quite mistaken, the animal is green; I saw it with my two eyes." "I saw it as well as you," cried the first, "and I am certain that it is blue." "I am positive that it is green." "And I that it is blue." The travelers were getting very angry with each other, and were about to settle the disputed point by blows, when happily a third person arrived. "Well, gentlemen, what is the matter here? Calm yourselves, I pray you." "Will you be the judge of our quarrel?" "Yes; what is it?" "This person maintains that the chameleon is green, while I say that it is blue." "My dear sirs, you are both in the wrong; the animal is neither one nor the other — it is black." "Black! you must be jesting!" "Not at all, I assure you; I have one with me in a box, and you shall judge for yourselves." The box was produced and opened, when, to the surprise of all three, the animal was as yellow as gold! In one of the Hindoo books we are told that "in a certain country there existed a village of the blind men. These men had heard that there was an amazing animal called the elephant, but they knew not how to form an idea of his shape. One day an elephant happened to pass through the place; the villagers crowded to the spot where this animal was standing. One of them got hold of his trunk, another seized his ear, another his tail, another one of his legs, etc. After thus trying to gratify their curiosity, they returned into the village, and, sitting down together, they began to give their ideas of what the elephant was like; the man who had seized his trunk said he thought the elephant was like the body of the plantain-tree; the man who had felt his ear said he thought he was like the fan with which the Hindoos clean the rice; the man who had felt his tail said he thought he must be like a snake, and the man who had seized his leg thought he must be like a pillar. An old blind man of some judgment was present, who was greatly perplexed how to reconcile these jarring notions respecting the form of the elephant, but he at length said, ' You have all been to examine this animal, it is true, and what you report cannot be false; I suppose, therefore, that that which was like the plantain-tree must be his trunk; that which was like a fan must be his ear; that which was like a snake must be his tail, and that which was like a pillar must be his body.'" Once on a time a pastor of a village church adopted a plan to interest the members of his flock in the study of the Bible. It was this: " At the Wednesday evening meeting he would announce the topic to be discussed on the ensuing week, thus giving a week for preparation. One evening the subject was St. Paul. After the preliminary devotional exercises, the pastor called upon one of the deacons to ' speak to the question.' He immediately arose, and began to describe the personal appearance of the great apostle to the Gentiles. He said St. Paul was a tall, rather spare man, with black hair

and eyes, dark complexion, bilious temperament, etc.
His picture of Paul was a faithful portrait of himself.
He sat down, and another prominent member arose
and said, ' I think the brother preceding me has read
the Scriptures to little purpose if his description of
St. Paul is a sample of his Bible knowledge. St.
Paul was, as I understand it, a rather short, thick-set
man, with sandy hair, gray eyes, florid complexion,
and a nervous, sanguine temperament,' giving, like
his predecessor, an accurate picture of himself. He
was followed by another who had a keen sense of the
ludicrous, and who was withal an inveterate stam-
merer. He said, ' My bro-bro-brethren, I have never
fo-found in my Bi-ble much about the p-per-personal
ap-pe-pearance of St. P-p-paul. But one thing is
clearly established, and tha-that is, St. P-p-paul had
an imp-p-pediment in his speech.' "

" Having lived long," said Dr. Franklin, " I have
experienced many instances of being obliged, by better
information, or fuller consideration, to change opinions
even on important subjects, which I once thought
right, but I found to be otherwise. It is, therefore, that
the older I grow, the more apt I am to doubt my own
judgment, and to pay more respect to the judgment
of others. Most men, indeed, as well as most sects in
religion, think themselves in possession of all truth,
and that whenever others differ from them, it is so
far error. Steele, a Protestant, in a dedication tells
the pope that ' the only difference between our two
churches, in their opinions of the certainty of their
doctrines is, the Romish Church is infallible, and the
Church of England never in the wrong.' But, though

many private persons think almost as highly of their own infallibility as that of their sect, few express it so naturally as a certain French lady who, in a little dispute with her sister, said, ' I don't know how it happens, sister, but I meet with nobody but myself that is always in the right.' " " I could never," says Sir Thomas Browne, " divide myself from any man upon the difference of an opinion, or be angry with his judgment for not agreeing with me in that from which, perhaps, within a few days, I should dissent myself." " Whoever shall call to memory how many and many times he has been mistaken in his own judgment," says the great French essayist, " is he not a great fool if he does not ever after distrust it ? " " Beware," said John Wesley, " of forming a hasty judgment. There are secrets which few but God are acquainted with. Some years since I told a gentleman, ' Sir, I am afraid you are covetous.' He asked me, ' What is the reason of your fears ? ' I answered, ' A year ago, when I made a collection for the expense of repairing the Foundry, you subscribed five guineas. At the subscription made this year you subscribed only half a guinea.' He made no reply ; but after a time asked, ' Pray,. sir, answer me a question. Why do you live upon potatoes ? ' (I did so between three and four years.) I replied, ' It has much conduced to my health.' He answered, ' I believe it has. But did you not do it likewise to save money ? ' I said, ' I did, for what I save from my own meat will feed another that else would have none.' ' But, sir,' said he, ' if this be your motive, you may save much more. I know a man that goes to the market at the

beginning of each week. There he buys a penny-
worth of parsnips, which he boils in a large quantity of water. The parsnips serve him for food,
and the water for drink, the ensuing week, so his
meat and drink together cost him only a penny a
week.' This he constantly did, though he had then
two hundred pounds a year, to pay the debts which he
had contracted before he knew God! And this was
he I had set down for a covetous man." "We shall
have two wonders in heaven," said the wise and
gentle Tillotson; " the one, how many come to be
absent whom we expected to find there; the other,
how many are there whom we had no hope of meeting."

It would seem that, as things are, there is nothing
so natural as intolerance ; and it is not to be wondered at that the language to express toleration should
be of modern invention. Coleridge was of opinion
" that toleration was impossible till indifference made
it worthless." Dr. King had a different view ; he
said, " The opinion of any one in this world, except
the wise and good, who do not aspire to be even tolerant, — who are too modest to be tolerant, since toleration implies superiority, — is of little consequence."
Hunt said of Lamb that " he had felt, thought, and
suffered so much, that he literally had intolerance for
nothing." Palgrave, in his Travels through Central
and Eastern Arabia, relates of Abd-el-Lateef, a Wa-
habee, that one day seeing a corpulent Hindoo, he
exclaimed, " What a log for hell-fire !" This fol-
lower of Mahomet had not only the intolerance, but
the conceit of super-excellence that the poor sectarian

followers of Christ too often have. "When he was preaching one day to the people of Riad, he recounted the tradition according to which Mahomet declared that his followers should divide into seventy-three sects, and that seventy-two were destined to hell-fire, and only one to paradise. 'And what, O messenger of God, are the signs of that happy sect to which is insured the exclusive possession of paradise?' Whereto Mahomet had replied, 'It is those who shall be in all conformable to myself and my companions.' 'And that,' added Abd-el-Lateef, lowering his voice to the deep tone of conviction, 'that, by the mercy of God, are we, the people of Riad.'"

Upon the subject of toleration and charity, read a part of the remarkable dialogue from Arthur Helps' Friends in Council : —

DUNSFORD. — It is hard to be tolerant of intolerant people ; to see how natural their intolerance is, and in fact thoroughly to comprehend it and feel for it. This is the last stage of tolerance, which few men, I suppose, in this world attain.

MIDHURST. — Tolerance appears to me an unworked mine. . . . .

MILVERTON. — There is one great difficulty to be surmounted ; and that is, how to make hard, clear righteous men, who have not sinned much, have not suffered much, are not afflicted by strong passions, who have not many ties in the world, and who have been easily prosperous, — how to make such men tolerant. Think of this for a moment. For a man who has been rigidly good to be supremely tolerant would require an amount of insight which seems to belong only to the greatest genius. I have often fancied that the main scheme of the world is to create tenderness in man ; and I have a notion that the outer world would change if man were to acquire more of this tenderness. You see at present he is obliged to be kept down by urgent wants of all kinds, or he would otherwise have more time and thought to devote to cruelty and discord. If he *could* live in a better world, I mean in a world where nature was more propitious, I believe he would have such a world. And in some mysterious way, I suspect that nature is constrained to adapt herself to the main impress of the character of the average beings in the world.

ELLESMERE. — These are very extraordinary thoughts.

DUNSFORD. — They are not far from Christianity.

MILVERTON. — You must admit, Ellesmere, that Christianity has never been tried. I do not ask you to canvass doctrinal and controversial matters. But take the leading precepts; read the Sermon on the Mount, and see if it is the least like the doctrines of modern life.

DUNSFORD. — I cannot help thinking, when you are all talking of tolerance, why you do not use the better word, of which we hear something in Scripture,— charity.

MILVERTON. — If I were a clergyman, there is much that I should dislike to have to say (being a man of very dubious mind) ; there is much also that I should dislike to have to read ; but I should feel that it was a great day for me when I had to read out that short but most abounding chapter from St. Paul on charity. The more you study that chapter, the more profound you find it. The way that the apostle begins is most remarkable; and I doubt if it has been often duly considered. We think much of knowledge in our own times; but consider what the early Christian must have thought of one who possessed the gift of tongues or the gift of prophecy. Think also what the early Christian must have thought of the man who possessed "all faith." Then listen to St. Paul's summing up of these great gifts in comparison with charity. Dunsford, will you give us the words? You remember them, I dare say.

DUNSFORD. — (1 Cor. ch. xiii.) " Though I speak with the tongues of men and of angels, and have not charity, I am become as sounding brass, or a tinkling cymbal.

" And though I have the gift of prophecy, and understand all mysteries, and all knowledge; and though I have all faith, so that I could remove mountains, and have not charity, I am nothing."

MILVERTON. —You will let me proceed, I know, if it is only to hear more from Dunsford of that chapter. I have said that the early Christian would have thought much of the man who possessed the gift of tongues, of prophecy, of faith. But how he must have venerated the rich man who entered into his little community, and gave up all his goods to the poor! Again, how the early Christian must have regarded with longing admiration the first martyrs for his creed! Then hear what St. Paul says of this outward charity, and of this martyrdom, when compared with this infinitely more difficult charity of the soul and martyrdom of the temper. Dunsford will proceed with the chapter.

DUNSFORD. — " And though I bestow all my goods to feed the poor, and though I give my body to be burned, and have not charity, it profiteth me nothing."

MILVERTON. — Pray go on, Dunsford.

DUNSFORD. — " Charity suffereth long, and is kind ; charity envieth not; charity vaunteth not itself, is not puffed up,

" Doth not behave itself unseemly, seeketh not her own, is not easily provoked, thinketh no evil ;

" Rejoiceth not in iniquity, but rejoiceth in the truth ;

" Beareth all things, believeth all things, hopeth all things, endureth all things. Charity never faileth : but whether there be prophecies, they shall fail ; whether there be tongues, they shall cease ; whether there be knowledge, it shall vanish away."

MILVERTON. — That is surely one of the most beautiful things that has ever been written by man. It does not do to talk much after it.

Channing closes his Essay upon the Means of Promoting Christianity with this remarkable passage : " If, in this age of societies, we should think it wise to recommend another institution for the propagation of Christianity, it would be one the members of which should be pledged to assist and animate one another in living according to the Sermon on the Mount How far such a measure would be effectual we venture not to predict; but of one thing we are sure, that, should it prosper, it would do more for spreading the gospel than all other associations which are now receiving the patronage of the Christian world."

At the White House, " on an occasion I shall never
forget," said Mr. Deming, " the conversation turned
upon religious subjects, and Lincoln made this impressive remark : ' I have never united myself to
any church, because I have found difficulty in giving
my assent, without mental reservation, to the long,
complicated statements of Christian doctrine which
characterize their articles of belief and confessions
of faith. When any church will inscribe over its
altar, as its sole qualification for membership,' he continued, ' the Saviour's condensed statement of the
substance of both law and gospel, Thou shalt love
the Lord thy God with all thy heart, and with all thy
soul, and with all thy mind, and thy neighbor as thyself, that church will I join with all my heart and all
my soul.' "

" You may remember," says Farrar, in his Silence
and Voices of God, " how, in the old legend, St.
Brendan, in his northward voyage, saw a man sitting
upon an iceberg, and with horror recognized him as
the traitor Judas Iscariot ; and the traitor told him
how, at Christmas time, amid the drench of the burning lake, an angel had touched his arm, and bidden
him for one hour to cool his agony on an iceberg in
the Arctic sea ; and when he asked the cause of this
mercy, bade him recognize in him a leper to whom in
Joppa streets he had given a cloak to shelter him from
the wind ; and how for that one kind deed this respite
was allotted him. Let us reject the ghastly side of
the legend, and accept its truth. Yes, charity — love
to God as shown in love to man — is better than all
burnt-offering and sacrifice." " In thy face," said

the dying Bunsen to the wife of his heart, bending over him, " in thy face have I seen the Eternal."

When Abraham, according to another old legend, sat at his tent door, as was his custom, waiting to entertain strangers, he espied coming towards him an old man, stooping and leaning on his staff, weary with age and travail, who was a hundred years of age. He received him kindly, washed his feet, provided supper, caused him to sit down; but observing that the old man eat, and prayed not, nor begged for a blessing on his meat, he asked him why he did not worship the God of heaven. The old man told him that he worshiped the fire only, and acknowledged no other God. At which answer Abraham grew so zealously angry that he thrust the old man out of his tent, and exposed him to all the evils of the night and an unguarded condition. When the old man was gone, God called to Abraham, and asked him where the stranger was. He replied, " I thrust him away because he did not worship Thee." God answered him, " I have suffered him these hundred years, although he dishonored me ; and couldst not thou endure him one night?"

" Ah! poor things that we are. We are all sore with many bruises and wounds. The marvel is that our own tenderness does not make us tender to all others."

" He shall be immortal who liveth till he be stoned by one without fault."

25

INDEX.
